Flesh and Bones

of

Frome Selwood and Wessex

In the year 934 at the winter court of King Athelstan of Wessex a nation is forged, a landscape speaks

Annette Burkitt

First published in the United Kingdom in 2017

by The Hobnob Press,
30c Deverill Road Trading Estate,
Sutton Veny, Warminster BA12 7BZ
www.hobnobpress.co.uk

British Library Cataloguing in Publication Data
A catalogue record for this book is available from the British Library

ISBN 978-1-906978-50-1

Typeset in Scala 11/14 pt. Typesetting and origination by John Chandler

Printed by Lightning Source

For my husband Tim

Cold Kitchen Hill and North Hill from Packsaddle, Frome.

You, prince, are called by the name of 'sovereign stone'.
Look happily on this prophecy for your age:
You shall be the 'noble rock' of Samuel the Seer,
[Standing] with mighty strength against devilish demons.
Often an abundant cornfield foretells a great harvest; in
Peaceful days your stony mass is to be softened.
You are more abundantly endowed with the holy eminence
    of learning.
I pray that you may seek, and the Glorious One may grant,
    the [fulfilment implied in your] noble names.

Poem to Athelstan attributed to John the Old Saxon. Trans. Lapidge,
M., Some Latin Poems as Evidence for the Reign of Athelstan', *Anglo-Latin Literature 900-1066* (London and Rio Grande, 1993), 49-86.

Contents

Flesh is a story. Bones contains source material, discussion and a tale.

Bones

Introduction

In 934 a royal charter dated 16 December, granting a land holding to the priests of Winchester, was agreed upon in Frome, Somerset. A copy is today in the British Library. It was witnessed by Athelstan, King of Wessex, Hywel Dda (the good) a Welsh sub-king, the Archbishop of Canterbury, the Archbishop of York, fifteen other bishops and twenty-five ministers. Its contents were debated at the royal palace which lay somewhere in the vicinity of the present church of St John the Baptist.

The Saxon king's council was meeting for a Winter witan in Frome (pronounced Froom).[1] It was continuing to decide the fate of Britain, having just waged a successful war campaign against the fledgling country of Scotland, Alba. Constantine the King of the Scots had been brought south as a 'guest'.

In order to forge a stable nation of the English, Welsh and Scots, much diplomacy was required. So were important saintly relics on which to swear binding oaths, if the new nation was to stick together. Religious belief and statehood worked hand in hand, bishops and kings equally important in this task. Mutual support for the dynastic ambition brought into being by King Alfred was vital.

For the tenth century Church, this was a challenging and changing time of reformation, not unlike the 16th-century Reformation in its severe strictures to adhere to dogma – but this required the population to follow Rome's dictates, not reject them. King Henry VIII put an end to the Middle Age's religious connection to Europe, ensuring that Britain went its own way. The early Church's problem of the Pelagian Heresy, produced by a Briton, remained part of the national psyche and still does. It wants to do its own thing.

In the fictional story of Flesh, one of Athelstan's court clerks, Nonna, delves into the deep past of the Celtic British, stirring memories which may unsettle or inform his view of the ambitions of Church reformers. In a chest brought from Glastonbury there are manuscripts which evoke the culture of the old British kingdom, Dumnonia, defeated by the Saxons two centuries before. Landscape stories are revealed, fossilised in the place-names of the former Welsh speaking kingdom. Celtic Christianity, legend and lore, heroes and saints clamour to be remembered. They disturb the tenth century scribe, who wishes to progress at court and wants a peaceful life.[2]

Roman Catholicism plays an important role in the development of the new nation of Britain. The landscape stories appeal to what is becoming regarded as the primitive and superstitious mind. They threaten to upset the growing trend towards greater control of the Christian imagination. Nonna wonders about the loss of a sense of wild freedom which his forebears apparently enjoyed. Hills, antlers and wild flying horsemen fill his dreams, all dangerous symbols; dangerous, that is, to the fledgling Christian state, recovering from recent Viking attacks which had threatened to overrun Wessex as well as northern and eastern Britain. Should he intervene to save these manuscripts or allow them to be destroyed by Christian editors of his time, or, worse, used to encourage a superstitious population into strict religious adherence? Will the echoes of former beliefs be used to portray a hellish destiny for those who refuse to follow the ways of Rome? A debate about the validity of the uses of Heaven and Hell imagery must have taken place in minds of the time. Sticks, as well as carrots, were evidently important to ensure progress, as the Lives of Dunstan and Aethelwold, two of the reforming priests of the 10th century show.

There is much at stake. Church and State must work together. In 934, at Frome, Athelstan must do what he can to force compromise between protagonists, British and Saxon, Wessex and Mercian, abbot and layman. Some may have thought that he did too much. He has only a scant appearance in the Anglo-Saxon Chronicle, as though he has been written out.

Flesh and Bones, story and sources, attempts to understand why.

The Dark Ages in which this story is set is the name often given to a period in British history between the cessation of Roman administration in 410 and the coming of the Normans in 1066, sometimes called the Middle Ages or early Medieval period. It is generally thought of in terms of prevailing ignorance and barbarism, when upheaval and disruption together with large scale movement of peoples across northern Europe led to domination, displacement, slavery or ethnic cleansing by one group of another.

The formation of kingdoms with their ambitious leaders, learning to hold their own against others who wished to rule, led to the growth of powerful dynasties, families who worked for their own ends over many years, producing fertile ground for jealousy and intrigue. The Wessex dynasty of Ecgberht and Alfred was one of these.

Displaced peoples coped in different ways with their new overlords, sometimes by wholesale abandonment of their land, sometimes by complete submission to and adoption of the culture and language of the newcomers. Others preferred a halfway house, clinging to a dying culture and language in their original territories. This appears to have been the case in the south-west of England. In Somerset, some of the post-Roman British peoples of the British Kingdom of Dumnonia hung on to live, if not thrive, in the expanded eighth century Wessex kingdom of the Saxons, as is clear from the Laws of King Ine. Written about 710, these laws accommodated them. In Somerset over 10% of place-names at Domesday in 1086 are comprised entirely of British elements or contain such elements, showing a survival of the Old Welsh language. 106 place-names have been identified as of British derivation and "this must be regarded as a minimum figure".[3]

Though the times were difficult and disturbed, thanks largely to the Vikings, the Dark Ages were not completely unilluminated. Flashes of cultural progress and enlightenment shone at various times, including at the brightly lit court of Athelstan in the second quarter of the tenth century. He held his witans throughout Wessex between 924 and his death in 939, with one of his favourite palaces and hunting centres being at Frome, in the forest of Selwood.

Frome is a market town in east Somerset on the border with the county of Wiltshire. In the mid to late Saxon period it had a monastery, church and royal palace favoured by Wessex kings. It was an important seat of government, owned by the king, a "Villa Regalis", comparable to Cheddar. At 1086 it is thought to have had a population of 4-500 people, with presumably a market. This would have swollen in number with the arrival of the huge court retinue and associated hunting.[4] In the early 11th century it had a royal mint.

The palace hall, positioned probably near St John's church in what is now Vicarage Street, would have been big enough to host a large royal assembly as at Cheddar, which has been excavated. This was found to be 100-110 feet long, plus ancillary buildings with a forge and fowl coup.[5] There would have been a brewery[6] to turn foul water into drinkable ale, something of great value to large numbers of visitors and inhabitants. The many springs on the church side of the town were a great advantage and a good reason to site a royal and religious settlement here, giving easy access to the hunting playgrounds of Selwood Forest. Another king is known to have frequented Frome: Eadred, half-brother of

Athelstan, who died here in 955, perhaps at a hospital attached to the monastery.

Selwood is the former royal hunting forest which straddled the area of the present county border between Somerset and Wiltshire in the early medieval period. It was predominantly an oak forest, covering the landscape north to south from approximately Malmesbury, Wiltshire, to Sherborne, Dorset. Gradually it was broken up into smaller woods and renamed accordingly.

Dumnonia is the name of the post-Roman British kingdom of the south-western peninsula, which included the later counties of Cornwall, Devon, Somerset, parts of Dorset and parts of Wiltshire. Its name is based on the former Iron Age Dumnonii tribe. It developed into a kingdom after the abandonment of Britannia by Rome, with administrative capitals at Isca Dumnoniorum (Exeter), Ilchester, Bath and possibly Somerton. Gildas,[7] writing in about 540 AD, refers to kings in Britain including Constantine, "tyrant whelp of the filthy lioness of Dumnonia". Its official religion was what we now call Celtic Christianity, though some earlier pagan elements will have survived and perhaps were gaining strength, judging from the tone of Gildas' rant. He blamed the Britons' religious laxity for their downfall.

Eastern Dumnonia came under Wessex rule by 710 AD in the area of Somerset, its last king, Geraint, dying in battle at Llongborth (probably Langport).[8] The Saxon kingdom of Wessex under a succession of kings, culminating in the long reign of Ine, extended its control westwards through Selwood to encompass the great monastic centre of Glastonbury. With its spiritual heart ripped out, Dumnonia, land of the West Welsh as they are described in the Anglo-Saxon Chronicle, collapsed. The Wessex based English kings ensured that no southern British ruler would be successful at reversing the Saxon onslaught. Only Cornwall, Kernow, hung on to its pure Celtic past. The Saxons became

Christian at this time, more attuned to the callings of culture and refinement than previously. The library of Glastonbury was spared from destruction, its Irish teachers and priests survived.

The Britons of eastern Dumnonia lived side by side with the incoming Saxons. They continued to use their own language. They taught the newcomers their place-names. Some names were adopted and many became fossilised in new spellings as the written word began to take hold, leaving an oral past behind. The myths and beliefs of the people of West Wales, stretching back into the pre-Roman period, the sound of the names of heroes and gods, exist today in some of these place-names, although the spelling may have become anglicised. They give us clues to the stories of our landscape. As in modern Wales, where the names of heroes, saints and legends can still be recognised on a map, they can also be expected to be found in the English borderlands of Somersetshire, Gloucestershire, Herefordshire and Shropshire where the Celt and the Saxon learned to live together.

Meanwhile, the Saxon apparatus of power became steadily more refined. Sometime in the tenth century an early form of a Chancery of clerks was in existence. It was a small group of trusted civil servants, some in holy orders, some not, who may have included bishops and their servants. These men acted as interpreters, diplomats, charter and law recorders as well as scribes. They constructed, under Athelstan, a recognisable extensive written code, powers of the state, bolstered by relic oaths of a powerful nature. They attempted to apply, throughout mainland Britain, uniformity and stability. The diplomatic nature of much of this law making must have been extensive, ongoing and wearisome especially as the requirement for the written word and for reading the King's edicts became established practice among secular court officials as well as those of the Church. The churchmen had a natural advantage at this time: they were taught to read and write from an early age. Most secular officials in the early tenth century had to struggle to become literate as adults.

Ministers and clerks, religious and secular, worked hand in hand during the tenth century to develop the nation of England. Wealth and power seekers were drawn to careers in the church. Drastic religious reformation was in the air. A man, even without land ownership, could fly high if he could get close to the king. Ambitious ministers took it in turn to do a three months' stint at court, returning to their own estates for a rest and to see to their personal affairs.[9] Kings from other regions were expected to come to the witans at the court's bidding. The Celtic kings became known, and signed documents, as 'sub-kings', acknowledging Athelstan's superiority.

Athelstan's court became internationally acclaimed for its brilliance. He was compared to Charlemagne. Little remains which can be directly associated with the person of the King, but we do have something of value: a ninth century psalter, an illustrated book of psalms, which is today in the British Library together with the Frome Charter and is said to have belonged to him. It presumably, miraculously, survived Thomas Cromwell's attentions in the 16th century. Today Athelstan has little recognition. There is an Athelstan Lane in Milton Abbas, an Athelstan fuel garage in Cirencester, a greater understanding of his influence in Malmesbury. There is nothing which remembers the King in Frome as yet. Flesh and Bones aims to restore Athelstan to his rightful place in the stories of Europe, Britain, England, Wessex and Frome.

1   Recent examination of charter evidence has suggested that the court's Christmas was kept at Dorchester, Dorset in 934 and that the court may have moved on from Frome on the 16th December to southern Wessex for 21st December with two witan courts perhaps producing documents for December of that year. For the purposes of this story and in the light of uncertainty over the dating and tampering with original sources it has been assumed that the court, meeting at Frome on the 16th December 934, stayed there for the festivities and

to hunt after a tiring summer campaign as suggested by Sarah Foot in *Athelastan, The First King of England*, Yale University Press, 2011, p. 88

2   A scriptorium producing manuscripts on the scale of Winchester or Malmesbury is unlikely to have existed at Frome, but for the purposes of this story the clerks of the court and relics would have to be working or placed somewhere and a scriptorium/relic room, albeit a small one, has been envisaged.

3   Ian Burrow, *Hillfort and Hill-top Settlement in Somerset in the First to Eighth Centuries A.D.* BAR British Series 91, 1981 p 54. (A copy is held by Frome Museum).

4   Personal comment of Professor Michael Wood to the author, 4 April 2017.

5   See Rahtz, P (1979) *The Saxon and Medieval Palaces at Cheddar* (BAR Brit. Series 65: Oxford).

6   A brewery would be essential for the usual inhabitants of a settlement the size of Frome and especially for the witan or other court meetings held here. Ale was preferred to water, not least because of the disinfecting effect of the alcohol.

7   Gildas, *The Ruin of Britain*, in *Arthurian Period Sources* vol 7, ed. John Morris, Phillimore, 1978.

8   For all major events relating to the movements westwards of the Saxons and retreat of the Britons, see the *Anglo-Saxon Chronicle* for the relevant years.

9   Asser, *Life of King Alfred*, para 100. Trans. and introduced by Simon Keynes and Michael Lapidge, *Alfred the Great*, Penguin 1983.

Maps

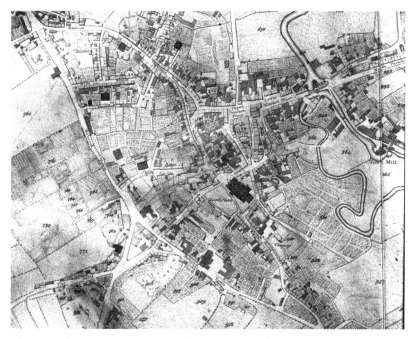

The core of Saxon Frome seen on the Cruse map of Frome, 1813. The church and tithe barn (on Behind Town, Christchurch Street East) are shown as darkened buildings.
(Longleat Archives, Somerset Maps 70 and 71. © Reproduced by permission of the Marquess of Bath, Longleat House, Warminster, Wiltshire)

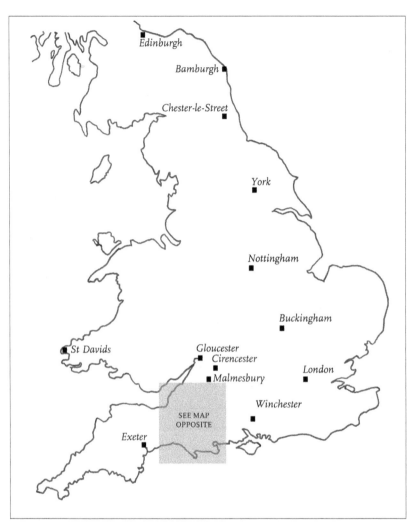

Map of Britain showing places mentioned in the text

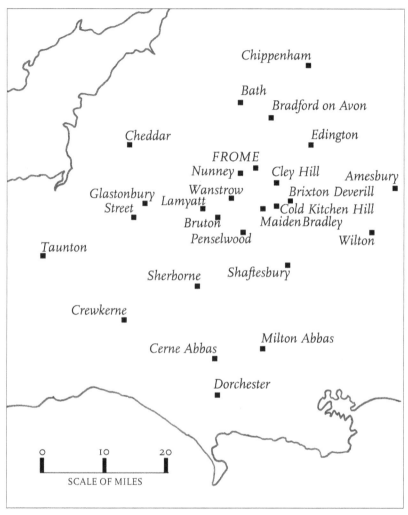

Map of Wessex showing places mentioned in the text

Simplified Genealogical table of
the Alfredian Dynasty

(Dates given where known. See also page 351 below)

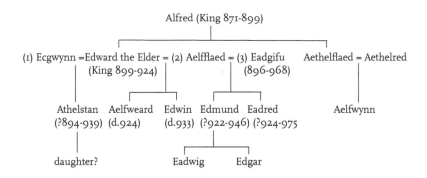

Chief Characters of Flesh

Royal Kin:

Aelfflaed, one of Athelstan's stepmothers. Edward the Elder's second wife, mother of Edwin.

Aelfwynn, Mercian princess, cousin of Athelstan.

Athelstan, King. Eldest son of Edward the Elder. Reigned from 924-939. Part of the highly successful dynasty of Wessex.

Eadgifu, Athelstan's stepmother, but younger than him by a few years. Edward the Elder's third wife, mother of Edmund and Eadred.

Edmund and **Eadred,** young half-brothers to Athelstan, sons of Eadgifu.

Edwin, son of Edward the Elder and Aelfflaed his second wife, half-brother to Athelstan.

Clerks of the Royal Court:

Dunstan, artist and scribe, in 934 becoming important at court. Later Archbishop of Canterbury and Saint Dunstan.

Leofa, scribe and interpreter, also one of the lay brother clerks attached to the Chancery of Athelstan. Fictional, but his name appears, described as a thief, in the Anglo-Saxon Chronicle under the year 946. He existed and had an important part to play in the life of the court in the mid tenth century. His name means "fluent" in Irish gaelic.

Nonna, the fictional narrator, scribe and interpreter, one of the lay brother clerks attached to the Chancery of King Athelstan.

Others:

Hywel Dda (the good), King of Dyfed, Wales.

Aethelwold, a rising star of the court in the 930s.

Constantine, King of Alba (Scotland). Known in the Anglo-Saxon Chronicle as 'the practised scoundrel'.

FLESH

Prologue

The Library of St. Augustine's Abbey at Canterbury, 3 pm 27 October 983

Two elderly monks are hunched together over open manuscripts on a table in the far end of a gloomy book lined library. The chains attached to huge books glitter as candles are lit by a scribe.

There is a muttering sound, a throat being cleared.

'And there it is again, that same name, different spelling.'

'Yes yes, Nonna, I agree that it figures in a few items, but that does not make it valid.' Dunstan coughs too, puts down a chunky eye glass.

'Then we will have, perhaps, to agree to disagree,' Nonna does not back down. He's too old; it doesn't matter anymore to him what Dunstan says or thinks. At least the old tonsure dispute has been put to rest: they are both bald anyway. That's one less bone of contention at the breakfast table.

These are scholars, wise ones, spared the wars, plagues, poisonings and devilish work that beleaguer others' lives. They still have ambition: to outlive each other.

Nonna has slightly the upper hand; he is three years the younger, but has had a wanton youth and is aware that that may tell against him.

Dunstan has God on his side, he thinks. So much so, that he has a secret fear of being torn apart for gilded reliquaries before Heaven can take him. Others may want to make him a saint (he hopes) but please, not before he's dead. He thinks, on a bad day, that Nonna, at heart, has the devil on his side and devilish intentions. He keeps a careful watch on him.

'By the way, it is forty-four years to the day since the death of Athelstan.' Dunstan knows that custom requires energetic genuflection at this point, a useful tool for deflecting adamant opposing views.

'And eighty-four years since the death of Alfred.' Nonna's memory is long, too. It's all the fish they have eaten. He considers his subordinate position, then does a double genuflection with appropriate enthusiasm.

Meanwhile Dunstan begins a voluble, lengthy prayer for the revered departed.

Pedantic, as usual, Nonna thinks. He knows Dunstan's interruption of his ideas would have taken longer if the prayed-for had been saints as well as kings, might have necessitated a visit to the choir stalls, the lighting of candles.

Should he push this place-name business further or wait until the older bones succumb to their fate? He would inherit, surely, the business of editing the early histories when the time came. He knows Dunstan's stance on this; he has spent his career living with the certainties of his superior's mindset and his uncompromising attitude to events in the lives of the many kings they have served. Perhaps tomorrow he might push it further. He has some leverage, after all. Like Dunstan, Nonna holds secrets which some would love to know. And what he knows, he knows that Dunstan is not sure that he knows. Malmesbury Abbey will reveal some of them, hopefully, in time. But time for them both is short. Neither will travel to Malmesbury again. Vikings are on the move once more.

Beginnings

Nonna

My name is Nonna. I am an old man, full of memories. Is it a curse or a blessing to remember so much, in so much detail? I am a scribe, trained by the Monastery of Glastonbury, Ynis Witrin, the Island of Glass. Before it is too late, I wish to record the story of my times. I have been witness to the reigns of many kings, some good, some less good and to many changes in our beloved Church. Forgive me if my history does not chime with your own version; I can only do my best, recalling what I myself have seen and known and reading the accounts of others where my memory is less sure. Here at Canterbury I am able to access most of the writings of past times and I have former Archbishop Dunstan to help me when I require. Together we spend all our days in the extensive library.

Let me begin in my youth, when we were both companions and court clerks to that mighty king, Athelstan. This is his story. He instructed me to write of his life. I will try to see things through his eyes as well as my own. He generously opened the door to a comfortable life for me and my fellow scribes from Glastonbury and I will always be grateful for that.

I was a good looking young man in the year of Our Lord, 934. I was 21 years old and neither wholly man nor monk, by which I mean I was not married. I was the son of a Dumnonian woman who hated to be called West Welsh ('a foreigner in my own land,' she would pout) and a Saxon father, a woodworker. He was dense, made of wood, thought like a tree, as hunters think like the animals they chase. I was their educated only living child. I was born in Frome, where the great oak forest of Selwood thins. I wished, even as a small child, to speak to the future of things I had discovered of the past.

I had ambition. The graduates of Glastonbury all did. I am grateful to have been raised so far at the royal court, from the hovel of a mother who was daughter of a slave and a ceorl father, to this. I took notes of the doings of the royal court for the Chronicle of our nation. Perhaps one day my histories will be read by those who may recognise the greatness of Athelstan and wish to emulate him. I fear there are still many who would malign him. The families of Winchester were never his followers. They detested his Mercian accent. He made them learn to read and to write. Writing survives, commands the minds of readers, he told us all. Listeners forget; manuscripts record. Truth may be changed in speech; the written word holds unchangeable fact at its heart. Our libraries expanded in size, the ability to read and to write was once again regarded as a valuable skill, as before the Viking wars. Athelstan was a faithful grandson to Alfred's wish for education and for the rule of law.

In 934 I was attached to the Monastery of St John the Baptist, Frome, as Assistant Regulator of Relics, with administrative duties for cataloguing and restoring. I spent much time in the reliquary room, the haligdom. Athelstan collected relics as you might collect the dead wings and bodies of butterflies with a zeal and jealous acquisitiveness. He spent much time with them, accessing their wisdom. My burden was heavy as he was always acquiring more, whether bought on the continent by a diplomat or brought nefariously by ambitious monks from other haligdoms. No questions were asked, as far as relics were concerned. He had inherited a great deal from his aunt, Aethelflaed and uncle of Mercia. They were his chief interest, but then, he did not have a wife and a man must have his obsessions. They told him what he wanted to hear, unlike some of the nobles and bishops at court.

He also loved to hunt, which relaxed him. Being a king is really hard work in these days, even without constant war. Would I wish to be one? No thank you. And I did not wish to pretend to be a virgin or live like a monk, though that has come, at the end.

My close companions in the King's chancery were Leofa and Dunstan. We worked closely together throughout our careers after the days of our schooling in Glastonbury, where we were chosen from the ablest group to be Athelstan's clerks. Eleven years of work as scribes, interpreters, soothsayers and spies, we had had, by the year I write of. The King said he couldn't do without us. We were his extra eyes and ears. In return he gave us much; best of all, his confidence. He was like an uncle. I miss Leofa and his laughter. He left us too soon.

Rather than chasing deer for leisure, the King's pastime to get in a sweat, we young men liked to practise stick-and-ball. We played against a rag tag Warminster side up the slopes of Cley Hill on feast days when we were in Frome, or arranged an invitation to view the court ladies' embroidery projects. Dunstan, a ladies' man, usually managed to get us into their chambers; he was an artist, regarded as safe. I did not wish to be regarded as safe. Safety is not, in my opinion, an attribute attractive to the fair sex. I wished to be attractive. Life in 934 was good. I remember Gwladys from Dyfed, dark Glwadys, particularly. Life in 934 was memorable, though, in other ways, as well. Hell was defined then. But you had better ask Dunstan about that.

And so my tale begins, where it should, at the beginning.

Priory of St Oswald, Gloucester, Autumn 918

'Oswald, Athelstan. He is the key to all that you may achieve of my father's vision.' Aethelflaed of Mercia lay back on her couch, exhausted by even this short sentence. The world was growing dark. 'You are my adopted son. You must unite the body parts of the great King and Saint. You know where he is. Together we have rescued much of the dismembered parts, now you must bring his soul and body together, unite the land as he should be. Oswald's head must be recovered. He must be able to stand entire on the day of judgement. My father's legacy requires it. Promise me.'

'But in order to do this, Aunt, I have to persuade the guardians of the tomb of Cuthbert in Chester-le-Street to both open it and somehow to extract the head which is inside, or take it by force.'

'Holy Cuthbert will advise you how this is to be done. It is essential for the good of the nation, for the joining of England from the south to the north, to the border of Alba and beyond.'

Aethelflaed, lucid, but sinking fast, clutched Athelstan's arm. She knew he was imbued with Alfred's vision; she had spent most of her adult life indoctrinating him from a very impressionable age. Edward would have neglected him, the only son of a concubine, even though Alfred had singled him out as a special child, had seen something in him which sparkled, noticed the star in his hand. Edward was much more pragmatic than his father, preferred a son not to outshine him. He had no time for anything sparkly. Athelstan was sent away from Wessex, his fate sealed, to Aethelflaed's gain. She had no son of her own, wanted no more children after the painful experience of bearing her daughter Aelfwynn.

Aethelflaed grew more urgent as her breath became ragged. Is it better to be conscious at death or unconscious? 'Promise me that you will join the parts of Oswald, Athelstan. Carry our hopes forward for England.' She gasped, her breathing now slow and short. Again, with her last strength, she touched his arm, the last touch of another's living flesh. She breathed out, died.

Athelstan, bending over his beloved aunt, whispered at her ear. She would perhaps hear him promise yet again to fulfil this most urgent task, the task and purpose of his life.

'Aunt, I promise.' He turned to look at Aelfwynn standing beside him, her arm around Athelstan's shoulder.

'We promise, Mother,' she said. On her other arm, the baby cried.

Glastonbury Abbey, noon, 29 August, 922

A middle aged monk and a fair, tall young man are walking in the cloister. Abbot Striward is robed in white wool down to the ground. You can hardly see his feet, even when he moves. The younger man is wearing an English court dress which stops at the knees. A short purple cloak, fringed with golden tassels, has an enamelled brooch to hold it on the shoulder. There is an enormous shiny buckle on the thick leather belt. Cross-strapped hose emphasises the calf musculature. There's plenty of it. There's no need for a dagger, but he wears one.

'And you say you have a few very promising youngsters, Striward?'

'Yes, my Lord, some very exceptional ones in the fourth year. Let me introduce them to you.'

The fourth year, four years after monastery scouts first went into nearby villages and farms, selecting boys and girls for the schoolrooms, the scholars of tomorrow. Gathered at eight-years-old, they will be ripe at twelve; almost men, almost women.

The two men duck under a cloister porch and walk along an internal dusty passage to the foot of a steep staircase. The Abbot lifts his long skirts as he climbs. Athelstan slows his pace to match the Abbot's. They emerge through a heavy door to a bright, clear-paned room, the length of one side of the cloister, the schoolroom. Thirty young heads turn as they enter, mostly boys, a smattering of older girls. They are the last intake of female children for scriptorium training. Double monasteries are going out of fashion. The separation of sexes is better for them both, it is thought.

'Carry on with your work.' The tutor nods at the visitors in welcome. The young heads respond as one, bend forwards, continue writing. The tongues of some of the younger ones at the front of the class protrude in concentration.

'Is this the Latin class, Elfred?' The Abbot points out the proficiency of his youngsters. No need. Athelstan has already heard how good these scholars are, how advanced in learning. Elfred, having expected the visitors, takes a little time to explain the current task, proud to be able to show off the merits of the abbey, its investment in the future, its role in the nation. The visitors allow him his moment of glory, listen attentively.

'Elfred, my Lord wishes to select three boys as his attendants. He wishes to form a core of students for his household. Whom would you recommend?' Some of the younger children look round. The older students in the back row are eligible for taking up positions elsewhere, this is their chance. Who will be chosen?

Elfred has already been made aware of the request, has been grooming three of his brightest for some weeks now. He addresses Athelstan directly. 'The three boys you see at the back right corner, my Lord, are the most accomplished of my students, Leofa, Nonna and Dunstan. They have Scandinavian, British and Saxon ancestry, as I understand you specifically required. They have achieved a great deal in the time they have been with us. They are fluent writers in both Latin and English, with the added benefit to your court, my Lord, of two of them being able to converse in their original foreign tongues. In addition Leofa has mixed parentage and has been encouraged to retain his mother's Irish Gaelic. All have shown great diligence and promise. Dunstan has the advantage of being of noble Wessex birth, but, I assure you, were it not for their imperfect early circumstances, the other two would grace a royal scriptorium or some such high purpose.'

Elfred signals to the three, one dark haired, one red and one blonde. They stand up. Leofa, the dark auburn boy, is tallest. Nonna is dark, short and plump. Dunstan, the fair one, is slim. A mixed race selection.

'Their ages?' Athelstan likes to know just where he stands.

'Leofa is thirteen years old, Dunstan fourteen and Nonna nearly twelve, my Lord.'

Striward turns to Athelstan, who nods.

'Come with us,' the Abbot beckons to the trio. 'Leave your work where it is.' They look at each other as they make their way out of the schoolroom and into the void of their futures.

Later that day the three boys and their new master are travelling physically as well as mentally forward to Malmesbury to take their oaths as clerks at the tomb of Aldhelm, patron of learning and culture. The wagon carrying them rolls easily along the high dry ground, the carthorse and driver both competent, young and magnificently liveried in red and blue. They are an example of attentive and encouraged training and patronage, not lost on the boys. They are in good hands.

'I will inform your parents of the change in your circumstances.' Athelstan wishes to reassure his new servants. 'They will be given small parcels of land to celebrate your good fortune. As you understand, I am sure, there will be many rewards for you, too, as the years go by, if you hold true to me.'

Nonna and Leofa glow with pleasure. It is remarkable that they have been picked out from so many children of lowly status to be potential students at Glastonbury Abbey; now they would be working directly for a nobleman, a son of King Edward no less. Dunstan is pleased, but less impressed. He wears a bland look of indifference.

Perhaps he was born with it, thinks Athelstan, looking at him sideways on.

Dunstan turns away from the wind and sun to meet

Athelstan's gaze. He is blessed by his pure Wessex background. He met Athelstan at court as an eight-year-old, remembers the graceful attitude, noted the psalter forever in his hand. He is a distant cousin of his new master, born in Baltonsborough. He is connected to the Wessex royal kin. That must be worth something.

The straight line of Dunstan's mouth says it all. Athelstan makes a mental note. *Watch this one.*

The breeze blows the young lads' hair around their faces as they cling to the cart's side, their few possessions in sacks on the floor. The end of summer shines in their hair; a new chapter of life begins.

'We will carry on to Gloucester tomorrow. Before we arrive at Malmesbury, I want to make one thing clear to all of you. I want you to call me Stone,' says Athelstan, 'when we speak in private. Whoever you become or I become, you are from today my trinity of boys, my extra ears and eyes. Remember to call me Stone whenever you have something important to tell me. That will signal my full attention. Repeat my name.'

'Stone,' Leofa says.

'Stone,' says Nonna.

'Stone,' says Dunstan and smiles.

Ripening cornfields stretch out beyond the wagon's rolling progress, heading north east from Wessex to Mercia, the late summer air behind them warming their backs, pushing them on. Stone the man and Stone's boys, on to the edges of their world, on to Mercia.

That same evening in Winchester palace, Queen Eadgifu, third wife of Edward, groans with pain as she does her duty. The aetheling Edmund is being born. A fourth boy has arrived to prop up the Wessex dynasty, one for the Kentish faction, this time. There will be plenty of boys to choose from when the time comes, never enough, so Edward thinks. Others wonder what's going to happen, fear too much choice. It's all very well having

wives from different kingdoms, different families, but too many heirs make for uncomfortable decisions. The naturally gloomy would say a choice of one is good, but then, so many die young . .
.

Palace of Chippenham, 29 January, 933

'So I said to Eadflaed that she will have to take what she is given. Either that or go to join her mother at Wilton Abbey. She didn't like the sound of that, she said. I think she will come round to our idea. Children think they have a choice in such matters; anyone would think a royal girl should be allowed to marry where she likes. She should never have had that Irish priest as her tutor, he has given her most peculiar fanciful thoughts. Did nobody investigate him?'

The gentlemen providing the male audience of Queen Eadgifu, dressed in her evening gown of purple and gold, displaying the latest floral embroidery, are uncomfortable with this often-repeated family argument. They shift in their chairs and cough.

It has been going on for at least a year, this discussion about Eadflaed's future and is close to becoming annoying to the hearers. The small inner chamber, windowless, heavily double staved, protected from non-dynastic overhearing or spying, is almost filled by the presence of the King, his stepmother and three of his chancery clerks. The chairs are comfortable here, made sturdy for lengthy, in depth family planning. It takes a long time to sort a dynasty's decisions. Individuals do not always take kindly to their inevitable royal destinies. There are deep drawers of wooden penitential resort, slapping sticks, for those occasions when the victim is young and in need of being taught his or her duty; boxes of dried fruit to encourage the willing. A long oak table serves for taking snacks during contemplation and for parchment or charter viewing. Bibles and psalters are ranged on dark walls, ready for consultation when no-one can agree. The leather cat whip hangs in a corner, seldom, but sometimes, used. It serves its purpose, dangling there.

Dunstan defends his old master, the tutor in question. 'The Irish are rather wild in their sense of what is fair in love and in soul matters in general. Perhaps he did no great harm in encouraging the girl to think there could be some sort of choice of husband...'

'Choice! She has the choice of marriage to whom we choose or no marriage at all. She is of royal blood and these are modern times!'

Eadgifu has command of the females of the family. There are many of them, a large brood of sisters and half-sisters left in the wake of three marriages by Edward, her dead husband. She is wife number three. She is called "The Abbess" secretly by the court clerks, though she shows no signs of wanting to found her own abbey far away from the court. Some hopes. Even Athelstan sometimes finds himself wishing she would. Perhaps a generous gift of land and a sack of gold might do the trick? But he knows she would not go without a fight. There is too much interest for Eadgifu at court. She loves to interfere; guide, she calls it. Shoving an ex-king's wife out of a royal court is no easy matter. His own wife, if he had one, might have done the trick. Murder would be easier. Anyway, anything for a quiet life.

Eadgifu storms off, slamming the door. She has to have a final conversation with her stepdaughter, must bend her will while she is weakened. The men will leave it until the girl is too old, or has spoiled her own chances by elopement with some young man of the palace guard.

The King and his young men of the chancery are left alone. They shuffle their feet, look down at them.

Athelstan restores equanimity. He's good at that. He pours wine into his goblet, leans back in his chair. Passing around the wine jug, he sighs.

'Well, Eadgifu is good at what she does. What would I do without her managing the palaces' upkeep for the witans; she's so experienced at the job. The details she deals with, the comforts she supplies for our foreign guests; she's indispensable, takes such a load off my mind. She even manages to make our stay here comfortable.' Chippenham is an old fashioned army barracks. The men love to be here, they can make a mess, but Eadgifu wants changes at all the Wessex palaces. It's another theme which crops up regularly, along with marriage.

The three younger men are less in awe of Eadgifu; an old woman is an old woman. Though not so old in reality; only thirty-two. Wedded to the court, she says she is, would not think of marrying again. Her sons, Edmund and Eadred, are Athelstan's adopted heirs. She has rights as their mother. She will be the Queen Mother of the next king. Athelstan is just a capable caretaker in her mind.

The young trio of clerks, the trinity as the court calls them, are all wise enough to keep their mouths shut on family matters. They have proven their worth as keepers of secrets, have been close to the King since early youth. Uncle Stone likes to encourage bright youngsters and these are three of the brightest, picked by the Glastonbury monks to take part in the great push towards making an educated England. Dunstan, Leofa and Nonna, all of a similar age, in their early twenties, already skilled diplomats, skilled language experts, skilled scribes. All schooled in the religious milieu of the monastery of Glastonbury, all aware of a religious duty to fulfil their early promise, of their unique abilities to help Athelstan to shape the future of the country. Piety, honour, loyalty are their watchwords. One is more pious than the others. Dunstan reaches for a psalter from the shelf behind him.

'It may help, my lord, if we consult with the Holy Ones on the matter which we were discussing earlier.'

Eadgifu had made an unexpected entrance to discuss her stepdaughter's potential marriage. The four men lean over the selected book to watch Dunstan, skilled and renowned at biblical prophecy even at his age, allow the psalter to fall open at a conducive page. A gilt and lapis image of angels and ploughmen surrounded by foliate decoration gleams in the firelight. The exquisite workmanship demands a thorough viewing. The words, though, gain Dunstan's chief attention on this occasion.

The book falls open at Job five, verse eight.

Dunstan picks up a nearby aestel pointer, refuses to stare at the great, mesmerising beauty of its handle. How did they make that? Things of beauty, he finds, distract him too much. He will return to look at it again in detail, some other time. He reads aloud in Latin, the language of the Psalms. All four know spoken Latin well. It has a meditative effect on those who know it from youth. It comes in handy at court, sometimes, when subtlety or secrecy is required. The secular court ministers will get around to it one of these days, but not yet. Latin is still a foreign country for them. It evokes empires and power, culture and self-discipline.

> For my part, I would make my petition to God | and lay my cause before him | who does great and unsearchable things, marvels without number. | He gives rain to the earth and sends water on the fields; | he raises the lowly to the heights, | the mourners are uplifted by victory; | he frustrates the plots of the crafty, | and they win no success, | he traps the cunning in their craftiness, | and the schemer's plans are thrown into confusion.

There is silence. Athelstan indicates that they should now kneel in prayer. Cushions are provided for such moments of concentration or prayer at the small altar at the end of the room. The King kneels on his cushion, the others behind. There is silence. Alfred's candle clock in the centre of the table, keeping the slow hours, sheds a solemn light across their backs.

These are the words of God. How to construe their meaning, bearing in mind the slight touch of craftiness the group had in mind before they were interrupted by Eadgifu? A king must do what a king must do to provide peace for his realm. If directed by God, the acts he must undertake, sometimes unpleasant, would surely be forgiven? Careful planning for the future, inevitably involving subtlety and subterfuge, has to be contemplated if the nation is to benefit. We must be brighter, better prepared, armed with law, Church, God and the Saints as well as an army, than the Others, whoever they are, who would bring us down. Mercia, perhaps. No, Athelstan is our protector. Wales perhaps? No, Hywel Dda is a friend of the King. Cornwall? Not much to be feared there, though they are sometimes a nuisance. Northumbria? Getting warm. Strathclyde? Warmer still. Alba? Ah yes, the heat of the enemy, showering down through the length of the land to tickle our toes, the Practised Scoundrel of the Scots, Constantine, King of Alba. The hairy old devil himself, his beard in two forks of a porridge coated tangle. A breaker of oaths, not a gentleman.

Craft is needed on two fronts, Constantine and Cuthbert. Three, if Edwin is to be dealt with.

What shall we do with Edwin? This is the cry of half the court in its dark corners. What shall we do with Athelstan? The other half weeps. The dynasty must be maintained; but loyalties to the dynasty representing which kingdom, Mercia or Wessex? Who shall be King of Everywhere?

Prayers of individuals on the matter come up with suitable answers, all different, all spoken by God. One man's dream is as good as another. Birds of a feather...the groups of Us and Them, accompanied by the pillow talk and ambition of wives and concubines, have come alight again since the talk of giving Constantine a bloody nose has resurfaced. Who will be King of Everywhere, if Constantine is not defeated? Will it be a Wessex puppet, a Mercian upstart, a Northumbrian, a Dane? Irish, even? Who knows? If Athelstan keeps spending on relics in the way he has done, there will be little left for weaponry, ships or soldiers. The bloody nose may only be a gentle boxed ear. Constantine could even become King, of England, as well as the Scots. That would be a turnaround.

Athelstan sighs, pushes himself up from the prayer cushion. His mind is clear that it is not clear on the matter under discussion. The other three men also rise. It is for the King, anointed and supported by God and personally backed by St Cuthbert, to speak first.

'The business of access or acquisition weighs heavily on me, my companions, but it seems there is no other way to gain the vision and backing of the northern saint against Constantine without close conference with the living flesh of Cuthbert and the mind of St Oswald. We cannot afford to waste any more time in fruitless diplomacy with the Columban monks. They have refused to sell his head to me, at any price. The only way to preserve the holy head, as my discussions with the holy St Aldhelm have told me before, is by ensuring its safety in the south, partnering it with the other remains at Gloucester, where it should be. Should it fall into the hands of Constantine, our nation of England would be imperilled, that much is clear. But if access is difficult, translation to the south will be impossible. I cannot see any way forward.'

Dunstan, eldest of the trio of young men, speaks next. Rank and birth are carefully observed by all at court. They are a matter of life and death. Get it wrong and you could be dead. Not here, though. Everyone knows their place and, anyway, Athelstan is a forgiving sort. The trinity are still his boys, even though they are now men.

'Would you have me make arrangements for a substitution, as discussed, my lord? Leofa and I, with your permission, could draw up a plan which will allow us to take full advantage of our projected visit to Chester-le-Street next year. While viewing the sainted Cuthbert, bestowing on him gifts, we should be able to rearrange the other contents of the coffin to our satisfaction. Leofa and I have already thought of a way...' Dunstan stops; he realises he is ahead of the thinking in the room. Have the others no imagination?

Nonna is amazed, his mouth hangs open. This is the first he has heard of a substitution plan. How to harness the thoughts of Oswald, dead King of the Northumbrians, he has been privy to, but not to an actual attempt to steal his whole head, sacrilege indeed. Unthinkable, he would have thought. But evidently it has been thought of.

'What do you think, Nonna? How would the haligdom of the nation fare with the head of the great king as well as his other parts?' Athelstan addresses his chief relic caretaker. 'Would I be forgiven the theft? Can it be justified in this case, is it a Just Theft?'

There is no credible answer to this. Eight years into his reign, the pious and noble King Athelstan has begun the descent into madness. It's best forgotten it was ever thought of, and Nonna firmly says so.

The Oaken Chest

Monastery of St John the Baptist, Frome, Kingdom of Wessex, 13 December, 934

A nation is being forged, as I speak. The King of Wessex is becoming King of England in these years, perhaps an Emperor. The court is engaged in helping to bring about a united country, a new Britain, comprehensive like the old Roman Prydein, but including Alba, Scotland. All the islands of Britain will be ruled for the first time by one king, Athelstan, my King. An Empire of angels with God and his Saints over all.

I operate as a clerical factotum between the secular officials of the court, the ministers and those in holy orders, bishops, priests and monks. I look and dress like a monk but I do not wear the tonsure, neither am I expected to act like a monk. Holy orders are something which may or may not come to me, as God speaks, but not yet. I am young, I have oats to sow. I am not yet confined to any monastery or only to pray for the souls of the dead, as monks are. On top of all that I have to do, I have a new task: King Athelstan, who is deeply interested in his family history as well as all manner of things to do with past territorial issues, has instructed me to make a pile of all that I can find of the history of his lands of Wessex west of the Forest of Selwood. I can only do my best. History and Truth, these will be my guides. And God.

While in Frome, my birth place, accompanying the court, I have promised to begin this work. A previously unrecorded chest of ancient manuscripts has been brought from the Abbey of Glastonbury for safekeeping to the monastery here. The floods of this very wet autumn and winter have wrought havoc to its library. Green mould on vellum threatens to destroy the written word, as effective as fire. Athelney and Muchelney monasteries are also at threat of subjugation by water, although as recently constructed sites, they are better able to fend off damp and decay than Glastonbury. At least their roofs are whole. In any case, they have little in their libraries as yet of any importance.

My King, Uncle Stone, is our ruler, grandson of Alfred the Great, son of Edward the Elder. He is not actually my uncle, only a guardian. I could not dream of claiming royal blood, nor would want to. He is forty years old this year. In nearly ten years of kingship, he has built upon his father's achievements, fulfilled Alfred's hopes. Skilled in outward diplomacy as well as inward wisdom, able to read the affairs of men as if by magic, he is a worthy successor to the kingdom. The line of Wessex has become England's dominant royal dynasty and now, rapidly, with the King's recent campaign in Scotland, he has contributed to the imperial legacy of Europe. Welsh monarchs have bowed to him, the Strathclyde king too. Alba, the Scots kingdom, has come under his sway. Acting together, we can hold off the Viking menace from our shores. Fractured and apart, well, that would be more difficult.

To simplify the inevitable question of succession and to satisfy the older Saxon kingdoms of England Athelstan has eschewed marriage, kept his private life apart from the usual infidelities and disturbances of the souls of young men. This is why some of us call him the Virgin King. He calls on St Aldhelm to help him with that aspect of his life. He was born to rule, married or not, charged by his grandfather to do so.

By promising to remain unmarried he is unassailable. The attempt by enemies to blind him as he acceded failed. He remains pure and beautiful, his head imperious, his hair golden, like a god's, combed, plaited and threaded with real gold and silver, shining like the sun. In the palaces of Wessex he performs the part allotted to him by fate and God. In private, with his closest friends, he sighs. Ten years as king: it is a heavy burden. No wonder he spends much time with his relics, exhorting the Saints to give him strength. I hear his sighs, wonder at his ability to sustain enthusiasm.

Along with monks of the Benedictine order, in whose company he feels most mindful, he values quiet prayer above all else as a solace to the duties of kingship which grow greater day by day. So does the number of administrators, each with their own area of expertise and opinion. The King expects much, delegates much. He loves to discover and encourage talent in young men, as he has in me, and to harness it. The life of the court is, as a consequence, much sought out by learned ambassadors from afar. The Mercian disputation, which was loud at his accession, has quietened. That was a backward movement. Naturally, old men remember better days; better, for them. But Athelstan has persuaded them to look forward, to progress outwards to the continent, to growth, not inwards to old quarrels, or so he hopes.

A growing kingdom demands energy from its leader. He must be prepared to sleep little. As well as the business of ruling and care for the succession, Athelstan has a superfluity of sisters to remind him of the pleasantries and alternative focus of womanhood, each one different, all with ideas of their own. The work of hostess is admirably carried out by his stepmother, Eadgifu, his father Edward's last wife. She is Athelstan's female aide, a capable, educated woman of many talents. She has provided my King with his uncomplicated heirs, late-born sons of his father, Edmund and Eadred. The throne is secure. Stone's other half-brothers are dead. Why add to the already very extended family, with all the potential problems of a disputed succession? There are always other ladies to enjoy, secret others, silent ones, if he wishes, but we know nothing of any private affairs. If children exist, no-one knows their names; they will never trouble the court.

Athelstan has studied and learned from the past. He knows its value. He is a natural historian. Like me, he likes to clarify and codify, pigeon hole and preserve. He never throws anything away. The written word is the record he can rely on. Oaths are not enough in a more literate world. Relics may constrain a potential oath-breaker, but the written word will take him to court, to the gallows, if need be. To break an oath made on a gospel book is to court a future in hell. To break an oath made on a sacred relic is to be doubly cursed. Men's memories he knows are fickle, subject to the emotional aspects of greed. Laws need oaths, peace needs oaths. The court of Charlemagne has shown how the written word cements the Law. All men of worth must be able to read and write. The thegns grumble. There is less time in the hunt than formerly. They are having to learn to understand the written word as seasoned warriors; it is not easy for them.

With the succession clarified since Edwin's drowning last year, all can breathe relief that civil war and shouting matches, or worse, in corridors will not occur at Stone's death. It was not always so at the death of kings. Many remember the difficulties of his grandfather and father, whose brothers and cousins were many, when the throne was often in dispute and the stronger, long-lived male was the gainer. We live in calmer times now, when by clear decision making and a vow to limit the succession to his young half-brother Edmund, arguments and the double dealing of the early years of Athelstan have faded. We move onwards, as the King often says. Reconciled now are the hearts who would formerly have torn out his eyes rather than have a Mercian sympathiser thrust upon them as their ruler of Wessex. But men will be men, and old grudges die hard.

A wife would soothe his soul, it is often said, particularly by his sisters. There are fewer of them about than formerly; some of their shrill voices and fair-haired loveliness have gone overseas to breed for rulers elsewhere, making new contacts and spreading the Wessex blood genes abroad. We are left with a quieter court. Their role in Europe is important, moving the fledgling British Empire's connections onwards, outwards. They do their bit.

Away from the busy court with all its challenging personalities, male and female, there is solace for the King when he escapes to his relics, with which he feels happiest, or when mounted, leading his team in the hunt where his skills with horse, dog and falcon are renowned.

As one of the interpreters for the travelling court as well as assistant charter maker and relic administrator, I often accompany Stone on hunts, when many intimate discussions between sub-kings, Welsh and English, occur. I operate what he calls my tuned antennae. I remain incognito at the edge of events but listen to conversations when alerted. Stone has a particular look and small hand signal when he wants close attention paid to a particular dignitary. An innuendo may make a difference to the business terms of an important matter. Later, alone, we discuss what we remember of motivation and intent and plan to use whatever diplomatic words may open up the mind of an opponent, to catch him off guard. Eadgifu likes to assist in this. We often have midnight meetings to try things out. Some of us are becoming more subtle at spying and listening; better this, than use the sword. Leofa and Dunstan, my friends of the trinity, are masters at this swordless diplomacy.

I am happy in the company of Stone, sometimes praying with him, sometimes escorting him to review his beloved collection of relics which grows daily as other rulers, anxious to please, send him gifts. They know he loves to receive the flesh and bones of saints. The cart which carries them from witan to witan grows heavy with the load; such is the value of the goods, the bones and reliquaries which contain them, that the flamboyant covered wagon has its own armed double guard. In each palace of Wessex a secure system of protection deep inside the scriptorium or library of the monastery nearby has to be constantly reviewed. Only Stone can give permission for his relics to be approached, though many would dearly love to see them on open display. He says in private that they are as valuable to him as the land of the nation; without them his power would be diminished. They should not be openly available to the public. There are plenty of other relics throughout the land for common pilgrims. These are his own treasures, like gold, silver or coin.

Athelstan is acutely aware of the status brought to the Wessex court by his collection. At special times, as on saint's days, he allows some of it to be approached. Each time a particular saint's reliquary is brought out, it appears to be even more gloriously endowed with silver, gold and gems. I wonder which is the more valuable, the relic or the reliquary. The anonymous artists (and those who are known) who embellish the reliquaries are magical masters, toying with our minds and hopes as gods may play with our fears.

Leofa and Dunstan oversee the anonymous artisans. Secretly, often at work in the workshops of Glastonbury, they produce marvels of beauty and craftsmanship to encase noble and saintly parts. They design the coloured window glass works and general metal and woodworking which is intended to adorn or embellish churches, monasteries and palaces of the land, as well as intricate jewellery of a religious nature. Everything in three dimensions is their remit and they have travelled throughout Wessex, from Kent to Cornwall, ensuring that standards at this time of educational and cultural renewal are ubiquitously high, reporting to Athelstan what needs improvement in terms of architecture and adornment. Stone calls them his wizards. Leofa likes this term, laughs when he hears it said by the King, but Dunstan meets it with a frown, or a straight mouth, a sure sign of his displeasure. Dunstan never remembers the last line of a joke. But he knows his strengths and weaknesses. He leaves jesting to Leofa.

I have my questions, which I keep to myself, about the expenditure of such vast amounts of gold, silver and jewels on the encasing of the dead. After all, did they not die from this world, intending to rise on the day of judgement? Would an unnamed knee joint or half a finger, thrown on a midden by some careless carpenter or artisan, charm the spiritual soul of a nobleman, if it were not encased in glittering metal? Would the holy blood of a sainted sister, poured into a glass and left in a dark corner of a side altar, unlit by flame, cold and unloved, attract the attention of a nobleman or hysterical peasant seeking a cure?

I agree with Dunstan that a dismembered part of a person, holy or not, is a more attractive thing when art has fashioned a cover, made it into a magic talisman, a talisman which can advise the King as much as a living ealdorman or thegn, but remain silent, unlike them, bestowing wisdom through the act of contemplation of their beauty, as at a glorious mass. However I tremble inwardly when I hear of the consequences of an overzealous desire for the relics of a particular saint; some holy men and women still living but aware of their saintly status have been known to beg for mercy to preserve their bodies whole, fearing the knock at the door of a knife wielding surgeon who may be prospecting for parts too soon.

Relics are just bones, fingers, knees, skulls and parts of skulls, eye sockets. Much of the collection of Stone is here at Frome, locked into the barred recess of the haligdom, waiting for its master to arrive for Christmas. The various items, some large, some small, sit alongside our own particular St John relic which remains here permanently, a piece of the rough garment worn by him and a finger bone, given to us by our founder, Aldhelm, who brought it from Malmesbury when he came to establish our house. Its reliquary awaits refurbishment and by the side of the King's fine personal collection looks a sad sight, its plain wooden coffin-shaped box weary with years and much handling. It has magic, though, its inlaid decoration woven into the wood in the primitive style of the Irish monks of Malmesbury. When lit from above, it sparkles almost as gold, revealing the holy one's name along its side. It gives a thrill to the occasional pilgrim who looks into the saint's display recess of the stone church on his feast day. It brings the monastery of Frome a little income, though pilgrims are few. The forest still holds a spell over them, the big oaks and wild creatures of Selwood still seem formidable to many, indifferent to the needs of travellers, like the bandits who would waylay them. Thievery flourishes in parts of our forest, despite tightened laws and the threat of punishment by hanging. The death penalty is not often utilised, but a young man of twelve, if he is a thief, may suffer this fate. The loss of Heaven as a curse which accompanies the convicted thief does not prevent crime in its entirety, though it should. Hell is not a destination I would wish for, under any circumstance. I would not risk the loss of Heaven. I could never be a thief, by choice. The Saints would catch me out. The descent to Hell, I am told, is not to be recommended.

Stone will be interested to see what the oaken chest from Glastonbury contains. It will divert him, he says, from the weary matters of court. He will arrange short meetings to occur at night, being a light sleeper disturbed with matters of state and documentation. State decisions, he says, produce dark eyed anxiety, history and relics offer security and wisdom. He strokes his collection of saints' parts as a lover does his partner. They provide reassurance, guidance, power, aid sent from above. I have never seen a person so craving the presence of parts of dead others, but each to his own. My preference is for the living, for the spoken and written word, whether sacred or secular, for legend, for poetry, story and song. The mind of a woman moves me and their company reassures me most. They are the strangest of creatures. In that lies their attraction, I suppose.

Athelstan tells me during our meetings that he is pleased with the way the learning of the court is progressing. He says that we three youngsters, myself, Dunstan and Leofa, are making a great contribution to the cultural life of Wessex as the first modern graduates of Glastonbury. The old Irish professors had their good points, after all. A few words of encouragement make a difference to our willingness to work alongside him, are like pearls in our hearts; in mine, at least. Dunstan and Leofa perhaps require and expect more than words.

The chest from Glastonbury, to be kept a secret from the casual eye, is less valuable to the King in terms of statesmanship than relics, but requires urgent attention due to its damp state and this is my chief concern, as we wait for his arrival from Chippenham and royal visitors from abroad for Christmas. It contains documents, Dunstan tells me. I can imagine, from the density of the wood, that it is both heavy as well as large, though much of the weight may be in the wood alone, it is so crudely thick. Its contents may be lightweight in many ways; I shall soon find out.

Renovations are being undertaken at Glastonbury which Dunstan says are vital for its upkeep and safety. The flood waters of many years having got into, under and through its ancient walls. The contents of its extensive library are being distributed to other nearby monasteries with better protection against the weather for the time being. The chest is safe here in the dry scriptorium of Frome. I will make a full inventory of its contents before the court moves on again, though as we are likely to remain in Wessex, I will be able to return to deal with any issues it may raise, as long as excessive court business or unexpected illness do not prevent me. I will open the chest this afternoon, as curious as Stone to see what will be inside.

In this dark afternoon before Vespers, I approach the locked portion of the scriptorium, the haligdom, with a candle in one hand and a large intricate key which Dunstan has passed into my charge. The oaken chest awaits at the end of the room like a living creature, watching me walk along the length of the scriptorium. As if it were a crouching animal, it seems to rise and fall with animate breath. I rest my candle on the sill of a small window beside the barred haligdom and unlock the metal door. The most cumbersome of the King's reliquary collection, brought in the cart ahead of his arrival at Frome for safe keeping and to be polished in readiness for the Christmas events, gleam in the low light. They appear to be alive, too, but their contents are caged. The Glastonbury chest sits on a plank table, conveniently sited for a man to view its contents without having to bend over. It reminds me of a stretched-out corpse.

Unlike the other contents of the haligdom, it is filthy. No one has been allowed to touch it as yet other than the kitchen porter and his boy who carried it here on its arrival. As large as a man's coffin, I marvel at its wooden carvings. I cannot help running a hand along the sloping top and sides, feeling grooves of tooled oak, dancing figures and creatures incised deep into the grain, the work of one dedicated to his task, like our Gospel mad, studious Dunstan. Some might call the work crude, but it has energy. The carving style is unlike anything Dunstan has designed. Its intricacy and wildness bespeak its age, of a primitive time before any Saxon court was in existence. Forest creatures, more visible in the landscape, more fearsome in the lives of men, roamed then, inspiring the imagination of Christians and the resurgent pagan community whose dreams and nightmares gave it birth. Men merged with animals in their minds. Grendel, creature of the deep, could have been born of this creation.

The oaken chest, locked by heavy metal bars, may harbour some of the history of a once solely oral folk, the British Celtic. It is said that they were determined never to write their stories for fear of theft or misunderstanding. They were and still are ignorant of the need to preserve in written verse or prose the doings of their people. Proud of their memories and traditions, they were determined that the time of the bard and scop, of learning and repeating an oral history of their communities would never end, that the written word would never supersede the honoured art of recitation. This chest may contain a small portion of these traditions in manuscript form, written by some who opposed these views. If so, they will provide a vital part of a history of a conquered people, the people of the Kingdom of Dumnonia, a historian's delight.

The carved figures on the lid dance in the candlelight; they writhe and sway with the breath and breeze of my heavy winter robes in the still library air. Some of the figures remind me of carvings in the stone of the crypt of the church and of the old preaching cross at the entrance to the village of Keyford behind the palace and monastery. Living stone, animal stone. I examine the details of the chest lid and sides.

I encounter, with trepidation, the powerful spells of animal shapes. They are similar to the font in our church which Dunstan loathes for its old-fashioned art style, feral creatures with improbable spinal twists, dancing, running, shouting, biting; erotic female forms with arms uplifted, large eyed males, part human, part animal, with branching horns for headgear, the glint of metal on their limbs in applied tin arm rings. Around me and beyond the chest, the eyes of the watching reliquaries and their studded gems awaken in the movement of the candle flame as I run my hands over the lid. I take a sharp breath, step back in horror. I am in the presence of a spiritual force. I say a prayer, let out my breath.

Nothing more happens. Perhaps my imagination is at fault. I settle to my task, bring out another key which belongs to a heavy metal bar crossing the top of the chest. The huge lock, also studded with small animal shapes, magic beasts, concedes defeat. The carved top swings back. The smell of musty manuscripts wafts up. Inside I dimly perceive the stacked, well ordered contents. The deed is done, the chest opened, the spell overcome, as Selwood, once protected by pagan spirits, was overcome.

Tomorrow Athelstan arrives, triumphant from his heavily armed foray into Scotland. He has travelled slowly through his land of Angels, this chosen people, to a long rest at the palace of Gloucester, overnighting at Chippenham and on to Frome for the Christmas court and hunt. Frome is one of his favourite palaces, set in excellent hunting territory. The great hall here is festooned with the huge heads of red deer antlers, trophies killed by former kings. Once he is settled he will want me to report what I have found in the chest. Dunstan will be eager to know, too. They are both, after all, primarily, men of letters and these manuscripts may be of value. State and Church, hand in hand, the past matters for the future of all.

The task begins. I begin to peruse the first of the ancient documents. There are many, heaped in bundles, tied carefully with different coloured ribbons. Their rescue has not come too soon. Yes, it looks as though what is left of the history of Dumnonia, land of the West Welsh, is here, one chest full of a forgotten kingdom's history. This is all there is.

Wilton Abbey, after Sext, Easter Monday, 933

Thank God the workmen are not here today. The heaps of spoil in the cloister are a damaging reminder of the modern world and its work, but at least it is silent at present for the Easter vigils. Tomorrow all will be in uproar again.

Aelfflaed grimaces. Noise, noise. Choir nuns learning anthems by heart are bad enough; random banging and scraping of metal instruments on stone and wood is worse. But if the convent works are to be completed for the winter reception of noble visitors, it is necessary, of course, just intolerable meanwhile. Aelfflaed continues walking around the roofed cloister, less in prayer, more in anger. She came here for peace. Would it be better at Shaftesbury? Probably not.

Her two daughters walking behind her seem less concerned with the current convent disturbance; they look forward to the availability of private washing facilities attached to their cells. Eadflaed, new to the order, fiddles with her wimple, which is too big for her. She is safe, she thinks, from marrying an unwanted suitor while she is here. She can put up with anything rather than that.

Cells? More like comfortable sitting rooms. Just order up your dinner if you don't want to speak to anyone. The large table provided in each will accommodate you and your friends. If you have to live in a convent, away from the court and all its social and diplomatic niceties, an item or two of luxury does no harm, keeps us quiet in our enforced separation from the complex but highly attractive gossip down the road at lively Winchester.

Aelfflaed's pace quickens. Her daughters pick up theirs to match. She can hear their prayer girdles rustling. That's enough of that, prayer. Ten times round the cloister, reasonable exercise. Now back for lunch in the common room. Then a snooze. Then, probably, Edwin will arrive.

She turns sharp right through the cloister entrance and down the steps into the nave of the church. She is sharp in all things, not a patient type. Sharp with her husband, sharp with her daughters and sons. Keen and long sighted, an excellent bedfellow for the insomniacs of her family, not so welcome to the quiet ones who have schemes of their own. She is avoided by some members of her family and they are many. She has elbows like knives, thoughts like pointed horns, her mind enclosed and encased in a delicate secular hood, her thoughts disguised. She has learned, too late in life, to conceal the steeliness of her mind. She will never become a nun. She is a paying guest.

Lunch for the guests is a bit boring, but nourishing. There are flies on the lettuce again. The bread is always good, a brown rustic cob today, a bit gritty for the teeth. Teeth are a worry. They are beginning to give up; already there's a gap on the right side; what fun is old age. To accompany the bread there is cave aged cheese from Wookey Hole and passable vegetable soup. Honey goes nicely with the bread and cheese. Freshly made butter makes the fare almost good enough for a king. It's basic fare for an ex-queen, in her opinion, but wholesome. Dried fruits follow, figs and dates from the Lebanon. Together with today's brisk turn in the cloister, that should do the trick to keep the Devil at bay. A glass of wine completes the meal, perhaps two.

Food soothes the sore mind, honey reminds one of the golden years of power in the palaces and halls with Edward, so often absent, like all good husbands, at war. If there are regrets, they are that she can no longer offer her advice to younger court members who used to sit at her feet. Nowadays they cannot come near her; even her chaplain advises against contacting the Archbishop of York, but she does. Wilton Abbey is meant to contain her interference, but though her body may be constrained, her mind isn't. Sitting back on a couch in her room, replete, she begins, as so often she does, the loop of her own history, the story of her past.

Athelstan's archbishops and bishops are Mercian sympathisers. The Wessex born priests at Winchester still hate him for what he did to Elfred, poor chap, taking himself off in exile to Rome. He went all that way for forgiveness and then fell down dead with the effort. Had Elfred succeeded in doing what was required, at the right time, she would not be in the position she is in now. Mercians and Mercian sympathisers rule the roost in Wessex, God forbid! A simple blinding was all that was asked, but Elfred mucked it up. Her son Edwin should have ruled instead, or even Aelfweard if he had survived. Who knows why her elder son had died. He should have been king; Edward wanted it, everyone wanted it. Why did he die so soon after his father? It all stinks.

The continual looping cycle goes round and round in Aelfflaed's mind. It is short, repeated incessantly and only assuaged by mealtimes, embroidery and gossip.

Athelstan, for thirty years a thorn in Aelfflaed's side. If not for Athelstan, her eldest boy, Aelfweard, would have been king. The priests were never able to sort out the mystery of his demise, but there were rumours. Athelstan was ruthless. She should have been Queen Mother, possibly acting as regent, able to direct, to dictate. Not now. Athelstan is her nightmare, the not quite Aetheling, the prince that Alfred wished for in his dreams, that Edward worried about in his. Books and relics were his world, the studious concerns of a boy who Wessex needed to be bloodthirsty, like his father, for warlike times. The Vikings were ever present, jabbing at our borders with their spears, laughing, ready to break their oaths for peace made a long generation before. Who would ever believe what they had to say? But Athelstan, soppy Athelstan, does. Like his grandfather, eager to hear the best of someone, willing to give them credit, unwilling to defend with the wit and wisdom of a negative outlook. The pessimistic views of some ministers, as Edward's voice faded through the years, were ignored. Sweetness and light, all will be well, said Athelstan after the agreement at Eamont in 927. The northern kings have promised to be good, he said. Pffff! Did he really believe that? A brainless killer, naive and bloodthirsty. That's what Athelstan is.

Aelfflaed grumbles to herself, the old sores revisited every day despite many hours of active prayer which usually turn to cursing. She was briefly the Queen Mother, wife number two. The short time that she had, arranging things for her boys, was not enough. She was high born, born to lead, made royal by marriage, as the first wife Ecgwynn never was. Her sons were safely born in wedlock to a king, not a soon-to-be king. They were true heirs, not maybes. She still has one son. There is still hope.

Ah, the bell. Edwin is here.

'Good afternoon, Mama, sorry to miss lunch. Are you well?' A tall well-groomed young man of about thirty years of age bends under the low arch to Aelfflaed's sitting room. He leaves the door from the cloister ajar. He never closes doors until he is asked to. Light green spring air floods the table in front of him, falls on the platters of colourful fruit and bowls of spring flowers.

Aelfflaed sighs. 'Shut the door, Edwin. I have something important to say to you. Sit down.'

Edwin collapses, ungainly, in a cross legged upholstered chair decorated with a crown and flowers. Mama has been busy with her tapestry designs again. Long legs splay out in front of him, disturbing a cat trying to sleep under the table on its cushion. His foot hits a table leg. The cat wails, shoots out of the door.

'I mean shut, Edwin.' There is more long limb movement. Edwin will never make a dancer. He doesn't know his right from his left. He sighs, ascends, knocks over his chair while turning, picks it up.

Aelfflaed tuts. He has been like this since he was thirteen. Awkward, not very bright. Never his father's choice for a crown, but he would do for hers. It may not be too late, yet.

Edwin closes the door. Eager to please, he begins to introduce his favourite topic and hers: life outside the cloister, life in the court. He knows she loves gossip. How else will she keep her finger on the pulse of Wessex except through him?

'Winchester is looking splendid for the Easter festivals, Mama, the Good Friday rituals were even bloodier this year than last and the risen Christ was attended by many confirmations. All the virgins of the town were there in white, ready to receive the blessings from on high, to begin their lives in Christ...'

'Enough of religion, Edwin. Don't you think that I get enough of it here? Of course I am pleased that God and his Saints are being well looked after by the folk festivals of the city. But I have important matters to discuss with you which have come from another quarter. Archbishop Wulfstan has been here. He tells me the matter of the North, Athelstan's great matter, is being discussed behind closed doors at the witans. The last two witans, in fact, have been largely taken up with agreements and disagreements about Strathcylde and Alba. What do you know of these?'

Edwin shakes his head, looks down and along to his finely shod feet. 'I know very little, Mama. You are well aware of my position at court. Mostly I am kept in the dark.'

'It is not good enough!' Mama has been expecting this; her son, her only son since the death of Aelfweard all those years ago, has little part to play in the current king's affairs, in the running of the kingdom. The loop begins again, always fresh to her mind. Aelfflaed rehearses it with Edwin.

Edmund is Athelstan's choice for heir, yet at the beginning of his reign, it was Edwin who was seen, at least by some, to be deserving of the chief aetheling's role. Winchester would have had him, if they could. If only she had courted Athelstan's favours more when he was young; but he was often in Mercia, often disagreeable to her, shunned her in the sewing rooms. He disliked her loud colour choices, she could tell. The feeling was mutual. You can only call someone a wicked stepmother once to alienate them. And with his own mother incarcerated, regarded as a failed concubine, repudiated and forgotten by all at court, it would have been difficult anyway to be friendly. You never hear about wicked stepsons or daughters. It's always the stepmother who is ridiculed. At least he did not call her a witch. Athelstan has good manners, most of the time. And he wouldn't fall over a chair.

'Listen to me, Edwin and keep those great feet still. Wulfstan tells me that there is going to be an important push by the army and navy northwards in the summer of next year to bring Constantine to bay. There is a chance that there will be disaster for the Wessex court if they get their planning wrong, do not consider the aftermath of any success. If Athelstan fails in some way, you will be the natural choice as a grown man to take over. The southern nobles will rebel rather than be taxed to pay off a ransom, for instance. Have you considered any of this?' Aelfflaed jabs at her son with a walking stick. 'You could be King in a few months' time, you know.'

Edwin is shocked. The world is mad. Why throw up a peaceful life in southern England to go to war? What is the point?

'Yes, Mama.' It is always yes, Mama. No, Mama is a rare treat and, he can tell, not an option today.

Monastery of St John, Frome, after Prime, 14 December, 934

In the monastery, the reflective time of Advent expectation is upon us. My home brotherhood of Frome, from which I spring and which has educated the child in me, struggles to maintain its income. Its private collection of relics is not large and needs attention; the King's travelling collection is much larger and better maintained, including many items collected by Alfred and Edward, his grandfather and father. Its library is only open to those who can read and they are few, even in these times. The hospital, however, is growing in reputation. We save many lives, make dying as comfortable as possible. War wound treatment is a speciality. Aelfflaed, when she was queen, began the organisation of a ward for veterans. Eadgifu, though she was not a close associate of her husband's former wife, has built up the facilities. The older men worst injured during the campaign in the north are here; the younger ones are being treated at Wilton.

There is still reluctance to become literate amongst even the highest in our land, particularly in this western part of Wessex. The West Welsh, low in status in the main, regret still the loss of their land. They have largely reverted to their old oral ways, preferring the recitation of edicts to written law abiding requirements. They want to keep room to manoeuvre. In the countryside beyond the forests, they tend their animals, defend them from the wolf, pay their dues and keep their heads down. They still speak their own Welsh language and have assisted, though unwilling, in the naming and dividing of their former country of Dumnonia. They eat, sleep, fornicate and expect little more. They will get nothing and go nowhere.

In religious terms, they have rejected, for the most part, an insistence by Saxon bishops on the formal adoption of the Roman Christian way. It takes many years to change minds, perhaps many generations. Rome is not their dream, though it is ours. It is their nightmare. I have had many discussions with my mother, who knew the British brothers and sisters at Keyford when they were in their last days, to try to persuade her that the English language of the Saxons and the art of the written word are key to the future. She bewails the visible destruction of huge old master oaks of Coit Mawr, her friends, she says, which have been taken by Saxon nobles for their barns and halls. Bridges and buildings add prestige. It is unnecessary destruction; such waste, she says. Huge piles of broken oak bodies litter the edge of the town, waiting to be used or abandoned, weathering and rotting. She marks the time of each one's demise, says she knows their names. Owl Oak, Herne Oak, Oak of the Green Antlers, her prayers are for them. She says they are the ancients, the wise ones. They are at least 500 years old. She puts offerings of food on their massive bleeding stumps. She still insists on the efficacy of the mind's memory and a religious focus on nature which the old people, she says, had. She even visits the grave of Kay, founder of the small monastery on the hill above Frome and lays greenery there at the four festivals. She likes making garlands. Her tears, she says, bind them all. Somebody must remember.

My mother rants on. She cannot appreciate the economic worth of wood. My father, much to my mother's dismay, contributes to the desecration of her forest home by insisting on using his skills to the full with his heavy woodworking axes and tools on whatever living, dead and dying wood comes to hand. He has sustained us by his skills, extending and maintaining the palace and its outlying hunt refuges, acting as an extra beater for hare hunts in open glades and as dog handler for the palace kennels. He brings home a share of meat which he has killed under licence for the bassets, blood and wolfhounds which are kept here in readiness. He shrugs when my mother wails at him, having noted the disappearance of yet another of her arboreal friends from the greensand hills where she roams. She reports that Gaer Hill will soon be completely bereft of its soul. My father is silent when she cries, only responding by pointing with his knife to the plate of food in front of him. He brings home the bacon. What can she do? Remember. Perhaps that will have to be enough.

She is good at remembering, though her memories, I suspect, are stimulated by an emotional attachment to her home and landscape and may owe a great deal to her imagination and traditional superstitions. My father says she lives in the past. She still thinks of herself as a Dumnonian. Like the other British nations in these islands subject to the Saxon conqueror, Dumnonia's history is asleep, its varied landscape now seen as a resource to be utilised, to be dug, chopped, mined. A forgotten land, lost land, Lloegr. Mother is easily set off on one of her rants. I fear death will be a blessing to her.

But there are compensations in being conquered by freshly Christianised Saxons, even for my mother, if only she would recognise them. Monastic scouts from Malmesbury and Glastonbury found me, playing in the palace yard as an eight-year-old, helping my father with the hunting dogs and picked me for educational drilling at Glastonbury alongside Leofa and Dunstan. Others joined us, born of all sectors of the nation, British, Irish, Dane and Saxon, some with connections to wealthy families, some chosen just for their acuteness or cuteness. A few girls added to the class's enthusiasm of youth. They would not be chosen now. There is a tightening of intent in these early days of education for all. Athelstan would like noble girls to receive teaching as extensive as the boys, but there is a trend against this which is gaining ground. The ealdormen and thegns prefer their family women to sew. Reading and writing are a threat to household peace, they say. The churchmen concur with the view that education is best dealt with in separate schools. They say it is progress.

As time went by, the small religious school at Frome which I attended as a child lost its teachers to Glastonbury, the library and school there having survived the ravages of the Danes during Alfred's time by some miracle or magic. We chosen youngsters boarded there and grew up in the peaceful, recovery times of Edward. Apart from suffering runny noses, which was probably something to do with the perpetual dankness of the place, we thrived. Fish, cheese and bread, with vegetables grown by the community, made us strong. By the age of twelve we were practised in reading and writing, could understand Latin and the Saxon tongue and were encouraged by our teachers to retain our mother tongues of Welsh, Scandinavian, Breton or other as a possible useful adjunct to our futures in scriptoriums, cultural workshops or as interpreters to the court. Some could even think of becoming diplomats. Ambitions ran high, anything was possible, even for the low born, as long as they were able and worked hard.

Leofa, with his Irish and Scandinavian ancestry, was particularly mindful of this and became one of the main means of intercommunication at Athelstan's court as the numbers of foreign dignitaries swelled during these safer years for travelling. Many were the journeys made to Rome at this time across the Christian lands of the Pope, though I never went. I listen to the tales of the fabulous lands of the warm south, to the doings of the cardinals and popes. That's what I do best, listen. I can see, feel, even smell those far off places when they are described by others. I live vicariously off others' experiences. I like to restrict my travel within a few miles of where I happen to be. That's chiefly within Wessex, short distances by foot or on horse if need be. It's not too far for the soul to stretch.

As we grew older and our best talents and inclinations were encouraged by the patient Irish monks, Leofa, Dunstan and I, the keenest of our class, in language and literature in Leofa's case, in manuscript and charter law in mine and in general arts in Dunstan's, we spent more time with the travelling court of Athelstan, learning our trade on the hoof, gradually becoming experts in our fields. Leofa and I exchanged places with each other at various times, listening and recording agreements and disagreements between various landholders at witans as the King moved around Wessex, settling disputes and noting requirements to his holdings, welding the nation in his written charters.

Increasingly we have to watch out for forgeries. Sometimes an unscrupulous thegn requires a friend or family member working in a scriptorium to produce a document to prove title. This may occur in lands newly acquired from the Welsh, where no written title has existed before, or in recovering land stolen by Vikings. Often these are, by right, holdings of the King. Our careful rewritings can make them so.

There are often lengthy disputes about ownership of relatively small parcels of land, particularly when being claimed by monastic communities as gifts from former owners to sustain them in their bid for a safe passage to heaven. Prayers offered for a soul equal the value of the land bestowed and gain income for the community. Greed, as ever and in every age, is accompanied by prayer. Prayers for something, prayers against something. Curses, some might call them. My mother says she would like to strike the lot of them dead. Then she remembers the imprecations of the Church about wishing ill on Saxon rulers. After that, she remembers her Celtic Christian benevolence and regrets her words, which she begs us to forget. More tears, more wailing.

The business of words, heard and written, occupy Leofa and myself continually. There is little thought of any family life of our own and yet we are not monks, for we do not occupy our spare time solely in prayer. We are certainly not celibate. We are too young. We have much to do with the secular organisation of the court and inevitably with the ladies and servants of the court.

Dunstan is different. He has had his encounters with women, but he seems to be completely taken up with the role of single-mindedly spearheading Wessex's cultural development.

Athelstan wishes to gain credence as a ruler encouraging the Arts, as Charlemagne did, as his grandfather did. Dunstan has found a niche for his ambition. Athelstan's father had less time for educational pursuits, but wished his sons to continue the process of civilisation and Christianity, to bring everyone under the Pope's yoke. The Roman Empire worked, on the whole, for the maximum number of people within its borders and the Pope's Empire is its replacement.

But Dunstan may be before his time. He is a rare sort, talented and determined. He may go far, in the right court climate. His work is beginning to be seen by some as the flowering fruit on the top of the bough of a well organised nation. Leofa and I are factotums of the state, but he is the deliverer of beauty, unnecessary accoutrements, the embellisher of reliquaries, the designer of stoles for saints.

He sees himself as a flower or vine, is trying to establish flowers, particularly the acanthus, as the archetypal motif for the architecture of the future, getting away from animals, the creatures of sex and fertility, which make him shudder. I don't mind both. The court ladies like his ideas. Eadgifu has them sewing embroideries based on his designs. Dunstan bends over her shoulder as she sews, encouraging the new floral motif, suggesting colours and stitches. Intimate. I sometimes wonder about them, when I see them together.

Dunstan is less concerned than Eadgifu with the exercise of power. He will make his way as long as he pleases Stone, if no-one else. His new friend Aethelwold is more interested in the development of the Church and its part in nation building. He is an opinionated revolutionary, to my mind. Dunstan's mind is more on artistic detail. He has been conducting, recently, a review of the interior decorations of churches in Wessex. When we were all inside the Minster at Winchester in recent months he was there as the King's advisor on treasure and art, making note of design, shape and colours used to paint the walls and pillars of the nave, tut-tutting at excessive emblems and the poor state of preservation of decoration of the seventh and eighth centuries. He regards the old style, he tells us, as primitive, dull and worn in many places, in need of replacing, of investment, creative thought. He is an artist who likes to deliver in fresh coordinated colour, says this has more impact on the eye and mind of the viewer, especially in a Christian context. Colours can be used symbolically, he says. He has been to Rome and Constantinople. He has many impressive ideas for redecoration and architecture, more than most of us can take in. We try to slow him down by asking for drawings. We haven't his phenomenal visual skills, we say. His enthusiasm is encouraged by Athelstan, but the more conservative quarters of the court are wary, like to keep things as they are. They mutter when he is around, but Dunstan ignores them. He is safe; he is one of them, a cousin to the King, a nephew to bishops.

When Dunstan gives his lectures, extolling the virtues of the Byzantine icons he has seen in the south, the deep, dark eyes of Justinian, the glorious folds of clothes sculpted in mosaic high on the walls of Hagia Sophia and Ravenna, the fullness of expression of a saintly hand raised in supplication, we roll our eyes and let him finish; there is no stopping him. He is my friend, but the gentlemen of the court find him too obsessive, too wedded to his art. He should be careful. He begins to bore too many. Eadgifu takes his part, says she loves what he is doing. What would we do without him, she says.

Who will win the day, the moderniser Dunstan, moving ever closer to Athelstan, or the conservative ealdormen and thegns, who have vested interests in the monasteries? Many members of their families, married secular relatives, belong to their communities. Money and prayers go hand in hand. They have given away much land to the communities of brethren and nuns to ease their way to Heaven. If he lives long and survives attempts by some to oust him, Dunstan will perhaps prevail. He has determination, can see the future, he insists. The thegns, though, have their own view of the future, and their swords may be mightier than Dunstan's pen or brush. Who will bully best?

All this is irrelevant to the British in our midst. Beyond the court, a few Welsh landowners sometimes cross swords with thegns or their reeves; they are renowned for their grumbles locally. They have little impact on court business and none on the architecture or artistic styles being debated in the palaces. They are dealt with easily in local courts. Sometimes there are disputes which claim the King's attention, but they are rare. The Welsh have become used to receiving scant justice, tend to order their own affairs behind closed doors. Court intrigues are of no interest. Let the Wessex dynasty cut its own throat, they think. My mother mingles with them on her walks. Most are bilingual, still retaining affection for their native customs, still very good at singing. We have musical groups to entertain the court occasionally. Knowing the language, I have sometimes interceded for them with Athelstan. Complaining is usually as far as problems go; they insist that they have been robbed. I fear the grudges will last for at least another generation.

They should make the best of their obscurity. Grudges and song, eating and sleeping. Not such a bad life. Better than a king's, in my opinion.

Wilton Abbey, 13 May 933

'Edwin, don't be so stupid. Of course you must.' Aelfflaed has got her "musts" about her. Edwin, feeling vulnerable, crosses his long legs.

In Aelfflaed's comfortable sitting room the spring light is advancing, throwing hatched shadows through the diamond cut panes. The windows are closed. The room is stupefying. That's how she likes it. There is a fire in a grate at the side of the room, recently banked up and blazing, for soothing older bones. For the male listeners present it is unbearably hot. Edwin tears off his outer garment. The Archbishop and two clerks wish they could. They clamp their teeth, drip into their black wool gowns. Wulfstan looks as though he might explode.

'Mama, we need the window open, please.' Edwin has noticed the discomfort of his male companions. His practical suggestion might offset his mother's theoretical and tactical theme, might divert the old girl for a minute while the rest have time to think. Their brains are getting cooked as well as their bodies. Aelfflaed waves a nonchalant arm.

'Madam, if I may offer a suggestion...' Wulfstan of York moves to the window, opens it, while Aelfflaed considers her next "must". Her chair, placed carefully in front of the window, is very much like a throne; high pointed back, comfortable padded tapestry. Impressively carved arms, a tapestry footstool to show off her embroidered slippers. All her own design, of course. There's a large embroidery frame by the window with a half done colourful altar piece on it. Heavy yellow floral tapestry curtains line the walls and edge the windows, useful for the winter, but staying hung up for the summer as they are so beautiful. All the visitors remark on them. It will take two years to finish the altar cloth. It features more yellow flowers and a nature goddess to her own design. Will she be granted the time to complete it, she wonders?

Wulfstan returns to his place, standing facing the former queen. The divorced queen. The queen of two sons and many daughters. Only one son now, Edwin. The younger of the two and not the best of the brood. One son down, one to go. All to play for.

'The King is proposing to take his army and navy to the north next summer. Constantine of Scotland is refusing to accede to Athelstan's requests. He says he will never be a sub-king to anyone and certainly does not owe Wessex any taxation. The North, with of course the Viking leaders, is sticking with him in this. In York there is much unrest. We are fearful and scornful in equal measure. If your plan for the aetheling Edwin is to come to fruition there must be some allowance made for their needs.'

'Hmpf.' Aelfflaed is in charge, here, today. 'We would rather hold the Northumbrian lands if we could, but some recognition of the rights of the North could be agreed, some lessening of taxation, if Edwin can gain the crown of England. We should concentrate on how this might be achieved. Close the window, Edwin, my neck is receiving a draught.'

Aelfflaed, by having the window closed, achieves a concentration of minds. Decision making is easiest when the room is too cold, or too hot, or there is no food and drink on offer or chairs. Edwin occupies the only other chair in the room, but it is Edwin who needs most persuading to act.

'Edwin, give the Archbishop your seat. He is your elder.' Edwin gets up. He makes a special effort to avoid the furniture, succeeds. He backs towards the door. There is a shrink crack between the door and the wall which may allow some air to enter.

Wulfstan needs no persuading, takes the unoccupied chair and leans forward with a conspiratorial waving forefinger, demonstrating his commitment to the project, he thinks. He turns to include and point at everyone in the room. He retracts his finger as his eyes meet Aelfflaed's.

'Madam, there is no doubt in my mind as in yours that Edwin is entitled to the crown of Wessex, should be the heir apparent to Athelstan. As Edward's remaining adult son of Wessex, born to yourself as Queen, he has the ability to receive the support of both Mercia and Wessex. There will be no danger to the overall plan for a united England. Progress will be made. That young Edmund should have been placed in a higher position as Aetheling by Athelstan is beyond belief. The days of a royal dynasty being able to practice choice between heirs is long gone, in my opinion. The eldest comes first. You know that is my view and the view of many others.'

Wulfstan looks round at the clerks as though challenging them to say otherwise. Dunstan and Leofa, as youngsters making their way, maintain their position as indifferent bystanders. The recording of history is their remit. They make notes, perhaps to report to the King. Dunstan looks at Leofa. They both raise their pens, unsure of their position in this debate.

An archbishop has as much power as a king in these days, if not more so. There are only two of them. The Pope commands them both. Perhaps the young clerks, beholden to the Church but preferring the company of the King, should not have accompanied this archbishop, a northerner, to Wilton on this occasion. But they are inscrutable to the ex-queen and her son, just black-cloaked clerks accompanying Wulfstan. Wulfstan is her choice for assistance in her cause, Edwin, but is he her choice for treason? This is the question. Aelfflaed looks at them both.

'Come here.'

Aelfflaed, her face in shadow, beckons to the two young priests. They approach the tapestry throne from the cloister door where they have been lurking near Edwin, doing their quiet duty, pens in hand. Dunstan reaches her first and stands in front of Leofa. They both bow to the waist.

'Don't I know you?' Aelfflaed has recognised the blonde young man.

'We have met at court, Madam. One of my uncles is Aelfheah and another was Athelm, Bishop of Wells. I was fortunate enough to be educated at Glastonbury, along with my friend here, Leofa.'

Dunstan stops, waits for Aelfflaed to interject, but she turns away. Men do not look like the children they once were and this man has done much outward changing since her days in Edward's court. Her daughters would know more about him, those who had not yet been shipped off to foreign courts as brides. She could check with them. Dunstan's fair hair will not have changed much. It was probably always a yellow mop. Leofa, behind him, is more interesting. Dark eyes. Red hair, freckled skin. He could provide the form for her next design, a nature god. Aelfflaed points at him. She needs to test his allegiances before going further. She indicates that he should stand beside Dunstan.

'And what are your connections? I see that you are both clerks, not priests.'

'Madam, I have none. I was born of an Irish land holding immigrant and a Scandinavian mother. I am a mongrel. Fortunately I was rescued from an obscure fate by the scouts of Glastonbury. My interests lie with the development of the court and my place in it. I wish to serve Wessex and whoever rules it.' Leofa bows again and when the finger flicks upwards returns to his place behind Dunstan.

Wulfstan elucidates. 'As things are in flux, Madam, and the nation's future depends on certainty for the years ahead, I can guarantee that my two clerks here present will remain silent about any course of action here decided upon. Naturally Edwin is considered the rightful heir, there is no doubt of that, and Athelstan has made a mistake in suggesting that he may be side-lined. But perhaps, if I may?'

Wulfstan, cautious, already armed with equipment for oath swearing if need be, pulls back his outer vestment to reveal a chain festooned with spiritual weaponry. Metal capsules of holy blood, pilgrim touch-relics, a finger of a saint in a small wooden coffin of its own, the armoury is revealed. Around his neck, hanging low, hangs a pendant talisman of holy hair as well as a large wood and metal crucifix. No wonder he clanked as he came into the room.

Aelfflaed snorts at the appearance of so much religious metalwork. She looks over to the embroidery loom to her left with its attendant hanging coloured threads. But each to his own. Monks and bishops are increasingly cluttered about the person by this stuff. It's Athelstan's fault, he and his aunt encouraged this relic collecting. An oath sworn on a piece of tapestry or embroidery, unless it has touched a sainted corpse and become a relic in itself, is not much of a guarantee of secrets kept, more's the pity.

It is time to swear. A holy oath on a holy relic. 'Come here.'

The two clerks move towards Wulfstan. He and the ex-queen are powerful figures in their lives. Their demeanour alone is forbidding. Together they make a great impression on the young men who have yet to make their way in life. Who should they choose to support, a younger son of a dead king or his half-brother, Athelstan, who has been in power for nine years but now chooses to name another half-brother, by another queen, as his heir, his Aetheling? Edmund is a child still and Athelstan is getting weary. But he is Uncle Stone and promises more.

The decision is easy. They are pragmatists, both of them. The oaths must be taken, the loyalty shown. They will do what they must do.

'Wulfstan, you will find in the wall cupboard over there,' Aelfflaed indicates with her languidly raised arm, 'a piece of parchment, ink and pen. Please bring them to the table.' Writing combined with an oath, now that's a serious business indeed. Not an oath to go back on. The two young men recognise the severity of their position. Law is being invoked. Law is their metier, better than religious symbols. Better watch out.

'I will quote and you will write.'

Wulfstan finds the items for recording what is about to be said. The three men move to the large beeswaxed oak table in the centre of the room. It has rounded legs like the sturdy columns of the Old Minster nave. Dunstan moves a patterned bowl of fruit, flowers in a vase and an ornate candlestick to a further end.

'Edwin, you may accompany them,' Aelfflaed indicates that he should get up to watch the writing of her words. He does so, hangs over the edge of the table, watching Wulfstan write.

'Put today's date. You can put in your usual flummery regarding God and the Saints later.' Wulfstan gasps. This is not a God-fearing queen. All pretence has gone. No wonder she is not welcome at court.

'Write this. In the light of the threatened challenge to the rights of the heir to the throne of Wessex and Mercia, Edwin, I here declare that I will assist in the just cause of his enthronement in due time. He will be the accepted chief Aetheling of Athelstan. I agree not to speak of this matter to anyone outside of this room on this day etc etc. I am aware that my life will not be spared of the torment of Hell etc etc, Wulfstan, you know what needs to be put here. Your oaths will be binding for life, on the relic of... who is it you have there, Wulfstan? St Radegund's finger you say? On St Radegund of blessed memory. Now sign, all of you. And Wulfstan, you keep a copy. Take it with you to York when you go.'

The three men swear and sign.

'You too, Edwin.' Aelfflaed is not sure that her son is altogether on board with the idea of becoming Aetheling again after so many years of happy obscurity and laziness. Hunting is better fun than fighting. And with a war brewing in the north, he would have to do plenty of that, if he was expected to rule someday.

'I'm sorry,' Edwin mouths to Dunstan.

If only his elder brother had survived. If only his mother was not as she was. If Athelstan had married and had sons of his own, things would not have come to this. Blast the Virgin King. And then there is Eadgifu with her brace of sons. Without the existence of young Edmund and Eadred, there would be no faction growing for the cause of his mother to right her wrongs.

The reach of a scorned woman from a convent can be long, longer than even a king's, sometimes. Aelfflaed will do what she has to do for her remaining boy.

With God on his side, Athelstan felt himself to be protected, as an anointed king would. With the Devil on hers, his elder stepmother felt that she might be his equal in power.

It would all end badly, that was for sure.

Monastery of St John, Frome, after Sext, 14 December 934

The kitchens and cobbled yards of the palace are in uproar. In the scriptorium, I, Nonna, am busy too, though less noisily, preparing copious writing materials for the witan. The King is arriving early tomorrow. Cold stores are full of freshly killed and jointed corpses, the animal pens nearby have been emptied of their occupants. Blood runs in rivers under the slaughter house gate. Squeals, lowing and quacking have been silenced. They have been replaced by shouting slaughtermen and women skinning, plucking, boiling and sorting of piles of flesh, chopping and scraping by cooks and their boys, everyone filthy with the excrement. The refuse is shovelled into carts which overflow with steaming waste material. Off they go to the tannery or into the aprons of peasant wives waiting by the gate eager for some of the fat, bones, tails and heads. There is more shouting about that, too. Food for free produces fights. Voices become shrill and quarrelsome. The male palace staff can't cope with it all. They pull down their hoods to try to escape the cacophony.

Something charitable has to be given away and will be marked by the steward, a gift by the King to the nearby township. Are the town's inhabitants really the most in need? I have my doubts. They are certainly the nearest to the palace and word spreads fast. The women of Frome, poor or rich, will be grateful for free bounty and will offer prayers for the safe keeping of the Wessex family. It's all grist to the mill on the journey to Heaven above. Give and take, mutual back scratching; everybody knows his place. We all get along.

The great hunt of Christmas is planned by the Huntsman who travels with the court. There will be several days of chasing hounds, hawks and horses. Athelstan admires the countryside of Frome and the opportunities which the forest provides. Sometimes Cheddar palace is chosen for the thrill of hunting in the gorge. He likes the west country, this westerly Wessex. It's almost as good as western Mercia, he says, in terms of the hunt but also the views. Somehow the former Welsh lands and their fringes have greater attraction for the beasts of the wild. They flourish there in coombes and woodland, hills and moorland. Stone is a bit of a lone wolf, says he would be one if he were an animal. What would I be? Leofa says a badger. Dunstan would be a fox. Leofa? I think a bird of prey of some kind.

I digress. About one hundred important guests, their families and followers are expected to be accommodated for the period of the Christmas court. Numbers vary with different courtiers arriving at various times to supervise preparations. There is much to plan for. Eadgifu takes charge of food menus, flowers, greenery for Christmas, toiletries. Edwin helped with stabling arrangements but that has become another area organised by Eadgifu since his death. She makes sure there are ponies to ride for the ladies. The grooms provide comfortable riding cobs for two archbishops and fifteen bishops, who usually have more girth than the noblemen. There is also a full stable of worthy hunters for nobles and a vast choice of freshly made saddlery and other hunting equipment, which will be gifts to take home at the end of the witan. There are many benefits to being at the Christmas court by invitation.

The witan will, as usual, be business mixed with pleasure. There will be courteous but vain attempts to impress foreign dignitaries, astonishment, real and feigned, of the cultural achievements of Athelstan's reign, flattery and in return the gifts of binding, mind boggling valuable treasure. Stone will bestow reliquaries which he has bought from holy sites throughout Europe. There will be displays in the church of some of these, closely guarded, before they are given as tokens of intention to seal rights and duties. You scratch my back... it's how all royal relationships are arranged.

All of the court pretends, whispers young Eadred the younger aetheling to his mother. She tells us about his astuteness. He should know better, but he is only ten years old. He sees things with the child's eye of truth. Eadgifu gives him a cuff. *Learn your manners.*

Pretence? What sub-king or noble can refuse to accept or fail to acknowledge the gift of gold, provided with a dose of flattery, particularly when combined with the holiest parts of a revered saint? A prince must learn to praise, must learn how to accept it. A gift of treasure makes up for having to adopt the new title of Sub-King. That's the fate of most of the former British kings who come here. Hywel Dda has come to terms with it. But who wants to be a sub-king? I'd rather be a poor clerk. I don't have to swear allegiance so often, can act as I think fit within reason. That is the charm of working as part of the Chancery. Being one's own man, keeping one's own counsel. Thank the saints, Stone is broad minded. It might not be as easy under another king.

Flattery and promises, binding promises, made in the presence and ownership of such treasures, with them and over them, seal an oath, the Christian oath, enable the court to function smoothly. Excommunication and a future in Hell is the penalty for a broken holy oath. Patronage, promises and Hell are the carrots and stick of governance, the oil making things work. The convinced Christian must be a fearful man. Athelstan is working, with Dunstan's help, on increasing the effectiveness of this fear of the consequences of oath-breaking, of binding his sub-rulers ever closer in Christ. They may bend the mind and soul even of the Practised Scoundrel, Constantine of the Scots of Alba, who has been forced to accompany the king south from his wild, rainy domain. The Holy Splinter or some other saint's relic should weaken his resolve. If not, perhaps the head of Constantine may make its way on to a display stand. Now that would be an interesting relic. But it's more likely to be on a stake, as St Oswald's was, than in a saint's reliquary. Some would like to see it there. Dangerous folk need controlling by strict sanctions.

Losing your head is a more certain way of losing power than a superficial blinding operation. Lurid punishments for a potential enemy are the chief talk of the court. I would wish to try to steer clear of this, but Stone wants to know what everybody thinks, so I listen.

A good dose of fear of the Otherworld might offset any ideas Constantine and the other sub-kings might have of raising arms. We could all live as Christians together in peace and with beneficial trade, Athelstan thinks. We can share music, art, linguistics, learn from each other, he says. He still has hope, even at forty. Only the Scandinavians are a thorn in our side, refusing, even though Guthrum in East Anglia bowed to Alfred's will to become Christian, to shake off their heathen beliefs, continuing to scream their bloody way to Valhalla. But they live in their squalid fortresses, hardly a stone privy between them, a long way off to the east and north, and in these years, thanks to Alfred and Edward, are little trouble. Their idea of culture is a good public throat slitting. If they came to court Athelstan would have difficulty getting them to sit still for a long-winded poem performance, unless it were one of their own. Loud guffawing at everything is their style, nothing serious, except a bloody tale with a sad ending of lost love. Then they cry like women. There may be some of their kind here in a few days' time; Leofa has been warned to refresh his father's tongue for possible interpretation requirements. I hope to see some; their dress is said to be outlandish.

The chief concerns of the steward of palaces, who, like me, has travelled ahead to prepare for the reception of the king and his guests, are shelter and food. The structures here in Frome are not modern and like Glastonbury much needs to be continually checked. Stone resists modernisation of all the palaces, likes the primitive buildings of his forefathers, says they have the smells of his early childhood in Wessex spent with his grandfather. While progressive in some things, he is conservative in others.

There is plenty of fire fuel to stoke the warmth of evening feasts to come and plentiful game as well as fowl to keep the kitchens in work. The people living nearby, together with villagers of Keyford, are willing to assist, for a few pennies, in swelling the ranks of servants who are permanently attached to Frome palace and monastery. Some are outside now, making that din in the palace courtyard. Forest folk have lately taken to dwelling just beyond and below the church, building daub houses along the line of one of the streams which issue from the north facing hill. Natural springs nourish the growth of the little town, keep it healthy. Drinking water and waste are catered for. The growing numbers of townsfolk take income from operating a toll at the bridge for passing travellers. They sell hunting mementoes and pilgrim badges of St John the Baptist and St Aldhelm to thegns and their followers who gain access and rights in the royal forest, though, it must be confessed, local metalwork does not match the skills of the lay brothers of Glastonbury. Dunstan scorns their pitiful efforts.

Frome is becoming populous, a convenient central township in the Wessex heartlands though the oaks of Selwood Forest still crowd at its edges. They cover the slopes of the hills and valleys where red harbingers of the new year, the red moss-cup fungi, grow in amongst damp fern and moss. My mother collects them still for display, places them in the church porch, insistent on keeping up her old traditions. I hope, for my mother's sake, that Frome will keep its rural character for longer than the other burgeoning townships of Wessex with their bustling trade and modern ways, their continual building and restructuring. The wild nature of these steep wooded hills resists market forces which prevail elsewhere in these peaceful times while we recover from the Viking onslaught of fifty years ago. The green gold of the oaks of Selwood have value beyond their usefulness in building; they should not be removed wholesale in one generation, Athelstan will see to that. Complete removal would damage the hunting of hart, boar and wolf.

Everyone who is involved with Frome palace and the coming witan meeting are focused on the great event, this Christmas court, the return of the King in triumph at his peaceful assimilation of the major territories of the lands of Britain, at achieving the peaceful submission of their rulers, grumbling or willing. They shall have his Christian support against mutual enemies. Wisdom will prevail. Stone's grandfather would be proud.

Some who inhabit Winchester will be envious. Will they bring their devious thoughts with them to our celebrations?

The Palace of Cheddar, 4 June 933

The light and airy spaces of the palace grounds and buildings of Cheddar, with their views out over the Summerlands, have been favoured by the King and his line for many years. Athelstan is wandering around with his master builder. Heaps of spoil cover the open yard and garden. It takes foresight to imagine what this will look like in a year's time, maybe less. Piles of sawn and weathering oak lie about. This is a holy day; the workmen have gone to their homes. There's a holiday from their noise, too, just gorge buzzards soaring overhead, crying 'I am'.

As with other West Wessex palaces, Cheddar is undergoing reconstruction. A new hall to suit new times with a nearby roofed latrine, designed for comfort, is being built reusing massive timbers from the original hall. There will be no more smoking central fire. No more red-rimmed weeping eyes. The ladies have won their argument. Inevitably some character is lost by the removal of the central hearth around which so many tales have by tradition been told. A brazier or grate in the side of a building is awkward for heroic tale gatherings. The circle is lost. Perhaps a rearrangement of benches in an arc may be acceptable. It was done in Roman times in the open air and in the north at Yeavering, Dunstan says.

Change is never popular, but people get used to things. The master builder is an enthusiast of the latest plans, is glad of the King's keen interest, welcomes his suggestions for details. He will be magnificently rewarded if he gets the job done before winter. There is an outside chance of using the new hall for the Christmas witan, says Stone. *That's pushing it*, thinks the builder, but does not say so. Too many internal fittings and decorations are required for that. But we'll see. We'll see. Athelstan doesn't like 'We'll see,' words often used by his father. He likes 'Yes we can!' better.

There is plenty of scope for modernisation, an appetite for

it amongst the noble women and plenty of money in the coffers to pay for it. More foreign leaders are expected each year at celebrations and witans and they are used to better facilities. Fines from the law courts have been rolling in, money fines instead of blood feud have become the norm. Use your sword, break the peace and you will pay. Some old families would prefer to have a good bloody fight to clear the air, but the argument of the King is that the air eventually goes foul again and he is deprived of yet another strong young man who could fight for him. He needs all the fighters he can get for the coming campaign in Scotland.

Meanwhile, major building goes on at Cheddar. Tomorrow there will be shovelling, sawing, hammering again. Today Athelstan chats to his hunting companions (this is a small, rare, private hunt for friends and family only) in the empty old hall with its smoky central hearth. He looks around, shares the memories of old times with his grandfather and father spent listening to the tales of Wessex, watching in his mind the elderly men who drank too much and fell off stools. He pictures familiar young faces across the central hearth lit up, rosy with laughter. He hears the tales of characters of battles won and lost, of war wounds healed and poisonings survived, of women stolen or loved, of treasure. The good old days, when men were men. When his mother was there. Before his father sent him away.

On the following morning as work resumes he wanders out to inspect the ongoing building, to view and chat to the different craftsmen. He wants to see carving being done of the creatures of the hunt and their mythical counterparts, wants to witness the swings and hoists of heavy oak being positioned.

If he could be born again, he would have enjoyed being an architect, as grandfather Alfred would have, too. Perhaps woodworking is in the blood of every West Saxon. Stone is a greater challenge, a different skill. Plans and parchment, mathematics and wood work. Mud, wood, stone. Fresh air. Better almost than being in a relic room. Discussions about weather proofing delight and distract him, discussion of the latest designs make him forget his cares. He views sketches of the details of Carolingian buildings, some of which are Dunstan's. Can we incorporate stonework? Tradition requires wood. But we might try some rough limestone footings incorporated into the foundations as support for the traditional massive posts. Then of course there will be a most impressive roof of best quality thatch from the reed beds nearby. Look upwards in your mind. Internally there will be intricate tracery of cross beams, glowing golden in the candle light of an autumn evening as you crane your neck. The fireplace causes most thought. No, it will not be central. Eadgifu has ordained. The women will have their way.

Looking upwards is what you do at Cheddar. Up to the gorge tops as you travel up the valley or down, up to the wonder of the natural world, of God's creation. A great depth of rock, rock of ages past. As impressive as the Alps which the bishops, who travel to Rome, report are so magnificent, awe inspiring. In the gorge there are the homes of ancient men and cave bears, caverns filled with the bones of pagans, born never to know the light of Christ. We shall pray for them. They were hunters like us, but how long ago? Before Saxons existed, before Dumnonians existed. What was before them? The unknown. Tribes who had metalwork knowledge, but before them tribes who hewed with stone. They carved earth and wood with it, hunting creatures larger and more frightening than the prey of our times. A slower world, with no taxes and no bureaucracy. Hunters and fighters and nothing else. Hunting, eating, sleeping and procreating. Not born of Woden, not born of the rib of Adam. Just men and their women, existing, now forgotten, their names lost. We have come far.

Athelstan loves to see the stars over the gorge on a summer night. They shoot over the earth, if you stare long enough, lying on your back. He has missed offices of the day in order to see the star show of the Pleiades in August. At midnight Stone shows Edmund and Eadred, his adopted boys. Shows Alain, Hakon and Louis too. While they lie on their blankets, breathing the enthusiasm of youth, boys turning into men, Stone feels that these are his sons, the heirs of Europe. Alain of Brittany, Hakon of Norway, Louis of west Frankia. His foster sons, all charming, all vital. All imbibing the future of the continent at his court, given protection under his wing. When the time comes, he will place each back into their own lands where they rightfully belong. When will that time come for each? He hopes he will live long enough. St Cuthbert tells him he will. St Oswald has promised he will. St Aldhelm has confirmed his dream. He must stay healthy to see these dreams into being.

The dream of the future, as he lies looking up at the stars, turns into a vision of the past. A vision of Aelfwynn. Athelstan is in public a Virgin King, committed to these boys and his brothers, his heirs of England, but he is a man like any other. His sister, Eadgyth and he grew up in Mercia with his cousin, Aelfwynn, Princess of Mercia. Delicate, sensitive Aelfwynn, the opposite of her capable, forceful mother, Aunt Aethelflaed. Like her mother, though, in beauty. Educated, like himself, in the most advanced of royal schools with learning from continental as well as English and Irish tutors.

At eighteen, the grown woman friend of his youth, learned and yielding, became a lover. Eadgyth did not realise until much later, when their father came at the death of his aunt to seize Mercia for his own, that Athelstan and Aelfwynn were as man and wife. They were cousins, unaware or uncaring of possible disapproval, two aethelings, joined by their love for each other, by their mutual interests, by their exchange of relic tokens, inspired to betterment and peace. Joined by the birth of desire after a childhood friendship nurtured by play and respect, they wished for a life enhanced by poetry and prose, prayer and meditation. A gentle form of Christianity was shared, a seeking of Wisdom their mutual goal.

Edward, the warrior king and father, father to two other

sons and with more in the offing when he could arrange things with Eadgifu, did not approve. The bishops would not approve. Lying on his back under the stars, Athelstan remembers the moment when his father came to tear apart the idea of a life with Aelfwynn. The shattering. Books thrown across the room, the swearing. Delicate missals treated as a Viking would. The temper of his father, worse than a sword cutting through flesh. The destruction of idealistic youth. He can see her now, Aelfwynn being dragged away, screaming, crying. The dressing down, the instructions given. Orders barked. No grey areas, just black and white orders.

Edward was now lord of Mercia as well as Wessex. He, Athelstan, was to be his proxy in Tamworth and Gloucester. He could have as many courtesans as he wanted, but not Aelfwynn. *Liven up, boy, this is the real world! Get your head out of the books you so love. And another thing: you may think you have rights to my throne as my eldest child, but I'm telling you, you have nothing. In Wessex you are nowhere. Your brother Aelfweard will be Wessex's heir; he knows how to hold a sword. Get used to it.*

Half-brother, Athelstan had replied. *Not my full brother. Younger than me. Your second wife's son. Grandfather chose me.* Explosion. Edward had made it clear that no son except of his choosing would be king after him. Aelfweard was his choice as king and of the court at Winchester. They would never accept a Mercian lad, wasn't that obvious?

Then why did you send me away, Athelstan had responded.

Because I wasn't married to your mother, of course. Being properly married is important nowadays. If you are a ruler it's become essential. You've heard the bishops. You are not married to Aelfwynn, either. Not formally, there's no acknowledgement in law. She would be unacceptable to the nobles, who have favourites. There would be an argument about children which would resound down the years in every royal family. Can't you see that? That baby is a problem. And Aelfwynn is a cousin. Consanguinity. That's a problem, too.

Athelstan never forgot the shock of his father's anger. He hadn't realised what love might do to upset a dynasty's plans; plans of Edward, at any rate.

Why don't you grow up, Athelstan? Why don't you grow up? Edward was livid.

'Why don't you grow up!' Stone shouts to the stars, waking the boys.

'Are you alright, Uncle?' Edmund sits up, his back silhouetted by the Milky Way.

Athelstan, an uncle. At thirty-nine years of age, an elderly uncle with no sons of his own. But Aelfwynn, Aelfwynn of Shaftesbury Abbey is his friend still, and her daughter is Leonada. They are sheltered and imprisoned by the high walls, forgotten royal kin.

He will go there tomorrow.

Haligdom of St John's Monastery, Frome, 15 December, 934

I cannot sleep, I am too curious. In the relic room on this dark pre-dawn morning before Prime the lid of the chest swings back, wafting the air, disturbing detritus on the floor, a damp smell rising from its interior mingling with the old oak aroma, the smell I now associate with the deep past, with mystery.

I see the collection of ancient things, mostly manuscripts neatly folded or rolled. There is a carefully prepared piece of vellum covered in the bold script of an old-fashioned hand lying over all, like a flattened sheet, a list. The language and style is Welsh, thankfully in writing which I can understand and have seen often before, but never in this quantity. I read by candlelight, written vertically in spidery writing, the words

Nenna has made this list.

There is no information about the maker of the list. I have heard from brother Asser's pupils of a monk of the last century, living in mid Wales, whose interest was the deep past and preservation of documents and who is rumoured to have made Welsh history his life's work. Perhaps this is his collection, brought to Glastonbury for safekeeping from and now to Frome from the weather. Perhaps he was the last person to see these documents. I like the fact that my name and Nenna's both smack of a western world, of a Celtic past. My mother named me, as Nenna was named by our brothers across the Severn Sea. Our names alone revive memories. The language of Greater Wales, land of Latins and Celts, minds which created flowing creatures, imaginations of lore led bards, is preserved in these simple words, visible even in this new Saxon land of Rome, of the Pope. Nenna. The name is the same as my mother's aunt. Is the collector female? If so, should I touch the contents?

Is this, then, the heart of the British cartulary of Ynis Witrin, of Glastonbury, the famous British monastery? It may be all that is left of a record in writing of an ancient past, stretching back to before the time of Our Lord, when the monastery was said to have been founded, when hilltops were still ablaze with the four fire festivals of the year, when rounded and man-shaped contours of old high fortresses preserved the names of their dead chieftains, their bodies lying, totems of protection, in barrows, round and long, visited by pilgrim descendants. Times of the Tribe. Were they better, in some way, than our own?

Once, long ago, the Saxons were a tribe, but we would not call ourselves that now. We are a nation of companions. But in old days, the days Nenna writes of here in the list, the names of the gods, foreign to the English ear, were raucous in the landscape. Then, the red and blue, the heat and the cold of the Otherworld and the horse-riding bearer of souls were the stuff of everyman's dreams, a place of rest and leisure beyond the stars where families could again meet their own, to feast together for ever in Annwn, Paradise. I now recall in a sudden rush my mother's tales from years ago. I had forgotten. Have I been asleep for so many years?

I open out the list, sure of what I have to do. Now the tantalising vision of the deeply dreamed past, mouldering and damp in front of me, fades and reduces to the practical necessities of preservation and the task of recording, while there is still time, the fragile contents of this chest of wonder. I must extract the manuscripts, lay them out on dry cloths, allow the drier air of the scriptorium to gently extract the humidity. The work begins. The lore of the past, of my ancestors, lies exposed in my hands. The first of many writings unfolds itself before me, as if my presence and care are deemed to be allowed.

I begin to read. The list identifies itself as referring to the contents of the chest. I squint at the miniscule hand of Nenna which scrawls in the letter shapes of the past. The language of the peoples on the far side of Sabrina the Severn, Welsh, is not unlike that spoken in the court of Brittany which I have heard in witans many times and seen in documents. I read a reference to the topmost of the manuscripts. It is evidently copied by Nenna from an older document perhaps destroyed or consumed by earlier floods at Glastonbury or lost in transportation through the years. Without laborious and painstaking copying by our brothers or sisters, where would we find and place ourselves in the so dim light of history? It is a pity that some are persuaded to apply their quill to the insidious task of forgery in these days, when bribery or compulsion sways the educated hand. But rich men have always grown richer by these means, except, sometimes, in war.

It would appear that Nenna's documents have not been subject to the forger's art. They are the product of a people of little consequence today in this land, their holdings taken over by Saxons. Do I feel guilt for my good fortune at a Saxon court? Should I? What chance would I have had to receive a king's support in Dumnonia? I think I know. Full-born Britons hold no power in the court of the King, except as curiosities. They figure as poorly dressed theatrical performers or servants in the kitchens and stables, pluckers of goose carcasses, menders of gates, collectors of tolls on the rain swept bridge. Half-born, speaking English with a Wessex accent, I am treated as a Saxon youth.

The first manuscript seems to be a preamble to a series of tales. The words Coed Mawr, the Great Wood, head the page. I know this title as the Welsh word for Selwood. This is the term my mother and King Alfred's Welsh friend, Bishop Asser, used.

Great Wood. Coed Mawr. The sound of the words stirs shadows of deep roots in me. Combined with the dark surroundings of the relics, chest and scriptorium behind me, they remind me of laughter, of times shared with my kin, of tales of heroes heard as a small child. I remember the sounds of Welsh speech which became layered under the later requirements of my schooling and strict Irish teaching. In my mind, I reach to pull them forward.

Coed Mawr. The Great Wood of the land of Dumnonia, now known as Sel Wood to the Saxons. I know it well. Its branches brush against the scriptorium window.

Nenna, in translation, has written, and I read.

THE GREAT WOOD AND KEEPER OF THE WAY, THE WATCHER OF CLEY HILL

At the first was the forest of oak and ash on clay wetlands and beech on sand, great trees in huge unsullied quantities burnishing the thigh of Prydein with green, gold and black, stretching from the mouth of the river Sabrina in the north to the south isle at Noden's Point.

Attached to the isle is the long golden gravel sweep of beach, which facing the sun is a causeway to Annwn for those who wish to travel there. From sea to sea Dumnonia, haunted by Roman legions on their roads, protected by the Great Wood of Coit Mawr, fought with all its might to exclude the relentless western moving fire of the eastern peoples, the Seax.

In our Kingdom-country of the Cymry there were many routes to the Otherworld, including that at Ynis Witrin. To the west of the Great Wood, the city of Isca Dumnoniorum, to the east, our Lost Lands claimed by the Seax, Lloegr. The city of Caer Badon, lively once to the sounds of the British tongue, Saxon now. Paladur, Llanprobus, lost. Now they are named in other voices, Exeter, Bath, Shaftesbury, Sherborne.

At a midway point along the Roman road from Bath is the tomb on the high hill of the Gate Keeper, the death barrow of the Guardian of the wood. It is The Place. Some call him The Watcher, the Keeper of the Way.

The Watcher keeps a tally of the robbers and bandits who roam below. There are many in these lawless days, hoping to pick off any pilgrim or market trader who dares to try to cross the entire width of the forest in a day. Wolves steer clear of this route, leaving the shock of assault to wild men of the Cley Hill heathlands. The Watcher knows their evil intent and curses those who would invade without permission. The power of a curse, as of an oath, is great. Robbers continue, despite this, to take what they can, regardless of the tirades of the Watcher raining from above.

Sometimes they have pickings from successful skirmishes with small bands of pioneering Vikings. Good luck to them. The Danes are a scourge. They ride through our lands as if they have no gods to contain them, will fight any foe, including their own, if they are known to have anything valuable about their person, or even if they have nothing. Vikings are the worst of reckless robbers. Danes and robbers alike, they are careless of curses and oaths. Young men and their too sharp weapons prevent the market trader from travelling to his sales. Eggs are broken deliberately, chickens stolen, vegetables thrown about and strewed across the road. Their owner is battered flung face down in the ditch, his daughter, travelling with him and his son, taken as slaves.

The Watcher sees all. He sees over tops of mighty trees to the holy hill of Coel Kutchen in the distance. Beacons send their flames at the gathering seasons, still, to the hills around. Young men play with their sticks, batting a leather head up the hill to the Watcher's barrow and back down again. They tickle the sides of the hill. I am the Guardian, he says, I speak now. Listen. Lift your eyes to bathe me with your prayer of remembrance. Watch me from the eastern hills, from the western forests, my brother Cernunnos running still with hare and stag through glades and groves. Villas, farmsteads and hermitages, churches of wattle, basilicas of stone, temples in valley bottoms and on hill tops litter the settled and civilised land. No longer the land of the sword, of gleaming bronze and iron and burgeoning warriors but a land of the word, the spoken word, a land of song, a land attuned to hear the signal shout, the high pitched yodel of the tribe.

Gwynn ap Nudd, my brother of the night, of the wind, who carries my soul and returns it to its resting place, tells me of the changes, the movement of new peoples who claim the land, usurping the peace.

The Watcher sees the newcomers passing below. There are strange sounding names on their lips, calling themselves Cynegils, Cwichelm, Aescwine, Cenwalh and Centwine. They are descendants of pirates, soon to call themselves kings, renaming the land as they go, making it their own. Their axes bite the oaks of Coit Mawr. Do not despair, they will never gain ascendancy, the thoughts of Arthur, the head of Bran and the Watcher's guardianship will prevail.

Turn to me, he says I will guard you. Believe in me. Remember me!

The rambling, direct plea of the Watcher unsettles me. He makes the groans of the Welsh which we hear everyday in the stables and kitchens of the palace yard sound tame. Is there still this magic in the land? I replace the first manuscript carefully, lock the chest and retire. Tomorrow I will have strength to see more, perhaps. Tomorrow the King arrives. He will expect an interim report on my findings.

Palace of Frome, None, 15 July 933

'Join me in the scriptorium now, Wulfstan. I mean now.'
Athelstan seems to have the mastery of his northern
archbishop. York is a long way off from Wessex. He needs to trust
this energetic man.

Wulfstan looks around for his aides. Have they noted the
King's tone? There is the other archbishop, elder statesman
Wulfhelm, absorbed in paperwork, pen in hand. Is he far enough
away from the courtiers at the other end of the hall for him to
have been spared the ignominy of being seen to be chastised
by the King? He is relieved to find that they are all engaged
with army matters and discussing warships. As was he, until a
moment ago when he was singled out.

'Dunstan. Leofa and Nonna, you come too.' Athelstan calls
down the hall, indicates some urgency.

The five men stride purposefully out of the palace and
across to the monastery scriptorium. High summer light and
shade of the shadow of buildings and church alternate, black to
bright yellow light and back again as the dark figures pass. They
run down steps to the scriptorium door, chase equally speedily
up stairs inside to the higher levels of wood and stone to the
scriptorium. The bright room is empty. The priests and scribes
are at prayer in the church. Wulfstan pants.

'Be seated.' Athelstan sits at a high writer's chair, signals the
others to do likewise. 'Dunstan, lock the door.'

Something serious has occurred, but what? What has the
King heard? Wulfstan is the first to break out in a sweat.

Athelstan turns to Dunstan who is now perched on another
high seat, looking his usual indifferent self. Nothing sticks to him.
Wulfstan remains standing. Leofa chooses to have his back to a
window and has picked an ordinary low chair. The psychology of
chair choice and its position would be a study in itself; the guilty
or nervous brazen it out or stand in shadows with their backs to a

wall. Sweating is a good indicator of the guilty. The King has seen it all. Reading character, spotting the shifty and the confident, Eadgifu is good at this and has taught Athelstan. She is excellent at guessing thoughts, as most women seem to be. If she wasn't a close associate of priests, she might be accused of being a witch.

'Now repeat what you have just told me, Dunstan.'

Wulfstan looks sidelong at Dunstan. Will he break the solemn oath he made only a few months ago?

'Leofa, I want you to confirm his account. I understand that you were present, too.'

Dunstan repeats the story of the planned attempt to oust Edmund from his position as Aetheling and to replace him with Edwin. Leofa confirms the exact wording used by Aelfflaed and Wulfstan, adding Edwin's reception of the plot. He has just sealed Edwin's fate and knows it. Pity, as languorous Edwin couldn't chase a chicken and kill it without either crying over the chicken or falling over. Aelfflaed could, with relish. Give her a knife and she would kill the chicken, skin, cook and eat it. A capable woman.

I see distaste on Athelstan's face. Just as the court is heavily engaged in planning for the war campaign, he is being diverted away from important business by having to consider family intrigue. This is typical of Aelfflaed. There is her cunning behind this. She chooses her moments carefully.

You have to admire her. If only Mercia could have counted on her scheming brain instead of Wessex.

'And was Edwin intended to lead the people of the North against me?' Athelstan is clear headed. He can see what this plot entails. Edwin is intended to become a puppet king, at the mercy of the tough necked Danes of York. He frowns at Wulfstan. The archbishop begins to stammer.

'My Lord, she insisted on her rights as mother to Edwin and on his position as eldest heir. You know she was sorely aggrieved by the loss of Aelfweard so soon after his father's death. She has seen the gradual demotion of Edwin and the usurpation of her place at court by Eadgifu. The princely gifts you gave to Edmund in front of the witan recently were the last straw.'

'I don't want to know the details, Wulfstan. It is enough to know that there has been traitorous intent. A court of law would take little convincing. Aelfflaed has troubles enough already. She has lost one son, may be about to lose another. Did Frithestan have anything to do with this idea?'

Bishop Frithestan of Winchester is not a friendly type. His ears are probably burning back in the palace hall. Athelstan knows you can't win them all, but is shocked to find an archbishop, one carefully chosen by him, involved in a plot to oust him and his chosen heir. Frithestan he can't do without, but suspects him of collusion. The Winchester faction is in the palm of his hand. The ramifications of any successful coup swirl in the room. If an heir can be ousted, why not a king, too?

Athelstan is aware of the extent of Aelfflaed's love for him. It's about the size of the head of her embroidery needle. She probably has a pin cushion in a cupboard in Wilton with his name on it. She might have instigated the plan to ship him off to Mercia as a child. She may have been behind the failed scheme to blind him after his father's death, might have arranged for Elfred to carry it out, waving her bags of gold, gifts from who knows who. A convent harbours the good, but also sometimes the bad, gives them immunity. But God has been on his side, God and Cuthbert. Alfred's ghost has hovered over the traitors, pointing at them. Eadgifu played a part in the discovery, too. There are ears and eyes everywhere.

I watch Wulfstan writhe. He might want to involve his compatriot, Frithestan, but that would be telling tales. He might need him arguing for him later on in a court, an ecclesiastical court, if not secular. Which would he prefer? Neither would be the best option. He decides to appeal to the better nature of the King.

'My Lord, Frithestan knows nothing of this. Edwin is a gullible fool. The court knows what sort of king he would make if allowed to become Aetheling. His mother drives him into territory he would rather not visit. And as you know, he is no soldier.' The sweat is streaming down. Athelstan stands in a cool spot, his face in shadow. Shadows are useful for the wise and patient, as well as for the guilty.

'Nor scholar,' Dunstan mutters. Athelstan smiles. Dunstan has been most helpful in this matter, making up for earlier mistakes. He would look out for a better position for him, perhaps a commission of art where he could show his merit, bind him closer.

'Leofa, what was the relic on which you were made to swear at Wilton?'

Leofa replies, tells the King of Radegund's bony finger.

'I think we can do better than that. Wulfstan, show me your relic.'

Wulfstan draws back his cape, detaches the coffin shaped box from his jangling belt and presents it to Athelstan.

'My lord, I apologise for my part in the encouragement of this foolhardy enterprise. You have my word that no such discussion or intention to replace your heir will ever occur again. Please accept this relic and its reliquary as a token of my sincere regret.' His hand shakes as he delivers the sacred box, part of his person since a young age, into the care of the King. It cost him much to obtain it, more to let it go.

Athelstan snatches the reliquary. He has a greed for these things. This is the first relic of St Radegund that he has touched. As the reliquary enters his palms, he remembers himself, kisses it and places it on the table behind him. He does not thank Wulfstan. He knows that this valuable personal relic, given willingly to another, holds extra powers. He nods to us.

'Bring out our monastery relic of St John, Leofa.'

'My Lord, Nonna holds the key to the haligdom.'

I rise to go to collect the relic. It will necessitate some organisation.

'Never mind, Nonna. The monks will be back soon from prayers. We will deal with this situation with my own personal relic.' Athelstan fishes out the golden chain from around his neck, revealing a variety of talismans, some metal, some feathery and furry. He detaches a delicately carved piece of rock crystal, deposits it on the table with reverence, mouthing a prayer. This is like taking off a holy ring from a finger. Not to be done often. Athelstan is married to his ring relics.

'The holy splinter.' He waits for our gasps and prayers to subside. A splinter of the true cross, encased in rock crystal, is about the King's person. A doubly blessed piece of ecclesiastical magic. Dunstan crosses himself energetically, falls to his knees.

Athelstan signals for the rest of us to kneel. We do, in awe at the nearness of such a holy item sending out its beams of power in the quiet scriptorium of Frome on this sunny afternoon in July nine hundred years after its separation from a faraway cross.

'Wulfstan, I need a superior oath from you if you are to retain my confidence. Swear on this holy relic that you will repudiate all connection with Aelfflaed and her son from this day. You are to go nowhere near her or to have any contact with her. No writing may pass between you and no encouragement whatever made to give her further hope of success in the matter she most dreams of. Her day is done. Her will must be broken.'

'But, what, my Lord, of Edwin? He is not naturally gifted and would not have considered any move against you on his own account. What will you do with him?'

'That is for me to decide. I promise you that no open court will deal with his disgrace or that of his mother. God will decide the best form of action to be taken for them both. Now swear. Dunstan, take the oath down in writing as we speak. There is pen and ink and there parchment. Write.'

Dunstan does so. Wulfstan swears his oath, binding himself to act for Athelstan, at pain of Hell's torture. He continues to drip into his cassock.

I watch the scene and see Leofa thinking hard. The King is less indecisive these days, more inclined to anger. More black and white. What punishment will Edwin receive for his part in this attempted coup, this corrosive distraction from the unification dream? Might he disappear or be found dead, like his brother so many years ago? The supine Edwin, found one day even more at rest?

The following day Athelstan sent Leofa abroad to buy or obtain more relics of Radegund.

The King's Arrival at Frome, 15 December 934

I go to the far side of the Portway at the eastern entrance to the town in the morning after Terce to welcome the King to his estate of Frome. He is a friend. He enjoys mentoring us young scribes, tells us we are the hope of the nation. In the private rooms of his palaces, with the presence of holy relics around us, he has told me much of his view of past events. I am his young historian, he says. He seems to trust me. I suspect he wants me to be his biographer. He is forty this year and is perhaps thinking of the next world and what it holds. An old man.

Athelstan has proved to be, in the ten years since his accession, the liberal, broad-minded and fair administrator, ordained by God, that Alfred, his grandfather, foretold he would be when he robed him and presented him to the court as a young child. Intense prayer sessions in the reliquary haligdom of Winchester and his inconvenient stomach problems may have caused Alfred to hallucinate. Pain and reality are often far from each other. He dreamed of a bright future for his eldest grandchild; perhaps he could foretell that, though he was Edward's first born son, there might be difficulties with a smooth succession. When was there ever one of those?

Alfred did not claim to have the magical skill of soothsaying, but with the help of his revered saints and their relics, he could pray a future for his dynasty. With St Cuthbert, holy one, on his side, he had hope for the future of the English race, for an England. Many did not approve of Athelstan's mother. Intrigues, prejudices and cares of the collective mind of extended families often create problems for those with more pragmatic minds. Alfred's intention was clear; his ambitious vision for Athelstan, like his visitation by St Cuthbert before the battle of Edington, was a certain, saint-supported projection of the future of his legacy for Wessex. England was there on the horizon, moving closer. In two generations it might be achieved.

A man of letters, as well as a competent warlord and administrator, Athelstan's father Edward was worried about the boy's early tendency, inherited from and encouraged by Alfred, to linger in the libraries of Wessex, particularly at Malmesbury. His mother was bookish too. The nobles of the court disliked this in a woman. She had to go. The child was fascinated by colourful manuscripts, thrilled by frightening but moral stories in painted gospels, mesmerised by relics of saints in their gilded enclosures. He went everywhere with a small psalter given to him by his grandfather, was seen to consult it constantly. Edward wished to replace it with a dagger, but Athelstan could not be persuaded to part with it.

A stepmother arrived, rapidly pumping out babies. Edward sent him with his sister to be educated at the court of Mercia with his aunt and uncle, where they fatally encouraged him even more in reverence for the saints and book learning. Half-brothers and many sisters came along in the fertile southern court of Wessex and yet more to a second stepmother, including Edmund and Eadred our aethelings. Edward was able to influence his sons with Aelfflaed and tried to make warriors out of them, but his third brood, with Eadgifu, were babies when he died. Athelstan teaches them. They will be pragmatic scholars, he hopes.

The daughters of Edward's second wife Aelfflaed, under their mother's tutelage, made fun of their half-brother's devotion to the written word and his apparent lack of lustiness, goading him to show an interest in their fashions, hairstyles and gossip. Not a vain man, though he uses his height and fair haired good looks to his advantage, he found their presence in large doses tiring and superficial. Thankfully he was most often at the Mercian court where the voices of women were serious, his aunt sharing equal status with her husband in the administration of the realm as well as a being a competent planner and executer of armed warfare during her later widowhood.

Edmund, son of Edward's third wife Eadgifu, and Eadred his sickly brother and their sisters were much more to the liking of Stone. There were fewer children of the third wife of Edward; Athelstan is their surrogate father. He is happy in the company of young children. He enjoys the role of foster father. He has told me that he could see promise in this last set of half siblings. The succession was secure, the mindset of Alfred would reappear, continued here in his descendants. Aelfweard and Edwin, however, had been too brainwashed by Winchester nobles and were too old to influence.

Aelfflaed, the mother of the second brood, proved tiresome and was sent to Wilton. One of her sons died mysteriously, shortly after his father and the other, Edwin, was less suited to the task of kingship, to put it mildly. What could you say about Edwin. He had hopes, I suppose, as any aetheling does, just not the talent.

Eadgifu, the Queen Mother of the younger princes, of a similar age to Athelstan, is now the chief hostess of his court, a capable and relatively quiet background manager of convenience and order. Quiet, that is, in public. As her strength grows from the acceptance of her son as heir, she is becoming impossible. She disappears for long secret sessions with Dunstan. I don't know what they do together. He is much too young to suit her tastes, surely? Is this the way of women? I am too inexperienced to judge.

Ah, the drums and trumpets. Here comes the King, riding along the road with his large retinue, pennants fluttering. I wave to him. He smiles at me. Some of the army have stayed at Gloucester, refilling the Mercian stronghold where they are based. A smaller core of armed men accompanies the wagons and horses of the returning warrior, the Aetheling Edmund and his splendidly attired but dour looking 'guest' of Scotland with his son of a similar age to Edmund. He does not look too downcast, considering his position. Hywel Dda of Wales is beaming, riding alongside Stone.

Carts carrying crates of hunting birds and dogs, large and small, travel with the stream of horsemen. There are carriages full of chattering womenfolk, mounds of foodstuffs from foreign parts, servants and huntsmen borrowed from other palaces and nobles with their retinues. Covered wagons trundle along, creaking as they go, full of mysterious, magical ritual goods accompanying the archbishops and bishops from all quarters of the land. Carts loaded with temporary lodgings for quick erection in the fields around the palace are pulled by muscular hairy-footed horses. Streamers of blue, black, gold, red and white, the badges and signs of chosen animals, bear, wolf and boar, declare the competitive interest and active intent to hunt and bear arms of their different family owners.

Colourful regiments of all the noble families of Wessex and beyond stream by. The soft, luxurious fur of animals, some from the deep dark lands of the hot continent, drape the necks and capes of those related to the royal family and they are many. They are tokens of wealth, of status, for all to admire. Leather is for the rest, the sturdy clothing of the winter hunt. Horse smell, wax and worn, hot animal skin pass me by, the aroma of power in action.

The sound of power is overwhelming. Trumpets are blown at random, there is drumming, barking, mewing, neighing, laughter. The line of the witan gathering enters the Portway, Cley Hill rising behind them in the east. Groups of freemen and their families of the town and nearby villages wave and shout. Mothers with their infants, ceorls and trusted slaves point out to their families the recognised faces of the military and diplomatic might of Wessex, of the present archbishops, all other bishops and likely saints of the next generation in their colourful glory. Church and State, hand in hand, ride together, law makers and law givers. The King's ministers, all twenty-five of them, bring up the rear, conferring on matters of state as they ride. There is much to discuss. The King will want to get cracking with the nation's business first thing tomorrow. Ahead there are smoking chimney fires of the huge kitchen area at the palace signalling a feast in preparation. The travellers are grubby, tired and hungry, but spirits are high. This will be their resting place for a number of weeks.

Above the monastery church of St John, which will see the King's mass priests perform the wonders of Christmas, is the tythe barn, filled to the rafters with grain produce from the summer. It overlooks the palace and monastery, has its own separate entrance from the road behind the town. Some of the wagons head off to unload in its courtyard. The mills on the river below have been busy all autumn, churning, grinding, producing grain from the barn for loaves which will fill the stomachs of famished visitors. Bakers with their ovens in Cheap Street add to the festive atmosphere with their own fire and smoke, catering for the gawping townsfolk, combining with the palace kitchen to make a pall of edifying aroma hanging over the monastery and palace like a heavy cloud of promising rain in drought. Frome has awakened. The King brings his life affirming presence back to one of his favourite palaces.

Many riders and wagons roll in after the elite nobility, all in hierarchical order as is proper and expected. They trundle by, like a slow and gradually less colourful carnival, downhill to the utilitarian quarters of the courtyard reception area of the palace. I walk back down the road towards the church to watch them dismount and unload, always an exciting and interesting time. There are friends to hale, girls to observe. A group of buff coloured townsfolk, unwilling to return to their duties while the spectacle is still available, join me. Their clothing indicates the humble activity of their lives in contrast to the butterflied hues of the court. Division by colour. It's cheaper to produce brown stuff than red and blue. Some of the locals are in dark blue clothing; they are the dyers. They have their guild at the Blue Boar Inn by the river. Weavers and cloth makers meet at other inns. The spinners stay at home. Everyone knows his place.

The clattering and clopping of slipping hooves and shouting to grooms ensues in the cobbled space of the palace yard. I stand inside the gate to watch. Palace staff, burly men fattened on venison and boar, unload the carts carrying utility items. Books, furniture, clothing, a variety of small comforts and items of sentimental attachment, things the visitors and King cannot do without. Leather goods, hunting apparel and weaponry. Spare items which it is difficult to conjure up or mend when broken, favourite lances, bows, saddles. Sealskins need to be removed from carts, protection from the elements now not needed for a few weeks, stored in barns ready for the reloading. This new nation of England could plan for and rule the world. Perhaps it will.

Individual wagons for each main hunting group, festooned with team colours, park along the barn sides. Their owners will vie in competitive peace, rather than war, for the best achievements in the field. None are more skilled than Stone. At hunting he is always top dog and loves to show his mastery. I suspect some let him have their kill. He cannot always win, surely? Many of the animal skulls on the palace walls are said to be his own trophies. The antlers and stuffed boar heads are not to the taste of the bishops, but the tradition of decoration in this old palace hall has been the same for centuries. Flowers have not yet been painted on them in their place, though Dunstan and Eadgifu have their plans.

Most notable of all and bringing up the rear, a well-guarded large wagon rolls to a halt, its hoops of fine material and decorated curtains indicating very special contents, the royal relic collection. The saints of the people, the parts, the bones. Sometimes flesh, too, well preserved. Flesh and bones. Some monks are practised taxidermists, they know their herbs. We clerks call these travelling relics "The State Guarantors of Peace" or "Skeletons of State". The large wagon deserves, and gets, four armed guards on horseback and two priests riding inside. They look drained, like dead saints themselves.

In the courtyard of the palace unloading continues amid raucous shouting. Edmund, heir to Wessex, Alain, Louis, and

Hakon, very young men in their early years of wisdom and understanding, glowing with the encouragement of the King and familiar with each other and the court, jump vigorously from their ponies. They all look splendid, vital and even virile in their furs and leathers. They attract the gaze of dun clothed kitchen girls. Younger royal children tumble from a carriage.

The travellers dismount gracefully or slide from their horses, depending on their age and vigour, or have wooden steps brought for them to dismount in comfort. Athelstan is not fussed how he dismounts. He uses the short stone mounting steps attached to the outer barn, letting his guests dismount at higher steps nearer the palace door. They are the less competent, perhaps he wishes to show. Certainly Constantine, the Practised Scoundrel, needs all the assistance he can get, and doesn't like to be watched receiving it. The northern guest and his son, who we are instructed not to refer to as "prisoners", eye the varied infirmities of those around them. Some are sporting battle wounds. It has been a long trek from Alba to the south and from Chippenham to Frome this morning. A goose feather bed is required for many and a good long night's sleep, preceded, probably, by a long afternoon's snooze. The palace staff have many rolls of mattresses for the nobler guests; even if they have to sleep in tents, they will be able to lie in comfort. The monastery will take care of the bishops with equal comfort. There is a great deal of catching up to do, in more ways than one.

Constantine of Scotland has been forced to sign his first charter as a sub-king, I have been told. He doesn't like that. There are interesting times ahead, I think. All summer long our Saxon troops have been on the move, fighting, harrying, the navy too. They travelled further into the north than even the Roman generals went. Stiff necks and limbs will be weary. Exhaustion and the mead vats and fresh ale drunk during today's siesta will make the guests more pliable, more open to our diplomatic suggestions.

The bishops hope so. Their scribes and spies will have them in their sights. Plenty of opportunities will be had, in the coming weeks of the Christmas court, to wrong-foot, hint, suggest and suspect, delicious conditions for ministers, diplomats and interpreters. Athelstan, at the top of his game, will extract a few promises tonight. Oaths will come easily after the feasts. Food and drink loosen tongues. Add music and you have full entry to the heart and soul of any reluctant visitor.

Sweepers swinging their brooms from side to side remove horse dung from the yard, take it to the compost heap. Male guests, willing as well as forced, enter the large open doors of the palace hall. The raucous noise subsides and transfers itself to the interior. Accompanying noblewomen are ushered to the smaller warm hall beyond the palace reserved for womenfolk, able to relieve themselves in privacy and rest before the evening gathering, the first feast of the Christmas court.

Let it begin!

Shaftesbury Abbey, the evening of 13 August 933

'Greetings, my Lord. I trust that you are well.' Aelfwynn looks questioningly at her king, does not lower her eyes. There is her former lover, forty this year like herself. Still slim, but he now has heavy bags under his eyes, darkened teeth. The lacy fringed wimple and loose, light over-garment she wears, the summer version of a nun's habit, disguise her recent weight gain; so she hopes.

Athelstan gives his horse's reins to Leofa, who has accompanied him on the ride south from Frome and tells him to wait, to take refreshment in the Abbey's hostelry.

'Aelfwynn, I am well. How pleased I am to see you again. I trust the Abbey continues to treat you well?' He can see that it does. She is still lovely, though her face and hands are all that he can see. Plaits of dark auburn hair loop below the sides of the headdress, hair he can remember. The scent of it. A hint of grey silvers the loops. Aunt Aethelgifu, the first Abbess of Shaftesbury has ensured a comfortable home for his cousin. From its walled rose gardens and walks in the vicinity of the hilltop town, the sun setting over the landscape of southern Wessex, as over their love, is a sad but beautiful reminder of a life that could have been led. If only they had not been parted, destined for other partners or none. If only they had not been born royal children, aethelings both, cousins.

The two mature, wise beings walk hand in hand along a paved walkway to a bench overlooking the vale. Together they may have a chance to witness the daily miracle of sundown, followed by the dramatic jackdaw roost.

'And how is the child?' The child. Not their child. The child. Leonada. They do not speak of her as having anything to do with kingdoms and heirs. There is no "Ae" at the beginning of the name. How did Aelfwynn think of that name? Her father might be taken to be a foreigner, even a slave. Good. It's best to keep it that way. She is safe, for now.

'She is well, Lord. You shall see her for yourself when we return to the Abbey refectory. She has just celebrated her sixteenth birthday, has been granted a few freedoms by the Abbess. She waits on visitors, enjoys listening to their stories.' A breeze, swooping up from Hambledon Hill, lifts an edge of the summer wimple. More lovely hair is revealed, then it vanishes again.

'I am glad. Glad, too, that she is a reader, a lover of books like ourselves. Life will bring her many joys as long as she remains here, unknown to the world.'

'She remains unaware of her origins, Athelstan.' Aelfwynn relaxes. She hasn't seen Athelstan for a considerable time. 'It still seems to be best for her. She is settled and happy here, knows nothing else. There is always Wilton Convent, perhaps one day, if she wishes to progress in her career, but of course she cannot go there at present.' Aelfflaed. From her comfortable prison at Wilton, Aelfflaed casts her jealous shadow, her influence over other lives a dominant force while she is alive. Aelfwynn does not demean herself by mentioning her name. 'But what of Edwin? What became of him? I can see you are troubled.'

There's no disguising it; this bother with Edwin is getting him down. Sleepless nights are not new to Athelstan, but now they come every night.

'I challenged him directly. For the first time he said what he really thought. He thought that I had deliberately killed his brother. He accused me of that! I wept at hearing of his death, despite everything. I told him as I have said many times to others that I had nothing to do with Aelfweard's demise, though of course I did not wish him to have you...' Athelstan puts an arm around Aelfwynn.

This partnership might have lasted a lifetime, has been a comfort on their rare chances to be together. The marriage veto of consanguinity for Aelfweard might not have been deemed a problem, but for himself and Aelfwynn it most certainly would.

Edward would have had none of it, would have turned a blind eye to his second son's relationship with the Mercian girl; it would have suited him to do so.

Only cousins of King Edward's choice could get together. Athelstan and Aelfwynn, given his blessing, might have produced a bookish Mercian for a king. Wessex had enough problems without that. And besides, Aelfflaed may be a bitch, but she was right about some things. Aelfwynn and Aelfweard could rule after him, a joint Mercian/Wessex project, but not Aelfwynn and Athelstan. Mercia and Mercia? Unacceptable.

Aelfwynn, refusing to marry Aelfweard, was bundled off to Shaftesbury on the death of her mother. The child accompanying her was kept a secret. Athelstan was forbidden to see her. Spoiled goods, she was destined to remain here. Aethelflaed of Mercia, Lady, had lived long enough to see her only grandchild and to know whose she was, but took the secret with her to the grave. No-one other than Edward knew of her parentage. Her only regret was that Leonada had been a girl.

Children, half-brothers, cousins. Where kingship was involved, love was never easy, never to be expected. Athelstan's love for this Mercian girl could only be maintained through surreptitious contact, but had survived. She had been his chief advisor when he needed to act on family matters. She was his ultimate secret relic, hanging about him like a ghostly whisperer near to his heart, his soul. But living, breathing, still.

Edwin. What could be done about Edwin? He had been a headache for the first nine years of Athelstan's rule. If only he had been another girl adding to Aelfflaed's large female brood. He acted like one. A bookish lad would have been easier to deal with, but Aelfflaed had insisted on a martial upbringing which did not suit his personality and by the time Athelstan was in power and Aelfweard his brother dead, it was too late. He was not acceptable as priest or bishop, good for nothing but being pampered and the occasional hunt.

Athelstan mused. 'Edwin was heard by Leofa to be making remarks about the uselessness of my intended push to the north. Leofa reported to me directly that he and Archbishop Wulfstan had been making plans to save northern lives by declaring Edwin king in York. He heard them during a drinking session, speaking more loudly than they should have. Edwin is a little deaf. Was a little deaf. They said that they objected to the waste of lives and expenditure on what they called a projection of vanity. They thought they could deliver an independent Northumbria as of old, with Edwin ruling it, able to challenge the south with a supporting army of Irish Danes, nest of vipers that they are. Edwin was not completely stupid; he might have been capable of cooking up some arrangement which would suit the parties in the north. I couldn't let that happen.'

Athelstan looked out over the south west lands, his lands. 'I love this place, Aelfwynn. Edwin didn't have the same love for the land of Wessex, though he was born to it. He used it, appreciated it, but had none of our grandfather's vision. He would have let the Vikings return, would have been weak. The bishops would have ruled him. Balance must be maintained. Church and State together, not one greater than the other. But you know that.' He turned to look at Aelfwynn.

'Yes, I love our land, our combined Wessex and Mercia, it makes sense to me, and if I were a man, I would have done what you have done. But what happened to Edwin?' These were comfortable words of great ease to Athelstan. He went over the case with Aelfwynn.

'He drowned. Edwin, escaping apparently from what he thought would be my understandable wrath, took a sailing boat from Wareham accompanied by a single squire. They seem to have made their way partly across the channel, but, inevitably, disaster struck when the summer's day, fine to begin, changed to storm. The wind and waves were too much for them, the squire reported. They struggled on a short distance to the bay of

Studland where Edwin, exhausted, sick and unable to swim, was tipped overboard by a large wave. The squire managed to retrieve his half-dead body and brought it back to shore. He expired in his arms. I was informed of the disaster within hours, ordered that no-one was to move the body. I arrived the same day, viewed Edwin where he had died. He looked grey, sodden and battered lying on the sandy beach. There he was, my brother, thirty years old, who had achieved nothing. Born to a king and queen, but as second son of a second marriage, adrift with the fates as he grew. Pleasant enough, but inconsequential. His hair, full of sand, spread lank across his face, his long arms and legs splayed out sideways, uncontrolled as in life. It was a pitiful sight.'

'Do the fingers and thoughts of witnesses point to you?'

'One brother dead and now another. Inevitably, yes. The body was taken up and carried to the church nearby. Prayers for the prince were said, candles blazed for the body and myself. Had I pushed him too far? But what can a king do in such circumstances? Order an execution? Try to ignore an attempted coup which might lead to instability? Edwin was useless at sailing, useless at swimming. Useless. He brought his own death to himself. Edwin, dead. You know what they will be saying in Winchester.'

'Oh, my love, this is just another minor setback. Edwin should not have conspired. Should have lived out his life quietly, perhaps gone to live on the continent. Perhaps that was his intention, to go to the heart of Frankia or further south, perhaps to be with one of his sisters. He might have done you no harm, but on the other hand...you did not wish him to be killed. He contributed to his own death. You know that. You are guiltless. What more can you do to convince your nobles and the Church of the necessity of your sacred mission to the north?'

Aelfwynn calmed him, but Athelstan was not comfortable. Already some of the Wessex bishops were baying for penitence, accusing him of having Edwin killed. Archbishop Wulfstan was capable of limiting Athelstan's power to act, could whip up court antipathy. Where one devil was slain, others appeared. Penance might have to be done to maintain the court's support. More might be required to ensure success in his attempt to make Britain whole. He fingered the relic of the Holy Cross under his cape.

What greater relic than this could he use to inspire the war campaign, to hold his plans for unification in one piece? There was something, something he personally desired, something which could emit a holiness which would hold the nation together. It lay in the north, waiting for him to join it to its body in Gloucester. He told Aelfwynn what it was. She remembered her mother's dying words to them both. What was it she said?

Get hold of the head, the very sacred head, of St Oswald.

Scriptorium of St John's Monastery, Frome, before Vigils, 15 December 934

After the sorting and disbursement of travellers I was invited this afternoon to Stone's quarters in private. He had much to tell me of various conversations on the recent days of travel, which I must record. Soon it will be the bell for Vigils, then back to the scriptorium. It will be difficult for me to sleep after hearing what the King recalled in detail and in some urgency related to me. He has emptied his brain into mine. He will sleep better, at any rate, I hope, while my work begins.

Tomorrow morning, after the evening meal and bardic performance tonight, which is planned to be a quiet time of recuperation and soft music to relax the travellers, the guests will have shaken off their travel weariness. Intense diplomacy will begin. I shall have a chance during these night hours to offload through my pen some of the characters and events and plans which Stone's conversations have brought to mind. There is already much to think about and to annotate. I have not yet begun to tell him about the Glastonbury chest. He will ask me about that when he is more rested. First I want to see more of its contents.

There is the bell. Vigils is calling the monks. I have returned to the haligdom at the end of the room from my temporary pallet not far away in the scriptorium. I have already outlined Stone's recalled events and conversations and will return to them later. The chest's contents call to me, drawing me to them as the monks are drawn to file down to the church by habit and the Benedictine requirements of faith. Stone would understand the pull of the chest and its contents. We both love to uncover the deep past, but there is little appetite for it amongst the courtiers, who are baffled by documents, think they are a monk's remit only. They slumber, lulled by their soft linen bedclothes and goose down covers, oblivious to any intense obsession other than hunting, or war, or sex.

I unlock and enter the haligdom. Athelstan's personal collection of relics, taken off the wagon yesterday, lie in orderly heaps. Precious wood containers of many shapes and sizes, some with gold, silver and gem embellishments sit on benches. Glass vials of blood, congealed parts of the saints of Britain, saints from Brittany, saints from the continent, decorated venerations, magical in their moral boosting efficacy, their oath bearing might, breathe their potency into the enclosed space, make their locked enclosure with their ugly metal bars seem like a cage of static wild animals. Are they locked in for security or kept from escaping?

I am reminded of how the King's visiting relics again make our permanent collection at Frome monastery look insignificant. I must ask him if Frome might have a few more. We could do with more income from pilgrims. The hospital is active and needs better buildings. There is a lot of money to be made from pilgrims. They would benefit, too.

Dust flares up in the candlelight as I lift the heavy chest lid. Sounds of late carousing from the hall produced by a few revellers not yet worn out by the evening's food and mead, new to the splendours and facilities of the timbered palace, echo in the palace yard. Candlelight shines on gems studded into the relics around, making them glow like living animal eyes. There are even more eyes now that the King's relics have joined the haligdom. I tremble in their presence. And now the chest, too, challenges my spiritual strength. I say a prayer and continue with my task.

The Watcher manuscript has attuned me to the type of document I may encounter here; to my mind it gives rather an authentic sounding, but crazed, version of the way things were after the Romans left Britain. Ridden with superstition, these are the minds and sensibilities of a tribal culture. The writing of history in our day by scribes attached to holy orders, schooled in modern monasteries, is different. There is a huge gulf in understanding between our cultures and our way of thinking, a different approach to truth and reality. Perhaps there will always be a difference between the British and the English mind.

A weather-beaten manuscript falls into my hands, in a writing style not unlike the last, but more archaic in letter form and more difficult to decipher. Like the last, I think this is not a copy, but an ancient original piece. It intrigues me. The deep past speaks again, a world away from ours. I pause before reading, sit back in my chair.

After Compline last night, catching a nap after my brief interview with Stone, I dreamed of the curving creatures of the chest, coming towards me as if they were alive, snarling, snapping, barking, hissing. They coiled and wound their bodies around me, dragging me down into a pit of doom. Dunstan would tell me to wrestle with the imagery. There are dark things lurking here which could take over a man's mind. He may be right; the chest's contents have allure to me, like a woman.

The old faded manuscript in my hand has me in its grip. Its promise of the insistent voice from the past, the words of an anxious scribe of long ago draw me forward. I shake my head. Dunstan will cast out any devils who may assault me. I begin to study the manuscript. It is the merely the words of man, not a god, or God.

There is much Welsh script as well as Latin here, I see, writing of the period just before the Saxons were present in this land. A Dane might see this during a violent assault on a monastery and spit at it, abuse the writing, tear it in half and wipe himself clean with it for a joke, making trivial amusement for his fellow Viking idiots. They wasted the beauty of words, of history. What did they care? For them, there is no past, only the present. Before and after there is nothing; only the perpetual revel of Valhalla counts. Christians die in bed. Danes die by the sword. Bloodily.

I spread out the manuscript on the nearby scriptorium lectern. On its upper left, there are Welsh words, spidery and foliate as though growing from a coppice of young trees, "Hywel, his hill". I say the name, remembering the way my Mother speaks,

"Kaw-ell", like the rough sound of a raven flying overhead. On the right side of the sheet, there is a small drawing of a mounted man. He or she has a large head and stylised curly hair. The mane of the horse seems curly, too. Both rider and horse appear to be laughing or shouting, their mouths open.

I read.

THE CURLY-HAIRED HERO OF COLD KITCHEN HILL.

I speak for Hywel. The incomers call him Coel. That's how his name sounds to them. His name is in many places in our Kingdom of Dumnonia, scattered amongst the trees and hills, places where the folk gather to dance. Often his name is linked to castles of the imagination, rising at evening with the going down of the sun, fading with the mist and dew at dawn. Castles in the clouds, the haunt of lovers, where all are equal, all young forever.

Hywel hugs and embraces them, safe in the Otherworld for a short space of time. He kutches them. In the moment, the lovers embrace, sleep in the arms of their god, their hero who comforts and guards their souls. On Coel Kutchen they are safe.

Crickhowell is one of his places, the hill of Hywel, in the heartlands of the Cymry. Wherever you can see the highest hills in the land, there the neighbouring youth will go to meet their brides, their husbands and to make merry. The forest groves are also used for their love. As long as the forest stands, the oak protects and the wolves stay away from the firelight, the young will meet their lovers here in the privacy of the leaves and antler boughs.

Hywel the hero, the curly-haired hero, protector of the land and sky, takes our soul with him to the Otherworld, Annwn, the red and blue, the heat and the cold, the great beauty. He laughs and sings as he rides his horse, dragging our souls through the sky from dawn to dusk, urging us, cajoling us in the wheel of our existence. Horse and man as one, his large curly-haired head, protecting the realm, the land of Bran the king-god who sacrificed himself for the protection of the land. Galloping across the sky, the stars, watched by lovers lying beneath on the grass, a shooting star of light. Gwynn, some call him still. He has many names, this God of the land and sky.

Now we come together at Lughnasa, the fire feast of harvest, the time of greatest joy, the time of hunting the husband, of meeting the bride. We climb the slopes of the hill ahead from our farmstead. Our cart is filled with foodstuffs, dogs, children, grandmother and father.

We travel most of the day, joining with others also making their way to the hilltop. Overnight, there will be feasting, dancing and singing and in the morning, the horse races begin.

We are pilgrims, heading for our hill of Hywel. Pots and jars we bring to make offerings to the gods, helped by the ritual priests who live permanently there, whose fires we see with comfort each night as we gaze to the south, to the meeting place of the tribes, the Dobunni, Durotriges and Belgae. The great White Sheet encampment of the Durotriges guards the route to the south beyond Coel Kutchen to the sea and Noden's Point. They stand alert at the toll of Long Knoll, taking coin for the passing of travellers through their territory, as we do, for travellers coming north to our city of Badon. Horse and cattle, ears of wheat, fertility and fecundity are our main concerns, our joys. The horse carries us through life, the wheel of life reminds us of the part we must play in our tribal community. Honour the tribe, remember your place.

Now we hear bells ringing on the hill. The priests make a clamour with trumpets and bells, ringing out across the land. Come to us! You are welcome! Come to the feast! We bang and clatter our metal pots, shout and sing. Stay at home if you are old and do not like noise. This is the marriage festival of summer, the festival of song, story and shouting, the sights and sounds of colourful joyful togetherness, all the senses jangling. We sing for Coel and Macha the goddesses. Three days we have of abandon, of our feast, our summer gathering, our Lughnasa.

We Sing, we shout. Dogs bark, horses snort, bells swing on the necks of oxen, bells trill around the garlands and sides of wagons.

There are bells on the legs, feet and arms of all the girls, bright rings
on their fingers, bells on their toes. A young man wears leaves in his
hair, plays music on a harp. He sings:

> Old King Cole was a merry old soul,
> And a merry old soul was he;
> He called for his pipe, and he called for his bowl,
> And he called for his fiddlers three.
> Every fiddler he had a fiddle,
> And a very fine fiddle had he;
> Oh there's none so rare, as can compare,
> With King Cole and his fiddlers three.

The Curly-haired Hero draws us on, waits for us on the hill.

We lift the young girls to the ground from the backs of wagons.
Their red ribbons stream in the wind. The red cloaks of the older
women, shawls of wool, red, blue, green, colours of the hero, glow
around the feast fire.

At the temple, the priests stand, greeting the crowds, the stalls of
votive offerings before them, guarding the shrine of all the gods who
will be honoured by sacrifice this day. Taranis, they call their main
deity, the god with brown curly hair. In the temple, the statue wears
a black, flowing mantle around him like the night, a wheel shaped
brooch of bronze on his breast. Standing by, admired by all the
girls, look, here is Taranis in the flesh, a youth named and dressed
to represent him in the drama, the god of thunder, of the sky. His
painted face, like the statue glimpsed behind the priest through the
open temple door, is coloured red, blue, black. The colours of Annwn.

The writing ends tersely, leaving me in suspense. Evidently more was intended originally, but could, or should, the excitement of the narrator be extended? What infusion had he imbibed? He was so filled with involvement and excitement of his recollection of the hilltop festival.

I remember a time when the four festivals, some more sombre than others, were kept. They were little more than small bonfires for families, a reminder of a way of life, now gone, which the British once had. They felt at one with their hills and valleys, with the cycle of the year. The English celebrate too, and know unbridled joy in living, but we are Christians. The Saxons have lost much of their former Germanic culture, separated from the forests and hills of Thor and Woden on the continent. The English do not yet have a deep sense of joyful belonging evidently once known in this land by its former owners, whose songs were born of long association with their place, as if they were taught by a living landscape, their holy land.

We prefer, in this young country of Wessex, the valleys to the hills. For some, hilltops are dangerous places. Priests are taught not to go to them. There is bad blood and devil worship on the heights, they say. I do not believe this. My Welsh mother could not believe this.

Sometimes I hear Dunstan talking about hills as though they harbour devils. The old Roman roads crossing on our nearby hilltop of Cold Kitchen, are just that, roads, with plenty of travellers, but now no revellers. Christian monks and priests have discouraged feast gatherings, their disapproval has stemmed the coupling meetings of the festival of Lughnasa. I know that revelling groups still meet at night at Hales Castle which is only an hour's walk into the forest from the monastery. The old ways prevail, though they are not what they were. Hywel's name lives on but is remembered by fewer as the years go by.

I look up from the manuscript on the table. While reading, I have been a witness of a ritual from the past, written in the

Old Welsh of the Britons, the Brythonic language. The joining together of communities to act together in celebration of their culture was a fine thing. The feasting here is different in character. The Christmas witan usually has politics as its main interest, with undertones of intrigue. This year, with the presence of Constantine the dour Scottish king, it is even more so.

The Welsh kings are less angry than the remaining West Welsh with their fate. They have become used to the responsibility of power being lifted from them. They smile, share entertainment, calm the Saxon soul with their harps and poetry as the English seek to calm the hearts of Scandinavians with their religious fervour. The Welsh have a grudge, but their leaders have accepted their role as under-kings. Better to live and laugh in the mountains than to die in battle in an English valley or a Welsh one.

Hywel of Wales, Hywel Dda, the Good, is particularly smug and attuned to English ways. His chief scribe and interpreter has told me before that Hwyel regards the Saxon court as bereft of the ability to appreciate subtle poetic understanding of metre or rhyme and has much to learn in the art of beauty and word lore. He enjoys sparring with Stone, showing off his ability with a musical instrument and poetry. He drives Athelstan to greater heights in wisdom and cunning, beats him often at Gospel Dice, which Hywell calls gwydbyll, shows his language skills as he converses with Bretons, English, Dane, Scot. He has honoured the King by naming one of his sons after his younger half-brother, Edwin, but Athelstan, sensitive to the name of his dead brother, has not invited the whole Dyfed family to our Christmas court this year. He is still sore about the Edwin episode, has to continue to do public and private penance. I think it is penance enough to be a king, but he says it is not enough. He must kneel and pray, do more time with his relics, asking forgiveness. The cat is often used.

I can hear carousing in the hall, carried on wind to the scriptorium, another version of the old song.

Good King Coel,
And he call'd for his Bowle,
And he call'd for Fiddler's three;
And there was Fiddle, Fiddle,
And twice Fiddle, Fiddle,
For 'twas my Lady's Birth-day,
Therefore we keep Holy-day
And come to be merry.'

It is Hywel's baritone voice. The past is not forgotten yet, quite. Who are these "three fiddlers", I wonder?

Questions. I return to the manuscript. The illustration of the horse and rider draws me. The manuscript description of Hywel says that he had vigorous curly hair. This hero figure seems to have been very important in the lives of local people. Who was this rider, what did he or she look like? Any rider of competence commands the gaze of a walker. His height from the ground imposes, his range of vision is greater. His comeliness, his robes, his demeanour, his strength, his at-oneness with a revered animal would impress his followers. What king could be without a horse and still command his army? And what of the horse. Must it have similar attributes, of far sightedness, of active virility, be of glorious colour or perhaps be white, or night black? That it should be tireless, willing, brave, we must take for granted. Then this horse, like the king or hero bestride it, must have, or be seen to have, very special powers, magical powers. Powers of flight, at least, as Gwynn ap Nudd's horse leads the Wild Hunt through the dark skies of winter.

A small, crudely made box comes to hand, safely stowed in a corner of the oaken chest. On its lid is an equally crude figure of a horse like creature, but stylised, with a heavy dotted mane, large head and pointed hooves. The lid lifts easy. Inside is a mass of uncombed wool. Three small metal figures of Roman gods are amongst it. One other small item comes to hand, a worn bronze and enamel brooch. It has a sprung pin on its rear, still sharp.

I hold it, closely examining the figure before me of what appears to be the large head astride a horse, like the illustration I have seen. The big-headed man or woman has short hair, incised as though it has the energetic character of curls. His body merges with the horse's and has no obvious arms or legs. Leaning back on the plunging horse, he has a wide-open mouth, shouting, screaming, laughing or singing. The ancient scribe has used this brooch as his model. The horse, too, has an open mouth and appears to have a smile on its face. The eyes of both horse and man are tinned and shining. The tail and mane of the horse are incised, like the man's hair and along the body of both of them there are patches of enamelling in red and blue. Is this the jolly rider of the skies, beloved of the people of the woods and hills of long ago? Is he Taranis, Hywel or Coel? Or all three?

I lean back again in the scriptorium chair. Luckily it has a cushion provided for those of us who spend hours here. What was the social life of the Britons who inhabited this landscape before the Saxons arrived? Was their demeanour really so different from ours? Was it charmed, in fact, by its poetic outlook, its association with sky, land and spirit? Are we missing something important in our times, when wood is seen as a mere commodity, stone as a resource? When trade is becoming our god and the minting of money a necessity for any borough of worth? When gold is not something beautiful but valuable and men's lives are measured in oaths and punishments? Is the King aware of a vital difference between the outlook of his two sets of citizens, the possessors and the dispossessed? I ruminate, the candle burning low. Ownership and the problem of theft are important to Saxons.

What could a biography say about Athelstan, if I write it? Would it include his own personal experience of theft?

Athelstan is a wise, some would say a cunning, king. He seeks sagacity. He has the advantages of being a sound warrior schooled in literate education, knows the power of the sword as well as of the pen. He has both strings to his bow. He is deeply religious, perhaps too much so, in my own view. The example of his grandfather, aunt and uncle in devoting much time in prayer and in encouraging the prayers of the Saints, particularly Cuthbert and Oswald to assist with far sightedness, decision making and on the battle field, has helped to determine his character as a man and ruler. He is adaptable and forgiving of the best of his foes, but banishment for his own people and execution for others are sanctions he is prepared to use. Athelstan is open to reason, though theft he cannot abide. If anyone stole a relic belonging to him, which he regards as part of the safeguard of sanctity for his people, there would be no punishment dire enough.

Stone has returned to Frome for the Christmas court fresh from his great victory. The Virgin King has proved himself to be an angel in Heaven's defence. With swords drawn, blessed by the presence of relics, he has successfully waged a holy, justified war on pagan British miscreants.

With ships and armies shown to be willing to invade and to fight, he has achieved what no English king has done before, or Roman army. He has obtained the submission of the Scottish king, Constantine. He has his body in mental chains, has enforced the baptism of his son. Constantine is cowed. He is an oath breaker. He must be shown that this has been a mistake.

During the long journey north and back again Athelstan has viewed the territory of Mercia and Northumbria and best of all he has viewed the remains, uncorrupted in his coffin, of St Cuthbert, who appeared to Alfred in a dream before the Battle of Edington, urging him on to fight and guaranteeing glory for him and his successors. The sight of Cuthbert in the flesh was a great boon. Rarely is a coffin lid or reliquary of such an important personage opened. At Chester-le-Street, where Cuthbert now lies, so close to the border with the Scots, Athelstan sucked in and wielded all of the saint's accessible power, temporal and spiritual.

He is the man who has seen, spoken to, even touched, the uncorrupted saint. He has him on his side, as his grandfather did. He left magnificent stoles, embroidered by Aelfflaed, to comfort the dead saint, to decorate his bed within the coffin with holy writings. St Oswald's head was also there in the coffin with Cuthbert. He has wanted to consult Oswald for years, he says.

I could write that sometimes the king can be over enthusiastic, in my opinion, in his requirement of confirmation of his Christian virtues. He is always looking for advantages by exchange, or a bargain.

I would not write that he is a worried man, desperate for the state of his soul.

Milton church, Dorset, 30 September 933

A kneeling, half naked figure is in communion with his God. A priest accompanies him in a well-known prayer, standing over him with a hand on his head. The prayer psalm is being listened to by a female figure who sits a short distance behind the king. Two half grown boys kneel by her. An older woman, weeping, sits behind the boys.

Three young men who might be taken for priests kneel near the entrance to the small church. It is a windowless crypt, lit by three candles. There is no need for light to read. Everyone knows these prayers by heart. They are all dressed in sombre colours.

This is a private requiem mass, a family affair. Dowager Queen Eadgifu, her sons and Aelfflaed the old queen are passive witnesses of the scene. The clerks hold his heavy cloak, his outer clothes, his bible, his sword.

The priest removes his hand from the King's head. Athelstan bends forward, lies prostrate on his belly, arms outstretched, like the sculpture of Christ on the cross which hangs above him. Aelfflaed stops weeping.

It's difficult to speak when you have your face on the floor, especially when the requirement is to speak in Latin, but Athelstan must do this. Latin is the language of drama and ritual. He moves his head to the side.

'I atone,' he repeats. 'I atone for the sins of omission and commission, for the neglect of my brother Edwin, for any wrong that I have done him and my family.'

And perhaps for his brother's death, too. Aelfflaed bursts into louder weeping.

The floor session lasts for a long time. Archbishop Wulfhelm of Canterbury, who is officiating, eventually touches Athelstan's arm to indicate that he should rise. He gets up, creased and dirty, from the floor. He turns to the small group of watchers. He takes a deep breath, opens his arms wide and speaks, seemingly to more people than are present.

'For my part in the demise of my brother I have agreed with the Archbishop that I will do a penance of seven years. I acknowledge the requirement for this act to signal the need for recompense. Let it be clear to all that fratricide will not be tolerated in my lands. My own behaviour will be an example. Edmund and Eadred, bear this in mind; do not let misunderstanding arise between you. Pray for forgiveness for any indiscretions either of you will make and pray for the souls of each other and your sisters. Always care for each other.' He turns back to the altar and the archbishop, kneels again.

Another burst of loud sobbing comes from the back row.

The Archbishop hands the King a long flail. His back is bare. The cat quivers in Athelstan's hand. He mutters a short prayer then begins to strike himself. Seven lashes, for seven years. For seven years of rule in place of a favoured brother and now guilt for the loss of another, the sons of the aged queen who is here, a sobbing ruin. Blood runs down his back. This hurts. A lot.

When it is over, the bloody flail is offered to the archbishop as though it is a reliquary of value.

'Thank you,' says the King.

Wulfhelm recites prayers and then there is a final period of silence for all to take in the magnitude of the penance ritual. Eadgifu goes to Aelfflaed and offers an arm. It is refused.

Dunstan helps Athelstan to dress, hands him his mud spattered dusty cloak. As he puts on his sword, he finds words to express his remorse.

'In this place, in memory of my brother Edwin, I will build a monastery which will last a thousand years, to the glory of God. It shall be known as Milton Abbas.'

A simple declaration, a simple intent. One which the hearers will appreciate. This is a big task. Like the monastery at Muchelney, this is yet another building project in honour of God. There will be a cost.

A cost as dear as a son's life? As a dream of kingship ruined?
Aelfflaed thinks not.

'I understand Winchester is reviewing recent Chronicle events.
Some rewriting is suggested in the light of the summer's tragedy.
That's a serious matter, isn't it?'

Leofa and Dunstan, waiting outside for the King to mount
his horse, are realising the effects of his near admission of
murder in the matter of Edwin. The pitiable figure of Aelfflaed
is bundling herself inside a carriage for the return trip to Wilton,
still weeping, but quietly now. Her red face shoots one last glance
at Athelstan as he raises himself in the saddle, wincing.

'Yes, it is,' Dunstan replies. 'We shall have to wait to see
how this business plays itself out. They suspect Stone may have
played an active part in Edwin's death. It may be enough that the
penance is activated and acknowledged; the Winchester faction
will be mollified, I think. There is anyway the coming war to keep
everyone amused. The winter is more likely to be taken up with
splendid thoughts of battle than personal revenge. And anyway,
what's done is done. What do you think, Nonna?'

Nonna sighs and shrugs. 'It looks as though Wessex and
Mercia are at each other's throats again. I thought all that
business was over.' *Will this jealousy never end?*

Demolition and building at Milton began the following
week. The small church and the crypt where Athelstan began his
penance was no more.

Monastery of St John, Frome, after Prime, 19 December 934

It is after Prime, the time before dawn on this day of Advent. I am exhausted. The great law court of bishops and ministers has thrashed out the latest amendments put forward by Christian administrators, hearing mostly secular ministerial objections, pushing through with continuous debate the requirements of the state, trying not to come to blows, retreating at last, bruised in mind, to the mead flagon.

Stone has double heavy mauve bags under his eyes. My hand hurts from speedy writing, ink covers my forearm. My mind is weary with catching the sense of conversations, interpreting the intentions and motivations of speakers. I am trying to keep out of the way of a Welsh scribe who would like to pull wool over my eyes. I have to insist, quite rudely, that my own Welsh translation will do, thank you very much. He walks off in a huff, grumbling. I must get some sleep before the next meeting.

We have been engaged with matters of state for a full four days. Decisions have been made, charters written. A flurry of parcels of land have been signed away to delighted courtiers, to envious bishops. Fair shares for all, the King says. Now play nicely together.

The ordinary business of the witan has been complicated by the unwilling presence of the chief guest Constantine. He attempted to slip the guards while the court paused at Buckingham in September on its way south. Athelstan has been working on him privately, trying to get him to see sense, alongside Hywel Dda, but has made little headway. He will sign no more documents as a sub-king, he says. He would rather eat shit. His interpreter is not much help; he appears to be biased. Interpreters should do their jobs, speak for the foreigner, not rehash his words. But it would be difficult to make Constantine sound worse than his face appears. He is not enjoying his host's hospitality. He is humiliated and not good at pretending.

But now for some light relief. The first hunt, a demonstration of skills of hawking by Athelstan and the Aetheling Edmund is to take place later this morning. The falconers are preparing their birds in pens beyond the scriptorium, bustling inside the fences and sheds, sending up feathers, screeches and hoots. From small prey to large, from mice and rats to hares, all will be hunted not far from the palace on the other side of the Portway. It will be a good chance to show off the King's stable of horses. For Edmund, it will be his first time showing his skill with birds of prey in public. He should do well; he is a promising prince. Nevertheless there will no doubt be nerves.

Many of my fellow lay brothers and those monks who remain in the monastery for working prayers have retired to their cells again for further contemplation or scriptorium work, or to make notes for the King at his chief counsellors' briefing which takes place after breakfast. More diplomacy, more pretence will be required. The church leaders closest to Athelstan and the trusted inner circle of his family will be involved. No doubt Eadgifu will get her oar in. She often sidles into session with a bishop on her arm. Some brothers will have gone to the kitchens to assist with preparations for the important midday meal to be taken after Terce.

Among the noises outside my window I can hear crockery clattering and the muffled sound of instructions about weighing and argument over portion sizes. There are swooshing sounds of large amounts of liquid being poured. Hopefully the high-born guests sleeping in tents are not made too tetchy by this early activity. After a few days of the larger witan meetings good manners are all that keeps some from taking out their daggers and using them.

The weather has been kind to our visitors, some of whom have never travelled to the hunting grounds of Selwood before.

The King has two access points into the forest, here at Frome and at the palace of Cheddar, which gives the additional thrill of gorge and wetland fowl hunting. Edmund and Stone like to watch the stars in a dark winter sky above the gorge while lying on their backs, trundling home in a hunting cart. They sense the deep past, the power of the heavens, they say, when they are there. I know what they mean. Edmund's brother Eadred also has something of the mystical about him. Perhaps an anointed king has a deeper relationship with the numinous than the rest of us, can see ahead and backwards through the ages with vision granted by God. Certainly this family seems unusually concerned with great matters of existence. I can't imagine the Practised Scoundrel eulogising about the belt of Orion.

Apart from Winchester, which holds no favourable childhood memories for him, Athelstan likes to be where his grandfather used to be. He soaks up his spirit in the old palace halls like Frome. Tomorrow there will be a full council meeting in public to which the guests will be invited. Leofa and I will be interpreters as usual. We have the afternoon off today. Dunstan, Leofa and I will confer, perhaps investigate the kitchens for a bit of spare food. There are some pretty ladies working there. I have my eye on a dark haired one in particular. I like to practise my Welsh.

Meanwhile I have another brief chance to delve into the oaken chest. This morning I choose a folded manuscript, its folds yellowed along its back. It opens out across an arm's length of writing table, displaying cracks at its extremes. It is written in the Latin of the British and refers to two cities at the north and south extremities of Selwood. Caer Badon or Bathanceaster as it is called now by the English is in the north and Pensa vel Coit, which we now call Penselwood, at the southern end of the Great Wood, a once famous city now lost in the trees since its capture in 658.

The story of these two places is related here anonymously. They are in a different hand from the last, again spidery and difficult to decipher, but evidently by one of the Christian faith as there are gospel references and slight, faded drawings of uplifted arms and hands of sainted figures in the margins. I shall have to speak now for the anonymous ancient monk who wrote these words in many centuries past.

In 516, he lists, was the Battle of Badon, in which Arthur carried the Cross of Our Lord Jesus Christ for three days and three nights on his shoulders and the Britons were the victors. In 665, a whole world away from those early days, he records the first celebration of Easter among the Saxons and the second battle of Badon. This is the place that Nenna has written about elsewhere, the land of hot springs, Bath.

I leave the table to wander over to the current records clerk's stall. He has the upkeep of the Saxon Chronicle as his chief remit. He is the source of the record of activity of kings and travels with the court. The diary of events is kept chained to his desk. There are some who would like to amend it in private or expunge it altogether, as it is frank and records evil deeds as well as good. It naturally favours the rulers of Wessex. Its jewelled aestel, the magical pointer, hangs by its side, also chained. The inkwell and quill lie nearby, ready at all times to record great events. It is to be supposed that the meeting of minds and warriors here at Christmas will be recorded. In my view this will be an important milestone in the career of Athelstan. Others may see the successful outcome of a battle as more noteworthy. Fracitus, the recorder, is fastidious in his notes. He normally allows no-one to interfere with the Chronicle. Nevertheless, he has told me much about recently written contents and on one occasion, privately, he allowed me to read it. I take my chance, open the book.

I can recall the nature of the early battle of 516 with the British vividly, as if I were there. It comes to me in dreams. I lift the heavy vellum, turn its pages, find the references for the year which I read before. My mother told me the story of the battle. It was a significant defeat of the Saxons.

But there is nothing mentioned for 516 in the Saxon
Chronicle. The first Battle of Badon does not exist in our history,
only in the oral traditions of the Welsh. Asser and Alfred evidently
did not think it worth recording. I have found that the scribes of
the time did not necessarily record all moments of tension with
the Britons; not all encounters went our way. This is the battle
won by the Britons against the Saxons. The Welsh have recorded
it, as well they might, but the English have not.

Why should I care about a long-ago battle? Because the truth
is important and fairness is a valiant goal.

The Saxons fought back in time with a defeat and
humiliation of the Britons in 577 at Dyrham, north of the city
of Bathon, when Cuthwine and Ceawlin slew no less than three
British kings, Coinmail, Condidan and Farinmail and captured
Gloucester, Cirencester and Bath. This time the successful rout
appears in our Chronicle. The loss of Bath must have been
difficult for my mother's people.

The poets speak of the awe of the Saxons when regarding
the work of the Romans, monuments to their great achievements
in stone, basilicas, baths and buildings. They were highly
regarded for running a common system of economy and religion
throughout the country of Prydein, Britain, which we in Wessex
as yet can wonder at. I have heard of such things in existence on
the continent, at Charlemagne's court and I know it is Athelstan's
dream to establish such a system of good, even luxurious
management in these shores. Perhaps he will, but the lifetime
of kings is often short and there is much to do. They have to
hope that their dynasty will carry plans through. Fifty years of a
consistent bloodline, perhaps a hundred, may be enough. At any
time, the Vikings might decide to plunder again. But not now, not
yet. They are too busy licking their wounds.

The excitement at first of the defence of Dumnonia and
then its loss must have been a source of many stories told around
the fires, on both sides, British and Saxon, though the British

are more likely to have sung of the disaster. They are pragmatic and do not mind sad songs. They relish gloom, I think. Once bright with gold, its former temple complex and hot spring baths designed to delight, respecting all gods and catering for all tastes, the fair city of Badon, with arcades of shops and beautiful public spaces and restaurants provided respite for the legions as well as the citizens of the ordered empire. Suddenly plunged into desolation and ruin, ravaged by the cavalier hordes of Wessex, it had been a glorious gateway to the south-west, a gateway which, however, the pagan Saxon kings failed for so long to penetrate. It became a forlorn, ill-managed place.

For another three generations after Dyrham, Saxon Wessex consolidated its members and settlements, moving along the river valleys, settling invited families, clearing woodland and scrub where former owners had abandoned their farms. The British moved abroad or married their daughters to the more peaceable of the newcomers. Some stayed to farm the land they had held for generations and hoped for the best.

While the monastery at Glastonbury survived, the city of Penselwood was destroyed and swallowed up by vegetation in Selwood. Today it is inhabited only by farmers and woodsmen. It is still the haunt of wolves and witches are said to live nearby, causing unease to the newly Christianised.

The forest's dark spirit lives on.

Monastery of St John, Frome, after Terce, 20 December 934

It is mid-morning. Terce has been sung, breakfast consumed by even the late risers. The sun is up and we can see to read without candles, even in the darker corners of the scriptorium. The sun sprays through the glass windows; they could do with a clean. The diamond panes set in lead are a fiddle. I watch the lay brother as he tries to remove spider webs which have inevitably grown overnight. It would be churlish to point out the bits that he has missed.

I look down to the courtyard below. There is movement, the stablelads are about, chattering instructions, preparing the great hunters. The large gates at the end of the cobbled area swing open. Eadgifu, queen and competent rider, is emerging through the gateposts into the shadowed stable area. She makes for the nearest dismounting block. A retinue of guards follows her in together with her two young lads riding on cobs.

I had heard that she had been away briefly to attend to work in hand at Winchester, taking the princes with her. She signals to the guards to unload the packages and purchases she has evidently made while there. It consists of rolls of material, mostly, by the look of it, more sewing and needlework for the ladies of the court, more new ideas for dresses, perhaps exotic threads for headdresses and collars. I have noticed that gold and silver have been making their way more abundantly into court dress, both for men as well as women. Bells are sewn onto female clothing; the ladies jingle as they walk. Bells are everywhere, accompanying the bell like tones of their high voices. We hear a lot of the speech of ladies, these days, more than the palaces used to. Once it resounded to the exclusive deep drum voices of men. Eadgifu is all for equality.

She is back in time, as promised, for Edmund and Eadred to listen to some witan debates. Athelstan will soon be taking over their full-time instruction as they travel with the court, interspersed with lessons at Glastonbury. The Aetheling heir and Eadred need to learn as much as possible, as soon as possible, about etiquette and diplomacy. Since Edwin's death last year their age has not held back Stone's wish to advance their experience. The sooner they learn how to handle the minds of men as well as to hunt and fight, the better, he often says.

Eadgifu tears off her riding gloves, tells her sons to hurry. Her shrill voice commands but does not bully. She can do what is necessary, like Aelfflaed could, but more pleasantly. She is dominant, but not pushy. She maintains her royal position very cleverly, in my opinion. Very graceful, most attractive, for an older woman. Dunstan may be right in his assessment of her. She still outshines most of the women of the court. She passes into the women's quarters.

A messenger comes for me. Stone wants me to wait on him in the palace hall. I put down my pen, close the chest, exit the haligdom and lock it, stride along the scriptorium, run down the stairs and along the passage out into the light. I climb the steps to the hall above, enjoying fresh, frosty air, pleasing to the senses. Another day in paradise. I am a young Chancery clerk to the great King Athelstan of Wessex, in this glorious year of 934. How good that feels.

I enter at the east end of the palace hall. This is an old hall, like Cheddar's used to be until they pulled it down to build a new one last year. It's eighty feet long and twenty feet wide, with the wind whistling through the central doors, but very beautiful. There's a hearth in the centre, just as Alfred used to like it, for when men were men. Eadgifu has her sights set on modernising this one, too. She may get her way as she often does. After next summer, when Scotland has bowed to us, Athelstan has told her. Not now. Later. He seems fixed on this. She will have to wait for her cosier hall, her attached latrine, her ordered buildings suitable for womenfolk as well as menfolk. I think Athelstan may want to keep this hall as it is and may try to resist her plans. He cites money as an obstacle, but everyone knows that there is ample for any rebuilding he wants done. *Defence construction for burghs is more important, Eadgifu,* he says. There is no real argument. Eadgifu knows that she can't win every time, but she makes progress in many small ways.

Athelstan is eating a late breakfast at the west end of the hall. Sunlight through the eastern door shines up into the rafters, pointing up the network of boughs and beams of oak, making them glow orange. Eadgifu and her sons join us. He indicates to us that we should approach him. He puts down his fowl's leg and bread.

'Welcome, Eadgifu, you come just as a fresh platter has been brought. Come, eat. And you too, boys. And you, too, Nonna.'

I am always ready to eat, despite having just finished breakfast in the refectory. I take a duck leg. Eadgifu and the boys take tearings of the large brown loaf, help themselves to the tankard of ale.

'Are you ready to tell me about your visit?' Athelstan is always interested to hear what transpires at Winchester. He does not often go there himself. 'And I want to hear how Aelfflaed is at Wilton. Did you pass by there?'

Eadgifu did. Went there on her way, came back there on her return. The boys waited for her outside the convent while she visited the old queen.

'How is she?'

'Mad, quite mad.'

The sun goes behind a cloud. There is silence. Suddenly he looks older. He shouldn't have asked.

Haligdom of St John's Monastery, Frome, afternoon, 20 December 934

Back at the scriptorium after a private meal with Athelstan, telling him more about the British documents, I unlock the haligdom door and the chest, get back to my pleasant labours. Stone has said that I should concentrate on its contents for the remainder of the day. Leofa or Dunstan will take care of witan matters.

A third manuscript from the oaken chest seems to record the loss of Bath by the British.

I read.

Sulis Laments

What is this? Outrageous war thunders in my streets. My land, warmed by luxurious heat, succour to the soldier, play-place to the minions, bathing place of my fellow gods, home of my shrine is insulted. Stone heaped on decorated stone, the delicate tracery of gold and silver in the arches of my halls, statuary to my brothers of the skies and earth, ghosts and heroes of the past, destroyed.

My brother Gorgon shakes his head in shame, hair like serpents crying out, calling foul for the panic in the land, assaulted by the dread, uncouth, fair haired invaders. They are untrained to hear my voice or care what I say, speaking another language of the mind. Usurpers of our hegemony, the land of Prydein.

They do not hear, they do not see. They have other images in their minds, from other worlds than this. Other gods, warlike invaders, drive them on. Their hell is not ours, their heaven is a different place.

I am static, open mouthed at the assault to my being, powerless to intervene with those who do not know the land, do not care for it. I must accept that my face will be abused, my head decapitated, my shining eyes dimmed as it lies upon the marble floor. I face the enemy askew, thunder pouring from my lips, but the new faith of my people forbids me to retaliate. Mutilated, I stand by as more of my powers are lost. Shorn by my people, attacked by the enemy, I drown beneath my own warm waters, warm like blood. Thick mud oozes around my feet, my temple steps, the healing heat neglected, flowing to the cold waters of the sea, to my brother god Nodens, who wails, like me, drowning.

I do not believe the new god, the new hero, will save my people. They smash my image like the enemy does, fearing that my face will look them in the eye and say 'No more, forget me and you die'. I curse you. The new god of their hearts is a gentle one who leads to a splendid life beyond the grave. But I did that, too. They only follow one, they say, you are too many gods.

I blame the priests of the temple who found that more of us would mean more for them. In the beginning there was only one, and I am his true daughter. There should never have been more, but the foolish and the greedy found excuses. So more and more of us became minor gods and goddesses, split by split, priest by priest, until the people of the new god cried enough, no more.

The soldier of these times, this Arthur, this bear, who invokes this god and his mother, will bravely fight. Secretly with the little power I have left, I assist. But I can foretell, it is in the pool of water, of blood, at my feet; all will be lost. And it will be the fault of my own people who neglected me.

Caer Bathon is falling. Dumnonia is falling, soon to be lost like some faery kingdom in the mists, subject of tales. Pilgrimage to my shrine will cease. New shrines will arise on top of mine, ignoring my foundations, flattening my floors, my beautiful paved areas where barefoot feet were safe to tread. There was once no excrement to tread in or glass to wound. Now there is debris everywhere.

The battle of the dark-haired and the light is just beginning. Like Gildas of the new order, I bewail the loss of saintliness, the increase in gluttony and self-regard. The Britons have become the eaters of all things, like their enemy; but not courageous like their enemy. Wisdom and simplicity and stout heartedness are not their birthright. They must be achieved.

Let bloodshed commence. The shadow of fear skims the hillsides, the cloud of all-encompassing change, grabbing, throttling, renaming, removing legends, heroes, shrines, beliefs. The enemy will make us subject to their laws, to their history. Choice will be the enemy's alone. Their history, not ours, will prevail.

What will remain? Peace will come, established by the sword, followed by taxation. We have words, grudges, the art of foretelling, of laments sung to the consoling harp, curses for the ill-disposed.

We have our words. Remember me. Remember my people. Do not forget.

Monastery of St John, Frome, evening, 20 December 934

I was shaken by the words of the goddess Sulis. During the rest of the day, attending the King and court after a hawking contest and between the office hours of None and Vespers I worked in my role as interpreter and scribe, assisting the Welsh and English bishops. The sense of loss of my mother's people kept rising through my inner being, crying foul, making concentration difficult. I felt emotional, unlike myself.

I could see Leofa across the hall attending Stone close at hand as his interpreter with the Irish and Danish guests, his head turning and darting between each as comments were made and noted. Several matters of great importance needed to be covered, several persuasive gestures needed to be made, with correct, firm emphasis. There was stony silence from the King of Scotland. Leofa kept his cool. He was always professional in his work. Getting everyone to speak in turn and not at the same time was nearly impossible, though Stone was able to bring his self-composed personality to bear, called them all to order.

Despite the impressive outcome of the Scottish enterprise, where Athelstan showed his might, ravaging as far north as Caithness, there are still difficulties with Constantine. He will not bend his neck in complete submission and seems deaf to entreaties to listen. He feigns sleep, yawns to indicate boredom, cackles irritatingly at inopportune times. Others look round when he does this; he knows the irrelevant laughter will stop them in their tracks. He is not to be trusted. Athelstan intends to keep him close by as long as possible; he hopes to influence him into being a less savage persona, at least to look at. But Constantine is old, past forty. An old dog, grey and hairy. He may prove impossible to tame. Archbishop Wulfstan has attempted to do so at Aethelstan's request and with Leofa's help, but it seems there is no favourable response from his religious sensibility, if he has any; Constantine doesn't care what the Pope and Wulfstan think.

Leofa has been asked to show some of the less valuable relic items to Constantine in an attempt to test the binding strength of his oath. Most men would blanch at the idea of breaking an oath made over these items. Ecclesiastical magic usually holds sway over men's minds. If he proves intractable or unimpressed by the wrath of dead saints he will have to be sanctioned in some other way, perhaps a permanent retention of significant hostages. His young son is a candidate; the lad seems more outgoing than his father, more open to reason, but like any son in this situation blood will out and loyalty will be due to any patriot's king and expected of his son. The encouragement of patricide might be an effective means of deactivating Constantine; but that would be the last resort of a Christian king such as Athelstan, who would prefer to encourage both father and son to seek his protection and oversight as sub-kings. We continue to consider what might be done to bend him. The forging of the nation depends on breaking the Practised Scoundrel's will, somehow.

Leofa has reported that even St Radegund's reliquary had little apparent effect on the King of Scotland's mood; he merely asked when the next meal would occur as he was faint with hunger and needed meat. Leofa went to find him a chicken leg while the mass priests guarded him and protected the relics. When he had eaten, he belched and tossed chicken bones on the floor. Was anything to be done with him? Stone seems nonplussed by the wiry haired loser. He is either quite stupid, or quite bright; he doesn't say enough, other than in grunts, to be able to tell which. Perhaps he is unaware of his present difficult position, in shock at the rapid summer success of the southern king. He certainly has no charm. He is a very different foe to Guthrum, Danish enemy of Alfred, who became pious, albeit temporarily. Constantine wouldn't even be able to fake.

Dunstan is nowhere to be seen. The kitchen staff say he was last spied coming from the nave of the church, covered in many hues of paint. He has neglected all the offices of late, though the mass priests see to it that the prayers are said, incense burnt, communion given. Usually he is never far from the rituals of the monasteries we visit. His project here in Frome is absorbing his energy. Stone wonders where he is, sometimes. We remind him of his own painting commission to Dunstan for the nave walls of the monastery church. He tells us to let him be.

In the evening, Leofa and I, having taken on some of Dunstan's court work, have a chance to meet over a hurried meal in the refectory kitchen. He is looking tired, his handsome eyes sore and reddened, though the whites are bright. He is stimulated by the huge variety of visitors to the witan and Christmas court. We have never seen such large numbers of different foreigners with their unfamiliar languages and gestures. Their dietary requirements, too, are causing a problem for the kitchens. The Danish visitors are easily pleased; they will eat anything. Their behaviour remains typically uncouth; the hall floor is littered with fish and fowl bones every night.

He, like me, like all of us, is having little sleep. It is difficult to reconcile all that is heard from the different voices, so intense is the requirement to understand the commitments about to be entered into, to swallow the vital importance of these challenging diplomatic tussles. Changing the shape of Britain's kingdoms is no easy task, but one which has become imperative. The physical battles have given way to psychological wars. The ultimate prize of an Empire of Britain is worth a few sleepless nights.

Leofa and I have been trained to work through extreme tiredness, to listen, to spy and to hold what we have learned in our hearts and heads for reporting in person whatever may be of use to the King. He wants to go down in history as the leader who left a significant legacy, a common wealth. Is he too far before his time? Will the dream crumple? Will it kill him in the making?

Where possible we must retain the exact words we hear from the various arguments. Added to Athelstan's own view point of the day's information, we three, together with Dunstan when he is not engaged in his artistic creations, add to the pile of nightmares and dreams which somehow translate into a plan for action on the following morning. We report to him at night, offload our information, sleep (or not), the King dreams, and wakes clear-headed in the morning, when he gives us fresh instructions on where our ears are especially to flap.

Whenever he gets wind of the appearance at court of an imposing foreign visitor, especially one with a Papal connection, Dunstan manages to appear in a corner of the hall. He is moving at present from the business of interpreting to what Aethelstan regards as a higher calling, that of culture, embellishing the political achievements of the court with his art. Aethelwold has taken over his spying duties. The workshops at Glastonbury ring with his hammers and tongs as he makes glass collide, metal bend. Here at Frome he is working on the King's commission in the church. It is a secret. Perhaps, on Christmas Eve when it is to be revealed, there will be a last chance to impress Constantine and to save Stone the heartache of having to impose a greater sanction, one which might involve permanent incarceration or worse.

Studious Dunstan, short sighted Dunstan. His eyes are better at focussing on the bigger picture, though his mind is as sharp as the King's and cunning too. He may go far. Cunning, rather than brawn, seems to be becoming a necessary requisite amongst these ministerial gatherings, they are becoming so populous and international.

Stone's age has begun to worry him. *Will I live long enough to see this through*, he often says. Can we and some of his sympathetic bishops share some of his load? Edmund, his heir, is still very young, and has much to learn. Dunstan has noted Stone's growing impatience, tries to offer advice, which sometimes backfires; Athelstan likes him, but Dunstan can be too voluble and too right.

Some members of the family, particularly the younger royal women, are not keen to allow Dunstan to have even greater influence. They laugh at him, at his stature and bookishness, at his sometimes over-sensitive requirement to impress. They do not wish him to join them at Gospel Dice and he annoys them by disregarding their fashionable presence. He does not flatter or charm. He does not show that they are important to his well-being. They plot to see him fail. Dunstan will not fail. In this household of the Virgin King, he is safe. Safe to climb ever higher.

If Dunstan rises, Leofa and I, as members of the trinity, will continue upwards with him. He does not see the distinction between us, which we are aware of, of that Saxon silver spoon in his mouth. It comes naturally to him to take advantage of the bloodline he bears, his progress assured as long as he makes no major mistakes. His art efforts in the reliquary line have proven superb; his wrought iron, glasswork and mural painting have yet to be appraised. He has seen for himself the adornments of the churches on the continent; he wants the same for the minsters of Wessex. No longer able to compete, because of his eyesight, in the scriptorium as a gospel illustrator, his wings have flapped and he has flown. The big schemes are his, the see of Canterbury is his goal. *Why not*, he says.

At work in the church, while the majority of the court is out hunting and hawking, Dunstan paints. The nave is out of bounds to all but the lowest of boy servants, a dumb creature, who takes him food. Sackcloth covers the walls and pillars of stone where he is working, rickety scaffolding disfigures the eastern portion of the nave. Priests and monks of the daily offices are able to use the quire, but beyond is the quiet, unseen work of the muralist that Dunstan, on this occasion, has become. He even works throughout the performance of offices, dedicated to his task, whatever it is.

All will be revealed at the Christmas eve mass. You can be sure, if Dunstan has been able to show in his works what he has been talking about to us, that it will be something stupendous.

Preparations for war, Chippenham Palace, January 934

I accompanied Athelstan throughout the year of 933 along with Dunstan and Leofa, watching and recording the decisions and planning for the campaign in Scotland. We visited Portchester to see the navy's work in preparation, saw fresh armoury being made at Glastonbury and elsewhere, noted the building work at Cheddar and in the burghs. We were to give the northerners a bloody nose. Vikings, Northumbrians or Strathclyders, it didn't matter. They had all proved themselves to be untrustworthy oath breakers. The nobles, old and young, were enthusiastic. They had been hankering after a fight for years, a chance to prove themselves.

For the early months of this new year we were based in Chippenham. It had been freshly refortified and was now a sturdy northern Wessex burgh. The witan's chief leaders, ealdormen and thegns and their retinues were comfortably accommodated by the barrack-like arrangements. Tiers of beds, sometimes four high and three deep, ranged up the side walls of the hall with piss buckets attached to ropes for convenience. The young men at the top could touch the rafters. Heavy plank tables extended the length of the hall either side of the central fire, bearing continually refilled leather jugs of ale, wooden bowls of pungent cheese and fresh bread. Pottery was not required in this soldiers' environment. When it shatters, it cuts your feet as you jump down from bunks. Much better to stick to leather and wood containers. It is what men are used to. They last forever. This palace was arranged to cater for men going to war. The basic requirements of fire for cooking and lighting, piss buckets and beds under cover were the only luxuries. Not for ladies with their embroidery, this hall. This was an army's headquarters. Eadgifu hated it.

The witan was discussing the naval requirements, men and boats. I made notes for Athelstan to peruse later on. War brings men together; they have the enemy to unite them. There was a growing sense of endeavour, of excitement about the coming trip north. In April the winter mud would be drying up; by May's witan at Winchester all that could be would have been achieved in terms of manpower and armaments, ready for the journey. The King was pleased with progress and with the mood of the court; the antipathy of the previous year when Edwin died had melted away with gifts and promises that he had made to the nobility.

Aldhelm is Athelstan's cultural and spiritual mentor, less tied in his mind with the defence of the realm, more of a personal deity and muse. When he feels troubled about women, he asks Aldhelm for guidance. When he needs advice for cultural pursuits, he asks Aldhelm. He likes to think he might have found a close friend in the seventh century monk. He often sends a prayer, a gift, to Malmesbury as an offering to his tomb, always visits when he is north of Bath.

Aldhelm was put to one side while war took over all thoughts; Athelstan needed all the manly vigour he could summon from dead King Oswald. We made a brief visit to Gloucester shortly after Christmas to consult the parts of him that lie there. Oswald's legs, however, were not as lucid as we thought his head would be. They could hold the power of the soul, like that of Bran, the old celtic god that I have heard of. Oswald's head needed the protection of the southern English. Athelstan had convinced himself, I now realise, that he had to see it.

And so that visit to Chester-le-Street was planned. At the very least, personal consultation with Oswald's head would be vital. A private visit should be arranged with only myself, Leofa and Dunstan, Stones-men. No-one else should know of the King's requirements. They might be outraged. Stone asked Dunstan to plan for a possible viewing of the head. No doubt Cuthbert's monks would require a significant contribution for any special privileges.

Oswald's head became an extra obsession with the King, meat and drink. He was thinner, despite Christmas excesses.

He was worried about what to do about it. He had dreams of it speaking to him. Leofa, Dunstan and I had to utter blood curdling oaths. We all have more than enough religious teaching in our souls to keep us from revealing the King's thoughts and intentions to anyone beyond our trinity. At night, when I reported to Stone on the day's gleanings and court gossip, told him about the grumbles and expectations of his soldiers and sailors, he almost wept. He wrung his hands.

'Can it be done, do you think, Nonna? Can it be done?'

But these were rhetorical questions, I knew. Really he was consulting Oswald. And Cuthbert. And Alfred and Aldhelm. And Aethelflaed, his Mercian mother. His own personal hagiology of advisors, held in his heart. Personally, I wouldn't dream of doing what he was suggesting; I would like to go to Heaven when the time comes.

Wilton Abbey, 21 April 934

A royal carriage swoops down from the Wylye track, bearing a queen. Eadgifu is going to pay her respects to another queen, Aelfflaed, another wife of her own dead husband. She likes the irony of this. The carriage comes to a halt. An outrider dismounts to open the door. Eadgifu emerges into the sunlight. The trip from Amesbury has been muddy and difficult, but the deed must be done. Love Lies Bleeding is flowering in the stone ringed flowerbed by the entrance.

Aelfflaed has died. Certain things must be wrapped up, arrangements made for wills to be read, daughters' interests must be looked after, though the ones remaining in England are both nuns and well catered for.

She allows the outrider to pull the bell handle for entry. A grill is slid, enquiry made. The heavy door opens onto a brick courtyard. Eadgifu steps inside. The outrider hands her a large basket of flowers and greenery which she has arranged personally and returns to the carriage, patting his horse and speaking to the driver. Horse breath in cool spring air rises; they wait outside at the Queen's leisure.

A nun approaches from an inner entrance. She bows to Eadgifu. 'Greetings, Madam. I will take you to Eadflaed. She is with her mother. She is aware of your intended visit and will be honoured, I am sure. As are we all.' The Abbess is always mindful of royal patronage. At such times much may be gained, or lost. They walk briskly to Aelfflaed's comfortable rooms, knock gently at the door. Eadflaed opens it. She curtsies to Eadgifu.

'Welcome, Madam.' Eadflaed takes the proffered flowers. 'Thank you.'

The three women approach the coffin on the table. It is surrounded by more flowers. Luckily the air is cool; no fire has been lit. Nevertheless there is a faint smell of decay. Burial will take place this afternoon in the Abbey cemetery.

'Eadburh sends her condolences, I was with her last night in Winchester.' Eadflaed nods and curtsies again in appreciation of her half-sister's message, from one nun to another. But they have never met. Eadburh is only a child, still. The Nunnaminster of Winchester has her as a novice in their schoolroom.

'Is she well, Madam?' No need to ask after Eadgifu, she is obviously in good health.

'Yes, and doing well with her studies.'

The new generation of nuns aims to be as competent at writing and illustration as scriptorium monks. In many ways they already are. There is a growing air of competition between the ladies of Winchester and Wilton. Shaftesbury, too, is joining their ranks as educators of women. They walk to the open coffin on the oak table.

'Was there pain in the passing?' Aelfflaed's corpse is looking well, there is colour in her cheeks. She may have received some painterly attention.

'We think she suffered a stroke, Madam, in the afternoon. She was unconscious when we found her. No, no pain.' The Abbess has learnt how to reassure the living of the softly opening gates of Heaven. It's best that way.

Eadgifu nods at the Abbess, who turns and retires through the door, leaving the royal kin to talk privately. The two women kneel to pray briefly by the flowery coffin, then light more candles at its corners, replacing others which have died down. The scene is a riot of colour. Bright orange and yellow hangings, shining with gold threads, reflect the heavenly scene. They rise and take two comfortable chairs close together.

'Naturally the will gifts the estates to the King, but are there other personal items which your mother wished to convey to him?' Eadgifu, the business woman, comes straight to the point. She sweeps her eyes around the room.

There are some fine stone carvings and bronzes here, some of antiquity, dug out of Bath and Winchester's ancient remains.

Statuettes of gods, red pottery dishes. Aelfflaed had a passion for artwork and the beautiful, a secular rather than religious sentiment. She crossed borders and religions.

'Mother wished to bestow her own embroidery work and that which was being done by her tapestry design and embroidery group on the King's household, to be used as you think fit, Madam,' Eadflaed indicates a large chest in the corner of the room. 'I have grouped her work together with her commissions. As you know, Mother considered the flower motif her greatest contribution to the art of today. Here are some of her best examples.' She indicates an open closet next to them.

Eadgifu inspects the variety of silk wrapped items, chasubles, albs, stoles, maniples, girdles, altar coverings, items worthy of bishops and archbishops. Here is a life fanatically dedicated to art, displayed on objects where all could see and enjoy intricate designs displayed on the bodies of the religious, on the fair frames of royal ladies. It is large closet full of sumptuous items, not to everyone's taste. Some of the items are gaudy in the extreme. She picks out several, avoiding the loudest.

'I will take these with me today after the burial. They will be well received by the King and I thank you, for myself. They are very beautiful.' *And very royal, worth a bit,* she thinks.

'Mother would wish her legacy to be seen as chiefly in the realms of art. Her whole life was dedicated to her needle, apart from her royal duties, of course. She would be pleased to know that her work will be appreciated and passed down through the royal family. Perhaps your daughters may like to choose from this selection?'

Eadgifu is polite. 'Certainly, we will take good care of these items. It may be that when the world has moved on and many centuries have passed that your mother's work will still grace the halls and homes of great men and women. She has set a precedent of workmanship second to none. Her output has been phenomenal.' She casts her eye around the room again.

Tapestry is everywhere, everything flowery. In the side room, a glimpse of a heavily embroidered bedcover. Curtains, too, evidently in the old queen's style. Rather remarkable, really, with white lily heads on a gold, yellow and orange background. Very lively. They would awaken the dead. She decides to make a request.

'Did your mother intend a new home for her curtains? They are particularly lovely. I admire the theme of gold and yellow, the large blooms which she has managed to convey so expertly.'

'I am sure that if you wish to have them, they can be brought down and conveyed to your carriage. I would be delighted to think that they might be viewed at court. They are somewhat heavy and as you see, long, to keep out draughts. I will bring a girl to fold them for you.' Eadflaed picks up a table bell, goes to the door and rings it in the cloister. The tuneful bell compliments the quiet courtyard of the cloister, the heart of the abbey. She is gratified that the visitor wants more of her mother's works. 'She was particularly proud of these curtains,' she adds.

They leave the body in its flowery boudoir and pass to the refectory to take refreshment. Cooking is a famed skill of the abbey; its scented honey and fruit buns are legendary. The level of comfort and the refectory of Wilton make it a very desirable retirement home for queens and their kin. Infirmary care, too is good. Many herbs, spices and potions make their way up the Itchen from Hamwih on the coast, excellent for baking, cure-alls for ailments. Wilton is known as a good place to come to die, but it also saves lives; infection medicine is being discovered continually as ships arrive from lands far away. Young men make good recoveries in Wilton infirmary from war wounds, if they can be brought here soon enough.

Eadgifu notes the new building and wall painting that has been achieved since her last visit. There is much colour about the place. Aethelwold, her chaplain, would not be amused. She must tell him of the cloister stone tendrils, the fine decorated tiled floors. She might persuade him of the efficacy of design in soothing, comforting. She knows what he will say.

When I get my hands on a monastic environment I will purge it of all unnecessary flummery.

Aethelwold has ambitions. Despite his hard-line attitude, he is good at heart and will go far, she thinks. But better not to mention his name here. Eadgifu enjoys her bun, refuses a second.

Dunstan, on the other hand, might approve of all this decoration. He is an artist, after all. But such secular decoration in a religious house might not sit well with him. They are both determined reformers. They seem to think that there is much to reform. Eadgifu looks around her, at the vases of flowers, at the tray of eatables, at the garden on view beyond the refectory windows.

I wouldn't mind ending my days here, she thinks.

After the quiet burial, attended by herself, Aethelhild and Eadfaed, both daughters of the old queen given to the Church, she returns to Amesbury, bearing the chest of embroidery to grace her own apartment there. Athelstan will be interested to hear her account. Aelfflaed was an old adversary.

On her return to Amesbury Athelstan makes a polite enquiry. 'Her heart should go to Winchester.'

'Too late, I'm afraid, she has been buried.'

'Pity. I think they would have liked the opportunity to gild a new reliquary.' Athelstan pulls a wry smile.

But Aelfflaed was no saint, no Radegund, even for her favourites at Winchester.

Bring me the Head of Saint Oswald

I write for future ages, who will perhaps have forgotten the beliefs and requirements of the souls of mortals of long ago. I hope and believe that the written word of the historian has a fair chance of surviving the vicissitudes of mankind. Perhaps we have seen the last of the disparagers of writing, of the recording of men's deeds. No-one could be as wantonly destructive as the Vikings. There would be no sense in it. Progress is driven by the written word and by men able to read it.

Athelstan's obsession with the head of Oswald, though it must be kept a secret in the present, needs explaining for future understanding.

The scholar Bede first tells us of the importance of the King of Northumbria who died at the battle of Maserfield in 642. The town of Oswestry forever marks where he fell. He was cruelly dismembered by the pagan forces of Penda of Mercia and his British allies. His torso, legs, one arm and legs were displayed on pikes, as if they were parts of a boar on offer for food at a street fair. His right arm was said to have been taken by a raven to a tree, then dropped and the earth where it fell made miraculous. Pilgrims dug a huge pit on the spot. Different rescued body parts were buried at Bardney, Lindisfarne and at Bamburgh. His head was later interred in the coffin of St Cuthbert and taken by fleeing monks (the Vikings were the problem, as usual) to Durham for safekeeping. Two saints in one coffin. Now that was a highly charged reliquary.

So St Oswald was scattered about the kingdom after death; his personal parts assumed magical qualities. Unusually for a king, he was sainted. Father Bede revered him for his holy deeds even in life, which added to his hallowed status, made him almost a god.

Oswald, being in bits, would have had difficulty in rising entire on the day of judgement, but then, many saints, their parts graced by exquisite reliquaries, shared that fate. Their dismembered flesh and bones were scattered widely over many lands, hanging in metal containers around necks, on belts, under hair shirts, beneath pillows, on dining tables, filling private altars in noble households, added as ash to holy water stoops, sprayed into the air along with incense. Great wealth comes to those who own these parts, this dried flesh, these bones. Pilgrims flock to publicly displayed items to try to save themselves from aggression, from illness, from witchcraft, from death. I do not care for these sentiments; I concur with Dunstan's opinion that there is too much made of these money-centred activities. There is the temptation to fake, too, which is troublesome, or even to steal. Monks have been known to succumb to the Devil's wiles in this way.

People think that they can secure a place in Heaven by the purchase or touch of these items and go, like sheep, to wherever they have heard there is something new to feel or kiss, grovelling on their knees. The more grovelling the better, they think. Dunstan thinks that the general populace should be encouraged to be kept loyal to the mother church nearest to them. Regular attendance at an inspired centre of Church teaching, with its rituals and iconography correctly displayed by priests who have been well trained, should be the focus, not traipsing around the countryside looking for fresh corpses to kiss, wearing out knees in the process. There are workshops in Frome and elsewhere which produce aids for pilgrimage including leather knee pads. They sell well.

The trappings of reliquaries come at a price and make a good living for the makers. Leather reliquary holders which attach to belts, belts, straps for wearing heavier items around the chest or back, carry bags for larger or more expensive items, purses of all shapes and sizes. Fashion for reliquaries changes, so prices go up and old leather goods are exchanged for metal, which require stronger straps, more belts and so on. There is something at odds in the way merchants deal with these pilgrim goods; their motive is clearly not religious in origin. Their prices go up on feast days, and they are many.

But better to have a healthy or unhealthy interest in religion and saints, says Leofa, than war. I listen to my friends, their thoughts; they are the thinkers of our times; I, Nonna, am merely a historian recording other men's deeds.

Monastery of St John, Frome, before Compline, 21 December 934

I continue, between Office times, to appraise the contents of the chest. After Vespers, having offloaded some political comments of interest to Stone, I return to the locked chest, a little fearful of the emotions it now provokes in me. Combined with my heightened awareness of the personalities and propaganda swilling around the court and tiredness in my daily duties, its contents seem all the more extraordinary.

It was as though the voices coming from the manuscripts of the chest were wishing to speak, through me, of the losses of power, of language, of culture, of the aboriginal peoples of the land around us. Families still living in Somerset, still speaking their own British language, had stayed on in disbelief that a rapid Saxon breakthrough could be made, sending their leaders into ignominy and out of the legends of history, confining their chief noblemen to the tiny section of the toe of Britain, Kernow. Arthur, the hero of the West Welsh and Hywell, Coel, Bran, would protect them, they had thought. The border of Selwood, Great Wood, would be respected, or feared.

Those clinging on to their Welshness thrive in outlying farmsteads, paying taxes to Athelstan, low in status, but able to farm, to take to market, to intermarry with the servants of Wessex. Some are free, some are slaves. Where they have become bilingual, they are able to enter the commercial life of the new realm. At least they have not been exterminated. This was a Christian conqueror, after all. Ine was a kind king. He let them live. Aldhelm, though he saw their intransigence in religious terms, encouraged peaceful integration. It was recognised that this would take generations. Had they remained stubbornly pagan, they may have fared worse. The monks of Glastonbury pleaded for their lives. They had been a cultured people, they said. They could bring literature and culture to the more boorish factions of the nobility of Wessex. The pagan ways which had returned to the countryside since the disturbances of recent years were only superficial. Beneath the surface, the British were a Christian people still, albeit Celtic.

So the British of West Wales were spared, tolerated. They would become absorbed, as the Roman rulers had absorbed the Celtic tribes. But unlike the pre-Roman tribes, the community identities of the British in our new nation of Wessex were gradually lost, their administrative zones dissolved, their place-names anglicised or hybridised or forgotten completely, except in the extreme west. In the land of Somersetshire laws involving fines were constructed to take account of their lesser status. It was difficult to swallow.

There was no need to consider the inhabitants of the land to the west of Glastonbury; mostly they had got wind of events to the east, packed and departed for Brittany and taken their culture, their songs, language and beliefs with them. The new county of Devon is still underpopulated, a good place to take land and to make new farmsteads in the Saxon way without having to take account of British sensibilities.

Immigration after Ine and Aldhelm came thick and fast, passing through the new, watery shire of Somerset and on to the fertile redlands of Devonshire. Much acquisition was made by new monastic communities in the expanded Wessex. Ealdormen, thegns, bishops and abbots, all required regalia and stonework to cement their position; churches and halls were hewn from rock and wood to meet the needs of the new men of status, springing up like beans in the spring throughout the former lands of Dumnonia.

Terce today was extremely beautiful, the low morning winter light shining through the quire windows of St John's church, red, gold, blue, green. The saints and martyrs were fully illuminated, their parts enshrined in oak and cherry wood and silver, glittering in their reliquaries on the altar and in the side chapels. New polishing of wax on the wooden containers, fresh for the witan meet, has burnished their ability to reflect; many candles, normally an expense kept to a minimum, displayed rich animal carvings on the choir stalls.

The wealthy attire of the diademed wives and concubines of foreign dignitaries adds to the cacophony of colour on these occasions. There is much detail to enjoy. In the corner by the high altar is the stave of Aldhelm our founder and opposite this the staff of St John, both encased in shining silver. The colourless sheets hanging over the nave entrance, blocking off the view to the west, seem to act as a focus on the high altar and its treasures, concentrate the mind on flesh and bones of the holy ones. Nearer to God...

It was Aldhelm, in partnership with Ine, King of Wessex more than two hundred years ago who brought the Roman Christian way to the land west of Selwood. Aldhelm was a reformer, like Dunstan is proving to be, wished to modernise and bring into line all Christians under the wing of Rome. The British, having lost their lands, were not willing to lose their Celtic style of faith and this battle of wills rages even now. The different hairstyle. The date of Easter. What did they care that in some northern land in the middle of the seventh century, someone had lost an argument. The Synod of Whitby of 664 was the Celtic Christians' ending as a force in the land.

The reminder that the British were first in the land to be Christian, by the unusual style of tonsure on display on every priest's head, had to go. Their stubborn attitude did not ensure survival of a kingdom; only of an idea or two. But in the lands of Wessex the British people have survived, alive, intransigent, grumbling. Their voice can still be heard in the names they use for places, in the names for hills and sacred spaces. Spaces that once were pagan but became Christian, places that remain pagan still, to Dunstan's chagrin.

When we were both young and in the classrooms of Glastonbury, I took a razor one morning and cut a tonsure on my skull resembling one of the old Irish monks. Dunstan was wild with fury, thought I was serious about taking up a Celtic Christian stance for life. He has never forgiven me for those moments with a razor, always reminds me of it at breakfast with a withering look at the top of my head. After my hair grew back, I did not repeat my sartorial insult. Symbols matter, I learned.

Palace of Winchester, 28 May 934

The air is foetid. Heaving bodies of men, unable to practice their normal ablutions, are cramped into the long aisles of the hall. Benches creak and groan with their weight. Some lean against the stone walls, their arms crossed, craning around the pillars to catch sight of the royal family as they emerge. There is a hubbub of conversation. Just outside the main door, the newly built latrines have failed to cope with the numbers. Noise, smell and sight offend and excite in equal measure. Pages flutter in and out of the few open spaces carrying pitchers of ale and wine to refill personal horns. They are the only fast-moving items in this stuffed atmosphere.

A trumpet blows. Here comes the King. Here come the princes. Here comes the Queen, Eadgifu. Behind them, but not much less in status, come the archbishops. They are robed almost as magnificently as royalty. No black today.

In the hall, facing Athelstan as he sits on his throne, are the all-important sub-kings, Hywel, Iudwal and Tudor of Wales, also looking colourful and bedecked with imaginatively designed metalwork on skilfully woven cloth. They favour many shades of the colour green, subtly changing through checked passages of turquoise to emerald and back. Sea and mountains, the emblems of Wales. They wear huge gold dragon brooches on their ceremonial cloaks. There is a glorious uniform about the Welsh kings. Their attire stands out.

Nonna makes a mental note of the events unfolding, this last important witan before travel northwards. Like Dunstan, his visual appreciation is his best sense. The varieties of colour chosen by the nation's leaders mark the differences between clans, between armies and navy. This is a meeting of men in their distinctive livery, the livery of war.

Everyone who matters is here. The only woman in the room is Eadgifu, but she is regarded as an honorary man. She wears robes which seem to emit power, seems to have herself grown a few inches. Look beneath her dress, you can see her high soled shoes. There's a lot of fashionable gold hanging around her neck and from her ears. The Welsh mountains have supplied her well. On her head, unnecessary for keeping the extravagant wimple in place, there is a significant piece of exquisite jewellery, made fresh for this occasion. It looks like a crown. It is certainly a tiara. The male crowd gasps as they recognise the regent who will rule in the King's absence. They bow to her and to Edmund, who accompanies her. He also wears a golden head-band as Aetheling, the prince and heir. Eadred, his brother, coughs. He is not happy in large gatherings.

Besides the King, Queen and the archbishops, there are 15 bishops, 4 abbots and 51 ministers of the land plus their supporters, restricted to two apiece on this occasion. All sweaty, all breathing, all awake to hear what is going to be said. Short and sharp this witan must be; the urge to go to war has captured all the hearts and minds. There hasn't been a war gathering like this for a generation. The younger men are ready and waiting. Swords have been allowed into the hall for this occasion; they make sitting even more uncomfortable.

Nonna nudges Dunstan. 'Eadgifu looks magnificent,' he whispers.

Everyone seems to be noticing the same thing. She is a remarkable woman, known to be capable and has earned the respect of many for her orderly arrangements for witans, for hospitality and gift thoughtfulness. She has graced and made possible the larger gatherings which have been taking place since Athelstan's accession. She has been behind the schemes for larger, more luxurious settings for the nobles and their families, planning tented arrangements, decorations to suit the status of attendees, the availability of food and ale, jewellery for the wives and concubines. A supporter of convents and abbeys, a smiling and attractive, diplomatically clever and courteous adjunct to Athelstan's court.

'Better than a queen.' Dunstan whispers back.

He should know. He spends a great deal of time with her, has been discussing in depth with Athelstan, Eadgifu and Edmund how the regency might work in the event of Athelstan's death in the north.

Leofa leans over. 'Time to get in position,' he warns.

The three clerks move into their roles as interpreters. They have their notes on the main edicts about to be announced, can give a brief summary as the King makes his speech to each of the sub-kings present. Nonna has the Welsh group of kings, Leofa the northern and Danish leaders. Dunstan takes his position behind Athelstan. He is doing well, can be seen to be a rising star.

The trumpet sounds again. Silence falls. A sneeze explodes from a back bencher somewhere. It could happen to the best of us. A long form of men rocks a little, there is laughter. At least no-one has fallen off or fallen over. The full benches sit rock-still.

'Welcome to my archbishops, my bishops, abbots, ealdorman and ministers. Welcome to you all in this rather full session of the witan. I appreciate that this is an uncomfortable arrangement; never before have we numbered so many in the confined space of our hall, but I will be brief.'

Athelstan indicates to the royal family and archbishops to take their seats, sits down himself. Unlike Eadgifu, he is wearing full soldier's gear. His sword is less ceremonial than practical. The only part of his apparel which looks kingly is his hair and head-band, which seem to shine with gold and silver braiding. There seems to be no difference between the metal and the hair. He waves his hands as he speaks. His fingers have several rings on them, most of which have hair relics as jewels. A saint for every finger. He begins the order of the day, the war to come and its preparations.

'As you are all aware, preparations for the forthcoming war in Alba have been going well. The funding campaign of two years ago was successful. Raids, forfeit and compensation resulted in extra profitable ventures for the crown, enabling the investment of considerable sums for our army and navy. I want to thank all those who have contributed to the wealth of our nation, including of course my archbishops, bishops and abbots.'

Athelstan waves his beringed hands at the officers of the Church, acknowledging their role. Some of the younger bishops have indicated that not only will they be travelling with the army but that they will be fighting physically as well as with prayer. They appear in colourful war clothes today as soldiers for Christ.

'Some of you will not be surprised to know that our forces will be supercharged with the actual attendance in the midst of our army by bishops of our realm in person.'

Many faces look around at compatriots. This was news to most. Fighting priests? Quite a novelty, but understandable. They are young men, too, spoiling for a fight just as others are. Have they been practising sword fighting in their silent cloisters?

Athelstan chuckles. 'That should give my soldiers and sailors something to think about. Imagine our good bishops notching up a head count above your own!'

Thankfully that is unlikely. But the point is taken. The hall of listeners chuckles, too. The bishops beam.

'Now, in all seriousness. Much has been done to prepare for this just war. All of you have made sacrifices, ordered your fyrds well. I have no quarrel with anyone here for your careful arrangements. This will be a brief but incisive incursion. Alba and the north will be given a bloody nose. There will be much booty and fame as well as fortune will be made. I will be grateful, of course, for the support which I know you will give Queen Eadgifu and her sons in the event of my death. The default position for the royal court is of course her regency until Edmund comes of age.' The hall is all ears.

'As for the detail, the army now numbers in total 23,000 men including a cavalry of 3,000. Fifty shallow keeled ships have been constructed which will act as troop conveyors, carrying another 5,000 men. They will be transported from the dock at Portchester to King's Lynn, travelling overland to our next witan on the 7th June in Nottingham. It will be important to show our strength to the good folk of the northern parts of Mercia, will rattle the imperious Danes who wish to move their armies south. This will give them pause.' Cheers and stamping from the hall. A few wave their swords.

'For those who require medical assistance, the sisters of Shaftesbury have offered the services of their trained nurses. They will follow the troops north, together with several brothers of the abbeys and monasteries who have amputation skills. Many are skilled healers. Any major injuries to you and yours will be treated on site and we will ensure all corpses will be returned to their families for burial.'

No-one cheers. No-one is going to die. The King is being pessimistic. That's one thing about him that they do not like. The mention of corpses might be a mistake.

Athelstan knows the reality of war. What some regard as pessimism is his normal state of reality. They will remember this comforting support system in time and be grateful for it. There will be casualties, there will be deaths. Both sides will have losses. That is war. Some older heads nod, put a hand on the knee of their sons. This will be of use to them. Warriors will be saved by the nursing attendants, the old heads have no doubt.

'I do not need to tell you, but it is as well to reinforce what this campaign is about. The agreement made in 927 at Eamont between the forces of the north and ourselves has been broken. The oaths made then have blown away in the wind. The Irish Danes, Strathclyde and Alba have united to resist our wish to bring the islands of Britain together under our rule and would overrun us if they could, hoping to restore the earlier British chaos aligned with a Viking kingdom. They wish to have a pagan future, to bring down all that we have achieved in the south of an English Christian future. Their humiliation is now at hand, the direction that this land will take is a forgone conclusion. Christ and the saints fight with us, there is no doubt of that and we shall win. This land will become a Catholic Christian empire.'

Cheers. Not so much for Athelstan's vision; they go along with that, but for the loot, the lands, the fight.

'Stand up, Eadgifu,'Athelstan turns to the Queen, gives her his hand. She stands with him in front of the witan. Athelstan orders another fanfare from the trumpet.

'I present to you my gifted support, Queen Eadgifu, without whom I could not rule with success. Eadgifu, mother of your Aetheling, regent of the realm in my absence. Swear to her now. Bend.'

The assembled throng stands, with difficulty, then kneels, with even more difficulty. But it has to be done. No-one topples over. The oath to the potential regent is taken. In front of the King, the two archbishops hold the most precious of the relics held at court for the swearing sessions, gold and silver heads of saints, some bones of Oswald. They hold the caskets aloft for all to see.

'We swear,' everyone intones. They stay down, waiting for the King to speak. They know what comes next. A ritual oath of allegiance, by him, to them. Their moment has come.

It is Athestan's turn to swear. He brings out the rock crystal cross remnant from his undergarment. His hands are holy enough, with all their rings, but here is the vital element, the presence of the living Christ.

'I swear to you, people of England, by all that I hold most dear,' he says as he lifts the cross fragment above his head, 'that I will lead this company to success, to the betterment of our land, to peaceful times and progress, to wealth. I will support you, my people, I will reward you. Your families, come what may, will prosper from this campaign. I commend you to Christ and the Saints.' He pauses.

This is more like it. Success is inevitable. There will be no woundings or deaths. Everyone will return unscathed. Wives and mothers need not fret; the prospects are good.

Faces in the hall start to lift. The King indicates that they may return to their seats. Older men are helped up by their younger compatriots. Acting together, they will succeed. This generation has never before seen a campaign as well managed, as well planned. For more than a year they have seen the preparations in full swing across the nation, from north to south. The construction of ships. The refacing of midland burgh defences. The investment in armoury and weapons; hardly a forge in the country has been untouched by request for swords, lances, shields. The furnaces have been stoked night after night, crops planted, reaped and stored in tythe barns against any future difficulty. All considerations of the possible outcome of the campaign have been acted upon. In the event of the loss of the King, Edmund and his mother are well positioned and popular. There is even his brother, Eadred, to fall back on. Wessex, at least, is secure.

Athelstan will take questions from the floor. He is a patient man, knows some which will occur and who will make them.

A minister, invited, asks his question. 'Will the Aetheling Edmund accompany us to Alba?'

Athelstan is happy to confirm that he will not. 'He stays here with the Queen. He is as yet too young at twelve years of age to play a part in this war.' The Aetheling Edmund looks rueful. The court can see that there has been much family argument about this. There will be no worries about the possibility of losing the main heir to the throne. Edwin's ghost rolls around the room. He would have gone with them, might have met a sticky end. What then?

'What does the King intend to do with the upstart princes of the north?' another minister enquires.

'We shall attempt to capture them alive. We wish to bring them to heel, not to murder kings.'

Hywel Dda stands to address the throng. Athelstan nods at

him. He wishes to make a statement, Athelstan knows. Faces turn towards him.

'We of Wales support our mighty King, ruler of these isles, in his bid to bring peace and plenty. Our swords travel with you and will play our part in the triumph of our times. Our bards and your scops will sing of our achievements for a thousand years.' Hywel signals to the three Welsh kings beside him, who all stand. His voice is deep, has a lilting but strong accent. He is the head of the Welsh contingent; the others have recognised his power in the English court. They raise their swords.

'I commend my Welsh forces to this task, more than willing to defend our lands as yours of England from the ravages of Alba and its traitorous allies. My compatriots join with me in our willingness to commit to this great project. We look forward to sharing song and story of heroic deeds in all our halls in the autumn to come.' Hywel and the other Welsh kings bow low. The simple act of bowing, how much it conveys. Athelstan does not bow. He waves his ringed hand.

'I wish you all good speed. Tomorrow at dawn, my lads!'

The hall erupts with more cheers. They are energised, united to make this Empire of Britain, to become rich, to be successful, to leave a legacy of deeds which will be repeated by firelight in the halls of the future, to resound down the years.

Athelstan thanks the Welsh kings, turns back to his family and archbishops, nods and leaves the raised podium. It has been a time of controlled excitement, needs the relief of fresh air and the latrine.

Next stop Nottingham.

Palace of Winchester, evening, 28 May, 934

S tone has called a private meeting. Not a council of war, more of tactics. Edmund is allowed to take part; he must learn of the wiles of men. Athelstan asks him to sit in the wooden chair near the fire. We are at the table. The twelve-year-old seems pent up, has something he wants to say and tries to, but his brother signals to him to stop. He knows what Edmund wants to say, has already half relented to the idea of taking him north with him at least some of the way. The young man must wait. The nation comes first. Edmund struggles to maintain patience, fiddles with his dagger.

'Leofa, Dunstan and Nonna,' Athelstan looks each man in the eye. 'You will be accompanying me as my personal attendants on this campaign. I want you to be, as always, my extra eyes and ears. You must inform me of anything you see or hear of interest to me and the State. Treachery, disagreement among thegns, any signs of misdeed need to be reported. You will know from our trip to Eamont all those years ago that we misread the apparent willingness of the northerners to do our bidding and how lightly they took their oaths. We are dealing with the pagan mind; they are not fearful of the consequences of lying and cheating. Their souls will go to hell in any case; what do they care? We need to strengthen our ability to turn them into willing client leaders. The alternative is to face the ruin of all that has been achieved by Wessex so far. Insurrection could one day be successful. I have a plan which will redouble our abilities to empower Wessex and our forces, though none should know of it. Sit down, all of you.'

Edmund sits up. This is interesting. What else does his brother have in mind other than fighting men, armour, weaponry and ships, the outward power of might? Would they not be enough to bring the North to heel?

The trinity sits around the table. This is where they have spent many evenings, discussing law making, reporting the words of the Welsh kings, contributing to religious and historical texts. The King sits with them, pours goblets of ale. Not too much; it's just something to do with one's hand while listening.

'I have been thinking over our progress north. We are, as you know, travelling first to Nottingham to join the naval force and then on to York. It will be a good chance to review the strength of feeling there, for or against Wessex. In York you will be particularly busy. We will hold regular meetings to update our views of the area we leave behind as we travel further. You know of my intention to visit the coffin of Cuthbert which is at Chester-le-Street. You also know of the importance of that saint to our purpose of bringing the nation together and of my family's desire to thank him for his assistance through the years of battle against the Danes. There is something else I need to do. When the monks of Lindisfarne were forced to flee their monastery, they took with them Cuthbert, but also the head of Oswald which I am told they placed inside the coffin. Do you remember that I talked with you about this matter after Christmas, last year?'

Athelstan pauses. Has he got their interest? Can they remember Stone talking about the head? Yes, but there is much else which has to be remembered. A man's dreams, even Stone's, are at the bottom of the heap of things to deal with. Leofa looks alarmed. Edmund, too, is on the edge of his seat. The mad obsession has come to the fore again.

'You must understand that Oswald's head is of particular importance to me and my family,' Athelstan nods towards Edmund.

'You have seen our arrangements in Gloucester at St Oswald's Priory where my aunt and uncle placed remains of his body. Other parts remain elsewhere, desired by all as a protector of the realm and as a boost to religious income. His cult is popular throughout Europe. In my view Oswald's role as supplier of income to the Church is not as important as is his role as protector of the northern border of England. What I am proposing is that we insist on viewing the head in the coffin in order to consult with his soul.

Dunstan gasps. But he has heard of this plan before, dismissed it as sacrilegious and probably impossible. 'Open the coffin of Cuthbert? That, Stone, is surely something the Lindisfarne monks would be very unwilling to do, even for such as yourself.'

'I am aware that in the north of England my southern credentials have little merit. So we must persuade them to open the coffin, somehow. I want access to that head. What do you suggest, Leofa? You deal with relics and negotiations for their sale or transference on an everyday basis. How can I get full access to Oswald, to his thoughts, prayers and support? King to King?' I have been anointed, have superiority.'

Leofa seems stunned, as does Nonna. Perhaps the trinity had assumed that Stone would not dare to act on his dreams of close association with an important saint's head. To prise open any reliquary, except in the case of an inadequate casing in need of replacing, is unheard of. The reliquary itself, containing the relic, is as much revered as that which it contains. And this is one of the most prized relics of all, one which many covet.

Dunstan recovers himself first. 'My Lord, Stone, I mean, I think it is unlikely that the Lindisfarne monks will allow us to open the coffin, though our cause and your piety demand it, both to ask for the aid of Oswald as well as Cuthbert. In my experience the guard over such precious items is constant. We know of other remains which have been stolen to order from great houses, even by brother monks. Of course the value lies to them in the income from pilgrimage, but in this case we may have a chance to soften resistance by lavish gifts. Could you, Stone, consider the gift of expensive items, perhaps even land holdings, which might help your cause? In effect, buy the opening of the coffin?'

'I am aware that my position as King of the English will have little influence on the northern monks; they look to York and Bamburgh for their leaders and supporters. In the event of my death or failure in the borders and in Scotland they will have little reason to be grateful to me or us. But I need to receive Cuthbert's favour before going further north and for that reason I am prepared to try to persuade them to open the coffin for a maximum time of one hour for full contemplation. That could be equated to a value. What do you think that might be, Leofa?'

Leofa, Dunstan and Nonna confer. The King gets up, wanders over to Edmund and whispers to him. Edmund nods excitedly.

'Stone, are the monks of Chester-le-Street aware that you wish to visit the coffin?' Dunstan has foreseen some difficulty. Athelstan returns to the table, signals to Edmund to remain where he is.

'Yes, they have been sent a letter of request to access. I have had no reply. Nonna, you wrote several months ago, did you not?'

Nonna nods agreement.

Dunstan continues. 'So they already know of your wish to consult Cuthbert. They may also be aware of your personal concern to consult Oswald and of your family's great desire to reunite his bodily parts?'

Stone pauses, thinks, walks about the room. 'They may have heard of this, Dunstan, but their primary concern will be with the access to Cuthbert. I think we have to state a price for access which they cannot refuse. They are, after all, a group of exiled brothers, in need of an income to reestablish themselves. Their Lindisfarne monastery has been almost totally destroyed and is vulnerable to further attack. They should be amenable to a generous offer. It is just a matter, I think, of how much.'

Dunstan consults Leofa and Nonna again. Athelstan talks quietly to Edmund who is now beaming.

'My Lord Stone, we three will put together a gift list which is suitable for your request to the brothers. The lady Eadgifu may need to be involved; she has many items of embroidered material which could be deemed worthy of the Saint. If we could persuade the brothers that Cuthbert, living, though dead, would receive comfort from such luxurious cushioning, then the coffin would have to be opened to put them inside. Naturally you would wish to place these items in the coffin yourself, thus ensuring that you had access to him.' Dunstan speaks for the trinity, as usual.

'Leofa? Nonna?'Athelstan checks with them.

'I agree this might be effective, Stone,' Nonna agrees. Leofa shrugs, then nods.

'This is likely to meet with some agreement as to access, Stone. I will go to the lady Eadgifu immediately, to see what she can offer in the way of comfort to the holy body. I think she was given a considerable amount of tapestry work by Aelfflaed's daughter when she visited Wilton for the old queen's burial.' Dunstan is up and running with his plan.

'Good. Do it quickly. Make sure there is enough in terms of valuable written works as well, in case the monks prefer to keep them outside the coffin. A copy of Bede's Life of St Cuthbert might not come amiss, to show we honour the great northern scribe. Some items of gold and silver, too, as well as money. Find a decorated chest, list it all and arrange it decently. The cartman can load it tomorrow from the hall.'

Athelstan walks around the room, his arms behind him. The others wait.

'There is one more thing which I suppose you will have thought of but which I have not dared to mention in recent months: you know that the head of Oswald is of inestimable value to me. I cannot tell you how much it means to me and my family. That it should be rattling about, uncared for, in a coffin with another saint is unbearable. Please, all of you, think carefully how we might access this on a more permanent basis. The safety of Wessex may depend on it. Do you understand?'

Athelstan looked at Edmund and back to his clerks. Yes, they understand. They would have to make this dream come true, somehow. And it was also understood that Edmund would be accompanying them tomorrow on the journey north.

Palace of Frome, 22 December 934

The morning light of the witan gathering of Christmas comes up with fine, pink and grey long horizontal stripes of clouds; there's no sign of any rain to dampen the parade of reliquaries due to take place later this afternoon after Sext. The wagons, decorated in the colours of the saints, and the men who are to lead and carry the smaller items, are milling outside the church doors. It's a fine day for the parade around the town. Not so the weather at Glastonbury, I am sure. It always rains there.

I make notes for Athelstan's biography. I should mention Aldhelm. At Malmesbury, where I have spent many hours in the library, there are many tomes on St Aldhelm our founder and his life, along with records of laws established for the two peoples, Saxon and Welsh. He is another of Stone's favourite seers. He first recognised the value of Glastonbury Abbey and did much to save it. In this third centennial since the taking of Dumnonia, much has been written of the piecemeal conquests and consolidation by the House of Wessex, in all its youthful vigour. Ecgberht, grandfather to our king's grandfather, with a strong hand and wise head began the glueing together of the nations across the south, establishing his kin as rightful owners of the southern slopes and valleys bordering the seas. Ine before him forged new frontiers in the west, biting deep into Celtic lands, severing them from connecting overland to their brothers to the north in Wales, making them the Wealas, foreigners in their own land. But the sea passages were still available to them, a hardy seafaring folk, along the route of the sixth century saints from south Wales to Watchet.

Glastonbury, ripped from its hinterland and separated from its believers and the influence of the Irish, fell into a ruinous state. Only now is it being renewed, with the energies of Dunstan and Aethelwold. They are the sap rising, the young vigour now in the minds and limbs of the Church and its courageous and cultured priesthood. It's about time. Glastonbury labours in disbelief at its fall to the English, its school has rotten floors and roof, black and green moss on its wintry stone walls. They are crumbling, mortarless, the dark wetness creeping down from broken tiled roofs to the surrounding ditches and dykes. Water weeds reach up to meet the mossy tiles.

Dunstan, wearing his hat as the nation's architect, has plans. The noble youth of Wessex needs new classrooms. He is a new broom, anxious to sweep and rebuild the former glories of the Abbey, for its students again to be proud.

The priests and teachers of Glastonbury, despite being English by birth, seem bowed down by their surroundings, defensive and withdrawn, uncertain of the reception at court of learning and literature. They have felt redundant for the last fifty years. The focus has necessarily been on survival in the face of terrible Viking intrusions. Perhaps a fresh beginning may lead to spiritual renewal. Thoughts and actions of past generations can sometimes be burdensome. A breaking may lead to a better mending. Something good will perhaps step out of the Viking shadow.

Dunstan follows Aldhelm in his bid to restore order. He is the new knight of this reform, this revolution. 'I am a visionary,' he says, and he means it. His vision of the recovery of beauty and culture is even greater than the King's; he will bring glory once again to the great monastery. Its heritage of history, the intricate story of the British in which it is bound up, is less certain of security, to my mind. The old histories are often put aside, except where they may help forward the progress of unity of belief, the order which reform may bring. I suspect that Dunstan has in mind using some of the imagery of the past to highlight the necessity of a fresh approach to religion by the peasantry; but he has said little of this so far. His visual artistry, so brilliantly exercised in the workshops at Glastonbury, shows that he has the skills to present a different imaginative world, if he sets about it the right way. Vision and artistry: a dangerous mix, or a courageous one.

I regret that the beliefs of ordinary folk of the land are disappearing. My mother spoke of ways of life and beliefs which honoured the woods and hills, connected with it in a way I do not see today, at least not at the court, on our travels around Wessex. This seems to be a particularly British sensibility, born of long attachment to landscape. The great library at Malmesbury has few references to it. Fewer still, since the Welshman Asser's day. Glastonbury has the most part of what remains, and now it is here, in the haligdom of Frome.

The spoken word, in British estimation, was mightier than the written. A speaker would elaborate the previous one, without thought for the original tale. The bard did his work, entertained, passed on the story but inevitably altered it. Soldiers become heroes and myths, even gods and goddesses. The inanimate becomes animate in the imagination, lore becomes sacred text. The more logical Saxon mind makes a mockery of their world and rejects wholesale nuggets of truth which may be hidden within. Dunstan wishes to supplant this superstitious mindset with another way to view the world, more in tune with the latest religious thinking. He and Aethelwold are sure this fresh approach is best.

I feel for my mother's kin. This spiritual reform has not occurred yet. The landscape continues to breed discontent and sadness, the pagan traditions are not quite dead. How much better it is to forget and to adapt, but these people do not easily forget and adaptability comes naturally to only a few.

But now to look to the future.

With the active input of Athelstan, with Viking wars over, Scotland conquered and Welsh kings submissive, a great push in investment in willpower, manpower and finance can begin to take place. Alba has been forced to bend its neck to us, the northern kingdoms of Britain have promised to look south for leadership.

Winchester shall be the capital city. Perhaps one day there might be a witan edifice for the whole world, whose edicts and rules will maintain order everywhere, covering the papal realm as well as far flung countries beyond even the Pope's remit, the unknown fringes of great seas with all their diabolical fishy creatures.

Church Reform is in the air in Frome. The bishops are muttering, some for, some against. Dunstan will succeed. He is the King's kin. Countries and armies are at our command, the triumph of the culture of Christendom is now within our grasp. Ministerial frowns born of impossibilities are melting to smiles which accompany the possibility of a new dawn of togetherness. They begin to believe that tribal origins can be placed firmly behind us, that we can move on to the brotherhood of man under Christ. Dunstan's visions may come to pass. He is young. Aethelwold is young. We have the hope and great skill of the written word to make this happen, the undoubted potency of valuable relics of holy men, of the Holy Cross, no less, to make men hold to their oaths, the promise to accept change.

Now is the chance to make a new land, Britain, under Rome, of course. This order will prevail, with the Pope's aid, an overarching guide to the best use of our resources. We pay to Rome what is due, but in return we receive many rewards.

To effect the further progress of this state of togetherness under Christ, Dunstan tells us, we must move to a stricter regime of monastic usage. He has seen it, across the seas. The Benedictine Way, as used on the forward-thinking continent, nearer to Rome and therefore more in touch with current practice, needs revitalising here, a shaking up. Aldhelm began the move to self-discipline but his ideas died with him.

There are too many members of the lower nobility buying livelihoods in the monasteries, too much vested interest in the prayer life of mass priests. There is corruption and lax morality; I agree with Dunstan about this. The second sons and third daughters of lesser land owners, placed in positions of authority by monetary promises rather than merit, have too great a part to play in monastic life in Wessex. They may have blue blood, but their casual approach to the religious life, their feeble excuses for not attending offices or from fasting leads to outrage among the truly religious and contrasts with the self-discipline exercised by the leading Benedictine orders on the continent.

Dunstan is full of it. He wishes to set an example of best practice, to show the ability of the Wessex court to aim for the highest accolades of spirituality. His ideas must start to be put into practice now, he says, so that within a generation Wessex may produce cardinals and men of conscience to rule the land in harmony with kings of like mind. In Athelstan and now with young Edmund, to whom he often speaks in private, he sees the chance to make a world of order, king and Church ruling together as one, balancing the life of the court with the life and intentions of the higher plane, a higher reality.

Many relics, retrieved from the holy land at the time of the rise of the Mohammedan, have arrived over the last few years in central and western Europe, where the highest bidder takes the prize. Athelstan's purse has managed to pull many of these to safety and it is these which he carries with him and which now adorn the haligdom at Frome. He probably has the greatest number of relics of any king in Europe. Some are smuggled parts of great value. Athelstan does not care. Where would these hallowed things be without the protection of the Christian kings of the west? There are so many now circulating the various courts and the lists of exchangeable relics so great that one wonders if there are not duplicates of some rare items. Forgery is punishable by excommunication; it would be unthinkable for any Christian to undertake the imitation of such valuable items; but perhaps others might.

Dunstan has been able to assist with these acquisitions, using his foreign contacts to great advantage. Instead of the dowries of old, a bride may be exchanged together with a precious relic. So much has been retrieved that it is advisable, these days, to have written confirmation of provenance. Dunstan or Leofa can usually guarantee and supply these. The written word is law and provides security, but when these two friends of mine speak, their word is good, too, in the lands throughout the Pope's jurisdiction, so trusted have they become in such a short time.

Becoming the champion of the Church, Dunstan and other young clerks and monks look forward to a new chapter in the life of the court of Wessex. St John's monastery and church will benefit by his enthusiasm. I have to agree, the past is what it is, gone. But something needs to be remembered.

I return now to my story of Glastonbury. Bregored, the British abbot of Glastonbury at the time of the capture of Dumnonia, was allowed to stay on after the demise of Celtic Dumnonia. King Ine and Aldhelm wished to be given a tour of its contents by one familiar with them. Dying in 661, three years after the conquest, Bregored lived long enough to ensure, by revealing the monastery's breadth of cultural acquisitions, that destruction would not be wholesale, if at all. He also managed, evidently, to secrete some literature which might otherwise become subject to purging by less sympathetic masters, and the oaken chest is proof of that. Perhaps the British documentation was merely ignored until its current reorganisation and rebuilding. Ine and the conqueror of Penselwood, his predecessor Cenwalh, fresh to the Christian faith, put a psychic ring around the monastery, backed by law, saving the discovery of its resources for future generations, manuscript lovers and scribes of the future. The encouragement of a sense that there was more than monetary value in such a place may be placed at the door of Aldhelm, already an influential great scholar, abbot of Malmesbury and kin to the royal line. A common bloodline helps, if you want to get things done, as it is helping Dunstan. It's who you know.

The priests of Glastonbury, despite objection by Aldhelm, continued to wear the adze like druidic tonsure, a wedge of hair from ear to ear, so remarkably different from the round halo style of the Roman church. They insisted on being different and thereby ensuring that any Saxon bishop, priest or abbot, sitting in meeting with them, felt the superiority of their longevity in the land. We were here first, they announced, waving their neatly shaven heads, carved fresh for display, at the forces of modernisation before them, making the Saxon religious leaders feel like foreigners or lepers. Very annoying. This is the style of hair which so annoyed Dunstan, that day when I surprised him. He does not let me forget his distress.

Gradually this style of tonsure has been dying out, though here and there, despite overt censure by the faithful and laughter elsewhere, some older priests adhere to it still. As the partners in crime at each monastery have died and they find it difficult to shave themselves, this may be the last generation in which this form of exhibitionism and insistence on difference will be seen. I would not dare to wear it nowadays. My position at court is too valuable to me. Only the kitchen porter here, whose wife shaves him and supports him in his usefulness as a lay brother, still sports the adze style at Frome. And he isn't even a priest. He does it just to annoy, to show he is Welsh speaking and a patriot. Sometimes the two of them can be overheard when they are in the kitchens, plucking fowl, bantering in Welsh, making me feel homesick when they sing together some of the songs my mother sang to me as a child. For a few hours, I feel nostalgic, weakened. Or do I mean strengthened? I do not know.

Among the documents which write of the last days of the monastery at Glastonbury are those of the lives of the Welsh saints, now almost forgotten, who named many of the hamlets and villages of eastern Dumnonia. They travelled here as white pilgrims, bringing the gospel to the superstitious peasantry of post Roman times. The influence of the old gods was still powerful, the agrarian year and its festivities exerting the mystique of the cycle of life and death. Cernunnos, horned god of vitality, was making a strong comeback and some of the chest's documents, as I have seen, are proof of that. A wave of saints from Wales came to these parts across Sabrina's Severn from the monastic centres there. Spreading out from Watchet and other ports, leaving a trail of their existence in their own names, founding new Christian religious communities amongst the hills and groves, they built preaching crosses where roads met, persuading the illiterate to return to the fold. From St David's and St Illtyd Fawr, Kay and Collen were two of them.

Like many of the saints recorded, from literature elsewhere at Glastonbury and which I have read in Malmesbury, St Collen had to face an ordeal with a devil. Dunstan had a similar ordeal while in the workshops at Glastonbury itself, when Leofa played a trick on him. He says it was quite a shock and did him no good at the time, but forgave him later. Devils spring up from where you look for them from hills, trees, people, animals. Leofa always was a daredevil as a child. He is no different now. *But better the devil you know,* I say to Dunstan, when he complains of Leofa's insistence on impromptu behaviour, which sometimes shocks the more studious types of the scriptorium. He has been known to ring a bell, sometimes, when there is no change of office, getting everyone wearily up from their work and out of the door, plodding towards the church, before informing them that they have yet another half candle to burn. There are many instances of his childhood antics which he is having to live down in maturity. Dunstan would never do such things. He prefers to impress, not to shock. Me? I am the quiet one, expecting little, grateful to be playing the role that I do.

The Welsh Saints, Collen and Kay, are mentioned in the writings of the chest, to which I will return.

On the road to Nottingham, 4 June, 934

There were cheers again throughout the mid-morning gathering of the troops at Winchester on the 29th day of May as it became clear that the Aetheling Edmund would be travelling with us at least as far as Chester-le-Street and Bamburgh. The youth and enthusiasm of the young man, after all only as young as many of the troops themselves and older by far than some of the pages and servants also travelling with us, made for an even more hopeful journey.

The navy had been sent on its way seven days before, hugging the coast around Kent and up the East Anglian seafront to King's Lynn, all the time being waved at and encouraged by the shore-living folk of the eastern kingdom.

'We must make a flag for this new nation to place on our masts,' suggested Edmund to Stone as we set off. 'Symbols are important.'

This became a focus among many during the days of travel. We were displaying our multi-faceted armies with a variety of animal banners. One symbolic flag would be a step forward in unifying us. Should it have a dragon? Too Welsh. A raven? Obviously not. A lion? What is that? A bear? Perhaps. What about a boar? A blue boar? A hart? Hunting might be a good association for a sport loving nation. This discussion continued. Dunstan made a note of ideas to report to Athelstan. He would be pleased with this. He could contribute his own ideas using more religious icons. He started to sketch ideas in the tent overnight, many on a flowery theme. We never reached a conclusion, but it occupied minds as we rode.

It took eight days for the army, travelling overland, to reach Nottingham. These were starry, hope filled, exciting nights of dreams and limited ale for the troops. This was not a jaunt but a very necessary statement of intent, as serious as the Alfredian encounters with Guthrum the Viking all those years ago. Failure to defeat the northerners could mean devastation for what was rapidly becoming an England which reached as far as York and hoped to consolidate much further into former Northumbrian territory, the land of the Earl Uhtred, Bamburgh Castle, Durham, and Chester-le-Street. These names became familiar in the talk by young soldiers sitting around war hearths at night, the stuff of legend. Older warriors advised the young ones, losing patience with their questions.

Would it be snowing in the north in June? No, you fool, it is summer there too. Do they have to wear skins and furs all day during their summer? Only if they want to look like Vikings. Doesn't the sun stay out shining at night? We shall see. What about the magic of the lights in the sky that the north is supposed to have? Will we be turned into green men? That's enough. Turn over and go to sleep.

Some twelve-year-olds are more informed than others.

But there isn't much known about the north, by anyone, in truth. Hardly anyone goes there.

Nonna and Leofa are amused by Dunstan's latest ambition to design a flag for the nation. Flowers?

'It keeps him off religious matters, at any rate,' Leofa's speciality in relics doesn't mean that he is interested in religion. Nonna smiles.

'It will be an interesting flag if we have to combine Strathclyde and Alba into the design as well, but that may not be Stone's intention. Does he really believe that we will end up as an empire of all the lands of Britain, or only of the southern and northern parts of England? It would be a push to include all of Northumberland.'

'And what about Wales? And what about the different languages? Then there is the question of what to do with all the

Danish immigrants. They will be throwing rocks out to sea to try to hole our ships in East Anglia at this present moment.'

Nonna laughs. 'They'd have to be champion caber throwers as I hear the Scots are, to be able to hit them. They are staying well away from the coast in order not to stir up animosity. When do we expect to meet the navy in Nottingham? I am looking forward to hearing how the new ships fared.'

'They will have arrived in King's Lynn by now, camped and left guards with the ships. The ship leaders will be joining us for two nights in Nottingham. They will be busy times for you and I. Stone intends to throw his weight around; there will be charters aplenty to write up.' Leofa pauses, turns to look at Nonna as he rides.

'Nonna, I have something I am bursting to tell you and only you. May I?' The excitement of the journey and the novelty of the circumstances have loosened the tongue of even the most secretive of the clerks.

Nonna is surprised. He is aware that Leofa has a charmed, perhaps a double life, but little shows in the character of his deeply intelligent friend in terms of weakness or compulsion. This sounds like weakness or perhaps both.

'Leofa, you and I have been friends since we were twelve years old and at school in Glastonbury. I liked you from the start. What is it?'

Leofa's eyes burn, his already deep voice lowers. He brings his horse closer to Nonna's. 'I am in love, Nonna.'

Nonna can tell this is serious. The double life was one thing; he had that, as well. But this is life-changing emotion. One of the trinity is in love. What does that mean for the three clerks, for Stone's men? It was going to happen sometime, but he had thought it would not be yet.

'Anyone I know, Leofa?' He is almost afraid to ask; Leofa looks so intense, in pain.

'You do not know her, but she is known to a few here, though I suspect not many.'

'Who, Leofa?' Nonna suspects his advice might be being sought. He is not used to this from Leofa.

'Her name is Leonada. She has dark auburn hair.' Leofa stops and waits while his friend racks his brain.

'That's not a Wessex name. Is she Danish?' Nonna can tell it is not a British name.

'Mercian.' Leofa looks closely at his friend. Does he know? But Nonna, though good at reading diplomatic thoughts in conversation with lesser nobles, is not so nimble in affairs of the heart.

'Ah. Mercian. Of what ancestry? Of course, who cares? It's the auburn hair that matters, you sly goat. Does she return your love or are you doomed to imperfect celibacy?'

'Of good ancestry. Too good, I'm afraid. That's what I want to talk to you about.'

Nonna glances at Leofa. The mood of hopeful battle, the thrill of travelling somewhere new, fades with the advent of afternoon. His friend has a problem, that he can tell. But what is it?

Monastery of St John, Frome, after Compline, 22 December 934

Where was I? Ah, yes, St Collen. I will give my version of what I have read. He was an early monk of Glastonbury. Wearying of close quarters in the monastery when he was abbot there in the seventh century, he moved outside the grounds to a hermit shelter on the slopes of the Tor. While in prayer one day, two yokels, who he naturally took to be devils, started to talk nearby him about the Tor. It was the entrance to the Otherworld, Annwn; Gwynn ap Nudd was its king, they said. They expanded on the notion that in Welsh lore Gwynn is leader of the Wild Hunt, in which the souls of the dead are snatched from their bodies and borne through the clouds to the gate of Annwn at the top of the Tor.

Collen, annoyed by the superstitious chatter, unable to concentrate on prayer, asked them to be quiet and not to speak such nonsense. The devils (they are everywhere and seek out holy men) were offended at this comment and said that he would have to pay for his disbelief.

Later, a messenger came to Collen, saying that Gwynn ap Nudd requested his presence at the top of the Tor. Collen refused at first to go, but after several visits from messengers who all pestered him to go to the top of the Tor and who were all dressed in red and blue apparel, he relented.

At the top he saw a magnificent castle. There were men-at-arms in shining armour, musicians playing, splendidly attired youths riding on horses. Everyone and everything was dressed in red and blue.

Gwynn ap Nudd then approached Collen, greeting him and inviting him to dine with him. Collen refused, observing only tree leaves on platters. The King of the Otherworld, being charming and craving flattery as devils do, then asked Collen whether he had ever seen men better dressed than those at his court. Collen replied that the apparel was good for what it was, the colours of burning and cold, to him the colours of Hell. He brought out his holy water sprinkler and dashed water everywhere. The castle and all its people vanished, leaving nothing but the green sward and leaves.

The red and blue. These colours keep on cropping up. Why should colours matter? I take out the box containing the horse and rider brooch. Red and blue enamel glitter on its front face. The horse and its rider laugh, mouths wide. Is this the work of the Devil?

A small thick, unfolded manuscript lies in a corner of the chest near the brooch box. It is soiled and written over many times, as if the scribe has been apologetic in constructing his prayer, aware of its unlicensed authority and source. It is not a Christian prayer that I recognise. It is in Old Welsh, the words faint and in places scratched out as if hastily constructed as a poem:

Inspiration to me be,
Give my life integrity.
Living it courageously,
Guard, guide, empower me.
Your wing is long, I hear your song.
In your hand lies my hand;
I go with thee.

On the back of the prayer, like the obverse of a coin, a later scribe has written in Welsh:

A token of Coel the Comforter, lord of the hills and sky, who carries your soul at death to the stars and on the wind to Annwn, land of hot and cold, of sunlit warmth and cool waters, where you will have rest by land and sea. All pain and ache will be gone, all memories of the best in life restored, fond relatives remet. The softness of the power of the sun, wisdom of the moon and stars, never ending, will accompany you, always walking in beauty. The Source lies with you, behind you and before you, guiding the soul in the light, heat and cool of the blessed Otherworld, in step with the wheel of time, the great chariot by which all beings come to live again.

How did the Devil become born of this?

Here is Coel again, master of sky and earth, the sun god of these heathen people, remembered by someone of the Christian monastery of Glastonbury, seat of great learning. This is a superstition deliberately kept alive by a literate scribe long ago. There must be something important about this figure that he should be remembered so well, should figure so prominently in this carefully kept chest.

Coel the comforter of the bereaved or weary traveller. Is he the Coel of Cold Kitchen, the long-topped hill that I can see from the rise of North Hill at Frome? I turn the brooch over in my hand. Only a small thing, the size of a large coin, easy to attach to a robe or cloak, a symbol of belief, of pilgrimage. A badge of comfort to touch when fearful or in peril, expectant of birth which so often means death is at hand, ready to snatch the young mother away, or a man about to go into battle, unwilling to leave his family behind. Is this Coel the Comforter, his head, laughing, curly haired, bright eyed, his horse the same? Together, the rider and the horse display confident vigour. *I will protect you, I will guide you, trust in me,* they seem to say.

With strong faith born of this land, no wonder the new religion of the foreign god of Rome took many years to replace the belief in restful, supportive joy. No wonder some beyond the burgh walls of the towns of Wessex cling to the rider and his horse still, in ignorance and superstition.

I replace the brooch in its wool and box. It is becoming a significant part of my time with the chest. It has power, it has purpose. Should I discuss this with Dunstan? Would he understand? Would he condemn my sentiment? I could not throw it away, it somehow seems precious, as any talisman or relic may.

I close the chest, lock it again. It is time to attend the King and to divert my thoughts to business. It reveals little of value, I shall report, just the words and trinkets of a forgotten people. I need time to think about this material and relevance, if any. I hold the key tightly in my palm, take it with me to my quarters for safe keeping. I hasten to the palace and Athelstan's private quarters.

'I am Nonna, come to assist the king'. But the guards know me, no announcement is really necessary. It's just form. In the darkness, with all the Christmas visitors milling about, they like to be sure.

I carry one of the manuscripts from the chest with me to show Athelstan, together with a letter I have found nearby, a recent one. It has somehow become mixed up with the ancient scripts.

I bow. Stone is weary, lying back on his couch, but alert. He waves to signal me to speak.

'What have you found, Nonna?'

I indicate that the letter is not of antiquity and I read it out to him. He appears to be exhausted. He sighs as he hears the familiar contents, frowns when he hears the date.

It is unusually entitled:

A WATERY GRAVE

From the Family of the Monastery of Glastonbury: To my Lord King, dated this fifteenth day of February in the year 934.

We the Abbot and brethren of the monastery of Our Holy Lady Mary do write to you, Lord King Athelstan, in due submission as we have been taught to do. We pray the offices for yourself and your heirs to continue with strength and health in the right ordering of this land.

We beg of you, our mighty Lord, your attention and interest in the material need of our monastery, which despite these welcome times of peace, spared from the wretched devils of the eastern lands, needs saving from the waters of the inland seas. The crumbling nature of our edifices is beyond our ability, small in number as we are and aged in years, to repair. Even with a further grant of land we would have to wait many years to carry out the major works which are now necessary. Ditches and dykes, once cleansed by the armies of the Romans, need to be dug out, acres of flooded land need to be assisted by knowledgeable engineering to rid themselves of green and foul-smelling waters.

The monastic buildings and their contents are threatened with destruction by the forces of nature which this year have been, as you know, particularly virulent. The rain and now the snow and ice have added to our recent woes. Cracks are forming alarmingly in our structures and already the outer walls of the enclosure have decayed, exposing us to trespassers, which, as my Lord you will understand, puts us at the mercy of any thief who supposes he can help himself to our treasures. We do not care for our personal belongings, which, in any case, are few.

As befits the finest school for able young men in Europe, a reputation which I hope we are recognised as having maintained, we wish to enhance the facilities for our teaching, to ensure that our buildings are comfortable and amenable and to expand opportunities to engage with skills in the arts such as metal and glasswork, which are presently limited.

Investment is urgently required. The tythes from our present land holdings have reduced recently with the succession of poor harvests and as you, Lord King, know full well, it is impossible to squeeze blood from an unwilling stone. It is fair to say that we have, of late, become poor, in spirit, in labour and in our buildings, with consequent detraction in learning and accomplishment by our pupils, with the exception of course of a few fine fellows who, despite the difficulties, have done extremely well, your cousin Dunstan of

Baltonsborough being one of our best pupils of whom we are very proud.

I am sorry to say that continual interference in the progress of our pupils, their style of education and the materials for their teaching as well as defective structural aspects of other parts of the monastery have become intolerable in recent times and we beg that parental influence in the care of our pupils be kept to a minimum. It is difficult to enforce a standard of care when some of the nobility insist on certain alterations in our methods.

We therefore beg that you by strict edict forbid your secular clergy, their families and friends, from entering our grounds, which as I have said are at present poorly defended from trespassers, with the purpose of attaching to themselves the few items of worth remaining to us, or of badgering our teachers with edicts which purport to come from your household, in order to gain preferment for their sons. Increasingly their material interest in our library and few treasures begins to worry us.

As you well know, thanks to the favours shown by your royal dynasty in recent years, we have many items of great literary worth in our unsecured premises, including manuscripts from earliest times, rare books, relics and other treasures laid by from many centuries of gifts from kings of many countries as well as lavish funerary gifts made by great families who have chosen to be buried here. We have treasures which the world itself holds dear, treasures which have been created by intense study, workmanship and other scholarly pursuit in imitation of the classical world, continuing the line of scholarly pursuits followed by the greatest names in classical literature, whatever their faith and profession, believing that the greatest and best works lie above and beyond the divisions of religion.

The items of great worth, of gold and silver, we do not require in order to keep this ability to learn and study alive. They may best be held in a royal treasury, relieving us of their burden. But it is urgent now that our library in particular receives attention to its structure which the ancient volumes demand for their preservation. We pray that some grant of a substantial nature be found to help in restoration and reconstruction of our grounds and buildings, for fear that the wet marshes all around us will soon suck all into the cloying mud of obscurity. We would remind you, Lord King, that as well as the many tomes of works by and about the ancient British held here, that there are also substantial works, original and copied, which pertain to the history and glory of the English nation. The works of both nations may be pertinent at this peculiar time of development in your house's plans to integrate the peoples of your realm.

We offer to make a celebratory book of the history of the English peoples, covering their arrival on these shores from the earliest times to the present day, which could be copied and presented to the court and foreign dignitaries. Your own reign could figure in this. It could be achieved speedily, bound in the best and most beautiful of covers, in return for your care and assistance in the matter of our material safety and forward preservation. We would also guarantee to you and to your priests of the court that any laxity in the adoption of the latest form of the Benedictine Way, which I admit we have been slow to foster, will be immediately overcome.

The style of tonsure persistently adopted by some of our older brethren and lay brethren and which I know rankles with your personal priests will be done away with as will many other differences of style of worship and dress modes which have become unseemly. To be modern and forward looking in all works will be our aim, with excellence our motto.

I and all brethren under my care agree that we wholeheartedly wish the various styles of clergy, whatever their original language, country or disposition, to join together in a process of harmonising, healing rifts and aiming for a central ground between an extreme form of religious practice and the traditional, local style which we have previously favoured.

The firmness of purpose as advocated by your new clergy, the clarity of intent with regard to Heaven and Hell, which, like the celtic style of tonsure, has caused argument, will be agreed upon and followed as the best course for the satisfaction of both clergy and laity.

To conclude, we welcome the presence of our former pupil, Dunstan, back into our fold to assist with our reformation and are now willing to accept his authority and guidance to this end as your representative and to act according to his advice. We would, however, require his agreement to his adopting holy orders in full. We look forward to your interest and assistance in all these matters and to the continuation and preservation of our great school of Ynis Witrin, Our Lady's Monastery of the Wooden Church at Glastonbury.

Signed this day, 15th February, 934 Ecgwulf, Abbot of Glastonbury.

'Dunstan must have been too busy in the Spring, helping with the northern campaign...' Athelstan has a reasonable excuse for my friend. But this letter should have been reported to him. There is a scribbled, draft reply attached, which he signals me to read.

To my friend and brother in Christ, Ecgwulf, Abbot of Glastonbury, greetings, on this day of March the 23rd, 934.

My Lord the King has passed me your letter of February 15th and asked that I reply.

With sorrow I note the great need of our former school and the requirement for copious resources.

As you know, I hold the memory of my time as a pupil and artist at Glastonbury close to my heart, ever grateful for the skills it gave me to be of use to the realm of Wessex and to my royal kindred. The enrichment of my spiritual life in the Wooden Church of Our Lady will live with me forever.

My thirst for devout behaviour and study was first fostered with your brethren and I am mindful of the great advantages bestowed upon me by the teaching and availability of the library and scriptorium in particular. The wooden benches in the latter,

I recall, were ancient even then and inscribed with many potent messages by the brothers of ancient times, of interest to the student of handwriting of centuries past but of little use to the future scribe in need of a wholly flattened surface. I am sure some funding can be made available at least for these in the first instance and I am sending our carpenter of Malmesbury to take measurements for replacements immediately.

As for the rest of the edifice, of course all that needs to be done must be done. I am making a case for the King to consider the requirements of the buildings in terms of cost and equipment. My Lord is at present occupied with considerations of matters regarding foreign campaigns, which you may have heard about, and has little time for material matters closer to home; however he has asked me to see what can be done in the foreseeable future.

I propose that I visit the monastery and yourselves, with your permission, on the third day before Easter, to share a Lenten meal with you and to discuss and look over the works required to be done immediately and to assess that which can be delayed for a later date. I will bring Aethelwolf, another of the King's trusted supporters. Together we will carry out a detailed assessment of the Abbey's physical needs and begin to make a plan for the carrying out of works.

If, as you say, the brethren are at last able to commit wholeheartedly to the changes which you and I have discussed many times, I feel the King will be able to be generous regarding the necessities so that works may be put in hand before the next round of winter storms.

Meanwhile I suggest that any valuable items of manuscript, relic or book which are in particular danger from the state of the Abbey structures and from inclement weather should be removed, during works which will be in hand in coming times, to a monastery of your choosing for temporary safekeeping; either Malmesbury or the smaller scriptorium at Frome where there is currently space in the haligdom for a certain amount of written material, having had new

shelving extended in recent times for just such a purpose. My friend
Nonna, based at Frome St John, would be pleased to assist in this
matter. Any items of particular interest and value such as the early
gospels which I have seen in the chained library at Glastonbury could
come here too.

As you know, I have a special fondness for illustrations of the late
British style. They have taught me much and stimulated my own
artistic endeavours. Perhaps you would consider the removal of these
latter in the first instance when we visit in March. I shall bring my
carter with me.

My grateful thanks to you and the Irish brethren for your
concessions in all these matters. My Lord King will be delighted, I
am sure, with movement towards agreement between our clergies.
With all my heart I will commend you to his good graces.

Dunstan.

Stone has been quiet during my reading of the two letters.
Now he looks hard at me, as though he speaks from his soul.
'Nonna, when the time comes I want you to write the story of
my life. I want the writer to be someone who is on my side.' He
waits for me to show I have agreed. But he knows I already have
notes on events of his reign. 'Promise me, Nonna, that you and
only you will make the summation of my time as King. I trust
you.' He continues. 'And I want you to be aware that I wish to be
buried with St Aldhelm in Malmesbury. He will accompany me to
Heaven, allow me through the gates of paradise. I shall need his
help and prayers. And one more thing.' He is very serious. 'I want
to be buried with my psalter.' His small book of psalms lies on
the table before him, never far from his person. He leans over to
caress it. 'It was touched by Charlemagne and Alfred.'

Athelstan slumps back in his chair, closes his eyes. The soul
has spoken. A few moments pass. The King returns, business-
like.

'Nonna, did the early Gospels as well as the manuscripts of

importance get here, despite the apparently unsent letter?'

'Yes, my Lord, Dunstan must have responded in haste, perhaps took a cart there in the spring as one became available. The rarest books and manuscripts are here with us, along with the chest, but no-one has yet had the chance to catalogue them. I think Dunstan has been acting alone, knowing your other great concerns.'

'After Christmas we shall have to get some aid to the monastery to save the rest. Get Leofa to arrange an engineering inspection immediately. What about the chest contents? Anything fresh to report?'

'Yes, another interesting item which signals the existence of early Christian activity in your territories, Lord.'

I read to him. The old manuscript is about Lamyatt, a hilltop near the small town of Bruton to the south of Frome Selwood. But more of this later.

Between Nottingham and York, 9 June 934

We were kept busy at Nottingham. The witan there was more spectacle than law-making; a few manumissions began proceedings, harking back to the coronation of Athelstan in 924 and reminding everyone of his generosity to the unfortunate defeated. Several slaves were freed, including Danish women. The King wore his entire Alfredian regalia, the sword, belt and scarlet cloak, to dramatic effect. The ealdormen and thegns of the south hailed him as he entered the Mercian hall and the Mercian nobility, who did not see enough of their favourite, shouted and drummed even louder. Both groups were reconciled, by now, to their lad of Wessex, Edward's son, Aethelflaed's surrogate boy. England was secure at least as far as this place. Any further north and the York influence would hold sway over hearts and minds. Wulfstan the Archbishop of York was reassuring, his northern accent purring encouragement into southern thegns' ears. He was the King's man through and through, he said. We all believed him.

Leofa said nothing more about his new love. He was of an age to think of marrying, and it was something Dunstan, Leofa and I had both aired with each other many times, though not seriously. We had all had access to girls and women, wives even, of near to royal blood, being not averse to the advantages and charms of the court, but there had as yet been nothing seriously considered as far as commitment was concerned. There was always the question of whether we would be required to take holy orders. Would our calling come first, or wives and families? Stone had intervened in one or two of our follies and warned us off some entanglements which all young men are bound to make, but this affair of Leofa's threw up different questions. Why test me out, instead of the three of us in the presence of Stone? It made me feel uneasy. His silence now added to my misgivings.

During the ride to York, I wheedled it out of him.

Leofa was in love with Athelstan's daughter.

There were two elements of surprise and unease here; no-one to my knowledge knew that Athelstan had a daughter or any issue. He had had affairs as a young man, we were told, but had not officially married any woman. And when he became King and had nearly been blinded to prevent that happening, he had sworn never to marry. He would be effectively celibate, would pass on the throne to one of his Wessex born half-brothers, Edwin, Edmund, or Eadred. The lawful state of celibacy seemed valid; it was a school of thought, developed by St Aldhelm and adopted by several nobles who were religiously affected, and Stone certainly was. It could even be possible. Eadgifu was in effect his wife; she was a similar age and took care of all court arrangements as a queen might; she had already borne the throne's popular heirs. They were a convenient trade-off for Stone's dreams for Britain. He would be left alone at nights to consult his relics, form his plans, to talk to us. The Virgin King got his name.

My jaw dropped open when he told me. Leofa, for the first time since I had met him, seemed genuinely out of his depth, didn't know what to do. He had first met Leonada at Shaftesbury Abbey when he accompanied Stone to a meeting with Aelfwynn, lady of Mercia. He said he had not realised until then that the two cousins had been so close. He could tell by their body language, as he watched them walking in the Abbey grounds that they were intimate. He could not help noticing the deep auburn hair of the girl who greeted the older woman as a daughter might, the same shade as the plaits which the older woman displayed. They looked alike. The years were right. They were mother and daughter, and the older woman was familiar with Athelstan. He said that his mind raced. Could this be a daughter of the King, an unknown soul, a relic of the family of Mercia, a great-granddaughter of Alfred?

Did she know who she was herself?

Leofa didn't think so. He had seen her several times since that first glimpse of love, the light nimbleness, the wind in the rising warm air of that August day lifting the auburn hair. Sixteen years old. And Leofa dark auburn himself, handsome, twenty-five years old, a clerk of the King, bound to turn heads. Leonada was that rare thing, an intelligent, educated beauty. She had been enraptured by his experiences, his knowledge, his worldliness. Love had come naturally, strongly, to them both.

When he had found that she was not aware of her relationship to Stone, he had wondered whether to approach him, or to approach Aelfwynn. Instead he had come to me. All winter long he had worried about the matter, hoping the revelation would occur to the growing girl, but she seemed not to want to know about her father or who he was. She had been schooled in self-discipline, was aware that his identity should be kept a secret. Her knowledge of royal family affairs was sketchy; her mother had done a good job of shielding her from information and the Abbey walls had done the rest.

It was only recently, on her brief and infrequent trips into the hilltop town for church services or to give alms, that she had become aware of some interest in her. The local townspeople had stared, remarking that she was their own little princess, the goldilocks of their fantasies. It was the hair. It's always the hair. It is glorious, said Leofa. And when she turned and smiled....

I had to stop him. He was smitten. Clearly he wanted badly to create another redhead as soon as he could. He might already have begun the process. To be beautiful is one thing. To be young, intelligent and educated as well a rarity. What was I to say? Don't do it? I knew that in his shoes I would feel the same, would be as desperate as him. I had managed not to fall this badly in love during my clerkship, though I came close when I was sixteen. Then the impossible was just that and even my immature mind was aware of it. But at twenty-five, for Leofa, a passionate man, the matter was entirely different.

Leofa had a good salary as a clerk to Athelstan, had been putting reasonable sums aside, as we all had, for years. There

was no need for expenditure on a day to day basis; all our basic
needs, bed and board and a horse when we wanted one were met
by the travelling court. We expected some day to retire as our
eyesight began to fail or our wits slackened and when the time
came to receive a modest pension and perhaps a plot with a small
amount of land to tend at a mature age, say about thirty-five. The
comforts of a home life, continuation of our personal studies or
interests, perhaps a family. After that, a good room in a caring
monastic community with a reputable hospital attached, like
Frome or Gloucester, the comfort of a priest well trained in easing
one towards the grave. A will intelligently and clearly written. Not
much. Just a sensible provision, a recommendation of the care of
one's children to the king whoever he might be. Edmund looked a
good bet. Already the trinity acted like uncles to him and Eadred.
They consulted us as if we were personal tutors and took care to
acknowledge us with a wave when they met us at court. Eadgifu,
their mother, sent us flowers to adorn our tables whenever she
was at Cheddar or Amesbury where she had extensive flower and
vegetable beds. We were all comfortable and popular, obscure and
happy.

But Leofa's situation, I could see, was perilous. Any liaison
with a daughter of Aelfwynn was bound to be fraught with danger.
She was a potential source of royal disagreement, of raised
Mercian hopes. They had never quite died, though the last ten
years had seen relative stability between the two factions at court.

Then there was the difficulty, which might emerge, that
Athelstan was not, after all, the Virgin King that he staked his
reputation on. His liaison with a Mercian princess, even though it
took place many years before he became king, would not go down
well with the Winchester crowd. Furthermore, if there were to be
issue from a secret Mercian child and it was a male, there would
be anxiety over inheritance, even though Leofa, as potential father,
was merely a mongrel without royal kindred. That made him safe
in his current position, but were he to have a son with Leonada,

this would raise her status in some eyes as a potential queen mother and that would be a threat to Eadgifu and her sons. At the very least there would be difficulties.

Leofa hadn't a chance. He was a poor royal clerk, that was all. No land, no money, no background. In love with a daughter the King would rather not have acknowledged in public.

'You'd best forget all about her.'

'I can't, Nonna. She is due to give birth in seven months' time.'

We remained silent for the rest of the journey to York. The joy and hope of the journey had gone. There were storm clouds ahead.

Palace of Frome, after None, 23 December 934

The Christmas court continues. I have read another, more puzzling, manuscript from the chest overnight. Like the others, it pervades my dreams, sleeping and waking. Lamyatt and its story, to my Christian sensibilities, is most dangerous. Soon I will come to this.

The raucous greetings of the early days have quietened down into gaggles of constructive or negative criticism, groups of like minds. Constantine has few admirers, but his gloomy looks have infected a few. He recovers in the hunt, though, throwing a boar lance with the best of the young men and showing great dog handling skills. He has ten wolf pelts already, beating Hywel Dda by several. In the evenings he glowers by the fire; even the King has given up trying to make conversation.

Constantine's young son is a different matter; he is bright and cheerful and as yet unbearded, seemingly glad to be amongst royal boys of his own age and showing off his own potential merits as a courageous hunter. Athelstan has hopes that his rule, in time, will be fortunate for Wessex and submissive in the required manner.

In the women's quarter, there is much disagreement, but not of a political kind. A troupe of Welsh puppeteers has arrived and amongst them is a girl who has set the hearts of the young men racing. She is not fashionably dressed. She is obviously different. She is ebony coloured. No Anglian, Saxon or Scandinavian headdress can hide the energy of her hair, no demure plaits can contain it or her blossoming vitality. Wherever she goes in the court bright colour seems to surround her, melting the cold air as she crosses the courtyards, warming porch doors as she enters, glowing in the wooden interior, complimenting the golden colour of the carved wood. She looks, in profile, like one of the nymphs lovingly carved on the staves of posts at the entrance to the royal bedchamber. The Virgin

King can take no advantage; he has stared like the rest of us, but only briefly.

Eadgifu has been watching her closely since her arrival, noting every detail of the clothing she wears, of the jewellery round her long neck, of her effect on the majority of the married men who view her intermittently and wish to see her more. And more of her. This is troubling. I can tell that her mother tongue is Welsh. She has arrived with the mixed sex contingent of bards, singers, musicians and acrobats from Hywel Dda's Pembrokeshire court. He is pleased by the shocked reception, knows that he has scored over Athelstan's cultural faction and challenges the tendency to conservatism where performance arts are concerned. Stone will not stand for bigotry amongst his courtiers and he knows it, pushes the boundaries of tolerance further with each witan he attends.

Stone's sisters are clucking; they are being outshone. Tonight the puppeteers will perform their tales. The dark girl will take a speaking part. Will her voice, talking and singing, be as enchanting as her looks? Will she fail at her musical accompaniment? Some may wish that she will. I will be there to watch and to enjoy, of that you can be sure.

Today the witan has had a busy morning, the elders discussing matters of state well into the dark of the afternoon, while younger family members of the visitors have been hawking. Louis, Hakon and Alain are coming on well with handling larger birds. We clerks have been kept busy with interpreting and making notes, elucidating where necessary, covering gaffes where required by the sleight of a hand, ever watchful, like an auctioneer, for the signal to desist or interject when things take a wrong turn. Raised eyebrows and a thoughtful pull of a beard indicate offence or a movement to outwit. We must be on our guard to respond at all times. It is exhausting.

I have retreated to safety, having wrongly interpreted once during discussion. Was it my fault or was it the intention of the

Scots to confuse? Was a promise an oath? Was it a promise to make an oath? The grey area baffled me. It led to the King giving away a look which may have indicated resignation, not a healthy look for a king to wear. He raised his eyes to the roof. The mask of pleasant indifference must be upheld, he tells me when we are in private conversation at the end of the day, berating himself for his lapse. A kingdom depends on the enemy being unable to fathom thoughts, unable to gain advantage from the smell of doubt or exasperation. As the witan continues, we must all guard against impatience and tiredness.

To add to the verbal difficulties of the day there has been a continual clatter of theatrical preparations outside in the courtyard with hammering, shouting and declaiming, along with short stanzas of musical trills as songs were being practised. The music disturbed me, led my mind to yearn for golden glades of woodlands and streams in summer, detracting from my ability to concentrate. A weary evening, a weary day, except for those out hunting, whose experience of healthy activity in open spaces will lead to further carousing this evening and on towards dawn, leaving the business makers in the palace ever more exhausted and fractious. I hope that a good night's sleep will be had at least by them. Some of the bishops have given up riding out and have taken to the scriptorium to record their thoughts and to contemplate their own contribution to the making of the nation to report to the King after Christmas. Some are also glad of the chance to sit down, stay put and to ease their cracking faces. The younger ones are not used to prolonged diplomatic smiling.

Meanwhile I must soldier on with the chest contents. Dunstan mentioned at supper that some of the Glastonbury effects may be taken to Malmesbury after twelfth night. I have told him about my finding of the letter from Glastonbury and his draft reply. He seems unperturbed, shrugs. The northern wars have made us all forget things of secondary importance. Glastonbury will be sorted, in time. There are more pressing matters. But he now knows that I know that he has reviewed the contents of the old chest. Why do I feel uneasy about this? Perhaps because of his suggestion of the removal of documents to Malmesbury? Perhaps because of his growing propensity to edit or expunge things he does not like? Aethelwold's influence grows daily. I do not like that man.

I am fearful that Dunstan may intend them to stay in Malmesbury for their safekeeping, in which case I may not get a chance to view the chest contents in detail without gaining limited access to a scriptorium not my own. I fear I may have said too much to him about the detailed nature of some of the manuscripts, but he seems to know some of them already. He is growing more certain of the need for urgent Church reform, getting anxious about it. Aethelwold, who is driven, is encouraging him in this. Aethelwold seems to have virginity and devils on his mind. Perhaps the fumes of the paint Dunstan is working with are overcoming him. Certainly he has plenty of time to create schemes while active in his artistic endeavours, on his own in the nave all day. I ask him politely if I may assist in his plans. He declines. I suspect his lengthy conversations with Aethelwold are having an effect. I'm hearing 'No,' from Dunstan quite a lot these days.

The daylight has long gone. The early evening darkness has not yet developed into the usual later evening loud entertainment. The fires of the palace are only just being relit for the first to come to the feast, which tonight, I understand, will feature much that is cold and carved from the roasted carcasses of earlier days. The cooks are allowed to rest before the coming Christmas eve celebrations when hell will be reconvened in the kitchens.

In the hallowed company of the oaken chest, I again unlock its portal, lift back its heavy lid and peer into its contents, which are now looking a little more disturbed. I have not folded or rolled the manuscripts or tied them with the linen ribbons; instead the read portions I have put to the left, the unread to the right of the floor of the chest. In their untied state, the chest looks even more dauntingly full. Nevertheless, like a tracker using a wool line in caves, I can see where I have been and tonight I start to read a fresh manuscript in Latin which seems to indicate that I will find a tale or recording of a Christian nature, though I have come to realise that the contents of the chest do not follow a pattern. There is much here, in Latin or British, which could be judged to be pagan. Having mentioned this to Dunstan, before he began with his 'No,' I am now worried for their safety.

I take out the carved box with the horse and rider brooch. Handling it seems to bring me in tune with the exotic flavours of the past suggested by the chest and its contents. I find myself adopting the breathing pattern of prayer, while my head tells me that this is inappropriate: I am merely a historian recovering documents, researching minds of the aboriginals of my place. But now I feel I have an added task: that of saving them. I remind myself that I have the only known key to the chest.

The virility and energy of the little brooch again surprises me. I recall a minor event of this morning. When removing a large snail from the earth floor just outside the scriptorium entrance, to save its life, I could feel the pulse of the creature's being in my palm. The brooch feels alive like the snail. I look carefully at it. The details used by the brooch maker to produce an object which represents a hero or god become more obvious with each time I approach it; turning it over and over by candlelight I can see the shining eyes of both horse and rider which he has tried to convey in the tinning around them. The smile, or shout of both is obvious, too, as is the slightly upturned open mouths which makes one think of the experience of joy. Bright eyes.

The wind outside gets up, as if to emphasise the sudden energy I can feel in the darkened haligdom with bones of the ancients all around me. Gwynn ap Nudd rides, howling down the winter. Branches will be broken off tonight. The full day's hunting planned for tomorrow to give the frowning court negotiators some respite from their cares may have to contend with floods and fallen boughs. Probably they will regard new riding obstacles as a challenge. The chance dangers of the hunt provide thrills but not too many spills. And the hospital here can provide for early treatment of any wounds received. A hunting scar is worth almost as much as a battle scar in impressing women. Being blooded is a necessary evil of being noble and a Saxon. The wind dies down temporarily, with a low whistle. I turn my attention to the chest.

The latest manuscript appears to have been consulted several times over the years; there are small tears at the sides and several glosses made in a different, English hand, in the margins. Access to the chest has evidently been greater in the past than in recent years, or interest in the pre-Christian era perhaps considered more worthy of study. That has not been the case in my time until now.

The Trinity of persons in our Gospels, is of course an important part of our Christian understanding. This manuscript is also about a group of three. What is it, I wonder, which makes three so important to us? And I see, which many would find particularly unappealing, that the trinity in this particular story is another religious one, but not of male figures.

At the beginning of the writing, heading the page, is a red line drawing of three female figures, swathed in robes, seated on a bench. They have trays of what appears to be food on their laps, abundance being offered. Plenty. This is what the goddesses will give to you. This is the female trinity, Macha. The name is written over the bench above their heads and underneath, the word Lamiae. A bird and a sword hover above them. Are they encouraging war or peace? The King has three sisters at court. It should be noted that together they are a formidable force. Their physical presence outshines any group of men in their self-confidence and grace. They could be kings if not for the chance of birth and their positions as later children of Edward, tools of exchange for the marriage market or, avoiding this, lives spent in the service of Christ in the richer nunneries, places of safety for those who do not wish to risk the hardships and risks of childbearing.

What of Macha. What does this mean? I am troubled by the ancient sounding harshness of this name. There is a mountain across the waters of Sabrina in Wales which is called Machen. In the unconquered land of Wales it has not received an English name, nor have any yet of the rivers or townships of the Welsh British in their own territory; it is to be hoped that even in submission, some old names will survive. And there is a sense of mystery, magic and poetry in those Welsh names, bespeaking myth and belief, rather than some of the prosaic naming undertaken by the English in Wessex. But that is just my view. Others do not share it, would wish that the only language of the new nation of Britain was English. They argue that culture and language survival encourages difference and diffidence in progress towards unification. Perhaps Hywel Dda, with his cultural superiority, has got wind of this. He hopes to show that Welsh is much more than the language of a submissive people.

Lamyatt, near Bruton. There's a name. Lambsgate might be the name as understood by the English, of the hamlet referred to in this document. Lambsgate is the obvious meaning of Lamyatt which we call it now. Small sheep going through a gate.

Lamyatt, Lamieta as some know it, is a hamlet not far from here, a high point overshadowing the Welsh rolling valleys so typical of these lands in the western part of Selwood. They are bandit country, could hide robbers well and must have done so, in former times. I see no suggestion of a sheep here in this name, though no doubt there are plenty of them feeding on the sunny slopes of the high hill looking across to the Tor at Glastonbury. Why name a place after an insignificant domestic animal? The manuscript is brief, describing the pagan temple and oratory which played a part in the religious life of the landscape and which was supported by the monks of Glastonbury, an outpost, it

is said, of their own evangelical missionary work.
I read

THE TALL WOMAN OF LAMYATT.

There were once three women who lived at Lamyatt, high on the hill. Sisters of mercy, sisters of God. With the blessing of the monks in the valley below, they brought the Word to a lonely place, inhabited sparsely by the pagan and semi Christian farming folk of the region.

Making their base in this formerly sanctified spot, visited in pilgrimage by many who also travelled to Coel Kutchen and the temple at Brean, they stamped the word of the Christian God onto the former pagan holy site, temple of Mars and other Roman deities. The women were known by the old pagan name, Lamiae, which had not been forgotten, despite their protestations at the localised conflation of two religions. These were early days for the newcomers, the Saxons, in our land. There was some confusion of belief and understandably customs of the farming folk took many years to change.

The three women, sent there by monks as they wished to live a separate existence from the men and to establish a form of female commune which could benefit local women in particular, practised a form of witchery which some generous citizens regarded as medicinal.

They were reputed to be giants. One witness who visited them on the heights spoke of the extraordinary height of one of the women. Even when sitting she appeared to dwarf any male visitor. The women had a male servant, a boy-man with a limp, who cooked and fetched water and was the first to be approached by any visitors. He protected them from the merely curious. Prayers were offered through fire, in keeping with some practices of old. It is said that the eccentricities of the women grew as they grew old. Their eventual practice of Christianity could hardly be told apart from old ways when so many in the rural hamlets were in danger of reverting to paganism.

At festival times the three and their followers lit beacons to remember the customs of the cycle of the year. The pagan Lamiae seemed to be reborn in the women, despite the warnings of the monks to the contrary. The monks' view was that hills had become dangerous places, turning the minds of those who lived there. When the fires burned, the monks below trembled. The hills were alive with pagan deities.

The tall women, in their hilltop residence, kept the flame of the old ways alight. By the time of their deaths, they had returned to their roots, the roots of the Goddess, of the Macha. The gates of Annwn opened to them and swallowed them, transported by Taranis and his magical flying horse. In time their servant the boy-man followed them there.

This was apostasy. It should not be possible to revert to paganism. Is this what Dunstan and Aethelwold fear? That others may find their own way to God?

Between York and Chester-le-Street, 15 June 934

We made good progress between Nottingham and York. The countryside seemed well tended, the rest stops were pleasant and adequately supplied by local merchants who had been warned of our needs by the scouts. The land was at peace, both with itself and the king from the south. There was no open animosity from Danish habitations as we passed; the former Viking pirates had become settled farmers and horse traders.

Our rapid movement north to York was tiring and troubling for me. Leofa's problem gnawed at my mind. He seemed unable to let the madness of his obsession pass. The further we drew away from the soft south and his love, the more he withdrew, knowing, both of us knew, that things were hopeless. This was one royal secret he could not discuss with Stone.

Athelstan was completely wrapped up in the war arrangements with his army and navy. Horses needed resting or changing. The logistics were a headache and absorbed much of everyone's daily sum of energy. Feeding and watering such a large travelling body of men was only done a few times in each generation; it threw up new issues to the inexperienced. The naval arrangements alone were phenomenal. Added to that, we were learning as we went along. We were mostly young men without previous experience of war.

Besides the logistics, Stone had to maintain an aura of invincibility. He could manage that quite well, had practised a certain aloofness since his coronation in 924, but I could tell it was becoming an increasing burden. The royal tent or hired room was vulnerable every night to the requests of thegns for reassurance and for prayers to be said in the event of a catastrophe. As we drew further away from our Wessex bases, the likelihood of insurrection grew stronger. Doubts began to creep in. Priests tried hard to maintain morale. The landscape looked more rugged as though it was unwilling to shape itself to our will. Rising up the steep Sutton Bank above Thirsk and looking backwards after the carts had finally achieved the summit we felt that we were in a land owned by different gods, as well as different men. A foreign, malign place began here, the Celtic North, with only a thin veneer of Christianity and a different sort of Christianity at that. The pagan land beneath its surface grumbled still.

Dunstan and I had continual discussions about the ongoing travel arrangements. Our journey north from York, where we had met up with the navy captains putting in at Hull, had slowed. Stone was becoming anxious about the visits to the resting places of his revered saints. St Wilfred, a contemporary of St Aldhelm and a staunch supporter of Rome, was beginning to take centre stage in his mind, encouraged by Dunstan and especially Aethelwold, who was Edmund's constant travelling companion.

Leofa reported that some troops were worried that the journey might become a pleasure trip of historic sites and pilgrimage. Their swords were getting blunt, they had already had too many nights on the road, wanted to get on with the battle, if there had to be one. Besides, the King had promised a short, sharp sojourn in the north. The northern barley bread was sour and grated on the teeth, homesickness was starting to develop. The alehouses on the road were not wonderful and some stomach troubles had started to emerge among the men. Nevertheless Stone, aware that he was unlikely to come this way again in his lifetime, insisted on making detours to places he had longed to see since he was a youth in Tamworth and Gloucester. The army was sent on ahead to meet the navy at Newcastle, while our trinity of clerks and a small contingent of troops diverted to the holy sites. Edmund and Aethelwold, now glued to the prince, came too.

We travelled in disguise, looking like a family of ordinary well-to-do Saxons, riding speedily to Wilfred's Ripon. It was evident to us that the two sons of King Edward were like father and son. Edmund was old enough and skilled enough with reading and penmanship to appreciate the sacred sites and in later years would often remind the court of the huge gift of experience he had gained with his surrogate father. He was captivated by the north, its splendour and roughness, its drama, stark moors and skies. Like Athelstan he appreciated and relished landscape, the starry night sky and all weathers. Unlike some of the more superstitious travellers, he wanted to see the green lights of the northern sky, spent time every evening, as we camped or rode into fortified habitations, sitting and staring into the clear summer sky, in the hope of seeing any phenomenon, any amazing sight. Most things are amazing when you are twelve years old, even when you are pretending to be older. But then, his was a poet's soul.

Leofa had given instructions to the mass priests who were staying behind with the baggage train to guard the relics travelling north. Fortunately he had been able to point out to Stone the difficulties of taking all of the usual reliquaries with us on our detours. Stone had been able to make decisions about what he really needed to take north with him. A reduced wagon load constituted the main part of his penance reliquaries which he said he could not exist without, but for now, to travel incognito, he was reduced to what he could wear above and beneath his clothing and a few bits more in the saddlebags on an accompanying pony.

After a couple of days Stone admitted he was getting used to doing without the comfort which his reliquary paraphernalia usually provided, but was expressing his ardent love of saintly flesh and bone in his excited talk and enjoyment of the idea of soon being in the presence of his family's hero, Cuthbert and most importantly the head of Oswald. He imbued Edmund with his enthusiasm; the two brothers, scions of Alfred and Edward, felt their dynasty's mission might be about to be accomplished.

We spent some time at Ripon, meditating on and consulting the great St Wilfred who was the North's equivalent to Aldhelm. This small place reminded us of Frome. Its religious buildings including a monastic community founded by Wilfrid more than two centuries before were flourishing, though the town consisted mainly of pilgrim hostelries. The old kingdoms of Bernicia and Deira had been generous in donations of land to the monastery from early times, but the main source of income was from its association with Wilfrid. His body still lay there and his tomb was visited daily by a stream of pilgrims. Their fervour to touch the resting place of a champion churchman was part of a round of journeys made by the religiously inclined, taking in our own chosen destination of Chester-le-Street to view the coffin of Cuthbert and Oswald as well as the Jarrow site of the monastery of Bede.

As we drew nearer to Chester-le-Street our scheme for the open coffin viewing of Cuthbert, in all his uncorrupted glory, was much discussed. Our evenings were taken up with arguments about how to best manage our intentions.

What would make the monks of Chester-le-Street willing to let Athelstan view the corpse of Cuthbert and the head of his contemporary, Oswald? We had not viewed Wilfrid in the flesh; given that he was well encapsulated in a solid tomb, it would have been difficult to arrange, though he was said to be uncorrupted like all the important saints. Still, exposure to air was not something the guardians of such relics liked to try too often. The uncorrupted state might not look quite so convincing after a number of openings, as I had witnessed myself on other occasions when viewing a shrunken, supposedly alive-looking corpse in a glass case.

It was decided that the monks of Chester-le-Street might be induced to allow a timed opening with attendant ritual with their own priests for a king and at a price. Dunstan was sent on ahead to negotiate a deal, returning after a day to say that the presence of the Athelstan and his heir at the open tomb of Cuthbert could be arranged for a fee and the amount would be up to the King's generosity. Naturally they would be only too pleased to accompany him in a ritual procession in their church and would provide candles and music to accompany the visit of one hour, long enough to view the coffin, the removal of the lid by its monk guardians and for contemplation in the cool of the crypt in private for the King and whoever of his small number of chosen companions he wished to bring with him, to a maximum of four. Contemplation seating would be provided for the individuals at the foot, head and sides of the coffin, to give an excellent view of the relic. Touching of the corpse would not be allowed, except by the King, as he would wish, no doubt, to offer gifts to St Cuthbert and to place them in the coffin. This would be the only time this had been allowed, they said, but as a special privilege...Nothing had been said about St Oswald.

Leofa snorted at this. Two centuries and no-one had opened the coffin or placed gifts inside? Not likely. However, one had to be pragmatic. No doubt the monks had to make hay while the sun shone. This was going to cost. It was just a matter of how much.

We spent the night before arrival at Chester-le-Street, where we would meet up with the army again, calculating how much to offer for the double pleasure of seeing and touching the Saint so carefully marketed by the monks. The baggage train had with it a number of items brought as potential gifts for these occasions. Wilfrid had warranted a few small valuable items; the monks there were surprised and delighted by our visit and were already wealthy landowners.

Wilfrid had left his monasteries in good repair in the firm hope that his likely sainthood would bring them more than enough to maintain an orderly house, and he had been right. The income from pilgrims alone had enabled repair and maintenance to keep pace with requirement and the monastic hostel had been a comfortable experience. Chester-le-Street would be a different matter. The monks had fled from Lindisfarne when the Vikings destroyed their home and had been wandering ever since. Their income was limited to whatever they could obtain from pilgrims and they had still to settle on a permanent home for their saint as well as themselves. They would drive a hard bargain just for access to the coffin, let alone to open it.

Dunstan knew something of their commercial mettle. He had read the lives of the northern saints with interest. Theirs were stories, like Aldhelm's, of the battle of wills between the ideas and practices of the Celtic Christian monks, particularly of Iona and Lindisfarne and those of Wilfrid's persuasion who represented the Roman Catholic tradition. For years the arguments about tonsure shape, the dating of Easter and several other difficulties of ritual and behaviour had raged, culminating with the Synod of Whitby in 664 which had seen the defeat of the Celtic group led by the Abbess Hilde. Wilfrid had been on the winning side. Thenceforward Roman ways were adopted, though, as in the south, pockets of resistance remained.

The Cuthbert monks were Roman followers. They bowed to the Pope's decrees. Cuthbert had been a Celtic Christian but had adjusted in his lifetime. Because of his fame, despite being known for his Celtic preferences, he had been a major source of necessary monastic income for the two hundred years since his death until the Vikings spoiled the pilgrimage route. Bereft of adequate provision for accommodation of pilgrims, the monks had built a reputation for tough negotiating tactics in order to squeeze coins from purses. They had developed a new line in personal guidance and prayer ritual which promised to take the visitor to places in his mind where no others had been before, a journey with Cuthbert, accessing his vision. One monk in particular was said to be Cuthbert's holy representative on earth. He could be induced to speak with Cuthbert's words straight from the corpse. This, of course, would cost a little more. The opening of the coffin, though, never occurred, they claimed, except on the Saint's day when it would be seen only by the private haligdom priests of Cuthbert's closest associates for cleansing and re-clothing of his remains. This was part of the commercial image put about by the monks. Dunstan understood the worth of such claims.

Leofa snorted again. He said that he had heard that the coffin had been opened and the corpse viewed by continental visitors on more than one occasion. We had some reason to hope, then, that an opening could be secured, something which the Athelstan needed badly. To see, to touch, to receive.

We had gathered a collection of valuable items from the baggage train. Eadgifu had thought that some of Aelfflaed's tapestries might be appropriate as gifts to dignitaries or potential sub-kings. A wife, if not a husband, might be softened by the offering of rich hangings. She foresaw that Athelstan might be able to gain access to the open coffin if he offered personally to place pillows or vestments inside. An anointed king's hands would surely be allowed to do this. She had agreed to Edmund's joining Athelstan after hearing of the planned attempt to consult Cuthbert. She wanted the aura of holiness to pass to her son, giving him, too, the added prestige of his blessing. Oswald was, she felt, more a Mercian project, but she could see Edmund's point when he, sounding and looking like a miniature Athelstan, made the case for the added afterglow of spiritual support by the two saints in one coffin.

The night before their departure from Winchester, Eadgifu had fluttered around the palace at Winchester, opened many chests, raided many cupboards. Athelstan had set aside a large sum of money, had asked Leofa to select books and gold items of significant worth. He would not come this way again, would not have a chance like this again. Edmund's presence with him would make the attempt to see the corpse even more relevant; the boy would be able to invoke Cuthbert and Oswald in the future in any palace or witan disputes. It was an investment.

'So, we have plenty to offer in terms of payment,' Athelstan had made a parchment tally. It would dent the travelling treasure fund, but not empty it. He would include three rare gospel books, a missal, a copy of Bede's Lives of St Cuthbert, two chasubles, an alb, a stole and a maniple to dress Cuthbert's corpse. He would also add a silver cup filled with coin which would go direct to the fund for restoring Lindisfarne, and grant lands which he was about to take from the King of the Scots to be gained with the help of St Cuthbert.

The tally looked impressive; never before had so much been offered for the mere chance of a sight of a saint in his coffin. Leofa rewrote the list into an official looking document which would act as a contract between the King and Cuthbert and his followers. Negotiations would begin in the morning with the guardians themselves.

'Tough customers,' Leofa remarked. We nodded. Even Edmund seemed to understand the politics of religious power, the market forces on display. Tomorrow Dunstan would be chief negotiator. Leofa would make the notes. I was to listen and watch. The madness was to become reality, Stone's dreams our nightmare.

Monastery of St John, Frome, after Compline, 23 December 934

I return to the contents of the chest.
Having read it, I put down the disturbing Lamyatt
manuscript. The writer was generous, considering his description
of the ghastly apostasy of the women. This was the first time I
had heard of anyone rejecting the accepted forms of Christianity,
of willingly growing backwards towards a religion which clearly
mirrored the natural state of their surroundings. Were they mad?
Do women have a tendency, left to their own devices, to have
direct contact with the Almighty, developing a relationship with
him without need for the guidance of higher male authorities?
Even an Abbess must employ a male priest to deliver Mass.
The chest had thrown up yet another shock. I picked up the
manuscript again to fold it carefully. On one of its four outward
sides I saw something I had not noticed before: the small
depiction of a horse and rider, both their mouths open, vigorously
riding, falling through the sky. More souls being carried to
Annwn. This is getting to be a common theme.

That night, I dreamed vividly about the tall woman. She
spoke to me.

NONNA'S DREAM

I am the Tall Woman. My command is this high place. My remit
is to tell the world of the great goodness of all who have faith. Antler
wearing, horse riding, feast giving, praying in stone halls, they are

the same, visible signs of inward spiritual grace. At the deepest level of our being, we are one with the Source.

My time on this hilltop, looking over the vale of Annwn, following the Gleam, is coming to an end. My white pilgrimage nears its journey's end. Only the lame priest remains with me now, thank the gods for his presence, and some of the village folk who have not turned against me leave me parcels of food. Unless they have an illness or their cow has the pox, they do not come near and children are forbidden. They call me the witch. Some think me black, a few, it seems, think me white. But I do not care. I am the Tall Woman and I have seen beauty.

I have no children to whom I can leave the legacy of my ardour. The Gleam that I see will not be seen by many, their sleeping will not be awakened. Only a few will hear the Shout of belonging. For most it will be noise, a disturbance. Silence the Shout, they will say. Do not disturb.

I am faithful still to my God, the saviour. I read his Book here on my hill. Few think that I do, but these words give me comfort and add to wisdom I have gleaned from the old ones. I write my own words to add to the continuation of the authority of joy which I have seen, to offset the fear of evil which I know to be misinformed, wasteful. I write now, after a lifetime of searching for sagacity, of my knowledge that it is always here within, the eye of the soul once opened, the cloud of unknowing accepted. There is a green door in our hearts which may be opened into the Source's domain; I urge you to open yours.

I must speak of the hilltop which induces visions. It is blissful to be sitting on my swing in the air of a low breeze, twisting to all quarters of the world, looking inwards to the hills of the new state of Wessex and to the ruins of the temple of Hywel, on to the course of the Roman highway over the downs to the north, southwards to the hillforts above the plain of Mere and their barrows of the kings of old, westwards to Sabrina and the great temple sites along her borders, to the nation of singers beyond which I can sometimes see, even with my old eyes, on a clear day. To the little town of Brumetone below and my people of Lamyatt who have spurned me.

But most I see the clouds and sky and today the great blue, tonight the stars over the great monastery of Ynis Witrin from where I came, schooled by the Irish; at autumn time, Samhain, sunlight on the deep pink spindle fruits nearby, golden honey of the hives of the farms of the moors at Lughnasa, red moss-cups and snow-drops of the valleys of the Welsh at Imbolc. All I have seen and loved.

And now, Beltane. The fresh greenery of the spindle in spring is almost as glorious as the pinks of autumn. I try to draw and to paint my thoughts of beauty. Its poetry overcomes me. I am the Tall Woman, I am the flagpole, I wave my joy to the human and animal souls around me, call to the passing fox and squirrel, the badger my night-time friends. They pause, look at me, agree with my hopeless joy and pass on. It is hopeless. In the evening I visit the graves of my sisters buried here by me and the lame one. The buildings are beyond upkeep now. I will be the last one to inhabit this sacred place.

Once there was fire and ice. The Gleam was a clear sword glint in the dark. Now, to me, the Gleam is green and gold, changing with the seasons and with my life. I bask in the returned sun, following the light with my heart. The Tor hillside below, the Gate of Annwn, waits to open to receive me. I will come when I am ready.

Soon I will go to my chamber, remaining there, as my sisters did, in tranquil hope. I have my prayers to comfort me, my brooch and cloak ready to take with me to the Gate, ready for the call from Gwynn. I have given instructions that my bones should be buried and left alone in the earth for the judgement day which may come; I cannot discount that it may. My soul is ready for change and recall to a spiritual place, but I hope not to judgement; my God should not judge. I hope for a feast of celebration at the end.

The lame one will not deflesh me as we have done to others before. I will not stretch out my limbs for the carrion. Long ago we undertook the work required of us in our hilltop sanctuary of dismemberment and parcelling of beings; no longer. The secret past required by the monks became a gruesome burden. We became the Witches of the hill because of it. The Ravens, we were called, the carrion harpies. Ground bones we would sell, to scatter on the wheat ground, boil in their cauldrons for healing and dreams. We passed our taxes to the monastery. Gaming pieces for the homes of thegns were our artistic offerings, made from the bones of saints. Skull pieces were our best sales to the remaining Welsh who prize the head. We filled glass vials with blood from corpses, packed limbs with fluid and herbs, made lovely the parts of persons known and unknown. Animals we preserved, too, for hunting lodges, their horned heads adorning walls. We placed glass eyes in empty sockets.

No more. My work is over. My burial slot awaits, the death bed is made. The lame one comes to take me in. I shall see with my own eyes the scene no more. My sisters, swaying in the wind, come to accompany me home. Gwynn, I hear your call.

Remember me.

I now have much to remember, if I am to try to maintain the legacy of beliefs of an earlier time. My head swims with the requests of ghosts. What is the Shout?

Wessex, Rome and the Witan of Frome

After Prime on the morning of Christmas Eve the King summons me to discuss the diplomatic difficulties of the previous day. I feel as if I have been hit hard on the head after the nightmare of the lonely female priest awaiting imminent death on Lamyatt two centuries ago. The concept of a man and a woman operating as priests together as equals troubles me greatly. The two together do not naturally occur except in lust in these present years; it would seem outrageous, inconceivable. Unholy. That may not have been the case with the British Christians. My inner mind reels with the concept. I cannot get over it. Male and female together in the priest's role? I try to concentrate on matters in hand though my head throbs. Stone and I talk quietly about our ability to bring around the Scottish king before he infects others to his way of thinking. Both of us are weary. Athelstan has gained a stoop. Will he survive much longer?

He has held a steady course and is still young enough to see it through. His body and mind are both strong; unlike Alfred whom he wishes always to emulate in his wisdom and holiness, he does not suffer from afflictions of the stomach. His taster, though, is always busy at the feast. Poisoning is not unknown. Many young aethelings have died without cause. They come into their prime, then, overnight, as if enchanted, they are gone.

Stone asks if I think a female member of the court, with subtle charm, might be able to penetrate old wily grey-hair, soften him up. If so, whom could I suggest? We are back to discussing Constantine again. What to do? Stone hints at the use of a mind-bending herb such as is used for pain relief in the hospital here. If all else fails, the wholesale removal of an obstinate old ruler may have to be considered. He asks me if I think that would be part of God's plan. Now I am certain that he is over-tired. I remark that Dunstan or an archbishop would be the better person to ask. Athelstan rambles. He has a powerful sense of his own God-given purpose. If the plan for the kingdom is to be brought to fruition, is it not right that a single ancient thorn, standing in the way of this, should be swept aside? But these thoughts are best shared with few and so I say.

This is unusual for Stone; clearly the worries of the last few days, despite the fresh air of the hunt, have been troubling him. I can understand the burden of decisions of a leader, especially one who must appear to be following the tenets of Christianity. I remember some of the ancient plans of Popes to carry out their brief to serve God. There has always been a way to progress, but the decisions to do what is required to attain it are not easy ones to make.

We concoct a plan. As the midwinter Christmas celebration of Our Lord's birth fast approaches, the centrepiece of the witan, it is agreed to try out a female approach. I have to talk privately to Hywel Dda. Stone would do this himself, but does not have enough Welsh to makes his wishes known in a subtle way. Hywel has some English, but he is like a cheerful form of Constantine, wily. You don't know whether he is pleasantly agreeing with you to make you smile or whether he understands and is happy to assist in court matters. Athelstan thinks him to be a willing ally, and trusts me to negotiate with him. Later I will go to him, or speak to him at one of the mealtimes taken before the chosen hunt for the day, a short journey into the forest for the hart.

The early morning sees the serious usual business of the witan; judgements on matters of law and tenure have been made, access to and maintenance of royal property as well as gifts to supporters and the Church are agreed and signed.

Well into the dark of the afternoon, the last pre-Christmas discussions have centred on the division of the powers of the projected kingdom of England. Athelstan and the sub-kings of Wales and Scotland, together with the chief negotiators of the bishops, have been closeted with us, the interpreters, for some hours. There has been little progress. The northern king, unused to having a bent neck, still refuses to compromise. He risks his head as well as his crown, but torture is not Athelstan's way. His war leaders counsel otherwise. But the old adage about cutting off a devil's head applies and he knows it. Talks will continue, weaknesses will be discovered. It will take time, but we have that luxury after the Scottish expedition's success.

When dealing with the Welsh an appeal through shared faith and discussions with bishops often broke a deadlock; with Asser and Alfred their partnership across states and faith worked well; here the shared faith is not a useful tool; any waving of a Christian magic wand seems to inflame the Scottish guest to greater intransigence. Something more prosaic, to do with wealth or passion, needs to be offered. Blackmail he does not care about. He has no shrill wives to fear, no public to admonish. Guest? The word is an insult. He recognises that he is a prisoner and says so.

The lesser courtiers, ealdormen, thegns and their retinues are weary with the reading and listening they have had to do. They are anxious to appear loyal but are desperate to get outdoors to hunt or to practise their skills with weaponry. Their horses, prancing and stamping in their stables with impatience, display a similar dislike of the confinement of many days. But the food is good and the women willing. Flirtations go hand in hand with the dancing. The sights and sounds of excellent hunting and the conducive competitive spirit of a large group of well-trained men make up for the sacrifice of having to attend a long witan. Justice has been served and thieves hung, their bodies taken to the hill a long way outside the town, Gibbet Hill, to dance in the western wind. There is a sense of achievement, of the successful rule of law. Things are as good as they can be.

My fellow scribes and secretaries of the court are growing increasingly fractious, making our way to and from the scriptorium where the writers of the wills, laws and verdicts are kept busy for the witnesses to sign while they are with us. Scribble, scratch, collect. Sign, copy, file. We run, carrying the words in our head to spill them to scriptorium clerks, bumping into others who are doing the same for their masters, recording for posterity and in writing the doings of the times, charters which can be held throughout the land as proof of their agreement signed by kings, archbishops, bishops and ministers. Britain is being forged. Oaths taken. God and all his Saints are watching.

I have interviewed Hywel Dda. His idea, which mirrors Athelstan's, is to try to soften Constantine with a trusted female of persuasive charm, to make him more amenable to a peaceful approach. Hywel suggests the use of the dark dancer. She is Gwladys, a moor, who has been brought up by his family, played with his young son Edwin as a child and become close to him. She has skills, he says, of the mind which she uses through her personal charm. She has gentle and persuasive manners which bely any man's unruly stubbornness. Born in Wales, she may be able to persuade the foreign King of the Scots that to bend his neck to the English king does not necessarily mean losing his Scottish manhood. And, as Hywel can vouch, the tax burden for mutual protection against Vikings is not overly burdensome, a few wolf skins, a chest of gold. Wales has plenty, land of song. Scotland has much wealth, too, many wolves. There are things of value other than the sceatta coin. Peace is worth paying for.

But old dogs, new tricks. Constantine does not read. He dislikes new things, holds on for dear life to the old ways, has a pagan heart despite many saints who are buried in his lands, despite their missions of Light. It worries Stone that Chester-le-Street, home of Cuthbert is close to his border. He is not to be trusted with oversight of the relics and is not impressed by their power. Athelstan needs someone who will honour saints, not destroy them. It is clear that Constantine has seen the single weakness of Athelstan, the power he gains from holding the relics of so many venerated beings. He dismisses with scorn the tributes, prayers and churches built to house their remains, preaching the need for peace. Peace! With unruly Scandinavians knocking on his door in the north? Bloodthirsty devils need to be met with swords, that is the only way to deal with them, in his mind. Forget saints and the Otherworld, if it exists. We make war to keep our enemies at bay. It is unfortunate that this time Athelstan, with his troops and navy, took him by surprise, caught him napping. Not next time. His eyes roll in dislike. Intransigent.

I interview the girl. Gwladys is a charmer, has natural beauty without artifice, outstanding in her clear headedness, willing to work for her lord and adopted father. She has performed her role admirably with the puppet troupe and remains on the edge of the court in the evenings, gladdening the hearts of most who see her, informing others of potential fashions. We make plans for her to be seated by the Scots king at mealtimes, to try what she can do to open his heart and eyes to a future for the peoples of the countries combined. She says he will be a challenge to charm; she has not tried before to speak at length to such an old ironfist. Nevertheless she will try, for Hywel.

Meanwhile Stone's young half-brothers, Edmund and Eadred rejoin the festivities. They will lighten the mood. Edmund is tall, promising to be striking. His younger brother Eadred is less imposing, slightly asthmatic, troubled in the stomach like his ancestor Alfred. It seems to be a family illness. They run into the great hall, surrounded by a crowd of yelping small dogs and puppies and two family wolfhounds, knocking over chairs and stools, but tolerated for the relief they bring with them to the atmosphere of the court. Laughter is a tonic after the serious nature of the witan discussions. Everyone is aware that, despite business being done, there is resistance at the heart of the negotiations, a tenseness which dispirits those in favour of a happy compromise. And the wish of some, now beginning to be apparent, to soon go home.

Will Christmas never end?

Church of St Cuthbert, Chester-le-Street, 16 June 934

S tone, now back in his royal regalia, accompanied by Edmund and Hywel Dda who had joined us from the Navy harboured at Tynemouth, walked in a small procession of his mass priests and close associates. The army leaders, rested from an uncomfortable trek from York in heavy rain, joined us in a show of dignity, the flower of the South. Wulfhelm of Canterbury was with us, just behind the King, but not Wulfstan of York. He had been left behind in York to bolster any required retreat. He was suffering from leg trouble, he said. We three plus Aethelwold carried the loot.

We lumbered along as sedately as we could with a chest with four handles, making the weight less onerous. Was Aethelwold going to become an essential part of Stone's private clerks? He seemed even more determined than Dunstan to make his way in the circles of power. His opinions, freely and often expressed, were already causing disquiet with some, which I had reported to Stone. But he liked a man to have opinions, he said. Besides, they usually calm down after a time. Personally, I found Aethelwold's potential strictures on morality to be offensively controlling, but there was some consensus about this which seemed to be growing. I kept my antennae clean and sharpened and reported all to Stone.

We entered into negotiations with the Abbot of Lindisfarne, a narrow-faced man who kept his hands inside his cope, hugging his elbows. Dunstan was his match, wiry and blond, active with his hands, blue eyes wildly exhorting the saintliness of Cuthbert, the requirement of the King to see the corpse, to spend time with him. We stood back, waiting for an agreement. It didn't take long. The hands emerged from the cope, shaking Dunstan's warmly. He turned and signalled to us to bring the treasure chest to him. We were in.

Athelstan shook the now proffered hand of the Abbot, whose features had disappeared into deeply wrinkled smiles. The Abbot and his ritual priests took up their positions. Regalia was hoisted, candles lit. Athelstan signalled to the army and navy commanders to follow him into the church. We four walked close behind the nobles. The monks inside were already intoning, evidently prepared for the event. No other pilgrims or local inhabitants were present, though some could be seen beyond the graveyard, being held back by our troops. We processed the length of the nave, stopping at the narrow entrance to a crypt with several steps down to a small door. The Abbot spoke to Athelstan, reminding him of the numbers agreed for viewing and of the small size of the crypt and its low ceiling height.

Athelstan indicated that only Edmund and his four clerks should follow him into the crypt. The monks made no objection to the larger number than that agreed. Hywel and the commanders took seats in the church, basking in the sense of being in close proximity to the saint. They would have a chance to view and touch the closed coffin later, if they chose, for a further fee. A priest moved towards them to show them a basket of pilgrim badges. Purses jingled as they willingly paid for sanctified aid in the battles to come. We descended the steps behind the Abbot and two monks, bent our heads to enter the sacred chamber.

Clouds of incense and bright candlelight were our first sensory encounters, enhanced by the sonorous voices of three monks singing high and low. A large coffin lay across temporary trestles in the far end of the small room which sloped upwards to a stone altar at the east end, approximately underneath the high altar in the church above. The confined space of exquisitely carved stone capitals on columns swirling and dancing in their cushioned designs, circles, dots and flowers, creatures biting creatures or themselves smelled of the earth and of the Life to come. We were in a very ancient or a very holy place, perhaps both.

Four prayer stools were placed at the sides of the coffin. The Abbot indicated to us to take our positions, with Stone at one side. Aethelwold was supplied with another stool to kneel beside Dunstan. The Abbot signalled to two monks to move forward with what looked like metal garden hoes but fashioned with finer materials. These were the coffin-lid lifting tools. How often were they used?

As the lid was raised by their leverage two other monks placed lead ingots, probably found in the legionary fortress nearby, on the sides of the coffin, giving a tantalising narrow view between the lid and the coffin contents of bedding provided for the saint but not much else. The singing monks continued their chant. A slight smell wafted from the coffin on opening which was overtaken by a fresh pass of the censor. We leaned forwards. We waited. Was this all we were to see? Material and a smell? But the drama was worth it.

We were being ritually teased. Four tall monks took up position as prayers were said, gripped the heavy coffin lid and lifted it over our bent heads. We were now nose to nose with whatever was inside the coffin. Another waft of smell and smoke blurred the scene.

I wanted to believe that the uncorrupted body of Cuthbert was what I saw. I tried desperately hard to do so. But what my eyes perceived was a half-rotted corpse, its mouth hanging open, the flesh of the eyes sunken back into the head, bony hands crossed on its chest. It still had hair, but the thing was ghoulish, the stuff of nightmares. But this was what made saints. There was no standard for "incorruptible" that I knew of; was it intended to mean recognisable facial features, muscular definition, eyes which looked back at you? What there was in abundance was nostril hair from a peeling, bony nose and not many teeth in a blackened skull. The cross "held" in its arms was glorious, gold and garnet, as were other items of disported jewellery about the body, but these served to make the saint's mortal remains even more pathetic and disappointing.

But it was holy Cuthbert and he was having an effect. Stone entered deep prayer and I noticed that Dunstan and Aethelwold did likewise. Stone's eyes rolled back on themselves. The sensory drama was superb. Edmund, kneeling on the floor next to Athelstan, barely peeping over the side of the coffin, was absolutely still, his hands in the upright position of prayer or fear. The singing and incense waving continued. There was a dense grey fog of incense around the small room.

After a time, long enough for Stone to recover his wits, having breathed the same air as Cuthbert for many minutes and consulted him in his deepest being, he turned and nodded to the Abbot, who had become the thurifer. This was the time when he might look deep into the coffin. He stood, touched Edmund on the shoulder and bent over the edge. They both spent a long minute closely regarding Cuthbert's face, touching his hands. I was not invited to have close contact, nor would wish to. What does one experience at such moments?

Stone indicated to Dunstan that he wished to have the gifts from the chest to place in the coffin. Not too much, there was not a lot of room, but perhaps the small gospel and missal books could be placed at the side of the body, to give comfort to St Cuthbert in his dark years alone, a piece of priestly tapestry to honour his continuing role as holy leader of the religious North. Dunstan brought them to Stone, who reverently lent over the coffin, parted the copious packing materials and placed them at the body's side.

I did not see anything else in the coffin, but Stone told me later that he had seen and touched the skull of Oswald, which was unceremoniously bundled in cheap cloth at its foot. The temporary nature of the hasty escape from Lindisfarne had not been conducive to enhancing Oswald's remains; besides which, Cuthbert was the greater draw as far as pilgrimage was concerned.

As Stone was engaged with placing his gifts in the coffin, the priests and monks withdrew into the shadow at the side of

the crypt, beyond the candlelight. The intoning ceased. I could
not see them at all. It felt as though the royal pair had been left
alone to pay their own private homage to Cuthbert, a gesture by
the Abbot to allow full communion, a recognition of the value
of the gifts he had given and which, it was to be hoped, would
contribute to the re-establishment of the Lindisfarne community
in a new monastery of its own. Athelstan expected Cuthbert's and
Oswald's assistance in the summer ahead and had paid well for
their prayers; it was fair enough that he should have exclusive
time alone with them.

Eventually the incense clouds reduced, Athelstan and
Edmund returned to the prayer stools, the coffin lid was replaced
in the same stages of drama as it had been removed. It seemed as
though the monks were trained at the ritual of coffin lid removal
and had done it before. Was this a rare occasion or not? But that
thought took over our minds later. For now, we were all stunned
by the dramatic look of the crypt, the contents and the dreams of
association. Edmund never fully got over his first intense religious
encounter. We stood and retreated back up the narrow steps
to the nave. The Abbot and some of the monks who had been
with us had already gone up. We met with them standing by the
ealdormen and followed them to the sunlit air and refreshment.
The nobles, patiently waiting in the church, were allowed to file
past the closed coffin. They then joined us in the churchyard,
looking equally stunned.

Tomorrow the army's entry into Scotland would begin the
humiliation of Constantine. Armed with the might of the sword
and the minds of saints, there would be no need of Wulfstan's
York defences. We hoped his leg was getting better.

Palace of Frome, None, 24 December 934

The terriers and otterhounds have been rounded up by the kennelmen, leaving the wolfhounds to sprawl in front of the fire. The hunt is over for the day, the darkness begins to fall. There is a break from diplomatic discussions, a time of rest before the evening's events.

Athelstan greets his young brothers, has words of affection with Eadgifu their mother, who has been officiating at the Christmas preparations for several months for the guests' quarters and kitchens with her usual skill. He is congratulating her, I can tell by her smiles and nods. Eadgifu plays a greater role in the witans as time goes by. Her daughters lead the sewing group for other highborn ladies. Much discussion of events, national and regional, cheer their hours. This year the arrival of Gwladys is causing a stir. The pursuit of gospel illustration involves a small number of them in a competition of their own to produce drawings of power and beauty. Some have taken part in hawking and one or two in riding with hounds, though the cold air and mud do not attract. Nevertheless Athelstan keeps suitable riding horses for the women of his family and other noblewomen when they wish to ride in the forest, bearing in mind the likelihood of wolves, though they are not as numerous as formerly. Hywel has seen to that in recent years.

Edmund settles alongside the wolfhounds in front of the fire, drinks his warmed ale. Ten-year-old Eadred is given a gospel book, new to his eyes, by one of the bishops, takes it to a corner and reads, obviously smitten. Both boys have been schooled well along with other noblemen's sons; in the schools of Winchester and Glastonbury they have been steeped in the expectations of their kin and dynasty. In future, the eldest son of the reigning monarch will expect to rule after his father's death; this break with tradition by Athelstan, his concession to have no heirs of his own, leaves the way clear for Edmund to take over on his demise. Edmund is very aware of his royal role.

The ghostly impact of Edwin is fading. It is possible that, weary, Athelstan may decide to abdicate and spend his remaining days and penance in Rome. He has often dreamed of this. But Edmund must be older than today before such a thing could ever come about. Of the two boys, the choice of heir, at least, is clear; Edmund will live longer and be stronger in physique than Eadred. You don't have to be a doctor of medicine to see that.

The two princes are already skilled diplomats ready to charm, schooled in gentlemanly behaviour, trained in politeness as well as in the arts and religious matters. The continuation of a well-rounded education for the two boys is proving a matter of pride for Eadgifu, who now comes into the hall from the kitchens to join her sons, her little aethelings. Her small daughters accompany her, queens in the making, also accomplished in grace. Their guards stand by in the shadows; protection is needed against betrayal; things have been known to go wrong for aethelings.

At the far end of the hall scops play and sing. Three musicians including a harpist and three singers including Gwladys are gently harmonising. A small group of admiring young men is seated near them, some making notes of the music or words, Welsh words, sung and spoken; perhaps composing poetry to be heard later, inspired by the sound of the singers and musicians which evoke mountains, rushing water and the sea, of golden oaks, of deep green valleys. They are moved by their own bubble of composition, helped by Frome ale and sweet mead.

Edmund is aware of the new beauty in the room centring on Gwladys. He observes her in silence, fascinated by her allure and apparent unspoiled talent. She feels his gaze, sees him, lifts her head to acknowledge. She has remarked him before, at the Christmas court last year in Wales, where he was visiting Edwin, Hywel's son and his other children. Edwin, named for the King's brother, before he died. Edwin, the brother of Stone's nightmares, reminding him of his first tentative steps to becoming king, of near blinding, of regret. The nightmares of kings: they must be many. Without nightmares there would be no throne. Madness accompanies both.

After this witan Edmund will remain with Athelstan, growing away from his mother's world, a man, now. Old enough to understand the needs of diplomacy, almost old enough to take a wife to continue the line. Old enough to entertain a concubine, perhaps. Not yet, says Eadgifu, he is too young. But never too soon to produce an heir some say and look, he is tall, could pass for 15. The pressure is on; Eadgifu must concede soon to the existence of another woman in her son's private and public life. Perhaps next year, she muses with the ladies. Next year, when I will be still the stepmother to the present king, mother of the next, controller of the household, stirrer of the household cauldron. The ladies laugh; this is a witty and popular queen, aware of her skills and powers. They are aware that she has many friends in high places, including our-up-and-coming Dunstan. They wonder about her preferences in men, but that is a private matter for her. There are no obvious signs of misdemeanour. She is known for her piety. She gets away with murder.

The evening brings more entertainment. Edmund has come prepared to offer his own poetry, encouraged by his father-brother. He wants to show his prowess at reading and the written word. He is known to be able, a fluent writer of English as well as Latin. He has already glossed many manuscripts, studied the art forms of the times, knows and has met the foremost scribes of the land in his short life. He is suitably pious but also boisterous as a young vigorous man should be, assiduous in his awareness of the daily offices as well as the hunt, a hopeful prince indeed for England. He will inherit, if Athelstan can arrange it, the most cultured kingdom of the whole of the British Isles and perhaps of Europe.

Leofa rings a bell to call attention to a performance of the Aetheling. The music ceases, Gwladys puts down her harp.

Edmund stands to declaim, his voice verging on the manly but still high, beautiful. In Winchester, he says, he has been finishing the composition of a saga like those of the Scandinavians, which tells of the doings of his ancestors who came as pagans over the sea. He promises to "scare and enthral" and to impress us with this tale, to be heard in the early evenings over the next three days, taking us through the eve of the birth of Our Lord, when we will all go in procession to the church for midnight mass and into Christmas Day and the day beyond. Musicians will be involved, too, we are told, to enhance the dramatic story of daring. Aethelwold has been helping him. He gestures to the young man at the back of the hall, who bows, acknowledging his part. Apparently these two cooked up the saga while they were in Bamburgh together. It kept Edmund's mind off the disappointment of being separated from the army.

Leofa has also been helping him with this drama, he says, indicating my friend standing by the door, stroking his beard, pleased with the progress and confidence of his artistic charge and his precociousness. Much of this drama, Edmund says, will be read by Leofa, whose voice, he laughingly says, will carry more weight when he reaches the gory bits. Knowing the deep gravelly sound of my friend's voice and his aptitude for drama, I am sure he will do a good job. Monsters, we are informed, will be a large part of the tale, monsters to make nightmares. As if we didn't have enough on our minds already. Aethelwold, I think, is too fond of monsters. I wish he wouldn't encourage them in the mind of the young prince.

Meanwhile the bishops and archbishops have been having their own witan in the monastery chapter house. It is a snug place, not yet modernised by rebuilding in stone, which is due to begin sometime in the autumn. It is so cosy, with the brazier in the middle, that some of their lordships have been known to snore in the warmth, squeezed in next to their fellows. All are English by birth, so no interpreters are needed, but as the

King likes to keep up to date on the thinking of the religious communities, I have hovered occasionally in the entrance to pick up a picture of their discussions. Dunstan is often here, covered in paint, taking a break from his work, which even the archbishops are not allowed to see until the Christmas Eve Mass unveiling. He has a keener interest in the progress of the Church than I do. I listen for any political debate; he listens for the slower moving talk of reform. I think it will be years before the collective bishops manage to agree on that matter. Dunstan is frustrated at their long-winded indecision. But then he is a young man, thin and keen. He says he will never become like them.

The bishops, having taking part in most of the court proceedings of the earlier winter days at Frome, are now free to discuss matters of specific importance to them, particularly the state of land grants to their dioceses and monasteries. The abbots have to put up a fight sometimes to protect their status, as the bishops, more secular, worldly wise and aware of royal aims, do the will of the State, while abbots think first of the will of the Pope. Age and wisdom make a difference, too; the younger brethren are at a disadvantage. Heirarchy matters. Blood matters; who you are, who you know.

Dunstan also keeps abreast of political controversy, loves to discuss opposing points of view with the protagonists, playing devil's advocate. In religious circles, he is the master spy. Often the two main factions disagree about the balance and overall source and size of revenue due to State and Church and the contradictory need for obeisance to either the King or Pope; there are some who would like to cut loose from Rome, such a faraway centre of religious power, but uproar ensues whenever they raise their heads. In extreme cases of intransigence, individual frustrations end in early retirement in the sunnier climes of Rome, sheltered by the sun of compliance, whether by choice or necessity. Pushing and shoving, the power games continue. At least heads do not roll. The cloth of religion protects a man from that fate. Exile or excommunication is the worst that the King or Pope is likely to prescribe.

Exile is the worst thing I can imagine. Not to be at Stone's side, not to be involved with the workings and progression of this nation. Unbearable.

The North Campaign, June-August 934

There was a lot of shouting that night after the visit to Cuthbert's crypt. A high voice, a low voice. Tents are not sound proofed, even when they have heavy material hangings and summer furs at their door. Athelstan and Edmund, whose voice was in the process of dropping, were having their first manly argument.

Of course Edmund wanted to see the fighting, wanted to stay with the army, or if not, sail with the navy, but Athelstan wanted him safe in Chester-le-Street or behind the solid walls of York far to the south. In the end they both compromised; Edmund would come with the army as far as the Tweed but turn east to occupy the presently empty seat of Bamburgh. Ealdred the northern English king had recently died and a new Saxon lord would be needed in his place to hold the border region; Edmund was persuaded that he could do an intermediate job, flex his royal muscles in a decisive presence in the old, important stronghold. It was agreed that he would be allowed to take part in whatever the army had to meet between Chester-le-Street and Bamburgh and so naturally his prayers were for fighting to commence, for the Scottish king to be bold and to invade southwards.

But he did not. Dunstan and Aethelwold and a significant army and navy presence turned north east to Bamburgh with the sulking prince while the rest of us marched or sailed across the permeable border into the Southern Uplands and Strathclyde. There were skirmishes, as expected, but little resistance from the Scots. Constantine and his son, sure that Athelstan had been bluffing in his threats to remove them from power if they did not submit to him, were in shock we heard and had retreated into the Highlands. Local leaders put up a gallant attempt to slow us down, but by July we were were marching into Edinburgh, having suffered only minor losses. Morale was high; the might of Alba was subdued. The legendary land of the ferocious Picts, Fortriu, lay ahead.

Athelstan was buoyed up by his successful bullying of the Scots; Hywel Dda with the navy joined him in Edinburgh to witness the taking of the city. The hall of the Scots king was deserted, milk had gone sour in jugs left behind on tables, the scramble to leave had been disorderly and panic-stricken. There had not only been a moral victory for Athelstan but a convincing strategic victory. Behind us, the troops acted as troops do who are away from home and happy to loot and destroy; but they were restrained compared to the Vikings. At this rate, they would soon be home again with their families and able to reap their own grain. There would not be much stored in the granaries of the eastern Scots and the oat crop would be poor for the Picts after we had set alight to their fields. Crop burning is a good way of bringing a wayward people to heel, as many kings have found.

We left a few troops in Edinburgh as guards while the main body of the army continued north to make the success of the campaign even more wearisome for Constantine. Athelstan, Leofa and I travelled with the navy from the Forth to Melrose which Athelstan wanted to see as one of the sites associated with Cuthbert and then on to Stonehaven. Here the combined troops, in a pincer movement, squeezed the known presence of Constantine into a small neck of land, unable to escape by sea and unable to flee further inland. With little bloodshed, he capitulated with his son to Athelstan, bedraggled and dispirited, on the shore at Stonehaven. His disarmed troops were allowed to melt back into the hills to lick their wounds, leaderless.

At Stonehaven we might have been satisfied with our victory and the overall success of the campaign, but Athelstan had yet another point to make. With most of his army leaders he embarked, in good weather, on a further mission to show his determination and might to the Norwegians who occupied the northern coastal territories. They had thrown in their lot with Constantine and shown their potential for treachery in combination with Strathclyde.

The ships sailed close to the shore around to the Moray Firth and northwards to the Norse-held town of Wick, where they landed and made a great show of force, slashing and burning crops, forcing the inhabitants to flee inland for survival. Destruction of property was significant, but Athelstan had given orders that there was to be no unnecessary killing of civilians. He wanted a pragmatic submission, not a century of grudge and retribution, a unification if not of the willing, then of the Scots and Pictish leaders who could come to terms to their own advantage, as the Welsh had done. Hywel's part in this transition to annexation of the land of Alba began; while the fleet harried to the north, he began persuasive work on the Scottish king, attempting to bring him into the fold of sub-kingship while escorting him south to Edinburgh.

It did not take long to convince the Norwegian Kingdom of Orkney to submit their mainland holdings along with their lords who had settled here. At Thurso they were forced to bend their knees to Athelstan, sign away land, give treasure. A weakened, dispirited force was left behind to enjoy what remained of the long summer nights of the northern reaches of Britain while we sailed back south to Edinburgh to meet up with Hywel and Constantine, who had been joined by Owain of Strathclyde. He had decided to submit without the need for army pressure. Constantine's hall resounded to the sound of English carousing, the ale of Scotland providing a glad backdrop.

Athelstan, Hywel Dda and other Welsh leaders worked on the recalcitrant Constantine with little success; physical restraint had been necessary for a while. Despite being an older man, he had strength. His hirsute appearance and gait simulated a wild beast. He paced the small room in which he was incarcerated, his own bedroom, like an animal in agony.

Language was a difficulty. Few knew the Gaelic tongue and Constantine was illiterate. He was pagan, so there were no priests or monks who could act for him. I attempted to gather some of the language; my ear is good, but in any case we would have time to deal with him; it was decided that he would come back with us to Wessex accompanied by his son. In the south, we would have leisure to unlock the soul of the North.

Palace of Frome, Vespers, 24 December 934

I return to my place in the scriptorium and the chest as the afternoon of Christmas Eve begins to fade to twilight. The days are so short now, always a surprise, like the great tides of each day on our shores which rise and curl with a sigh. Sunset and sunrise, miracles for each of us to witness each day, perform their splendour during the working day. The long deep-souled night of winter exudes its atmosphere, the twilight blackbird calls an alarm as it flies to the distant grey woodland. Frost begins to reform on thatched eaves. Ice sparkles on the cobbled courtyard. I make a note to myself not to hasten. A sudden wind brings yellow snow clouds across the darkening sky; jackdaws chuck, rising and falling in their dance before suddenly swooping to descend to their roost.

There is a sense of growing urgency about my viewing of the contents of the chest; I am aware that many of its contents could be viewed as subversive by some. I have taken to coming here only after darkness has fallen; a visitor or monk, seeing my entrance, might become intrigued by regular daytime visits. Perhaps one of the visiting bishops or abbots might become interested, which might be more dangerous. I cannot afford to have anyone looking over my shoulder at some of these drawings and at the brooch in particular. I realise I have become protective of it and what its image conveys. I have seen the way some of the hoards recovered from the Vikings, originally taken from pagan lands, have been treated. The gold has only a material value as a glorious metal even though it is fashioned as a symbol of faith. The items and manuscripts of the chest, picked over, would be noted for their outlandish idolatry without thought for any value as former cultural history or beauty before being consigned to the forge or fire, reinforcing the latest strict attitude to goods made by other cultures, other faiths. The Britishness of the contents of the chest would condemn them to a similar fate.

Rome rules the soul of the nation. The bishops and abbots do its will. A time is coming when the grey area of an individual's faith will be tested. Vagueness of spiritual purpose, the state of not quite believing, my state, is being edged out at court. Stone senses this and like me is wary of the growing harder line of belief. Younger bishops are gaining power, their will is strong. The old ones sleep. The young will win.

A single scribe, influenced by the growing tendency towards dogma, could destroy my chest, contents and all. The furnace at the end of the palace yard would do. All those hills. Tut tut. Dangerous places.

Gwladys has had her first interview with Constantine. She says he needs good quality wine to get him going. Only the best will do. She took him sweet figs to butter him up and some pickled walnuts. There must be some way to the old man's heart: through his stomach, perhaps? He is impervious to other means, having been caught out in that way before, but he does seem to enjoy his food. It may be a better use of time to work on his son, Gwladys reports. Pleasantries were discussed and he relaxed a little, but the sense of unfairness and contempt for luxury combined with his sombre personality will make progress difficult. When alone, he is not difficult to prise open, but his cynicism is ingrained, suspicious. Years of gruel in the morning have hardened him.

Intelligence and hardship have turned inwards to self-pity, she thinks. She will try again. Athelstan will not be too pleased with this report. Defeat in battle at the hands of a mad Viking axeman or the will of the Lord may carry him off, may perhaps solve our problem for us, if he is ever allowed to go home.

The chest, open once again, reveals a new item of interest. Turning over the rolls of manuscript, the name Kai on one attracts my eye. It is a brief unfinished hagiography.

Something occurs to me. I try to remember what is being suggested by my memory. Someone once told me that 200 years ago, when this monastery was first established, that there had been a small foundation of the Celtic church in the hamlet close to ours, at the top of the hill to the west and that it had been established before the conquest by a white pilgrimage monk called Kai. I read on, with interest. This is close to home.

SAINT KAI.

Kai, Kay or Cai, came to this place near the river Frome at a crossing of the forest in the sixth century, as one of the many brothers and sisters who brought the Word from the monastic schools of the north shore of Sabrina. He established a small teaching settlement at the crossing of a stream whose spring rose just above his hermitage, which when blessed by him, cured many diseases of local people and their animals.

Caivel, as it was known, Keyford to some, became well known as the resting place of the Saint, who it is said was one of Arthur's twelve knights, a soldier turned priest. Like many others we have heard of during the sixth century in Dumnonia, he chose the white martyrdom of a wandering preacher, reliant on the goodness and assistance of those he met. He gathered a small group of followers, hermits like himself, who acted as an enclave of Christendom in the surrounding forest. Selwood was dominated by the physical presence of wild animals as well as the spiritual forces of Cerne and Gwynn, horned one and horse-riding one. Another holy place he founded was at Lantokay at a place which became known as Street, near the Tor of Glastonbury.

When Aldhelm came to Frome in later years, some groups of monks and nuns may have been in existence in the Selwood area for more than a hundred years. Between Bath in the north and Sherborne in the south, both centres of Celtic Christianity, Aldhelm perhaps built upon a former religious community's meagre effect by establishing his own base nearer to the river, commanding the lower spring and the crossing of the river at the mid-point of entry to Selwood. His missionary community began mass conversion combined with market control. It soon grew in importance, with a palace built nearby for the kings of Wessex to enjoy the hunt.

This short account, written hastily, provides a reasonable explanation of the existence of monastic remains at Keyford, only half a mile from our monastery of St John. They consist of the base of an old preaching cross and some ruins, now cottages, which have religious carvings, at the lane where the road dips to enter the outskirts of the village. Frome lies to the north, beyond the ford of Kai. Which was founded first, I wonder, Keyford or Frome?

The huge oaks of Selwood have provided for the many large and smaller buildings in the small township, well-constructed and stable. The street known as Cheap and a few others which have sprung up in the shadow of the church and springs constitute the settlement and its market called Frome, on the central river of that name, there being three other Frome rivers which straddle the old border between eastern and western Wessex.

Today Frome, a small town, thrives by the visitation of huntsmen, in particular the kings of Wessex and their families and by being at an important toll of the bridge for traffic passing through Selwood. The cursed Danes came by here in Alfred's time and disturbed it, but went to find richer pickings elsewhere. Their destructive activity was quickly rectified by our skilful carpenters.

Aldhelm, great Christian reformer that he was (already the Church in our land was in need of reform; it had become dissolute since the days of Father Bede), was able to further his mission to the pagan Saxons and to keep back the tide of those, Celtic or Saxon, who believed in the old gods of both peoples. Dying at Doulting, he was buried at Malmesbury, where he had been taught by the Irishman Maildubh. First Bishop west of

Selwood, he had established monasteries along the length of Coit Mawr, rooting out what he saw as heathen practices.

Malmesbury. Yet again it features in our history, our Anglo-Saxon past. Today it is a great monastery, with perhaps the best library in the west, rivalling Glastonbury. Will it always be so?

I muse, sitting back in the scriptorium chair, my candle burning low. What was the development of the faith of Christ in our area? What was the nature of the early interface between Celtic Christianity and the Roman Christianity of the Saxons? I know a little about its history, having studied this matter at both Glastonbury and Malmesbury alongside Dunstan.

The monk Gildas, whose records are kept at Malmesbury and the goddess Sulis, whose lament I have found in the chest, were right to despair. Gildas, writing shortly after the departure of the Roman masters of Britannia, considered that the woes of the British were brought on themselves by their wicked ways. Sulis blames no-one in particular, but bewails the trashing of beauty and faith. Priest and goddess, both were losing the battle against destruction and secularism, against wanton vandalism and treasure seeking.

Superstition had taken hold in the hiatus left behind by the inevitable ending of the authority of the Celtic Church and the Roman state. Roman pagan gods still prevailed in places, particularly in the countryside. Neither provided a satisfactory way forward as an official religion for the fledgling state of Wessex as it moved westwards. Well-ordered religious ritual and belief had fled. In its place came the gods and myths of a people from a place far away, the Saxons, followed recently by a similar flood of pagan Vikings with plunder as their main goal. There were many changes between indifference, localised idolatry, full Celtic or

Roman Christian imposition by conversion and then again back to Viking. There were pockets of localised survival of idolatrous religious imagination in a hybrid of cultures, a hybrid of beliefs. Belief in Something seems always to have been important, in times of ever changing values and nationhoods. When backed by force or law the need for belief may make slaves of some, kings of others.

The pagan Saxons brought their own cultural myths to the mix on the ever-extending borders of Wessex. Bloody celebrations of Woden, ghosts and ghouls had been substituted for the feast days of martyrs and saints of the early Celtic Church. They made it up as they went along. There were no synods of discussion; just whatever took their fancy. Order had been abandoned by the British. They returned to their cultural idols, Cerne or Herne, Gwynn, Rhiannon, Epona. Multi-faceted, a god or goddess for all requirements. Gods must be invoked for safety. Who knew how long each man's days might be, when their possessions and homesteads might be burned or snatched from them, their wives and daughters taken as slaves?

Alfred bemoaned the lack of structure in the Church and religious life in general in his time. Because of the Viking problem as well as pagan Saxon conservatism, few had been able to maintain Roman Christian traditions and faith. There had been a relapse into the old beliefs, which persist to this day. God had not kept the people safe; perhaps the old gods would. They were certainly more fun. The monks of Glastonbury held the core of Christian magic in the west and led by Irish monks and teachers they endeavoured to use whatever "spells" they had in their armoury. Today we use the word "prayer".

The Celtic monks bravely held on. Fearing the worst for the souls of the people of Dumnonia the scholars and monks of southern Welsh monasteries encouraged a new wave of missionary work to move across Sabrina's Severn River into the heartlands of its eastern area. Individuals fired with the zeal of white martyrdom came this way. They left their familiar communities and travelled far away for ever, seeking new hermitages around and beyond the magical gleaming Tor. The hermits, trying to spread the Word by their exemplary lives of solitary communion in spots chosen for their natural beauty, influenced many. Sometimes loosely attached to small monastic communities which grew up near them, brave souls attempted to bring about a wholesale conversion of Dumnonian recidivists.

Travelling out from such centres as Llanilltyd Fawr, the monastic school founded by St Illtyd in the sixth century, they managed to rejuvenate Celtic Christian life throughout Dumnonia. More isolated areas retained their distinctive and determined new paganism, which bothers us still today. Once having taken root in the imagination, the old gods die hard. Even Stone and some of his followers shout out the names of ancient Saxon gods as they go in for the hunting kill. Dunstan reminds him regularly that this is giving a mixed message to the younger men. He always begs his pardon, says he will mind his language in future. When emotions run high, the old devil will out. He confesses this fault in his devotion at the mass at the end of each day of hunting.

St Dubricius in Porlock, St Decuman in Watchet, St Gildas in Glastonbury, St Kai in Street and Frome and many others scattered around the east of Dumnonia came to rejuvenate the Christian spiritual will of the doomed Welsh. The Saxon advance was not certain but inevitable pressure by settlers moving along the river valleys and where forests were thinning called for renewed psychic strengthening. These were Celtic Christians trying to hold back the tide of pagan Saxons, attempting with their own magic to preserve the land from the foe. Perhaps it was hoped that strengthening the religious wall of Selwood with an opposing force would keep out some of those who might fear to tread inside Selwood forest.

Alfred is to be thanked for bringing a moral Christian revival to Wessex and for learning and literacy in our day. He began a process of discipline and justice which continues to our day.

Chester-le-Street, Northumbria, 28 August 934

The army was happy, the navy was happy. They had had their rewards in terms of loot and land and an adventure, well planned, well executed, successful. The long arm of the English nation had reached into the northern fastnesses and returned triumphant. Athelstan could relax. He had shown his mettle yet again as a king, but there was a considerable cost to be met in payment, despite the treasure and land holdings taken. The ships which had been built, the fyrd taken away from its harvest, the armoury and general travelling costs as well as expenses of the Church in support with prayer, ritual and general man-management meant that serious account and treasury adjustments would have to be undertaken. There were large numbers of religious employees in tow, backing up the psychic needs of all, performing at each major centre where we camped or took advantage of monastic hospitality. Athelstan was not mean, but he was frugal. It hurt to waste. The tally of the campaign would be minutely examined. Balance and fairness would be achieved.

There was one more act needing to be done. During his journey to the very tip of his empire of Britain Athelstan had conceived a plan which involved giving grateful thanks for his success to Cuthbert, who was now a living being in his mind. He would not rest, he said, until he had revisited him. He wanted to offer his prayers to the man he considered had granted him his family's wish.

The pattern had been established. We reunited with Edmund who had to be told in detail about the adventures in Scotland, but soon the trinity plus Aethelwold met with Stone to discuss returning to view Cuthbert. A baggage cart stuffed with hangings and embroideries, intended to impress the kings of the north during conferences, had been left in Chester-le-Street to make travel faster. Many of the reliquaries and other valuable but cumbersome items had been deposited with Edmund in Bamburgh for safe keeping; after the first visitation to Cuthbert the religious items had been deemed less necessary for the campaign. Every part of the baggage train was now in position to make the journey back south via York. All Athelstan's thoughts were on securing the unity he had gained. That entailed not only thanking Cuthbert, but consulting Oswald. Saint and King, Church and State, the successful combination for the future needed to be actioned by suitable prayer.

The army had camped, resting and rejoicing, on the outskirts of the town. There were no secure buildings which suited Stone's present requirement for absolute privacy to discuss matters, so we accompanied him, together with Aethelwold and Edmund, riding for a few miles into the dale country, reputed to be fine landscape, while the long journey home was prepared. There would be no lengthy stays on the way south; the forging of the new enlarged nation needed debating and recording. Heavy court work would begin in earnest once we were safely back in Wessex. After an hour's riding we stopped beside a fast-flowing river, admired the sights and sat down on the valley side while the horses grazed below.

'Leofa, all of you, you noted, didn't you, that we were allowed a short time alone with Cuthbert during the viewing ritual?'

We agreed. I was surprised that Stone had been aware of this, he seemed in such a reverie in the crypt.

'Did any of you see Oswald's head?'

No, we hadn't seen it. Only Stone and Edmund had been allowed to touch Cuthbert, to lean into the coffin. That was the deal with the Abbot. Edmund had had eyes only for Cuthbert. He didn't like to touch the body, he said. Stone remarked that he may have another chance to do so.

'What do you think it would take to achieve a second viewing of the open coffin?' Stone wanted a new formula. 'I want to thank St Cuthbert for his support for our mission, of course, but also to have closer contact with St Oswald. He holds the key to maintaining unity between north and south. Dunstan?'

Dunstan thought. These were holy relics belonging to the Church, but he served an anointed king. There would be compromise. We could guess what Stone really wanted but could not say.

'Perhaps another cup of coin, as before? Or more of the excellently embroidered material we have brought with us?' Dunstan took charge.

'Try for another visit tomorrow with what you have suggested, Dunstan. The Abbot may negotiate, I'm sure he will, but begin there.'

He did, on our return later that day. He called us together in the evening. We rode back to the valley in the evening light to hear his report.

'The Abbot is willing to let us have sight of the coffin tomorrow and will take what we have agreed to offer, but says he must have more. He demands 1,500 shillings.'

We were astounded. 1,500 shillings! About half the cost of the campaign, far more than we carried with us. This was a coffin opening too far. Aethelwold recovered himself first.

'It is impossible, my Lord,' (he had not been admitted to the familiar Stone name use at this point), 'these northern sympathisers wish to undo your power. They cannot win in war but they wish to manipulate the peace.'

'Dunstan, what do they say they will offer in return for this huge sum? There must be something new in the equation. Surely they would not have let something slip with our previous visit?'

Leofa and I watched Stone and Dunstan hammer out a way forward. Edmund sat on the edge of a waterfall, listening to us but also watching the water. Aethelwold joined him. It was thought that the Abbot might be induced to offer a longer time in private with the coffin than formerly, if the price was right. He suggested a sum of 1,200 shillings might be offered as a counter.

'Do you think he will agree, Dunstan?'

'Yes, Stone, I think so. The Abbot is a practical man. He knows the value of the open coffin but can also estimate the potential cost to you. There is a balance somewhere.'

'But how can we pay so vast a sum? Leofa, Nonna, what do you suggest?'

Leofa came up with the best idea after some thought.

'Has the army gained a great deal in cash during the Scottish raiding, Stone? Is there much lining the pockets of the warlords? Could they be induced to part with some of it before our journey south?'

'To the tune of more than 1,000 shillings? I doubt it, but there could be a repayment package set up to return their losses in Wessex. It might keep them on board for some time after we return. We shall need most of the army landowners to stay at court while we tie up this business and catch up with other work of the summer.' Stone thought aloud. Edmund turned away from the water.

'Stone, didn't you say you wanted to have close communication with King Oswald and how important he is to our family, never mind the nation?'

Edmund saw Athelstan's requirement, which was now his as well. The King and his heir were as one. This must be done, at whatever cost.

We returned to Chester-le-Street. Dunstan hastened to an interview with the Abbot, who stuck at 1,200 shillings for a full viewing with five minutes of private prayer time. He returned to us as we finished attending the office of Compline and were filing out to supper.

'Complete withdrawal of the monks from the crypt?' Leofa questioned Dunstan.

'Yes, five minutes alone is guaranteed. That was worth the 200 extra shillings. Without them, he may not have been willing.'

'Good, you have done well, thank you, Dunstan.' Stone was pleased.

The coffin visit was arranged for the next day. Athelstan broke the news of a levy to the army commanders that night. They were so drunk and joyful that there was little resistance. It would hurt, but they could expect greater reward and a pay back from the coffers of Wessex, now soon to be overflowing with tribute from the North as well as Wales. Many did not share the King's enthusiasm for crypts and relics, but they acknowledged the Church and its saints' part in the successful campaign. It was a temporary loan which they could bear. They turned out their purses and by midnight the sum of 1,200 shillings had been achieved.

In the morning, with a less grand entrance than formerly, we were received again by the Abbot and a small group of monks, prepared again with their ritual coffin opening equipment. Dunstan handed over a chest full of coin, plus another cup-full from the King's private purse, to an attendant. The Abbot led the way down into the crypt as before. Intoning was not required this time, the ritual was basic. Time was short; the troops were anxious to return south to their families. Leofa and Aethelwold carried more vestments and some embroidered yellow curtain material which could have passed for a beautiful altar cloth.

We took our places at the prayer stools as before, Edmund accompanying Aethelwold at the head of the coffin. We began our prayers as again the lid was lifted. Incense was used copiously as before and candlelight fused with it to create the same harmony of drama, but the motivation of the viewers as supplicants and pilgrims was different. We were not impressionable pilgrims this time.

What were we? Something had changed in our attitude or that of the Cuthbert monks. It was a transaction this time, less magical, more pragmatic. We were all playing a part.

Silently, but noticeably, the monks withdrew from the sides of the coffin. We heard whispers as they ascended the steps of the crypt, closed the door behind us. We were alone with Cuthbert, able to thank him in our own way and to consult the head of the dead King of Northumbria. We had five minutes to do so, the observance of a short, small candle length. That was Edmund's part of the heist.

That was when I realised what we were. Thieves.

Palace of Frome, before Compline, 24 December 934

Leofa and Edmund are the main attractions of tonight's entertainment. The first part of Edmund's horror story is to be told, followed by Leofa's saga of Edington.

Leofa and I have spent some time reviewing the sound of the saga of Alfred's battle with the Danes, practising it together. I was going to be the chief relater of the tale, but a word from Athelstan has made me doubt my future at court as a bard; he says he prefers his secretaries to remain in the shadows. Leofa is risking his anger. He says that the old oral skills must not be lost in this great push towards the written word and there are few who can better his mastery of that, besides which, Leofa loves to perform.

To start proceedings, the scops enact a mumming play. They will have full reign on Christmas Day, when the rest of the court looks to the professional players to provide all the entertainment.

Athelstan comes into the hall looking weary; he has again been trying to persuade the Scottish king to capitulate. Constantine is increasingly frustrated at his absence from his own winter court. He is becoming more distant and unhelpful as the days progress. He trails into the hall with his son, a gloomy picture.

The Welsh kings by contrast appear cheerful. Hywel Dda has even offered to sing alongside Gwladys' harp playing. He and Athelstan get on well, have a love of high culture in common and an ongoing competitive relationship with the board game of gwydbwyl. The current score is even, I am told. Edmund, too, seems to flourish in his company and is learning Welsh as well as other foreign languages.

Constantine asks for drink and food. These are almost the only matters he will discuss. Much of the talk in the court today has been about the possibility of combined forces of sub-kings holding out against the Viking threat which centres on York and Dublin. Constantine, it is to hoped, will act as a bulwark against them. He, of course, will require assistance in the matter and demand to know what reward he will get for such activity, which may after all be injurious to his forces and expensive too. Constantine will not parley, but his ministers, skilled debaters, hold informal talks with ours. Another task for us clerks. Another chance to spy.

So the talks will continue over the full period of Christmas, thrashing out the present and the future. Constantine is aware that he is in no position to make proposals which favour his view of the world, a separate, northern, Celtic world. The Saxon Empire is growing and is unstoppable. The main body of clerks is engaged in writing deeds and agreements of the previous day, trying to keep up with interpreters' interpretations and trying to stay abreast of the chief negotiator, Athelstan, in meeting his needs and wishes. At all times, the assistance of God at all levels of discussion and the presence of the Saints in their reliquaries is called upon. Genuflection is becoming more extreme, more commonly seen. A mere show of hands used to be what was required for decision making at the witans of old; now the court must endure longer sessions, lasting several days each time, as the labour of the written word is involved. No wonder so many hate the onset of writing, but its slow remorselessness is here to stay.

Edmund begins a short introduction to his horror tale, which he says will continue on the following evening. He wishes to whet our appetites, he says. We cheer. Edmund bows and retreats. I have a feeling we will hear this tale many times in the future. A story written by an Aetheling, especially one as popular as Edmund, is sure to be a hit. The chief character of the story is a hero called Beowulf. He has been reading the Viking sagas again.

A low voice, central in the hall, gets into its stride. Leofa has begun an introduction to his tale, the last performance this evening of the scops. The older members of the audience smile.

They can drift off to sleep at the sound of an expert speaker, not have to pretend to pay attention to a stilted reading by an inexperienced youth, stumbling over his or more likely someone else's written words. They have smiled at Edmund's introduction to his story, pretended to look forward to more tomorrow, done their duty to the heir apparent. They reserve their overt judgement; it may turn out to be one of the best they have heard, or the worst. How can such a young man have written such stuff? Aethelwold is smug. We of the trinity know whose fault this is.

Official interpreters have taken their places by the foreigners. Most have heard this tale of the Battle of Edington before, even those from overseas. They have heard it in many languages and many times. They have heard it at every Christmas feast hosted by the King and his father. They know the tale will be cautionary and one which will provoke the unease of Scandinavians present, unless they are friendly in purpose and self-deprecating. They will be reminded of the defeat and humiliation of Viking might, of the success of the Alfredian dynasty. For dignitaries from other English kingdoms, now subject to the court of Wessex, the story will be a warning. Stay in line.

The hearers even join in occasionally when invited to do so, by the bard, "Tha ofereode, thisses swa maeg", that went by, this may too, they sing, when the bard waves them on. A slight disturbance to the Scandinavian psyche, a reminder of the recent past and their part in the savagery of their heathen assault will do no harm; we have, for the present, the mastery of them. Luckily, they have humour and can usually see the funny side of things. The loudest laughs are usually Scandinavian. I am very fond of my friend Leofa, who has many of their traits, as a man born of Irish and Scandinavian parentage. He knows how to laugh at himself.

There's a throat clearing. The title has been announced, a harp has been twanged, a bell rung to call order. The hall listens or peacefully slumbers. Leofa starts his tale. It is so well known to most of the hearers that they are tempted to talk to each other, but they are aware that this is the King's moment, the story of his dynasty, of Alfred's defeat of the Vikings. This is the beginning of the story of why we are here in this palace hall today, celebrating. Edmund and Eadred hear it for only the fifth time. The blood, the battle, the feasting of birds, Ecgbrihtesstan the meeting place of the warriors. Wessex triumphs and will again.

An hour passes. At the end, marked by a long harp chord, the voice of the bard pauses. There is silence in the hall, broken by a snoring sound from one dark corner.

The light within my mind of the passage about the battle starts to fade. Leofa has come to the end of his tale. I awake from the trance-like state of the reciting scop which I shared with Leofa as he spoke. His voice was mesmerising, with rich tones of drama. He should be an international diplomat. I can see the ladies like his voice. They are sitting upright, even Eadgifu.

Athelstan wakes from his dynastic dream. This was his grandfather who had been eulogised. Would he be, too? He rises from his chair, walks to Leofa, who still sits, exhausted from the recall of so much. Stone puts a hand on his shoulder and whispers his thanks.

The King turns to the still silent audience. What response does one give to a performance of history and saga which many present know to be real, as they see it pass into heroic status, the land of Wessex and its stories, a tale which many of their immediate forebears witnessed in its making? The glory of taking part in a vital and defining nation-building moment in the history of Wessex is a rare and heady delight, a force for binding individuals, a legacy which Alfred's son and now his grandson can build on to make a land of culture and wisdom.

And to prove it, in less than fifty years, Europe is represented here this Christmas-tide. This new nation hosts guests of Breton, Norwegian, Irish, Welsh, Gaelic and other representatives of the continent, ecclesiastic as well as secular. All the major languages of Europe are being spoken around the pillars in this hall, these hunting stables, this church, this monastery, this palace and centre of culture at Frome in the forest of Selwood. I am proud to be a part of this, pleased to have been born here.

Candles burn low. The end-of-evening musicians take up their places in the dying firelight, begin to play their instruments, to sing their light yodelling melodies, lightening the mood of the hall once more. A fine high voice leads the song, the chorus follows.

Compline in the church will be being said now with prayers for the recently dead, prayers for the King and his heir. Keep them safe, secure from their enemies. Safe from poisoning, treason, blinding. Give the King time, we pray. Time to enjoy his success. And to save his soul.

Feeling as one who has been listening to a voice from the past, drunk with words like a Viking after too many mushrooms, I eventually awake from the dream of the story of the battle of fifty years ago and return to present times. I look about the palace hall.

There is this cultured court, its faces turned away from mine, relaxing as more food is being brought around on trays together with fresh goblets of wine and ale. Soothed by low chatter, pleased to relax their minds from the intensity of listening to the flashing pictures brought by the words of Leofa, their eyes wander over the pleasant form of a girl who dances to the light sounds of music and song.

My eyes take in a group of young men who stand at one end of the hall. There is Dunstan and his young friend Aethelwold, both holding filled horns. In front of them a dancer sways to music. The black girl, Gwladys, gyrates, fascinating the watchers. Stone is evidently delighted with the fresh element of exotic movement, of 'primitive' dance movement. He is for all things new and multicultural.

Dunstan wears his practised look of indifference. I can see that Aethelwold's lip is curled.

I retire quietly to the scriptorium. The hour for Vigils is approaching, the night before the great day of the birth of our Lord. Later this evening Dunstan will reveal his artistic works to the court and make his name or fade to obscurity. There were some who would like to see the latter; he is too cocksure in his self-belief, too certain that order matters and that Hell is the retribution for non-believers.

For some of the audience in the hall belief in the afterlife and the existence of Hell is less important than a humane awareness of diplomacy and management. Family life and the pressing necessity of education of the younger family members are their concerns. There is already less time for hunting, more requirement for the occupations involving a seat and table, the pen and vellum. And why is virginity and chastity being sold by the priests as the best form of human existence? If they are to get ahead, it is clear that more time will have to be devoted by the young to these new requirements of the court. Then there are the wives. They will want some of this, too, for their daughters as well as themselves. More bother. There are not enough hours in the day to be law makers as well as soldiers. But we can't leave everything to the priests and monks. Trouble lies ahead, they think. There are new challenges for everyone as arrangements for the State itself become more complicated. A book learning regime is coming. A man's spoken word is not enough any more. A duel is no longer the way to settle a matter, or a feud.

In the church there will be a night full of the sacred light of candles, whatever the cost. I can hear across the courtyard the sound of refrains, Christmas songs, songs of greenwood and snow, of stags and hunting, solo and chorus, the old favourites, notes rising and falling. In the church, the candles will be being lit. Dunstan will be removing his dust sheets, ready for the spectacle of midnight mass.

Leofa, having come round from his trance as bard, told me later that the jester performed after the songs came to an end, lewd and silly, throwing doubt on the whole aspect of the fashionable court, on even the magnates from afar in their continental finery, bedecked with gold, sparing no-one his witty barb. His job was to wake the audience up, to shake it into readiness for the procession to mass. The jester is the oldest man among us. He has seen the ramshackle birth of the town, the maze of narrow streets and wooden shops. He has watched the building and growth of the tanning and weaving yards, market corrals for sheep and cattle from the Mendips and Witham Vale, hunting equipment manufacturers, sheds for the making of pilgrim badges as well as the working scriptorium and other buildings of the monastery. This is itself an industrial site with much wood and metalwork being undertaken, some for the church which seems to be extending each time I visit as well as the monastery hospital and outhouses for guests. Woollen cloth is woven by many and is sent for sale beyond the bounds of Wessex. Mills grind corn and beat cloth. The fulling trade is renowned. There are many jobs for freemen and slaves and more to come in future years of peace as promised by the King. Trade is encouraged and controlled by the men at the gates and on the bridge. There is talk of having a mint, a sure mark of a town's achievement. The market is lively. This is an important place. Frome is doing well.

Leofa told me that the old jester called the self-belief of each listener into question, presented a mirror of mockery, a vehicle for self laughter, brought us closer together as we laughed at each other and ourselves. He is a skilled, ancient performer who served the old king. He was even present at the court of Alfred as a young man, witness to the lowest ebb of England and its highest. We have come far.

After the jokes, a short time is allowed to sober up. The hall doors open to the night. Men and boys must piss. The liquid of past hours, stored during the listening and drinking, pours out into the drain, down into the spring water and away to the river. Midnight mass will begin soon. The procession has started to form. Priests claim the interest of the revellers. It's their turn to add to the drama of the night has come.

I gaze at the oaken chest. Tonight I will not view its contents, there is too much action in the present to be able to take on yet more of history and particularly the past of the sad vanquished. I wonder at Hywel Dda's ability, despite his inevitable awareness of the fate of his people, to overcome what must be a considerable grudge against the English to attend this court. But then, needs must. And perhaps he feels that much is to be gained from a royal partnership. Certainly Stone likes him and keeps him close by his side. He is a guarantor of Welsh aid at these times of sensitive diplomacy, when Strathclyde, Wales and Alba must be persuaded to submit fully to Aethelstan's overlordship. Hywel is intelligent, a skilful, smiling diplomat. We rarely catch him out.

I look out of the window. The first snow of the dark half of the year is falling. The procession will have to wrap up warmly for its slow ritual walk to the church. The east wind will be grabbing their hems and sending them flying up, chilling the under-parts. It may help to wake them up, at any rate.

A dog in one of the outhouses sings at the sound of the hall doors opening. The bishops, abbots and priests are shuffling into hierarchical order, their heavy staffs of office swinging about like ecclesiastical armaments, the cords of embellished standards flapping. A wolfhound inside the hall replies to the dog outside. They start off other dogs along the valley, shop and farm mongrels joining in with howls and barking. Light pours out of the hall as the inebriated nobles and their families manoeuvre into their positions, conscious, like the churchmen, of their order of entitlement. The first will be first. Elbows are out. I watch the developing scene, the making of a procession of power. I chuckle at the delicate shoving and shifting. It is like the tense moments before a much-prized race of children across the fields in summer. But this is serious; knives have been known to be used when honour is impugned in the all-important hierarchy of a procession. Lifetime grudges held by families are common. The door guards, standing watchfully, view the antics; they too have seen it all before.

The walking order required by status is eventually completed. Old high-born statesmen have been given their staffs. All are standing, waiting to set off in the cold air. The snow billows about. *Get on with it* is what the faces say. Small children are sheltering under their mother's cloaks like ducklings in down.

The secular lords are torn between the need to be pious and practicality. Some shrug at the idea of the mid-winter festival; the old insist it is not like it used to be; they have seen too many. Smiling delight at winter magic and colour, even the food, becomes more difficult with age. For most it is a time to indulge, to relax, to use up some of the store of goods laid by in the harvest, to tell tales by firelight, to restore the sense of belonging to the present, to the past. To plan for the future, for crops, for war. For intrigue.

For the servants and slaves it means hard work, but a time also to feast from the leftovers and for their children to add to a coveted collection of the lost, dropped and borrowed items of the rich. The midden is a good place alongside pigs to scavenge for discarded items of worth. The odd piece of material discarded from the ladies' sewing room, the broken leather strapping of a horse mount sometimes with the metal mount attached; small items of jewellery shed by the drunken unwary. In the pissing place, there are often items of worth to be found, even coins.

Christmas has more than an ecclesiastical requirement of the psyche; it is a time when the families meet on the same day throughout the Christian world, with the same feeling of a different awareness, of belonging to a greater family, of a feeling that they can be better or be good for a day, that they are a part of a mysterious cycle of life. The special nature of the day heightens their consciousness of the role which they or their children may play in shaping the betterment of the world. The time exaggerates the feeling of the existence of magic powers and otherworldliness, of forces which if only they can be perceived and harnessed will bring things into order. But the priests are here to help to do that. Tomorrow, when the wine and cider and ale have their revenge, this will seem impossible. But tonight, the potency is uniquely felt and we are at its mercy: the ritual staging of the midnight mass, the ending of Advent, the coming of the Lord. More than the Church, but staged by the Church. There will be a bright future. The year turns. The circle begins again on the magical night of Christmas Eve.

The line of people still waits, holding candles. Snow falls on them. A trumpet blows, a drum rolls. They shuffle and sway, obeying the archbishop who now moves forward slowly, taking his time. A mighty metal cross is hoisted high in front of him, leading the column of God. The other archbishop and brethren move forward, their copes swinging side to side. They move with the walking motion of the older, mature man. The abbots and priests behind them begin the plainsong chant. The ritual song and the snow combine in sound and visual beauty. The court moves forward in small half steps. Incense is flung into the depths of the dark by a swinging metal thurible, creating clouds of odour in the air. It falls across the faces behind. A man coughs. The performance of the procession, its ritual drama, forces thought. Inside the scriptorium, watching, I muse.

What choice do any of us have? Our place is given to us by fate or God. Are they the same? What is this mysterious otherness which we can perceive here, on this special night? Is it caused by the wine, the hour, the togetherness? Is it more than that? It is our destiny to grasp and hold the possible which is given to us at birth. Only a king can be raised higher than a mortal man, anointed by God to rule. The holy can be sainted and rise to great heights, but not in life. They are mortal like the rest of us. But perhaps an anointed king is not. Perhaps he has God within him in his thoughts. What of Cuthbert and Oswald, did they have God within? And what of St Radegund, symbol of the Holy Mother, whose reliquary is tonight presented at the door of the church?

The procession passes through the snow to the open west door of the church. The splendid gilded reliquary is at its entrance, festooned with greenery, displayed on a carved oak stand. It is of wood inlaid with silver, copper and gold, carved exquisitely, presented in a surround of fine embroideries. Eadgifu has overseen the seamstresses of the family, bending for much of the year over her work, supervising her daughters, devising, drawing up colours, ordering threads, considering longevity.

This is for ever, her gift to the reliquary. She doesn't know that it is presently adorning a northern Saxon saint's head, the seat of his learning, unless Dunstan has told her. He probably has; she wheedles most things out of him. Radegund has gone somewhere else on a temporary basis. Who knows who or what the reliquaries contain? Does it matter? It does to Athelstan, who knows whose head he would rather revere on this, his special night.

Whether she knows the secret or not, Eadgifu makes much of the female saint. She owns small portions of her parts herself. Radegund is an exemplar of piety and courage for noble women. She stood up for herself against tyrants. She encourages emancipation for women. She inspires nuns, comforts young wives. She is Eadgifu's advisor when she prays. She sustains the Queen in her many duites. Besides her embroidery Eadgifu's role as host has provided safe conduct for the guests, ensuring a smoothly run court for Christmas. She has ensured the availability of gear for hunting, gear for dancing, gear for lawmaking, provided a hook and a cupboard for everything. Eadgifu runs the stock list of clothing and linen for the extended royal family at the palace of Frome, attends to the production here of embroidered edging for tunics and cloaks, the needlework and lace which marks out the nobleman, the wimple of the nun. The woollen cloth that she chooses to be made into royal cloaks is second to none. She inspects workshops, spinners, mills, rewards makers and gives good value for the work of manufacture. She is a quiet revolutionary, a gifted woman, clever and careful. This is her night, too. She kisses the reliquary as she enters the church.

The jewel-spangled crowd files past Radegund, touching, kissing. *Radegund*, they mutter, *we receive the mark of the holy one. We touch the piety, the pure virginity, the reminder of the Mother of God and draw it into us.* The reliquary will be a little more glossy after tonight. The nobles will get more than they think from this virginal saint, a double dose of saints, like Cuthbert's coffin.

The procession moves into the church, the doors are closed for the service to begin. I hear a collected cry of amazement, before the voice of the archbishop welcomes the congregation. Dunstan's painted Doom has been seen.

I turn back to the chest. I cannot resist; I must view one more manuscript before I, too, succumb to the otherwordly fever of the day of Christ's birth, the mass hysteria.

This last manuscript, tucked under a thick layer of wadding

which appears to have been protecting something else falls into my hand. A small, folded item this time, barely legible, the ink cheap and faded, the style antique. There is no illustration, only a brief description of something or someone. It begins *Ego, I am*, and then lists names, perhaps names of places, written horizontally across the page. One or two names have been scored through emphatically in recent times with a bolder, stronger hand, as though in anger. Someone has been here before me and very recently.

I move the candle closer, attempting to decipher the letters which cross the folds in many places. The vellum, dirtied by years and sheep fat, smells rank.

Many of the names, about a dozen that I can read, have *hern* or *erne* as part of their endings. I recognise some, including Crewkerne, a place where one of the students I knew at Glastonbury was born. I read on, then dream.

My mother whispers in my ear, I am six years old and sitting on her knee. She is telling me about Herne, the shortened form of the name of the old pagan god of fertility, Cernunnos, who ruled the land before the Romans took us to the One God. Herne became an idol once again to the country people when British Christians retreated from the Saxon arrival. They needed a spiritual hero. The priests dwindled in number, the lawlessness and lack of education in the disturbed land allowed the old gods to grow in popularity. Cernunnos is still here in the countryside and deep in the forest. His horned presence enters my dreams. Dunstan says he is the devil. But Dunstan calls everything a devil when he does not agree with it or them. The trees, the hills, they are Herne's, Cerne's, abode.

Remember me, says the manuscript at the end.

I have much to remember, too much. The chest has become my burden.

I ponder the words scored through. Who has done this? Why? I lean back in my chair. A sigh from my lips stirs the candle flame. The horned god is almost forgotten except by small children being frightened into obedience by their mothers. He belongs to the oral tradition of West Wales and to the time before the Saxons, or even the Romans. He is no longer a threat. Or is he? Evidently someone thinks he is, and I think I can guess who.

I replace the last manuscript in the bottom of the chest.

Why I missed it before, I do not know. Perhaps the wadding around some of the items and the general darkness and gloom at this corner of the scriptorium concealed it. My hand, scrabbling the floor of the chest, feels a rough hard point attached to a branch. It is something organic. Animal heads, preserved from the most memorable hunts, dotted around the hall walls, have the same feel: stag horn, undying mementoes of the domination of a wild creature. They never dissolve into dust. There are antlers from many generations of kings on the palace walls, outside as well as inside, some more magnificent than others. If more people hunted, says Athelstan often, there would be less war. The skills of the hunt are many and if carefully drilled, the best and most skilled at hunting can gain fame through showing trophies of their skills in as lasting a way as any leader in battle. Armour, weaponry and stuffed heads, the symbols of leadership and command. Competition for the position of best hunter is fierce. There are magnificent prizes awarded each Christmas by Athelstan personally.

But this is not a hunt trophy. I pull out and hold up the antler, accompanied by another, to the light. They are attached to a piece of leather, less well preserved and stiff to the feel. Some Glastonbury mould is starting to grow on it. The antlers are threaded onto the leather to make a helmet. Men wore this on their heads, or at least one man, or woman, did.

As soon as I realise the significance of this anthropomorphism, I cast the man/deer mask back into the bottom of the chest, regardless of any damage. I am in shock. This is the most magic laden thing of all; it reeks of unholy ritual, drug taking, mind-blowing earth ritual, dance and drama of the deep past. It evokes a time when there were no farmers tied to the land, a time when the earth's resources were plentiful after the son of man first walked here, before the barrows and barrow-wights came into being, when oaks, bears, huge wild cattle and giants ruled the world. The antlered man dancer, the magician, the dark lord of fertility ruled the mind of man. Dunstan's ultimate devil is here. He is right to consider the backward, superstitious and multi-deity view point of rural folk wedded to the cycle of the agrarian year as anti-Christian. He wishes to bring enlightenment. Like the King, he wishes for peace. The peoples of the land of Wessex and elsewhere must be taught to move forward into the light of Christ, to leave their old imaginings behind. He and Aethelwold have much in common.

There is much of colour and imagination in the Church as she is becoming. Relics have taken the place of animal and multi-god worship; the magicians and wizards have become monks, priests and saints. Miracles happen on an almost daily basis where there is strong belief. The old superstitions, Dunstan says and says often, must give way to the newest forms of Roman Christianity. All devils, past, present and future, the shades, must be cast out. Rituals to encourage illiterate rural folk should be employed. Shouting out the Devil is one thing they are beginning to enjoy at old religious sites. Clipping churches, surrounding them and shouting is one way to harness the energies and minds of young and old. A roar of protection in an otherwise silent world. Silent, except for the stag call, the howling of wolves, the cry of the raven. The Dumnonians love to shout.

Where the people cannot be induced to turn away from him, whatever form he may take, whether black dogs, horned men or white women, they can be persuaded to fear his abode of Hell. Dunstan has made it his mission to speed up the process of transition to the celebration of the defeat of the forces of evil and the old gods of the past. His Doom painting will impress many, frighten some. As impressive as the shriek of the Welsh? We shall see.

He is dedicated to ridding the land of some of the dance and song festivals which the small landowners had begun to revive in recent years: the horn wearing, waving, stamping and stomping rites of spring and fire feasts of the countryside where the Danes have done their worst, ravaged religious houses, destroyed the Faith, left a void for the Devil to fill.

The shouting, Dunstan will allow for now; the other symbols, good and bad, the colour, the Church can harness. The people will have celebration, but they will also have the stick. They will have the freedom to choose: Heaven, or Hell.

And here he is, the man-devil, in the bottom of the chest. I have become possessive about the oaken chest in only a few days of this Christmas festival. I feel it holds many things of value to remind us of former ways of thinking, to tell us that we can be brainwashed by religious imagery, that order is required, order of the imaginative world. The wheel of the year of old times now travels in a straight line, to Christ. For some of the Benedictine Reformers, perhaps, a straight line to Canterbury and on to Rome.

I consider. We are at a religious crossroads. Pagan virility does not sit well with the encouragement of virginity. Saintliness is to be sought, but it is not for everyone. Must joyful ceremonies and celebrations, enjoyed through thousands of years, be lost? Can this sense of belonging and connection to Nature be suppressed? Should it? Then there is the matter of superstition, which some say holds up progress in the arts as well as learning. Antlers were used at Lamyatt, antlers occur at Cold Kitchen. A vigorous giant straddles the hill at Cerne. There are signs of the horned Devil everywhere, soon to be discarded, soon to be shouted out. The old gods will become myths, forgotten. Living with devils, tolerating them, will be punished.

The way is clear. In this year of our Lord, this Christmas of 934, we know better; this is a new world, the world of educated men and women, able to see the light ahead. A new Britain, a new Europe, harmonising the saints and their enlightened ways, the ways of the great Father in Rome, to whom we all look. For the king with whom he shares the power of the land, look no further than the greatest: Athelstan.

But something still rankles within me. Something is not right. The past expresses itself through its beliefs. Are we right to destroy this history or misuse it?

Soon the chest will move on to the haligdom of Malmesbury. Perhaps a monk in the future will find and remark on its contents in a time when there is less determination to discard and destroy the history of the pagan forbears of Wessex and England. I have noted its contents, felt its magical presence. My children, if I have any, will be Saxon, will know no British speech. The legends of the British will die away. When the chest is opened again and its contents examined, there will perhaps no longer be prejudice. In future times there will be little understanding of the existence of any Dumnonian ancestry or West Welsh language to guide or soften an investigation, to evoke sympathy. The British of Lloegr are becoming full members of the English people. One hundred years from now it will be easier to regard the pagan past as valid history, no longer a threat. What seems now to be challenging will then be seen as quaint. There is nothing here which should worry Stone. Dunstan and Aethelwold will take care of this aspect of his reign. I write a short note to add to the chest contents. I take out the small box with the horse and rider brooch and place my writing inside.

Nonna will remember. Frome, Christmas, 934.

I shut and lock the chest for the last time.

The bell for the night office of Lauds rings. The crowds have gone, midnight mass has been successfully enacted. The revellers now sleep in heaps in the hall with the dogs, with horses in the stables, piled into their down coverlets in tents. Bishops snore in their dormitories. A few dedicated monks make their way quietly to the office of the night. I enter the church with them. Dunstan, Leofa and a few older monks are here. Aethelwold enters behind me from the direction of the scriptorium. I was not aware he was in there with me. Did he see me at work with the chest?

The hard work of Christmas Eve, for the priests and monks, has been done. The Doom, designed and painted by our genius artist, Dunstan, still lit up by candles, shocks the senses. I see it for the first time, arching over the nave, its colours shocking to the eye, its figures of Christ and angels bright in their seated majesty, its falling human figures turning to red and brown as they tumble to the depths of Hell. At the base are two-legged creatures with animal faces, ready to receive the damned with pitchforks, brandishing their tails and horns. Freshly painted, a huge devil, mouth gaping, leers out to the congregation, antlered, dark faced like Gwladys, laced with a massive tail and talons. The stuff of nightmare, of the tales of the old. Not shouting in joy, but eating your soul. The Horned One.

Beware!

Leofa

Thick cloud sits low on Whitesheet Hill, ice feathers the short grass in freezing dew. Pink and grey streaks hang in the southern sky. The January morning of 935 has dawned, but only just. A solitary rider, dressed in dark grey and black, cloaked and hooded, leans forward as the horse stumbles down the chalky slope of the carriageway towards the stone built village of Meare.

The rider could be any age, but his willingness to stay in the saddle on this steep incline suggests that he is willing to take risks and is therefore young. He is also in a hurry, like the young. There is a lightness of later morning ahead, the sun coming out wanly and intermittently over Duncliffe Hill. Leofa has made his excuses to the King who is still in Frome after the lengthy Christmas witan. He will arrive at Shaftesbury by early afternoon, God willing, bringing the wishes and gifts of a grandparent as well as his own as a new father.

In the hospital of the Abbey of St Mary of Shaftesbury the nursing nuns have a new charge, recovering, the Lord be Praised, from birthing. The seventeen-year-old Leonada, daughter of Aelfwynn of Mercia, reared by the nuns and intended by them to grace their house, has given birth. She is not married, but then, so many are not. Cohabitation is an arrangement to be decided privately and the Church has not yet decreed that coupling will be governed by law, though it threatens to do so soon. The nuns are not unhappy; they will regain their student, no doubt.

Leonada lies in a comfortable room set apart from the other inhabitants of the hospital, who are mostly older nuns. In some separate chambers there are young men whose wounds received in battle or blood feud are being treated, some successfully, some not. Feverfew cannot work every time, but cleanliness and continuous nursing and vegetable broth brewed from the fresh items from the kitchen garden may bring a proportion of them through the terrible infections which so often accompany even a slight wound. A woven willow cot stands by Leonada's bed. She calls softly.

'Mother, Mother.'

She wants to wake her mother, not the contents of the cot. She has come round from the danger and efforts of the day and night preceding and sees her mother lying asleep on a day bed in the corner of the room. A brazier nearby lights the stone wall behind and beeswax candles, safely high up in sconces, shed a warm glow and shadows around the uneven pattern of stone and flint. Leonada continues to call softly to her mother.

Aelfwynn wakes eventually. She has travelled this birth ordeal with her daughter, felt for her, held her, bathed her, breathed with her. She knows the dangers of this terrible, joyful time. Her own mother had no more children because of the pain and anxiety she endured during childbirth. She herself came close to death giving birth to Leonada. The birth canal was too narrow, they said. Would Leonada survive? She hears the familiar voice calling her and focusses on the presence of young life in the room.

These are two women, ensconced in an all-female abbey, locked away for the most part of their lives, in the case of Aelfwynn and for all of hers, in the case of Leonada. But the locking-up has provided security and safety. The prison that is the Abbey of St Mary of Shaftesbury has proven to be a sanctuary as well and many friends have been made, much learning undertaken. Distant travel has not been possible, but the confines of the walled abbey have been breached on occasion, when festivities or holy days have relaxed rules to share food and offerings to the town's poor. Visitors have sometimes been allowed and the comfort of suites for nobility and those women who have risen in the community's ranks by force of personality or piety or organisational strengths is second to none.

There is fresh air and exercise to be enjoyed working in the productive kitchen garden. Nuns make excellent cooks and the light filled refectory is a popular place. Even Wilton Abbey, which competes with Shaftesbury for its share of royal endowment, cannot outshine the wealth, cultural advancements and beauty of this house. Wilton has its beautiful river, but Shaftesbury has views. Set on a high promontory with steep hills to three sides, it commands the southern, western and northern vistas for many miles over the terrain of central Wessex, with fields, coppices, ancient burial grounds and forts, a patterned Christian landscape of farming toil, settlement and culture. Here the seasons display their colours and bring music to the soul in their rushing winds, their orange sunsets, their deep snows and promised springs.

At Shaftesbury there is always something of interest to see and experience. Even restrained meditation walks within the walls of the Abbey grounds make one conscious of all of Nature and human behaviour beyond the gate and grill, so close the country and the town are to each other. At one end of the garden wall a small metal viewing window can be opened and shut for those who want to be reminded of the startling reality of the world beyond the wall, or of the loveliness of its forms. Sometimes the limitation of choice makes the view from the small opening to the present world seem restricting, but to most who live within the confines, this minute view is enough to remind them of their security and higher calling.

Aelfwynn stretches. The familiar voice of her daughter is calling her back to the present, away from dreams of Athelstan who had appeared to her as the young, handsome man he had been when they were together in Mercia.

'Mother, are you awake?' The slightly louder request wakes a baby. It waves a hand and grizzles, then re-enters unconsciousness.

Aelfwynn gathers her wits, sits up and rearranges the wimple over her hair in a deft movement familiar to all females in the Abbey. She makes a second movement to push a long tendril of grey and auburn hair back behind a shoulder. During these adjustments she contemplates her daughter, now a mother herself. So young! But there have been younger mothers at Shaftesbury, not all of them royal and not all with such happy outcomes. Midwifery and herbal cure are a speciality of the nuns, but the Lord does not look kindly on all conjunctions of human desire, whether mutual or political.

It seems that the love match of Leonada may have pleased God, for here she is, calling softly to her from across the room, by her side a cot with living content. Here is a warm fire against a winter day's gloom. A flood of thankfulness overwhelms Aelfwynn. She rises, crosses the room to Leonada and holds her hand.

'Thanks to the Holy Mother of God, Our Lady Mary,' she whispers, giving her daughter a hug of congratulation and relief. 'I feared for a time that the effort would be too much for you. I will call Sister Ena.' Aelfwynn goes to the door of the cell, opens it and walks a few steps to a nearby parlour. A heavily garbed nun responds immediately to her call. Her robes flap as she walks quickly along the paving slabs. The expected request makes her movement urgent, but so does the weather.

'Sister Ena, my daughter has returned to us, she is awake. She appears to be in good health.'

Ena enters the room, notes the calmness and composure of the atmosphere, sees the fire is getting low, the new life asleep, the young mother looking exhausted and in need of washing and perhaps a warm drink. The fever has abated, all is well. There is a rosy glow on Leonada's cheeks. Her nurse's instinct tells her that there is little that will not be improved with normal human intervention. She fusses over the girl, helping her to sit up, gently reorganising the immediate surroundings of her birthing bed and checks the cot.

'The sisters are at None at present, Madam. I will inform them so that they may say prayers of thanksgiving at Vespers.' The nun bows and goes off to organise the first healthful concoction of warm ale for both mother and daughter together with a light meal. Another nun, alerted by Ena, enters soon after with items for washing the new family. The business of preparation and readiness for the lives ahead ensues.

Mother and daughter are eventually left alone again to enjoy the relief of safety after danger. They hug each other, captives by choice in this reign of Athelstan, secure in the stone walls of this wealthy and permanent holy place of order, protected from the extremes of jealousy and violence which would wash against the outer walls should others know that they were here, should others know who they were. Aelfwynn has enlightened her daughter. She now knows who her father is.

The women contemplate their future and that of the offspring. They will need all the protection of the King and the walls, too, if they are to thrive. There is a loud wail.

The first milky feed of the next generation of the House of Mercia at the breast of the great-granddaughter of King Alfred is underway.

Leofa sits on a bench in the reception area of the porter's lodge of the Abbey, thawing out from his half day ride from Frome. A generous log is alight on the open fire cradle, cornered by snake heads, in the centre of the room. He has arrived hours earlier to be told by a nun that the lady Aelfwynn is not yet ready to receive him, but that she will bring him into the visitors' rooms as soon as she can. An added aside, which Ena has given him through the grill, is that 'all is well'.

He is waiting. He is good at being patient. There is much

recent court business in his mind to amuse the passing of time. He is grateful for the moment of reflection. Many recent events command his thoughts, require adjustment. His amazement at fatherhood and shock at the consequences of his love making and the responsibility of the reproduction of a potential Mercian heir are uppermost in his mind. The transition between earthly duty to his king and to his inner soul is making a review of his position a necessity, bringing with it all that a life changing event can with its heightened sensibilities.

At times he opens the Latin psalter, a black shape held against his dark brown inner garment, which he always carries with him, more as a random guide to support and wisdom at times of indecisiveness or emotion than to read doctrine or to quote text. Its words provide comfort and admonition in equal amounts at each opening. The soft leather jacket of the small volume, illustrated with simple black and white drawings at chapter headings, is a friend, better to him that any reliquary or jangling piece of Christian jewellery. His other source of advice, which he often feels for at times of heightened emotion, is the silver-hilted dagger which he wears at his belt, its decorated scabbard lumpy with embossed snarling creatures biting each other's tales. Familiar to his touch and polished by years of fond handing in court situations when the talk or interpretation process became heated, a caress of the ever-present hilt calms him down, grounds him. He has never personally used the article to harm any living thing. It belonged to his grandfather who was a Viking Dubliner. It is likely that the blade has touched flesh through him, but as a pagan, living in a world where reaction to the need for personal safety was often called for, allied with flowing ale, this was to be expected. The blade is his touchstone, a reminder of violence which need never be used, of the improvement of culture by the Word, of self-control and clear-headedness.

There is much to mull over while he waits to meet his lover's mother. Athelstan had taken the news of the pregnancy of his only acknowledged offspring, Leonada, in a surprisingly sanguine manner. Nonna had known about it through the autumn and winter and both had faced up to the inevitable difficulties that it would cause in royal circles. How to tell Stone that his secret daughter was pregnant by one of the trinity had become an extra burden during the witans of the autumn. There was never a good moment; the court and King were busier than ever. The distractions of the summer campaign in Scotland, the diversion that had been Constantine, King of Alba and the strain of the long winter witan of Frome had worn the patience of most of those involved. There was no time or energy for anything else.

Athelstan, still at Frome, resting after his Christmas labours, was returning to his nightly visits to the reliquaries which comforted him and had retreated from daily contact with ministers. His archbishops saw him in the mornings when he felt freshest, but for now the plans which had been made and the consensus about aspects of the nationhood and the laws pertaining to control of the northern border needed much thought. Everyone needed time to allow the situation to mature in their minds, not just his own.

Had Athelstan gone too far, expected too much? The campaign had taken two years to plan; ships had been built, troops had been armed, no expense spared; there could be no failure. England, in danger of being swamped by northern treachery, could easily have become once again a pagan, Viking and British hegemony where Wessex, Mercia and East Anglia and the Christian religion could have been snuffed out. The northerners were not to be trusted. They did not care for oaths taken on the Christian Bible. What did it mean to them? But it was everything to the southerners. The south had won the battle of religion and state, but it must be made secure for the future, for England's continued existence, for the heirs to the throne of Wessex, for young Edmund. There were rumours of continued resistance to the southern king, some emanating from his own witan members. He might have to employ force to ensure loyalty. Athelstan was privately showing signs of insecurity. He badly wanted complete agreement. Would he abdicate and go to live in Rome, as others had done before him? Leofa feared for the King's mental state.

He considers the position of Athelstan's court. He, Nonna and Dunstan together with Eadgifu and Edmund had had many late-night discussions recently about the nature of the peace which should follow conquest, trying to equate and satisfy the requirements of a suddenly much larger kingdom, one which encompassed not only the south of Britain and the midland shire of Mercia and East Anglia but also the vast area of the former Northumbrian kingdom including the important centre of York. No king before Athelstan, no court centred in Wessex, had ever had to deal with this in terms of finance, law making and taxation. It is a headache, though there are examples of control factors for a new state which could be emulated from across the channel in the Frankish state.

On the continent the subjugation of indigenous peoples, the Gauls, had been a much more straightforward affair. The Latin and Celtic speakers there had influenced the incoming Gothic nations and their later Viking usurpers in northern France to a greater extent that the British had managed to do with the Saxons. In Europe, the blending of the Gauls with the newcomers had been balanced and fruitful; they had settled legal matters with reasonable amicability to their mutual advantage. Perhaps a closer physical relationship with Rome, as the power of the Pope had grown, had been a uniting factor. In Britain the differences between the old Celtic style Christianity of the post Roman Britons and the requirements of the Pope's empire were still visible. It seemed as though there was something in the nature of the inhabitants of these islands which set them apart from the continental character. The old Pelagian dispute of the idea of God raged on. It seemed to be part of the gene mindset of many who objected to rule from Rome. Vikings and northerners, determined to resist domination by the south and the Pope, used their independent pagan sensibility to defy change which would weaken their territorial power. The Roman Church would not find them easy to convert, as Athelstan was discovering.

The King and his courtiers were caught between the pig-headedness of the north, as they saw it, and the requirement to please more noble families throughout the land which stretched ever further away in geographical terms. The requirement to delegate was obvious, one king could not hope to govern directly; but to whom should the rule be delegated? Constantine, who remained at the King's leisure together with his young son in Frome, was obstructive and ill mannered. He was unlikely to carry out any southern instructions; besides, he would not or could not read the King's edicts. Wulfstan, Archbishop of York, who was the natural choice for leader based there, was under suspicion as a northern sympathiser. There were excellent thegns and ealdormen of notable families in Mercia who could be trusted to assist Athelstan in his task, but their utilisation would make the old Wessex families jealous, as time had shown throughout the King's reign.

The strains of an expanded kingship, bringing about the vision of his grandfather Alfred, had made an old man of Athelstan. At 41, he still had golden hair and an upright stance, but his shoulders had rounded, his eyes were permanently bruised blue and black. Sometimes he complained of stomach cramps, recalling his grandfather's ailment which had plagued him throughout adulthood. He smiled less and less, except in the hunt, when for a few hours he was able to forget some of his duties. When he was with his godsons and half-brothers, sharing their keen interest in literature and holy script, he felt content. Edmund was going to be a worthy prince; at nearly 13 he behaved like a son to him, looked like him, was almost as tall as him. Between them, he and Eadgifu had done a fine job of educating a future king of the line of Wessex, one whom no courtier would dismiss as too bookish, too hot-bloodied, too naive. Edmund had already composed and read his poetry to the court at various times; as the boy's voice broke and his intelligence became apparent, along with good sense and a natural tendency to be diplomatic, few objections were raised against him as the potential ruler of an expanding empire. His youth might be a difficulty, but Athelstan was still alive and wished to continue the dynasty's project as far as he could. Leofa's role at court was likely to continue into Edmund's reign, he had no doubt of that. He and the Aetheling were good friends. There was the matter, however, of his Mercian child. How would Edmund deal with that?

Leofa's thoughts stray away from the court and back to his present circumstances. The snapping log and a dancing flame light up the darkening room. A cat which has squeezed past the porter's door rubs against his leg, attracted by the warmth and horsey aroma of his woollen riding cloak and the passionate person within it, bringing him back to the present. The wooden settle is becoming hard.

He will have to stay in Shaftesbury overnight. Should he arrange to hire a room beyond the Abbey or would there be quarters for male guests within the walls? Some monasteries, like Frome, catered for all travellers and particularly pilgrims, including whole families, as part of the means of income for the house; the lodges were basic but comfortable. But Shaftesbury Abbey is a high-status house, peopled by ladies of noble birth and their female relatives, some of whom will be in training as novitiates, others retired as widows or unmarried women who had chosen or been forced to take the protection afforded by the high walls. Casual visitors are restricted and the inner sanctums of the monastery, where the nuns chiefly live, are forbidden to everyone but their sister nuns. Leofa's young male presence might be deemed to be superfluous to the convent, particularly overnight.

The porter, returning from his janitor duties at the gates to feed the fire and the cat gives him information about the inns which line the market street of the town, recommending one on the edge of the urban area known as The Ship, which brews fine ale and houses farmers visiting on feast and sale days. Leofa thanks him and makes a mental note to go there as soon as he has satisfied himself about the newborn, Leonada and Aelfwynn. Surely this must be soon. They know he is waiting. He returns to his thoughts of the King.

Athelstan had sat with his fingertips pressed together across his chest, leaning back on an embroidered oak chair which had rockers attached to its feet. It was difficult opening a conversation with Stone on the subject of a pregnancy of his only, supposedly secret, daughter. The trinity and Stone had shared a private meal together, remarking on the progress of the court, congratulating themselves on a relatively successful winter witan. No-one had killed another visitor; there had only been one serious brawl. The other clerks had gone off to make notes in the scriptorium. It was a reasonable moment to approach the King on an altogether different matter. Leofa turned back from the doorway of the King's private room and asked for a private audience. Stone granted one immediately. It was the late afternoon of yesterday. Where to begin?

'Stone,' he had started, checking the King's face to see if the moment was conducive, 'Stone, there is a matter which I must discuss with you which concerns your family, though I of course know full well that kin matters are usually none of my business.'

Athelstan nodded to him to go on. The next office of the day was two hours away. Compline would mark a quiet time for the court, a preparation for the bedmaking servants to set out sleeping apparel and a simple supper of bread, cheese and fruit to eat with a goblet of wine before retiring. Most of the bishops and ministers had returned to their own palaces. There were few secular visitors left at court. The temporary tents had been dismantled and carts had trundled off in a variety of directions, taking equipment and gifts with their owners. Things were returning to normal. Athelstan was soon going off to the haligdom to meditate amongst his precious relics. Leofa had waited a long time for the moment to come to blurt out his news. Stone would either be enraged or cool; he was not sure which. He considered excusing himself, then rejected the idea.

Leofa breathed deeply. He would either be alive after thirty seconds, or he would be dead. He decided to be direct, as Stone had always encouraged him and the other Chancery clerks to be when revealing or discussing matters of court importance. Leofa did not think of himself as a spy, just trained from youth to be naturally curious and to wish naturally to report anything which might be useful to his master, but a spy was what he had become. Some in the court were aware of his role, so close to the King, but occasional visitors were not and they were the most vulnerable to the system of information gathering which Athelstan had maintained from an early stage of his kingship. Without it he might not still be ruler. The reporting system had been begun by his father, King Edward and was one aspect of his more warlike reign which Athelstan had to agree was essential to good order.

'Stone, I know that you have a daughter.' He paused.

Athelstan remained silent and still, pursed his lips.

'I know that she is sheltered from outside meddling by the walls of Our Lady Mary's Abbey of Shaftesbury and that she is unknown to the court, being named unlike your family or like the Mercian kin from which she springs.'

Still no response from Athelstan. The candlelight behind his left shoulder shone onto Leofa's face, kept the King's in deep shadow. The younger man could not tell if there was disturbance or tolerance on the older man's brow. What would Stone think, do or say when he realised that his clerk was now his kin? Leofa eyed the cat whip which hung on the wall behind Stone. What other weapons might be to hand? He had his own dagger and presumably Stone was wearing his, too. A guard stood not far on the other side of the conference room door. Alfred's hour-marking candle was burning low. A wolfhound under the large table in front of Stone stirred and sighed in its sleep.

'Stone, you told us long ago, when we were boys and you found us at Glastonbury, that we were to come to you if we had anything distressing or important happening in our lives. You took us in, mentored us, gave us our education as court clerks and all our wherewithal, made us what we are and I am grateful for the chance to use what skills I have to assist in your goals. I am forever indebted to you, as I know Nonna and Dunstan are, too. I have always been honest with you and loyal to you. By all the saints, I would die for you. You know that.' Leofa paused, hoping for a response from Athelstan. There was none. Athelstan waited for the young man to commit himself still further.

Forced to continue, aware of precious royal time passing and the deep nature of the King's attention, Leofa decided to plunge in. 'Stone, I have fallen in love with your daughter, with Leonada and she with me.' He waited again.

'Go on.' Athelstan's face twitched briefly. Perhaps he could guess what was coming? Leofa hoped so, but knew he was going to have to confess all, would get no assistance.

'There is no help for it sir, we must be together. She is young and free spirited, but confined. I happened to meet her by chance last summer, before the campaign in the north, when I accompanied you to see the Princess Aelfwynn. Leonada says it was meant to be, that I would be her support and saviour. My Lord, she is captivating, a lovely, learned young woman and I know I do not deserve her, but...'

'No, you do not.' Athelstan rose from his seat, suddenly appearing terrifyingly invigorated. Leofa dreaded to tell him more. His hand went involuntarily to the hilt of his dagger. 'You do not need to use that, Leofa. I will not harm you. You should know by now that is not how I resolve disputes. How far has this affair gone?'

'My Lord, Stone, she is delivered of a child this morning.' There was no other way to say it. Love combined with access and lust inevitably ended in an unavoidable outcome. At least this sounded, to Athelstan's ears, as though the outcome was positive. There would be no bells tolled for a funeral and a grave, perhaps. The girl was how old? 17. She was in her discreet home of the Abbey, not abducted to the devil knew where, not raped by a marauding Viking or other pirate, still a secret to all but himself, Aelfwynn, the Abbess and now Leofa. He admired the younger man, was glad of his keen brain assisting him with the business of the court, but this was an unexpected intrusion into his personal affairs, one which might have dynastic repercussions. He decided quickly to dispense with emotion about the revelation. There were serious matters to discuss, now the deed, evidently, had been done. He was looking at his unexpected son-in-law.

Leofa waited for the King to summarise his thoughts. Naturally he would be in shock. Aelfwynn knew of the development of the relationship, which over the months had blossomed during rare interviews at the Abbey, in its autumn grounds and in a nearby hostelry, and must have approved or Athelstan would have heard of it. Athelstan rarely saw Aelfwynn, the lover of his youth in Mercia and had been too busy with the campaign and its aftermath to take note of any family matters. Eadgifu usually dealt with these, but even she did not know about Leonada. If she did, she had never mentioned her. It looked as though this was a disastrous, but contained disclosure.

'I cannot pretend that this is welcome news, Leofa.' Athelstan had risen, placed his hands behind his back and walked to the fire. The light was again behind him as he faced the younger man. The light trick was ingrained, had proved productive on many occasions during interrogations of suspects. He signalled to Leofa to sit at the table.

'You appreciate that even Leonada has little knowledge of her family position or history, though no doubt she is learning fast. There is danger in the fact of her existence becoming widespread knowledge, danger both to her, her mother and...' Athelstan was about to say 'me' but deflected the personal nature of the conflict which he had been bearing for 18 years, 'my family'.

Both men considered the ramifications. The royal family. A difficult subject. Many half-brothers and sisters had complicated the line to the throne of Wessex in the early years of the tenth century after Christ. Would-be kings and their supporters had been prepared to wound, maim, blind their rivals in order to become the chief man in the Anglo-Saxon world. If whoever gained ascendancy happened to have an acceptable partner, one promoted by the winning side in the battle for power, all could be quickly resolved. But even now, eleven years after Athelstan's reign had begun, there was still argument, a seething resentment about his legitimacy to rule. Mercia, which saw his youth, and Wessex, which did not, were uncompromising. Before the rise of Wessex as the chief power in the land, Mercia had ruled. The statesmen and some of the churchmen of each side were always seeking to undermine each other. The balance could swing back to Mercia. This matter of an unknown Mercian princess and now her offspring was a delicate matter.

'What is the sex of the child?' A boy could mean civil war. A daughter could be hidden or disguised.

'I do not know, Stone. I will go to Shaftesbury tomorrow, with your permission.' Leofa dared not rise from his seated position. Athelstan prowled the length of the table behind him, thinking hard.

'It is a pity you did not seek my permission on previous occasions.'

What would be the repercussions of this unexpected development in dynastic terms? What could be done to avert the interest which would inevitably be shown in the continuing line of Mercia? And this, just as things were beginning to settle between the two states. Mercians would for long regard themselves as superior culturally, with their well-established monastic libraries and ancient lineage; the Alfredian line of Wessex, though successful, was a newcomer to the Saxon heroic stage. *Bumped up spear throwers*, the Mercian leaders thought. The Wessex thegns and particularly some of the characters in superior orders in the southern dioceses of the Church had similar views of their Mercian courtier comrades. They had held their views of each other in check during the summer campaign, but arguments had risen again during the winter witan, as the complications of sorting out England and dealing with northern kings had set in.

'I would come with you, but I must see the prisoners and the archbishops tomorrow at dawn and there are other matters which must be attended to. Leofa,' Athelstan now leaned heavily on the table by the side of Leofa and grasped his arm, 'go as soon as travel is safe, go alone and do not be recognised. Take this,' he took off a reliquary ring from a finger, 'and give it to the mother – to Leonada as a token of my familial interest and tell her that I will be with her and her mother as soon as I can. Leonada must now be made fully aware of her kin position and must take my advice for her protection and that of the child.'

Athelstan looked closely into Leofa's face and eyes. 'My advice,' he emphasised, 'not yours. You have a wise head, Leofa, but in this matter you are lost. And so am I, if there I do not think of a very good plan to recover from what has occurred. Now get up, pray, sleep and prepare for what may be the most dangerous ride as a messenger that you will ever take.' The King pushed up from the table with a sigh. 'Leave me.'

Leofa was glad to do so. He could not see Athelstan's expression but he knew what it would be from the gruelling nights of discussion of tactics which he had spent with him trying to ascertain a plan of action or to manoeuvre into weakness an obdurate or potential foe. Court politics were becoming impossible. He stood, bowed to his father-in-law, uncle and mentor, supporter and friend. He had not been killed, not humiliated. He had seen the King at his best, when it mattered, shocked, recovered and skilful, ready to adapt and to plan. That was why he had lasted this long. That was why he was deeply unpopular in some quarters, loved by others.

Leofa loved him, and it seemed that the King loved him, too.

The porter startles him awake to consciousness of the room. A door to the freezing outdoor weather opens and shuts, letting another cat sidle in out of the rain.

'Well, young man, I have word that you are to be allowed into the guest chamber for the evening and night, where the servants will see that your needs are met. Come with me. The Lady Aelfwynn is ready for you.'

Leofa follows the porter to the inner door of the abbey, then a waiting nun along stone lined corridors, oil sconces glowing at intervals. Heavy wooden doors indicate nuns' cells tightly closed for individual prayer. He can hear the unique cry of a small human, a sound uncontrolled by diplomacy, dogma or sin. It is a cry of being, of new life. Then another cry, slightly different, then together.

Two babies are voicing their lustiness in the world, demanding attention.

He is met at Leonada's door by Aelfwyn. She nods to the

astonished young man.

'Yes, Leofa, you have twins and I am pleased but also sorry to say that one of them is a boy. There are two new aethelings for Mercia. You had better come in.'

Epilogue

Palace of Cirencester, 20 May 935

We are back to normal. After a visit to Exeter last month we have been passing between Mercian estates, tending as usual to concentrate on floating between the western sites where Athelstan has close associations. He wants to revisit his early youth, it seems. I fear he is getting gloomy; nostalgia has taken him over. Constantine has grumbled a submission of sorts, put his rough signature crosses on documents and has been allowed to return to his home. Half the court thinks that Athelstan is mad to let him go; Stone thinks that generosity, as in the case of Alfred and Guthrum, which he keeps citing as an example, will reap rewards. He thinks his main work in life is done. He hopes so, because he is feeling exhausted. Archbishop Wulfstan argued for the northerner's release, said he would stand surety for his behaviour. His leg is better and he has travelled back on horseback with him. He's another one to have to watch.

Peace reigns. The troublesome cauldron of the north has been brought off the boil; its malicious contents should settle for a while, long enough to establish some ground rules. There's no settling Constantine; he remains awkward and uncommunicative, but we have retained his son for the time being, a bright lad who will do well after a year or two in our school at Glastonbury. He will go back home before he is completely grown and may do our work for us. We take a long view.

Stone and the trinity have been visiting the Priory at Gloucester, tending the relics of Oswald. Stone has had his heart's desire, the unification of the nation and of the holy body, but he does not seem happy. Radegund's reliquary is empty. The manipulation of holy parts is weighing heavily on him. He has gained one thing but lost another. He and Dunstan have had long discussions into the night about the events in Chester-le-Street.

Dunstan tells me that Athelstan regrets some decisions made while on campaign, blames the exuberance of the journey and his hopes, feels he has overstretched himself in religious terms, perhaps damaged his soul. Dunstan has tried to counter his arguments to set his mind at rest, but Stone continues gloomy. He mutters to himself.

'He's as bad as Constantine, sometimes,' Dunstan remarks. I have to agree.

Today, in the King's private chapel, I deal with the arrival of letters. The other members of the trinity are working quietly in the scriptorium nearby on the next set of charters. One of the letters today is set with the seal of Lindisfarne. Stone sees it and groans. 'Open it, Nonna.'

This has taken a few days to travel here and comes to light at the bottom of a saddle bag full of requests and questions from Wulfstan of York. I break the seal and read.

To the great King Athelstan, Emperor of Britain, greetings. May 15th 935, from the family of Cuthbert.

The sainted one in our keeping, Cuthbert, sends his greetings to your Lordship and to your brother the Aethleing Edmund who we were glad to meet during your recent journey and sojourn with us.

We wish you and all the royal family the best of health and wealth in this world and will continue to pray for you.

Since your noble visit and the observance of prayer in our little crypt in our temporary home of Chester-le-Street we have had no opportunity or wish to disturb our saints in their slumber.

However, our reliquary priest, as is usual at this time of year, checked recently to be sure that all was well with our founder. He had remarked on slight damage to the outer coffin which needed repair, which had nothing to do with its last opening. On lifting the coffin lid to re-establish the comfort of St Cuthbert and to remove any items which might be causing him discomfort, he noticed that an element of the contents of the coffin had changed, namely the item which we had placed at his feet.

The skull of King Oswald appears to have altered. The priest in question and later myself, examining it, are certain that the head in the coffin is not the same as when it was last opened. It is smaller, the eye sockets are different and the teeth are better. We have tried to discover, through prayer, the cause of this, but have been forced to accept that more than holy forces have been at work.

We have reached the conclusion that the last time the coffin was opened, which was when, great King, you were visiting us, the original head was taken and another substituted.

Are you able to shed light on this affair? What do you suggest we, as poor monks, should do for the best? You know the value of the head of Oswald to many courts. Perhaps someone in your entourage has covertly acted as a collector for one of these?

Naturally we will no doubt be able to come to some amicable arrangement which does not involve revealing what could be commonly known as theft. Alternatively, if the original head can be found and returned, nothing more may be said or done.

I look forward to hearing from you with a proposal of restitution. If necessary one or two of your associated clerks may wish to travel north to parley in discretion.

With all due respect to you, my Lord, and wish for your continued health and happiness.

Signed, the Abbot of Lindisfarne in Chester-le-Street.

Stone sighs. Then roars.
'DUNSTAN!'

Palace of Dorchester, 19 December 937

Another Christmas witan comes along, another reading of the tale of Edington, another display of finery by Eadgifu's girls and Athelstan's relics. The burgeoning court is descending tomorrow from everywhere in England to this place. As usual, I have been sent on ahead to prepare the paperwork for the law making and records.

Things are not quite as usual. This has been a difficult year for the King. Court business is becoming more awkward with each witan. The Welsh kings are staying away and Stone has no appetite to force them to attend. The Wessex faction continually remarks that he is losing his way and his reason and Aethelwold is ramping up his requirements for Church Reform. Stone hides away with his relics but seems to get little help from them. He looks ill.

He used to be the master of charm and persuasion, but Athelstan has become less and less inclined to bother to try to persuade and like Constantine he has taken to grunting in response to questions or comments. With us, the trinity, he is more voluble, but the sighing and moaning has become continuous, accompanied by the wringing of hands. It is a pitiable sight. This once vigorous warrior has been reduced to a person horribly aware of death standing close behind him. He wishes to be taken, he says. There is little we can do to cheer him. Eadgifu has given up trying to bully him into a positive frame of mind. She sends Dunstan and Aethelwold to pray with him but their lengthy penance sessions with the cat-whip seem to make matters worse. He is guilty about Edwin still, and regretful about Oswald, too, though events at Chester-le-Street remain a secret to all but the trinity. It must be of some help to have us to share his burden?

Stone has physical wounds which will not heal as well as mental ones. He received a sword blow to the arm during battle at Brunanburh this summer from which he has not recovered, making his only outdoor joy of hunting impossible. Tendons and muscles were disturbed which may never heal, despite the salves and potions of the nuns of Shaftesbury and Wilton. Stone packs his arm into a dressing filled with charms and small relics each night when he retires, but they do no good. He is old and healing from wounds is slow. He moans that his mind and body are both being snuffed out at the same rate, wishes the pace would quicken to take him to his grandfather. He hopes that he will see him in Heaven, but is beginning to fear that all kings inevitably end up in Hell, by the nature of the job.

Constantine and Owain of Strathclyde, true to form and the opinion of most of the court, broke their oaths, joined forces with the Danes of Dublin and launched an attack on Athelstan's Northumbria. During this summer, after a long period of disorderly indecision, unlike the King, we struck back at the disreputable foe and killed many of their leaders. It was a long and bloody fight. Five kings were destroyed and the Danes sent screaming in fear to their ships. Constantine escaped with his grey hairs intact, but his son, who had been educated for a while by the Glastonbury monks, did not. He lay stretched out in the sun along with the other dismembered and mangled bodies. No-one had seen so much blood spilled in one place. Ravens and sea eagles feasted well on the youth of the north. We brought home the bodies of two of our own, the great warrior brothers Aelfwine and Aethelwine, Athelstan's cousins.

The treacherous conglomeration of the Scots, Strathclyde and Dane has been dealt with, but the success of the battle and the need for it have struck a deeper blow to Athelstan's view of the nature of mankind. He is disappointed. *Practised scoundrels, every one*, he keeps muttering. *They're all the same. Mad, mad, bloodthirsty fools. Oh Lord, take me.* The self-imposed, continued penance for Edwin's death has produced weeping sores on his back and other cuts have appeared on his arms. Stone appears to want more wounds, says that the worse he feels, the better it will be. He is in a hurry to end it all.

Edmund is a tall fifteen-year-old, reaching his full adult powers. Unlike his half-brother Edwin, he is able to command his handsome limbs. In effect, he and Eadgifu are in charge. Since Brunanburh he has been taking over many of Stone's court duties. While Stone retreats, Edmund makes more appearances, wearing a head-band of high office. Eadred accompanies him often. They are practical, outgoing, vigorous, generous, seemingly able to deal with the Mercians and Wessex lords alike and welcomed by the Church as helpmates in the process of Reform, which under Aethelwold's instruction is now well under way. They are fresh to the diplomacy required to compromise all arguments while pushing forward their dynastic requirements. Their energies, combined with their mother and Dunstan, are effective at steering the English.

Constantine is back in Edinburgh, close to death, having also received wounds from which he cannot recover, we learn. Archbishop Wulfstan, who had treacherously encouraged the northerners in their attempt to wrest control of England, has disappeared behind the walls of York. He still sends out messengers throughout the north midlands, trying to enlist help to prevent Athelstan and Edmund from reclaiming his territory, but there is little appetite to fight. Brunanburh has been a huge shock to all fighting forces. Too many on both sides have been killed.

There is peace in the land, but for how long?

Priory of St Oswald, Gloucester, 27 October 939

It is done. Athelstan has breathed his last. Edmund, Eadgifu and Eadred were with him yesterday in the hospital and took his will with them to Winchester. It was clear to all that he would not be with us for more than a day or two. For fourteen years and ten weeks Athelstan had done his duty, carried out the dreams of his dynasty. His was a glorious and successful reign. Edmund, well trained in the arts of governance as well as of culture, will take his place in a smooth succession, as the Virgin King had planned. No part of England will quarrel with that.

I regret that Leofa could not be here with Dunstan and myself; I miss him and his cheerfulness. His exile, along with Leonada and the aethelings of Mercia was a loss of great talent to the Wessex court and to Stone in particular; he kept the King sane with his laughter when things were likely to go badly. I hear he is doing well in Dublin where some members of his family still live. I am sure he misses the intrigue of the court, but has become an important part of the scriptorium work of the Church there. I receive news of him occasionally; he writes short letters in Latin, but because of pirate interference and the King's wish for secrecy, I do not often hear from him directly. A visitor to court from Ireland mentioned him two years ago and said that he had settled well and that his family was hearty. He did not mention the children by name and I do not know anything about them. Perhaps that is just as well.

Aelfwynn is here; she arrived as Eadgifu was leaving. The two women passed in the cloister but did not recognise each other. She has spent the night by Stone's side, speaking quietly to him. Dunstan was attending office while she bathed his head; he did not know who she was, assumed she was his sister or some other obscure female. We all have some of those littering our histories. As Athelstan, clutching part of St Oswald to him, faded, Aelfwynn retreated to leave him to the monks and priests.

Unconsciousness came as a relief; the last breath was taken to the accompaniment of plainchant. The Virgin King has gone to meet the living souls of his saints. *Aldhelm, be my guide* and then *Grandfather, what is this coming to me?* were his last words. He went into his future, no longer concerned with the past. His face relaxed, he looked at peace.

The King is dead. Long live King Edmund and his fresh young Queen, Aelfgifu, and his son, the Aetheling Eadwig.

And his mother, Eadgifu. Long live them all.

Outside, Gwladys and Hywel wait to ride with Athelstan on his last journey to join Aldhelm at Malmesbury.

I like Gwladys, very much. She is improving my Welsh. I learn it best at night. It will be useful at the future witans of Edmund.

The Library of St Augustine's Abbey at Canterbury, 26 October 983

I remember it so well. Tomorrow it will be forty-four years since Stone's death. We carried him to Malmesbury. The Priory of St Oswald wished to retain him; it would have been good for their business to be buried alongside his aunt and uncle of Mercia, but Athelstan's last wish was to buried at Aldhelm's monastery of Malmesbury, alongside his cousins who had died at Brunanburh. He wished the nation to remember this last great successful exploit, this last great attempt to maintain unity in the land. Aldhelm would protect and watch over them, he said and the Vikings would never dare to lay hands on the precious treasures held there with his own and his cousins' warrior presence sleeping within.

So it was that Athelstan came to the Wiltshire monastery, in a journey full of pomp, stopping at all major towns and villages along the route to receive the blessings of his people. They came to touch his coffin and declared that miracles and cures had occurred because of the nearness of the King, but he was no Oswald. His death had been in a bed, not a battlefield. He would become no saint. Dunstan officiated at his funeral. Aware of Stone's regret about the Oswald affair, he acceded quickly to the Winchester faction's request to downplay the eulogy. They were still, despite the success of the reign in general, sore about the perceived Mercian imposition. Fourteen years and ten weeks and counting; their notes about Athelstan in the Chronicle of our times was a continual, conscious grudge. The Charter recorder was one of their own. Athelstan's reputation was belittled, But I have written his story, for others to read and I have placed it among the chained books in Malmesbury where only the most studious will find it. Athelstan will one day be recognised as the great king that he was.

In Malmesbury Abbey, too, inside the barred reliquary room of the modern scriptorium, lay the oaken chest, the container of the histories and legends of the West Welsh. The King and the stories of Wessex were lying together within the sound of the bells of the Abbey. Athelstan is still there, but his spiritual protector, St Aldhelm and the chest have recently been brought to Canterbury. Vikings are beginning to threaten the realm once more. Significant treasures are being brought to Canterbury for safety. Dunstan wants to examine their contents. He has done as much editing as he can, he says, on English history and the reigns we have witnessed. Now he would like to take a look at the deeper past. He has decided that Aethelwold's reforms and is own part in pushing them were not necessarily fair to the West Welsh and wishes to see if there is anything of use from the Celtic Christian position which might offset the witch and devil driven dogma which seems to be growing amongst the laity. Old women have become vulnerable to the accusation of witchcraft; there seems to be no stopping of the popular imagination once it is harnessed. It needs toning down.

The Head of Oswald is a problem. We often discuss what to do about it. Should we reveal what really occurred in Chester-le-Street since we are soon to be worm fodder? To do so would ensure that Athelstan is forever denied a place in the history of Wessex and England. Should the reliquary of St Radegund be understood to be other than it appears, with the head of an executed thief now having taken her place? Should we confess that she graces Cuthbert's coffin? And how would this admission affect Dunstan's reputation? It seems that whatever we do or say, a trip to Hell may be the consequence. We will meet many old friends there. It may be too late to alter the course of history, of what men have been led to believe. This may be what history is: a truth of sorts. What will be, will be. The secrets may have to remain as they are.

Hell, or Annwn? I shall go to one or the other. The small brooch, which I took so long ago from the oaken chest, reminds me of another, British truth, of sorts.

The Shroud

I am of the earth, the land of the dead. I lie face down in the sod on the hill, unmarked at a crossroads like the burial place of a gibbeted thief or a suicide, alone. I eat my assigned dirt. Discarded as a relic, though I have touched many saints' parts, unwanted by a reformed religion, my life's work rejected, my world, myself forgotten.

I am entire, not torn into shreds for others to kiss my severed parts. I will stand to receive my Lord's will. No saint am I, no miracles are told. My father and my father's father loved it here among the oaks. I lie now on a bleak hill. I see the land I loved. I have been granted my last wish, to remain here forever. Dunstan afforded me this.

The small township across the river water from my anonymous grave faces me, clustered around the stone church and empty monastic buildings. There is the stout but comfortable dormitory where once I slept and ate. The monks of my youth are gone from the place; no-one remembers me. Brown stone buildings, their walls studded with dead creatures of the sea, crowd new streets where there were once trees. There is the great hall still and workhouses, wooden beams of great oaks for lintels and roofs, windows with glass for the noble fortunate, water flowing as before when I lived here between wooden framed shops and merchants' homes. Streams and springs along the hillside are still plentiful; ale tastes better here than anywhere. I miss the ale of this place. I miss most the pleasure of eating.

I am in a Wessex town and market, familiar to me though many years have passed since I lived here. It is silent on a hot day in July, clamouring with bells and people on holy days. At Whitsun, there are fluttering banners and bunfights. It is sad in rain, with its dark brown tiles and darkened walls. Its people are much as they were, but more numerous. Weavers and wheelwrights, market folk and shopkeepers selling hunting leathers, spears and lances, shoes for the runners. Priests pray for the sinners and bury the dead in consecrated ground. But not me. I am an outcast, one for the Devil, for the north. I was an apostate at the end.

Am I a king, am I a saint? Am I a thief, a hanged man? Am I a mugger's victim? A monk? I am bones in the earth. What does it matter? Do you care?

Remember me, the body in a bag.

Malmesbury Abbey April 1539

Here they come, the new owners of this sacred place. We all turn in our graves. Aldhelm is safely at Canterbury, saved for continued sainthood by Dunstan. He will be remembered. We are still here, the kings and princes of the state, left to fend for ourselves. Dunstan thought we should do so in death as in life. There are my two cousins on either side of the altar and myself in my tomb. We helped this place to become and remain the great monastery of its day, its library second to none. We are about to be disturbed by rough hands.

In their irreligious vandalism, they come to twist and turn us, sifting through our corpses, hands around our skulls, not to honour our bones but to take any loot our bodies may conceal, something they can treasure on their way to Hell. They turf us out, wantons, from our resting places, caring not that we cannot defend our remains. Our protectors, the monks, wailing, have gone, booted out.

The library groans; the ancient pages have become stops for beer barrels and props for creaking tables. A thousand years have been torn up. Crumpled, bleeding, the product of hours and years of toil by short-sighted men and women, scribbling in the frosty dawn the deeds of kings and princes, bishops and abbots. Ashes now, filth.

Out I go, tipped onto the floor, kicked in my shroud to the edge of events. Never in my life was I at the edge, always the middle. My cousins, who fought so bravely at Brunanburh, cast out too. Bodies in bags, just another set of bodies, the place is riddled with them, high and low, but mostly high. That's why I wished to stay here to judgement day, with my educated peers, lovers of books and relics. We were a privileged royal few, attractive to the poor. We could cure and forgive, almost as a saint would.

Now, in the dust and shadows with destruction and

decapitation going on around me, pieces of history carved into the niches and walls destroyed, smashed in a day, I sprawl, bent and broken, the gold thread of my hair falling onto the abbey floor. There is no label to identify me. I am separated from my named tomb, from my gospel book that ever accompanied me, just another bag of bones.

In the dark, later, a cart comes and two hooded creatures lift me up. Farewell, cousins, I am gone to yet another resting place. Someone has thought of me. This man, this boy, touched my tomb and were cured. I have the King's touch still. They will take me to a burial place, one that will not be defiled. A common baker and his boy, watching the day's events, take me to their lodging. I remember now, I did this man some good. Not as a saint, that was never granted me, though many kings had that honour, if they were ruled by priests. Shall I follow Aldhelm to Canterbury? To Edmund at Glastonbury? Will they take me to where my bones can lie undisturbed on an island in a lake?

Do not separate my bones, leave me entire, I beg. I must be intact, ready to rise to meet my Lord. Bury me somewhere nearby in this place that I have loved, please. And remember me.

Offices of Thomas Cromwell, Palace of Westminster, May 1539

'The dust in here makes my eyes water,' a clerk kicks a heap of bagged bones.

'Don't do that, you'll only make things worse.'

Two black hatted clerks are sorting the new batch of assorted treasures brought by cart up the great Roman highway from the west from Glastonbury after the execution of the Abbot and from Bodmin, Muchelney and Malmesbury.

'They haven't brought the Abbot's bits as well have they?'

'Don't be daft. There'd be blood everywhere. Probably shipped off his quarters to landfill in different counties. They wouldn't want to make a saint of him.'

They continue sifting, sorting. Clouds cover the sky, darken the low-ceilinged interior.

'There's not much in this lot except the deceased and their bits. Mostly bits,' reports the first clerk. 'Some rubies in this one, though,' he tears a piece of metalwork from a reliquary of uncertain date, tosses it into a pile marked *Worthwhile*. 'There's a pretty book,' he holds up a small worn psalter. 'Think this one should be saved?'

His companion looks across the room at the leather and gold tooled cover. 'Nah, it's just another of those old idolatrous picture books. It's too small to be worth anything. Throw it out.'

Out it goes. Motes of dust rise up like ghosts from the growing pile of rubbish as it lands on one of the sacks near those marked Discard which wait for the rubbish cart. A cat, sleeping nearby on another sack, objects. Bones, books, more bones, endless bones.

'Bones. They do jangle in yer throat. Pass us the ale.' The black hats drink, continue their unending task.

Unwinding years, leaving the past
to the past.

North Parade, Frome, May 1931

I am the spy in the air, the spirit of corvid. Rook, crow, raven or jackdaw, it doesn't matter which. We operate together when flesh is available. We have our leaders and our calls. We are brothers of the bones, Corbies. We span the centuries, have witnessed many things. We keep the histories. You should listen to us, but you never do.

The breeze in high chestnut trees rocks our nests on North Hill in the green town of Frome. It is May, 1931 and we are Rook Tribe, in full breeding mode. Hormones of the ages, of millennia, urge us on. Our usual roost in the valley abandoned for now, the chicks of our race need height, to fall or fly. The road below is becoming busy with the combustion engine, smart cars and quarry lorries groan through the town and up the hill when heavy laden, their gears grinding. We will be here long after they have gone.

Frome is a pleasant home, there is water, plenty of broken woodland for nests and safety, fields with seeds and their eaters, larvae and worms. We need not go far from our homes in the sky to feast. In this spring of bright air, the winter survived, the urgings of our ancestors in our blood drive us to nest-making. We must rejuvenate, bear fruit and multiply. Our duties are clear. But we still look out as spies, always on duty. We are the look-outs. We see all. We greet Raven visitors from Orchardleigh, come to join us for their daily excursion. There are plentiful leatherjackets in the fields and gardens here. We do not mind sharing. We are birds of a feather, the Corvids. When we can, we eat flesh, we feast on blood. There is plenty for all.

The road used by the vehicles of man forks below. One way goes to Fromefield and off to Bath, the other to Berkley, relic part of an ancient forest, Selwood. Up past the old Roman road crossing at Clink it goes. There is blue sky above, air fresh for breeding, for watching. We wait for our young to hatch, swaying in the branches.

Below, two humans are at the fork in the road, digging a hole. It is warm, but these men are hot; they have no shirts on their bodies and have red faces and necks, bodies of winter clammy white below. One digs, the other leans on his spade. The resting man is wearing a flat hat. He must be in charge. A green car goes past, then stops, backs up. A black-hatted man gets out and comes to the men. They mutter. Black-hat, with the help of one of the workmen, gets down into the hole they have dug. There is much talk and pointing. The voices and shiny metal implements, smaller ones now than the spades, keep us interested. We caw and preen, watching. There may be food. Have they found food? It is approaching midday, sandwich time. Yesterday there was a discarded crust.

A young woman wearing a red hat puffs up the hill, leaning over her large infant who is harnessed and sitting up like a miniature monarch in a heavy pram. She reaches the top of the hill, relaxes into upright mode and makes for the group of investigators in the hole. She joins them, peering down, her hands on her hips, her chest heaving, still recovering. The infant looks too, its mouth hanging open. We shuffle sideways on the branch overhead to get a better view of proceedings, cock our heads to listen.

The flat-hat man has a sandwich in his hand as he speaks to the black-hat man. A piece of ham has fallen on the grass beside him as he gesticulates. He may forget it is there. I nod to my wife, who has left fussing with her nest building for a moment. We wait.

'Well, what is it?' Red-hat enquires.

'Somebody's bones, not recent. Ages old. Buried a long way down.' Black-hat's voice. He is a man to command a situation, knows what he is about. He does not have a sandwich in his hand.

Flat-hat speaks. He has a strong, deep accent. Rs roll out of his mouth like treacle. He points to something in the hole. 'And that's 'is 'ead.'

'A skeleton! I suppose you'll have to tell the police?' Red-hat is now fully recovered from the terrible hill climb. Next time Billy may have to walk despite the inevitable loud objections.

'I'll deal with it,' Black-hat seems assured, educated. 'I'll ring up the county archivist, he'll know what to do. It looks like a lone burial, but it's as well to take note of these things. Someone in the future may want to know about it.'

'Was there a cemetery or church here, then?' Red-hat persists. This will be something interesting to tell her husband at lunchtime, when he comes back for his dinner hour from the office in town. A good twenty minutes each day, up and down the hill, keeping him fit and hungry. They usually eat lunch together in silence. Meat, mash, cabbage and carrots. Apple pie. Cream today, market day, followed by the usual short nap.

'Not to my knowledge. There's been nothing built up here on the top. It's always been fields and trees. The church, town and its buildings stayed away from North Hill. Devil's territory, the north. It's unlikely to be a Christian burial. It would have been in the church cemetery, across the river from here, where the monastery is supposed to have been. So perhaps the body is Roman. The fresh water springs are all on the other side of town, too, where they would have had their houses. For ale making, you know.' Vicars know about brewing and religion. They go hand in hand, in history. The group nods to itself. Here's a puzzle.

Body, bodies. Any chance of being able to scavenge, for us birds? Anything shiny to please us? There's always a chance. But there is no flesh on bones this old. The ham sandwich and its contents continue to be our focus. We understand what they mean about bodies, we know the English tongue. No battles here, no hope in the offing of gory mess. Pity.

Red-hat, satisfied for now, pushes her heavy load into Berkley Road, disappears through the gate and door of a newly built semi-detached house to park Billy in his play pen and to make her husband's lunch. It's been quite an interesting morning.

Black-hat stays at the hole. He is a retired vicar, it turns out, and is interested in all things old and fleshless. Flat-cap and his young silent mate continue digging while the vicar watches. Black-hat is resisting going home to telephone to contact his friend the antiquary; he doesn't want to miss anything. I fly down to edge closer to the crust and piece of ham on the grass which has been discarded.

A blue charabanc rolls in from the Bath direction, carrying market shoppers from Beckington. It slows down as the workmen are approached; the young digger waves it past the low red and white striped shelter at the site. The charabanc passengers lean over to look down the hole. Something interesting there, something to talk about. There's our old vicar, at it again, peering down holes. There's the old shiny suit, knitted waistcoat, black hat. Still alive, then. The charabanc moves on down North Parade.

The day wears on, low clouds in a blue sky. Spring maypoles will be hoisted at the coming weekend. Cuckoos shout in Cuckoo Lane and all down the road towards the forest gate at St Algars Farm it is lousy with cuckoos and cuckoo spit flowers.

I'm near the group of diggers and vicar, now. I can observe at close quarters what is going on in the hole and listen to the conversation aimed into it.

'And it's face down, undisturbed until now, I reckon, nothing else buried with it. Could be Christian, probably not pagan, they'd have put something in the grave with it. But why face down? That's unusual.' The vicar rubs his chin.

Flat-cap like to think himself educated. 'Perhaps like Dead Maids crossroads up at Berkley, someone got killed here and buried for convenience?' he offers.

The younger digger stands up, puts down his tool. 'Murder?'

'Or perhaps a hanging? They could have had a gibbet here at the cross roads. But there is Gibbet Hill at the other side of town, looking out to Nunney.' The vicar has decided to share his excitement with the original finders of the bones. Would they have reported them, though, if the vicar had not come by?

But now he has exhausted his enquiries, managed to put a halt to any further destruction of bones until they can be viewed by the authorities. Some have evidently already been carted offsite. It is the least he can do, as a local antiquarian, to help towards an understanding of the past. Who knows what someone may be able to piece together in future about this little understood neck of the woods? All we know is that Frome was founded by Aldhelm, Saxon scholar and Saint. What about what went before or after? These are questions the vicar cannot answer, but perhaps others may, in time to come. Meanwhile what remains will be recorded. A small box of bones will be stored. A note will appear in a learned journal. A good deed for the day has been done, as good as helping a blind beggar.

At night, the vicar dreams. A face down burial. What does this mean? He wakes up remembering something he has read about which is similar, recorded by others in East Anglia. Another face down burial, this time in a cemetery, used from Roman times and on into the Christian era. The translation of a holy man's corpse, it was surmised, in a shroud. A shrouded skeleton might be buried face down by mistake. The body of someone important. A saint, brought to be near a church or graves, to pass on his supposed efficacy at healing and miracles.

A saint? Or an executed sinner? Or a king? A renegade monk, condemned to lie in unconsecrated ground? Probably no-one will ever know. We can only surmise what might been the history of this fellow. We are allowed to guess. That will have to be enough.

BONES

Glossary

Aetheling: prince.

Aestel: a pointer, used for reading gospels or other scripture, often with a precious gem or carving on one end. The stem might have been made of wood, but might have been bone or other material. The aestel was a valuable item. It resembled a magician's wand or conductor's baton. Alfred had many of these made and given to churches and bishops.

Alba: Kingdom of the Scots.

Annwn: British word for the Otherworld. It had red and blue as its symbolic colours suggesting heat and cold.

Apostate: a renegade from his faith.

Bard: British name for a musician, poet or performer.

Burgh or burh: Saxon market town, often fortified.

Ceorl: low born freeman.

Clipping (the church): a festival ritual of parishioners surrounding a church to 'shout out the devil', as practised until recently at Rode, Somerset. See the Ritual Shriek.

Ealdorman: Saxon equivalent of an Earl.

Ecgbrihtesstan: Possibly Brixton Deverill, Wiltshire.

Fire festivals of pre-Christian period: Imbolc (February), Beltane (May), Lughnasa (August), Samhain (November).

Fyrd: Saxon army.

Gloss: note added to an original written work.

Gwydbyl: Welsh board game. Gospel Dice was also played. They may have been the same game.

Hagiography: a saint's biography.

Haligdom: a room or place where reliquaries were kept. Sometimes known as a scrinium.

Kutch: Welsh word, meaning to embrace, comfort. As in Cold Kitchen Hill, Wiltshire?

Llan: Welsh for church.

Lloegr: Welsh word for England, the lost lands (of the Welsh).

Midden: Rubbish heap.

Mor: Welsh for sea, hence Somerset moors, inland seas.

Reliquary: container, often highly decorative, for a saint's relic.

Revels and Routs: village festivals, often rowdy and involving shouting out the devil from one place to the next as in the rhyme *Rode Revel, Beckington rout, the Devil's in Frome and cannot get out.*

Sceatta: coin.

Scop: English name for a musician, poet or performer.

Scriptorium: the writing room for scribes in a monastery.

Thegn: Saxon Lord.

Thurifer/thurible: priest in charge of incense, metal container for burning incense.

Tonsure: the style of shaven head of a monk.

Witan: Saxon parliament; met in different places around the country.

Ynis Witrin: Welsh name, meaning Island of Glass, for Glastonbury.

Place-names, Culture and History

Much has been written about the place-name Selwood and how it came into being. As with all early place-names, there is much conjecture. This is a fresh offering to those who might wish to rethink the thorny problem of the meaning of some place-names in eastern Somerset and west Wiltshire where Britons and Saxons lived together.

We first hear the name of Selwood in the late seventh century when the Saxons, having beaten the Welsh at a battle in Bradford-on-Avon in 652,[1] broke through the British (Dumnonian) frontier forest of Coed Mawr, Selwood, at the battle of Penselwood[2] in 658. The details of conquest will be discussed later.

A rapid westerly Saxon advance forced the British to retreat beyond the River Parrett in what is now central Somerset, which became a new, temporary boundary. This left the important monastic site of Glastonbury (Ynis Witrin, Island of Glass of the Welsh) vulnerable to looting and damage. Luckily, the victors, newly converted to Christianity, were by this time becoming conscious of the worth of historic holy sites.

Penselwood was then called, in the 8th century Welsh written form of the collection of the cities of Britain, *Cair Pensa vel Coyt*. It may have been an important habitation site at the southern end of the forest, *pen* meaning *end* in Welsh. The word *coyt* or *coed*, as written in English, means *wood*, *mawr* means *great*. The English scribe, hearing the Welsh name, Pensa vel Coyt, leaves out the obvious reference to a town or city, Caer (as in Cardiff and Caer Bathon, Bath) and writes down *sa vel* wood, joining the words *sa* and *vel*. Selwood comes into being. We can check how this might happen by looking at another place-name which has the element *vel* in it.

Keyford in Frome was at Domesday an important village community just outside of Frome, Somerset. It was spelled *Caivel* in its Latin form. If we separate the parts of the word form, we can see that *Cai-vel* could, in these times of general illiteracy and attempts at spelling, by Welsh, English and Latin writers, chime with the *sa-vel* of Penselwood.

Sa-vel and *Cai-vel*. Here we might be homing in on Celtic British or early Welsh written forms of the sound of the place-names. A local inhabitant, asked by a scribe to tell him the name of the place he was wishing to record, would supply a verbal rendition. The English scribe, anxious to report to the new lord of the place, would write an approximate spelling in his own language. Only local knowledge would do for a king or thegn in actively constructing a fresh administrative area, unless he wished to completely alienate its inhabitants or to exterminate them and it is clear from the historical record, particularly Ine's Laws of the early 8th century, that British inhabitants were living in the newly established western part of Wessex in considerable numbers. The word *vel* in Latin is a conjunctive word, meaning *either, and/or, even,* or *indeed,* according to its context.[3]

Assuming that *Sa vel Coyt* and *Cai Vel* both have, or could have had, hyphens in their names, (and would have had, were they to be heard and written down fresh by some incoming army of scribes today) and that *vel* is simply used here to mean *or,* then we can remove it and rejoin the words *sa* and *coyt* which means an original speaker, being interrogated by a king's scribe, may have referred to his neck of the woods as *Sa,* or *Sa Coit.*

What comes out of the mouth of this Welsh speaker, as heard by the English scribe, is *secoit.* The English scribe is well aware, in his dealings with others, that *coit* means *wood.* He writes down *se,* or *se wood.* It's is much easier to say if another letter is added, for instance *l,* to sound the forest name, and so, over time, the *l* sticks. In many place-names we see these changes in spelling and sometimes pronunciation occur for ease of use and subject to local dialect. For instance, Bull Mead Lane, a lane to a field at Trudoxhill near Frome, was pronounced in the 1980s as *Boomy*

Lane by an elderly, long term inhabitant of that place. The dialect form of a name is another consideration to take into account when hearing and particularly writing the form of any place-name.

To Selwood from Coit Mawr may seem a long stretch from the original Welsh name of the forest given in Asser's biography of Alfred,[4] but one must bear in mind the flexibility and fluctuation of the written spelling over many centuries before the permanent modern forms were set by popular usage and Victorian typesetting. The original form of Bath is another case of this need for analysis. Over years the rendering of a place-name sometimes becomes invisible to the modern historian's eye through its variety of forms, spelling and sounds.[5]

Saxon scribes had a busy time in the early eighth century, no doubt on a mission of recording not unlike the Domesday clerks of 1086, and they also, like the Norman French, had a language problem. Should they rename everywhere afresh for tax collection purposes? Should everything become marked in English or Latin on their spreadsheets? If Somerset had been emptied of its Brythonic Welsh speakers, the Britons of Dumnonia, this might have been an easy task.

Considerable numbers must have been absorbed, along with their language and customs. Sammes, writing in the 17th century, records the place-name 'Nant Twynant', Old Welsh for 'warm valley' for Lympley Stoke valley, near Bath, Somerset, which indicates some, at least, of the old words were still being spoken despite a long established English equivalent being in common use.

In cultural terms the Saxons were not the savages they had been in their supposedly more brutal takeover of the eastern kingdoms. Historians and archaeologists are still uncertain about the nature of the British loss of power. The newcomers in the south-west had become softened by the lure of cultural pursuits, were beginning to value things other than treasure, as the Vikings later on and earlier the Gothic hordes of central Europe had been. Christianity softened warriors, opened their eyes to something more gratifying than mere looting. Glastonbury monastery, a great seat of learning, was not erased, but prized by Ine. In the seventh century Cenwalh gave land to Sherborne community, known as Llanprobus to the British. The Saxons were learning to care for their souls as well as land. The birth of modern education had occurred; scribes began to record charters involving land and other rights; writing and reading became desirable for those who might wish to claim and hold onto their possessions or to rise through the ranks at the royal court. The Saxons found Devon (central Dumnonia) nearly empty of British inhabitants; many emigrated to Armorica (Brittany) and elsewhere along the Atlantic seaboard as evidenced by language changes there. Somerset seems to have been less empty. Perhaps the late seventh century defeats and rapid move westwards by Cenwalh, the Saxon leader, took them by surprise. Perhaps the British inhabitants of Somerset were less fussy than Devon families about who they mixed with.

Saxon scribes, rifling through the contents of Glastonbury library, may have come across gems of the written history of the Britons, parts of which have survived. There may have been, probably by Ine's orders (he was particularly interested in the cult of Indract, an Irish saint) and subsequent kings, a deep respect for some of this and for the promotion of learning by the Irish monks established there. Perhaps because they were Irish and not British (British priests had scorned to convert the pagan Saxons), the monastery was allowed to continue. It survived later encroachment and threats from the pagan Vikings, as did Malmesbury. This may have been due, in some part, to the magical or holy status of these communities. There is a story, recorded by William of Malmesbury in the 12th century of the miraculous protection of Malmesbury from Vikings by the spirit of St Aldhelm whose shrine was there before translation by

Dunstan in the tenth century to Canterbury. Perhaps Glastonbury had a similar sobering effect on the superstitious. These were early medieval minds, easily affected by the possibility of the vengeful effects of the supernatural. The word *perhups* should always be added during writing any supposition of these matters. They are very grey areas indeed.

Speech is a divider of nations, of communities. Some speakers of minority languages have been rated as inferior by the more dominant and the prejudice against some accents, particularly that of the west country is still a factor influencing social mobility today. As such it supplies evidence for an understanding of the relative positions of Celt and Saxon in the south-west. Some Somerset place-names are clearly of British origin, heard and written down by English scribes in English, their Welsh spellings and forms fossilised, in many cases, in the written language of the newcomers, but this has made them all but invisible to the English historian and caused much academic debate.

British might have continued to be spoken for about 300 years after the initial demise of Dumnonia, it is thought, which would take us to a reasonable bilingual state at about the time of the Norman invasion. It might well have been necessary for wealthier British speakers, in order to move up the social ladder, to adopt English as their mother tongue rapidly after conquest, leaving the lower orders to carry on with their own customs and language. Such a process is still seen in the valleys of Wales and elsewhere in recent times, where some have deliberately dropped their Welsh accent in favour of an English accent. These are human tendencies which would have been just as relevant in the time of the early Saxon/British interface.

Topographical features are often a part of this admittedly minimal language survival (*cruch*, hill, being common, in various spellings), but so were beliefs and myths. The area of Somerset and parts of what is now western Wiltshire were occupied by ancestors of the Welsh over many thousands of years with little apparent disturbance, plenty of time to build up story associations, religious lore, heroic tales and superstitions. River, sea and hill names are often strongly redolent of a mythical attachment to the landscape, as in Wales, an association of belonging which the Saxons, a mere two centuries away from their mythical homelands in central Europe could not hope to understand or probably wish to.

It is not surprising that the Place-name Society of England has not yet published an up to date version of the place-names of Somerset. They are not yet fully understood. All sources of history, archaeological, geographical, religious, folkloric, not merely the topographical and linguistic, need to be synthesised for this, a mammoth task and the same applies to all the border counties of England which were late in being taken over by Saxon scribes and kings.

The conquest of the West Welsh, as the British inhabitants of the south west peninsula came to be known by Anglo-Saxon Chronicle scribes, left them divorced from their Welsh cousins across the Severn. The Saxon Hwicce tribe (who however may have been predominantly British in origin), took over the Severn mouth, enjoying the ruins of Bath, ensuring no reinforcements could easily arrive to assist the West Welsh remnant army. The sea, however, remained an important means of inter-British communication and in the sixth century it had been the route for saints pouring out from such early monastic centres as Llantwit Major (St Illtyd Fawr) to reconvert the recidivists and apostates of Dumnonia. They may have been seen as in danger of revitalising old pagan beliefs, particularly in the countryside, bringing back their pre-Roman deities and myths. Cernunnos, a well attested god of the pre-Roman Iron Age in north west Europe, became Cerne or Herne, perhaps allied with Hercules as at Cerne Abbas, a potent symbol of the natural forces of the world and fate surrounding a people in need of saving from the oncoming tide of the Saxons.

By the time Asser, Welsh Bishop of St David's, was associating in the late ninth century with the keen student Alfred and assisting him with his Latin and biography, the respect between, or mutual loathing of, the two peoples must have begun to die away in inevitable acceptance of the permanent state of Wessex. Assimilation after 200 years in West Wessex is to be expected, though memories of the culture of Dumnonia must have remained. The Welsh of southern mainland Wales, for instance Hywel Dda, had accepted that it was best, at least in diplomatic terms, to play along with the idea that Wessex and England were inevitably in control, to their mutual advantage. The kings of Strathclyde and Alba (Scotland) were not so happy with the arrangement. The example of devolution of government in the present day may well herald the breakup of what the 10th century English hoped would be a permanent arrangement.

Using a synthesis of approach to the history of this dark age in the south-western peninsula we can peer into a world where it is clear that the land of Summer, Somerset, clung on to some of its original Brythonic language and to some of its ancient customs, pagan as well as Christian, for much longer than perhaps has been so far realised. We can see the ghostly shreds of a sense of belonging, of the stories which attached the people to this landscape of Selwood, fossilised in placenames. Not all the Britishness has disappeared. Something of this land of Greater Wales, the Lost Lands, Lloegr, is still to be discovered, after over a thousand years of neglect.

Much has been said elsewhere about the two active protagonists of Saxon dominance in the south west region. The early eighth century King Ine and Aldhelm, Abbot of Malmesbury, Bishop of Sherborne and founder of the monasteries of Frome and

Bradford-on-Avon, were State and Church personified. This came to be the dominant partnership of governance for the next 800 years. The Anglo-Saxon Chronicle, looking back from Alfred's time in the late ninth century, informs us of the general movements of peoples.

Cenwalh began it all. An early king of Wessex, he fought the pincer movement against the British at Penselwood in 658 which rounded the corner of the southern extremity of Selwood. This meant that with the earlier fall of Bath at the battle of Dyrham,[6] an overall conquest of eastern Dumnonia was within his grasp.

Cenwalh died in 672. His wife, Seaxburh, was powerful, perhaps a cultured influence, reigning after him for a year. The kingdom then passed beyond her immediate family to Aescwine in 674. He died only two years later, when Centwine, brother of Cenwalh, took over the Wessex kingship. Family and factional discord may have been a factor in these rapid changes.

In 682 Centwine "drove the Britons as far as the sea".[7] Theories abound about the positioning of the Wessex forces throughout the late 7th century. So many of the British/Saxon encounters cannot topographically be fixed accurately and we are confined to best guesses in most cases. Which sea and where it was remains a mystery, but we can guess the coastline north of Taunton, since we know from charters that Centwine was in possession of land as far west as within three miles of Taunton by 680 or 684 at the latest.[8] He reigned for a relatively settled time of nine years, then abdicated, dying later the same year. Ine then became king in 688.

With Ine came consolidation of the western wing of Wessex. The whole of what would become Somerset was absorbed and parcelled out to relatives and followers, thegns and reeves of the royal court. Sherborne, granted lands by the king, was given its English name, having previously been the British St Probus' base, Llanprobus. It seems that Celtic saints had reached far inland from their south Welsh origins, perhaps as far as Frome.

Sherborne became a new bishopric to cater for mission work west of Selwood, separated from the old diocese of Winchester which had become too unwieldy and large for one Bishop to manage. Aldhelm became its first bishop. Aldhelm had a great deal of work to do, perhaps dealing not merely with pagan Saxon settlers but also pagan Britons as well as those re-converted by the earlier Welsh saints.

Colonisation was regulated so that Anglo-Saxon immigrants could not take on more land than they could cope with. British subjects became slaves or continued as land owning peasants or farmers. Intermarriage, over time, smoothed things out.

Selwood remained a significant barrier to easy travel east-west across country for a considerable time (a group of bandits is reported living at Gare/Gaer Hill near Maiden Bradley in the 18th century),[10] though it gradually became whittled down into manageable chunks of woodland. Frome may have acted as a travel conduit for trade and immigration, a staging post. The oaks of Selwood were a valuable resource. Saxons, Alfred included, were almost as keen on woodwork in its various forms as hunting, it seems.[11] Palaces at Cheddar and Frome provided hotel arrangements for witan meetings and for festivities, including the winter witan at Frome in 934, when Athelstan, with his sub-king Hywel Dda of Wales and all his archbishops and bishops were present.

The so-called Frome 'gap', where the woodland was presumably less dense, and which seems to have been a thoroughfare through to the Severn coast at Brean (another Roman temple) and on to Wales, may for many years have been a natural route from the chalklands (via the great topographical feature and sign-post of Cley Hill) of southern Britain to the west and vice versa.

Asser, the Bishop of Dyfed and later of Sherborne, biographer of Alfred at the end of the ninth century, refers to Selwood Forest in his Life of the King,[12] calling it *sylva magna* (great wood) in Latin and *Coit Mawr* in Welsh (British). He refers to the men of Somerset, Wiltshire and Hampshire joining forces to support Alfred at Ecgberht's Stone (Ecgberht was a 9th century king of Wessex), "which is in the eastern part of Selwood Forest". No-one has been able to pinpoint this place precisely, but the Victorian monument, Alfred's Tower, at Stourhead in Wiltshire, is probably not far out. Brixton Deverill/Cold Kitchen Hill may be brought into the mix, Brixton sounding similar to *Ecgberhtstone*. Evidently the meeting place of the warriors was well known at the time of writing and may indicate some place of settlement. The finding of a significant Roman villa in 2015 in the valley at Brixton Deverill may have some bearing, with evidence of post-Roman wooden structures. There is no specific battle or other famed site known as Egbert's in the area which could be suggested.

Asser talks about the recollections of Alfred of the coming battle with the forces of Guthrum the Dane in 878, who had taken over Alfred's fortress of Chippenham. At Egbert's Stone Alfred made camp for one night. The next camp was a short hop away, north eastwards towards Chippenham. They set off at dawn to "Iley" for another single night's camp. This must be somewhere between Egbert's Stone and Edington, where the battle took place. Some have suggested Iley Oak, which is apparently a name near Warminster. More likely, as a Welsh speaker, writing in English *y glea*, which is the form of spelling used by Asser, is his record of a place he may not, as a native of Dyfed, known personally, but hears it from the King, who does, whose scribes have picked up the name from Britons, *y lle*, which in Welsh means *the place*. We end up then, with an anglicised form of *y lle*, the similar sounding Cley hill (note: this is a chalk hill, not clay). Iley/y glea/ Cley Hill, on the edge of Warminster, a significant chalk outlier, a one thousand feet island hill in the landscape, former Bronze Age burial ground, early Iron Age hillfort and easily defendable, may have been the site of the last night of Alfred's camp before the battle at Edington.

During Alfred's time in the *mors* (Moors) of Somerset (the inland seas, again a Welsh word), the Danes were free to maraud the eastern boundary of western Wessex, still partly bounded by Selwood. What they did during the winter and spring of 877/878 is anyone's guess, but they were probably utilising all the skills they have become famous for. Aldhelm's monasteries of Frome and Bradford-on-Avon probably suffered.

In 1997 the Warminster Jewel, a rock crystal aestel head (gospel pointer) of the type which Alfred is known to have commissioned and given to his bishops, not unlike the famous Alfred Jewel, was found by a metal detectorist in a field near Cley Hill. It is now on permanent view in Salisbury Museum. The presence of bishops and the relics of saints were essential to the attempt to defeat the Danes. Cuthbert had promised much to Alfred in a dream. A lost bishop's valuable aestel on the night full of religious ritual before battle? A small price to pay.

1   For a summary of the battles, Briton versus Saxon, see Tim and Annette Burkitt, 'The Frontier Zone and the Siege of Mount Badon', *Proceedings of the Somerset Archaeological and Natural History Society*, vol. 134, 1990 and earlier article, 'Badon as Bath', *Popular Archaeology*, April 1985, vol 6, no 6 (at Bath Central Library).

2   9th century writer, Nennius in *De Civitatibus Brittanniae, Cair Pensa vel Coyt* is assumed to refer to Penselwood, Somerset. John Morris, ed., *British History and the Welsh Annals*, Phillimore, London and Chichester, 1980.

3   Latin Conjunctions-Ancient/Classical History-About.com, N.S Gill.

4   Asser's Life of Alfred, in *Alfred the Great*, trans. Simon Keynes and Michael Lapidge, Penguin, 1983.

5   Annette Bennett and Tim Burkitt, 'Badon as Bath', *Popular Archaeology*, April 1985, vol6, no 6 (at Bath Central Library).

6   Anglo Saxon Chronicle for 577AD

7   Porter, H.M., *The Saxon Conquest of Somerset and Devon*, Pub.

James Brodie, 1967.

8 Porter, ibid p 30.

9 Porter, ibid p 39.

10 Collinson, *History of Somerset.*

11 Alfred's statement, in *Alfred the Great.*

12 Asser, *ibid.*

Places and Items mentioned in the Text

Known or speculative British place-names shown in italics.

The Old English letter, the thorn (ð) is pronounced *th*. Latin speakers and writers do not have a *th* spoken sound or letter to represent it. They most often write *d* or *dd* instead.

Alice Street Farm, Leighton, near Nunney, Somerset, lies on the line of the Roman road E/W from the Mendips to Cold Kitchen Hill. The name Street indicates a possible Roman connection. *Alice* may derive from *llaes*, long, (Welsh). Long Lane is nearby.

Bath, *Caer Badon*, Somerset, *Aquae Sulis* of the Romans, *Baðon* and *Bathe* of the Saxons, *Caer Bathon* in modern Welsh, probable site of the 517 Battle of Badon (Arthur's defeat of Saxons). 'One of the hills around Bath is commonly known by two names: Lansdown and Mons Badonica.' Sames, 17th antiquary, in Britannia, quoted by Wood, J.C., in *A Description of Bath* (18th century), Kingsmead Reprints, Bath 1969.

Bradford-on-Avon, Wiltshire, monastery founded by Aldhelm c.705. Disappeared by the time of William of Malmesbury in the 12th century. (see Frome, below).

Bruton, Somerset, township beneath the hill of Lamyatt. *Brumetone* at Domesday.

Cerne Abbas, Dorset. The chalk giant, whatever his origins and date, has been identified as Cernunnos. Here he may be conflated with Hercules as he holds a club. A medieval Christian community established below the hill tries to offset his obvious virility. Aethelwold, one of the chief protagonists of the tenth century reform movement, spent time with the monastic community at

Cerne and it must have affected his thinking. There is a decorated metal strap end at Winchester museum with a figure incised on it looking very much like the Cerne chalk-cut figure.

Cheddar, Somerset Site of a Saxon Palace, excavated by Philip Rahtz 1979 *The Saxon and Medieval Palaces at Cheddar* (BAR Brit. Series 65 Oxford).

Cley Hill, near Warminster, Wiltshire. Geologically, a chalk outlier of the Salisbury Plain chalk hills, an island of chalk upland lying near the greensand ridge of Longleat to the west. Victor Strode Manley, who collected folklore of the Warminster area in the 1920s (his notes are held by Warminster library) talks of hearing of the men of Somerset and Wiltshire meeting (within living memory) below Cley Hill for an annual contest. 'A free fight with fists and sticks took place to see which side of the county boundary one party could drive the other. As men were laid out they were flung up in the hedge to clear the road'.

Katherine Jordan (*The Folklore of Ancient Wiltshire*, 1990, Warminster Library) records that a revel held on Cley Hill on Palm Sunday involved burning the grass here 'to burn the devil out'. She comments that a revel was a funerary feast commemorating an ancestor. Strode Manley records a game of ball and sticks on the same day. The ball was played uphill by a line of men armed with curved sticks.

Cold Kitchen Hill, *Coel Kutchen* (guessed spelling), near Maiden Bradley, Wiltshire, significant crossing place at or very near two crossing Roman roads. A pagan temple site and extensive settlement is associated with it. Some excavation took place in the 1920s. See Cunliffe, B in *Victoria County History: Wiltshire* vol. 1 (pt. 2) p 416. A masonry wayside shrine, temple and other structures probably associated with ceremony and a market was found. To *kutch* is to enfold or cuddle in modern Welsh.

For references to The Curly-haired Hero and Cold Kitchen Hill see *Pagan Celtic Britain*, Ann Ross 1967 repr. 1992 Constable. Archaeological Gazetteer in *Victoria County History: Wiltshire* , vol I (pt. I), p I, 1957.

Who is the hero enshrined in the horse and rider brooches found at both **Cold Kitchen Hill**, **Lamyatt** and many other sites throughout Britain (brooches have been found in many different places)? Perhaps he is the St Anthony of earlier times, the travelling companion and protector of the journeyman. Hywel/Coel could be the sheltering protector named at the many Cold Harbours especially in southern England. It has been suggested that these may be wayside rest stops.

For **Taranis**, curly brown-haired god of the Iron Age on the continent and probably here as well, see Ross ibid p 476.

Bran the Blessed is known in the Mabinogi of Branwen as Bendigeit, 'blessed'. He was said to have a wonderful, talismanic head which supposedly protected London when buried, after battle in Ireland, at the White Tower. He leads his people into battle, guiding ships to Ireland, carrying musicians on his back, a patron of the arts as well as a war leader. He is consistently described as a giant. He wades across the sea to Ireland. His head presides at the Otherworld feast. His name meant 'raven'. See Ross ibid, p 322.

Two headless skeletons were found in the temple or feast midden at **Cold Kitchen Hill** in the 19th century, *Wilts Arch. Gazeteer*. Bran is associated with the widespread cult of the head in Celtic society.

We seem to have a conflated hero/god at **Cold Kitchen Hill**, associated with the sky, a popular mythological figure to be revered and seen as a major character of feast times associated with the agricultural year, from at least the second century AD in southern Britain and at Cold Kitchen earlier than this, perhaps pre-Roman. Much the same feasting and gathering at the four festivals would have been widespread throughout the pre-Christian era and even into it, the gods becoming adopted and conflated into saints in the Christian culture which followed. Some echoes of the festivals remained as stubborn reminders of a former, freer or more primitive past which celebrated the wild hunt and fertility in ways which came to be seen as disturbing to the developed Christian culture of later Saxon times.

The **wheel brooches and horse and rider brooches** found at Cold Kitchen and Lamyatt are possibly pilgrim badges, perhaps a talisman for the traveller or just a reminder of the gathering and the hero in whose name it was held. The red and blue enamel of the horse and rider brooches suggest strong associations with the **Gwynn ap Nudd** legends of the **Wild Hunt**, related in the story of sixth century St Collen (Porter, *The Celtic Church in Somerset*, 1971, p 64/5), where the saint is invited to visit the red and blue dressed court of Annwn, the Otherworld, through the portal of **Glastonbury Tor**. The Wild Hunt is said to have raged in the early winter at the time of Samhain, when beasts were slaughtered, when stormy weather in the darkness carried the newly dead along in the sky.

Crewkerne, *Cruc Herne*(?), Somerset, hill of Herne. Crucherne, the Welsh spelling for the place the English spell Crewkerne today, like Crickhowell. The *herne* element in place-names is common throughout southern England. The port of Concarneau in the southern kingdom of Brittany, where so many of the Dumnonian folk went has it and acknowledges it as a reference to Cernunnos in its town history. The Bay of Herne in Kent and the hill of Herne there preserve it. There are others across the land of Wessex. Some of them are spelled in different ways. Instead of an e, they may have an *i*, or a *u*. But they all sound the same to the ear. The village of Horningsham, Wiltshire, is another notable example, lying below and within sight of the looming Cold Kitchen Hill.

Many of the *-herne* names have *h* as a first letter. Sometimes they begin with *c* as at Cerne in the county of Dorset, sometimes

two words with *k* as at Crew-kerne. Cornwall, known to the
Cornish as Kernow, means Hornland. These *-horn/hern/hirn/hurn*
names are common. They have a harsh *hhh* sound at the back of
the throat, somewhere between a *hair* and a *chair* sound.

Crickhowell, Wales. Welsh word meaning the hill of Hywell.
Another placename with the hywell (pron. in English *coel*)
connotation, like **Cold Kitchen Hill**, but without the 'kutch'
(cuddle) element.

Egbert's Stone (or Ecgberht). Said by Asser in his biography
of Alfred to be the meeting place of the men of Wessex before
the Battle of Edington, 878. The site is uncertain, but has been
assumed to be somewhere along the route from Athelney in
Somerset to the vicinity of Warminster in Wiltshire. Stevenson,
W H, *Asser's Life of King Alfred*, Oxford 1904, suggests that it may
have been near **Penselwood. Alfred's Tower** at Stourton is another
suggestion. The crossing point of two major Roman roads on
Cold Kitchen Hill near the present village of **Brixton Deverill** is
more likely, for two reasons. The first is that this hill was on the
eastern side of Selwood (the Anglo-Saxon Chronicle talks of it
being 'to the east of Selwood', which Stourton and Penselwood
are not), and the place-name Brixton. The Anglo-Saxon Chronicle
calls it *Ecgbryhtesstan*.

Frome, Somerset, monastery founded c. 685 by Aldhelm. Visited
by Wessex kings for hunting and entertainment, an important
Wessex palace site. Possible site of British monastery of St Cay/
Kai or Key. (Keyford was a manor at Domesday, now part of
the town of Frome). There is no mention of any monastery at
Frome in 1086. Porter H M in *Saint Aldhelm, Abbot of Frome*
(Frome Society for Local Study, 1984) points out that William of
Malmesbury (12th century) reports that the church was built in
honour of St John the Baptist and it is still there. Faritius, Abbot

of Abingdon, writing before 1100, also mentions it. William of Malmesbury reports that the church was still there but not the monastery, which has "followed the fashion of mortal things and disappeared, leaving only an empty name, although it is hard to decide whether we should blame the fierce wars with the Danes for the destruction of these great buildings or the rapacious altercations of the English". (William of Malmesbury, *Aldhelm and Malmesbury Abbey*, chapter 198, Aldhelm's Monastic Foundations).

King Eadred died at Frome on 23 November 955. He was sickly all his life, so it possible to surmise that he may have died in a monastic hospital, which Frome might have had. If so, this would suggest that something of the monastery of St John survived at least until this time. The church and its lands were taken over by the Abbot of Cirencester, who had a tythe barn on the site of the present St John's school, demolished in the early 20th century.

Glastonbury, *Ynis Witrin*, Somerset (island of glass) of the Welsh, site of probable Roman, post Roman and early medieval monastery renowned throughout western Europe as a great centre of learning. It survived the Danish assaults. Reformed and rebuilt by Dunstan in the 10th century, it became a Benedictine centre of great wealth until the Dissolution of the early 16th century. Its abbot, refusing to surrender to Thomas Cromwell and King Henry VIII, was hung, drawn and quartered.

Hales Castle, (earthwork), East Woodlands, near Frome, and Cole Hill on which it stands. Both may refer to Hywell/Coel.

Horse and Rider brooches. At least 17 Horse and Rider brooches have been found in Great Britain, dating from the early Roman period to 2/3rd centuries. Two, including one found at **Cold Kitchen**, can be viewed in the museum at Devizes. Along with

wheel brooches, which may be representative of Jupiter, perhaps
conflated with a local deity, these are a sign of a commonly
worshipped divinity throughout a wide area, of a shared interest
by the southern Romano-British population. The horse and
rider brooches always have the same characteristics of incised
hair, large head of the rider (he could be said to be all head with
little body) and red or red and blue enamelling. The open mouth
of both rider and horse is also usual. There is no indication of
weaponry. Some appear to be more crudely made than others, but
in the best preserved, the tinning around the eyes is clear, done
presumably to show the brightness of vision, perhaps joyfulness
or magical powers attached to the characters of the two by the
imagination and priests who sold these pilgrimage badges.
Five similar Horse and Rider brooches were also found during
excavations at **Lamyatt** near Bruton at the temple site there.
Others have been found in Norfolk.

Refs: Ed. Peter Ellis, 'Religion in Roman Wiltshire' in
Roman Wiltshire and After, Papers in Honour of Ken Annable,
Wiltshire Archaeological and Natural History Society 2001 157 fig
8.11.

'The Excavation of a Romano-Celtic Temple and a Later
Cemetery on Lamyatt Beacon, Somerset', Roger Leech in *Britannia*,
vol 17 1986 pp 259-328. See The Ritual Shriek, page 381.

Lamyatt, *Lamiae*(?) Somerset (place of the three Lamiae) Lamyatt
Beacon Roman pagan temple site, near Bruton in Somerset, above
the small hamlet of Lamyatt, was excavated in 1985 by Roger
Leech (*Britannia* 1986, vol 17 pp 259-328). It was extensively
robbed in the years preceding, but excavation was able to reveal
a great deal of its character. Many votive objects were uncovered,
including a variety of metal miniature Roman god statuettes.
Antlers cast by deer had been buried as ritual objects as at **Cold
Kitchen** and five horse and rider brooches with remnants of
blue and red enamel, of the same style as those at Cold Kitchen,

were found. The burials of at least 16 people were recorded, in close association with the antlers, buried east-west, indicating a Christian bias, though Romano-British pottery was present in some of the graves. A mid sixth to mid eighth century date was given for the burials. The tallest of the female burials was 1.780 metres, the skeleton being described as tall and slender, with a square chin.

At **Lamyatt** and at **Cold Kitchen** there are **antler burials.** Here we have yet another mythical figure being remembered and revered. Cernunnos, the horned god, is well attested on the continent and appears on the Gundestrup Cauldron from Denmark. Antler wearing appears on cave art of the Palaeolithic period of the last ice age and even today in the Abbots Bromley horn dance.

The place-name Lamyatt is said by Ekwall to mean "Lambs Gate". Another possibility, which records the actual use of the site, could be *Lamiae*, a reference to the triple goddesses, sometimes known as the **Macha.** The excavation revealed structures including a sunken room with fire evidence, similar to that found at Benwell in Northumberland. The Romano-Celtic temple at Benwell was dedicated to a group of three goddesses called the Lamiis Tribus, or Lamiae. (Ann Ross, Pagan Celtic Britain p 285). Their altar was found in a subterranean room, reddened by fire, as at Lamyatt. The Latin name for the goddesses belies the Celtic concept of the goddess type; it is noteworthy, however, that Cormac, a king of Ireland, glosses Macha, the war goddess, as Lamia (Ross p 313).

This triple war goddess is found often in references in the British Isles. Sometimes referred to in the myths as the Macha (Ross p 267), ravens are often alluded to, as are horses, so that the idea of the three female godesses links to Epona and Rhiannon, horse goddesses, but also to fecundity and childbirth. Sometimes they are associated with war and the taking of heads, so common a theme in the Celtic imagination and culture.

Lantocay: Kai was one of those who came towards Selwood to try to shore up the magic of the Christian god. He had been a soldier, so it was natural to him to take an advanced position. He set up a church at Lantokay at Leigh in Street near Glastonbury, at Landkey near Barnstaple (ref. Glastonbury Charters, Porter p 60) and Kea near Truro. He was a contemporary of Gildas while he was at Glastonbury and said to be the son of a king of Usk.

There is debate about the position of Aldhelm's monastery in **Frome.** He may have built upon earlier Christian sites when establishing his new monastic centres and new diocese of Sherborne. There may have been a Celtic Christian religious house of some kind at **Keyford.** This may mark the site of a foundation by Kai, who as we have seen was active throughout Dumnonia. At Domesday the manor of Keyford, treated separately from Frome, is called *Caivel* and *Chaivert* in two separate entries. Perhaps a site at Keyford, a Celtic Christian foundation, was gradually shut down by Aldhelm's foundation of St John which was probably nearer the river, half a mile away, in the late seventh century and that for a while they coincided. The palace of the Saxon kings is also likely to have been near the river bridge and close to the church. The record of religious remains at Keyford remain a mystery but the place-name may contain the clue as it does in all the other placenames where we know Kai to have been active. A family by the name of Cayford lives in Frome to this day.

Llanilltyd Fawr: Lantwit Major, south Wales. Monastic centre of St Illtyd, 6th century.

Machen, Glamorgan, south Wales and **Machen Mountain**: its name is more than suggestive of the pre-Christian triple goddess, the Macha. (Ross, Pagan Celtic Britain). Another hilltop religious/folklore connection?

Malmesbury, Wiltshire, site of the Irish monastic foundation of

Maildubh, tutor of Aldhelm, seventh century.

Penselwood, Somerset, the southern tip of Saxon Selwood. Said to be a city by Nennius, 9th century monk (*Nennius, British History and the Welsh Annals*, ed John Morris, Phillimore 1980.

Shaftesbury, *Paladur*, (Geoffrey of Monmouth) Dorset.

Sherborne, *Llanprobus*, Dorset. The Church of Probus, Celtic Christian, which was the bishopric of Aldhelm's new diocese west of Selwood in the late seventh century.

Wanstrow, *Wodens Treow*(?), Somerset.

Frome Place-name

Eilert Ekwall, writing at the dawn of place-name study in
England in the early 20th century,[1] considered that Frome,
certainly a British place-name, stemmed from the Welsh word
ffraw, meaning fair, brisk or fine. Local historians since then have
accepted this without question. Ekwall's opinion has never been
challenged and we are left wondering why a description of a not
very impressive north Somerset river has stuck as a meaning. The
county of Somerset has not been updated yet by the English Place-
name society, who have, since then, developed their extensive
understanding of philology.

The first mention in the written record of Frome is as
From in or about 701, when Aldhelm received a Bull from Pope
Sergius to build a monastery here.[2] The Latin reads: '*Fecit et aliud
cenobium juxta fluvium qui vocatur From*'[3] (and he made another
monastery close to the river which is called From).

Modern readers see *From* making the same sound as the
modern preposition from, but perhaps as with Bath (Badon)
there was some difficulty in writing down the local and probably
abiding sound of the pronunciation of Frome as *froom*. Let's
suppose that a scribe in Rome was doing his best. In 1252 a scribe
writes the place-name of Bishop's Frome (Herefordshire) as *Frume
al Evesk*. It is useful to compare the other Frome name spellings,
all pronounced *froom* and all to do with the British river name in
border areas between Wales and England. Someone, as late as the
13th century, is trying to write the *froom* sound. The modern name
Frome, involving habitations and rivers, occurs commonly in the
Dorset, Somerset and Hereford areas.

Frome St. Quintin (Dorset)
Chilfrome (Dorset)
Fromes Hill (Hereford) Canon Frome (Hereford)
Bishop's Frome (Hereford).

Castle Frome (Hereford)

Related names may be:

Frampton (Dorset)
Frampton (Lincs)
Frampton Cotterell (Gloucester)
Frampton Mansell (Gloucester)
Frampton-on-Severn (Gloucester)

Why did Frome (Somerset) never become Frampton? Was it perhaps because it had the name *Selwood* attached to it? It would be useful to follow, through written evidence, the development of the Frampton names. Why did Frome receive an *e*? Perhaps this makes the name more obvious to a medieval eye as reading with a long *oo* sound.

The next known written appearance of Frome after 701 is in the charter of 934, where, again in Latin, it appears as *Fromae*. The Anglo-Saxon Chronicle was being written probably during Alfred's time for the earlier years; it records Frome as the death place of Eadred in 955.The OE spelling (Parker Chronicle) is *Frome*.[4]

At Domesday in 1086 Frome appears in all citations as Frome. There is no mention of Selwood. The Selwood appellation was at least occasionally in use by 1599 as a parish name.[5]

Place-name experts consider that Britons living in or displaced from early-middle Saxon territory in England were tending to develop Celtic-British speech into either Old Cornish, or in the eastern part of south west England into Old Welsh. Perhaps modern Welsh might provide a few clues to the spelling and pronunciation of Frome.

Ffraw is the name we are invited to look at by Ekwall, describing moving water. That does not suggest the sound of the place-name Frome or froom. The *m* sound would be more prominent, we should expect, in all these different places which produce the same sounding name.

Let's try another word. Modern Welsh provides us with *Ffrwm*, which sounds like the English pronunciation of Frome. It occurs at Caerleon, the legionary city in south Wales, as *Ffrwm Caerleon*. *Ffrwm Road*, Machen, also in south Wales, is another instance.

Ffwrwm is the name of a modern arts and crafts centre in Caerleon. The name must be recording a memory of something older. The centre includes the partially reconstructed gate entrance to the Roman legionary fortress. *Ffwrwm* is said to be derived from the Latin 'forum' and is modern Welsh for *seat* or *bench*. The forms which were benches in school gymnasiums spring to mind, as does Kingsettle Hill, near Brewham, near Bruton, Somerset. It is worth bearing in mind that *seat* could indicate *seat of government*, or *throne*, c.f Arthur's Seat in Edinburgh, Cadair Idris in Wales.

Both *Ffrwm* and *Ffwrwm* might be better places to look for the origin of Frome as a town name than *Ffraw*. The use of the 'w' representing the *oo* sound would not be used by an English scribe. Perhaps it means the *King's Seat*? Canon Frome and Bishop's Frome (Canon's Seat and Bishop's Seat make sense) might be pointing that way. Perhaps, as Athelstan and his heirs were important 10th century figures, a name involving the word *king* either was never attached or was unnecessary. However, Frome at Domesday was clearly an important early medieval town, owned by the king.

Then the question arises: why did not other places in the south and west involve the British word for *seat* or *bench*? Why is the river name of Frome so dominant in the area bordering the edge of 6/7/8th century kingdoms of Wessex and Hwicce/Mercia? The Hereford, Gloucester, Somerset and Dorset Fromes all lie close to the edge of Anglo-Saxon territorial gains by the mid Saxon period (c.6th/7th centuries). The Somerset and Dorset

Frome names are close to the supposed border between Britons and Saxons, the possible eastern Dumnonian frontier, at this date. Could there be the suggestion of an administrative, if not defensive, boundary here, stretching perhaps with the Cole river of Dorset and the north/south extent of Selwood forest to act as a post-Roman, pre-Saxon official boundary between Dumnonia to the west and the post-Roman Belgae administrative area centred on Winchester to the east? This was a very permeable border, changing rapidly, like the changes in administrative boundaries in the latter half of the 20th century.

The suggestion here is that the kingdom of Dumnonia came into being after the Roman withdrawal in 410. It may have been established by the time of Gildas,[6] writing in about 540. It combined the former smaller administrative regions of Kernow, Defnaint and another, unnamed eastern region. This might have been called Gwlad yr Haf, modern Welsh for *Land of Summer*, or perhaps a word similar to *Sumorsaete*, with a major administrative centre at Somerton, captured from Wessex, only a generation after Dumnonia had fallen, by Aethelbald of Mercia in 733. The place-name Somerset appears to derive from the original inhabitants, the Sumorsaete[7] and was adopted, unchanged, by the Wessex Saxons and Mercians.

Do the Frome/Ffwrm names indicate a boundary of some sort between Britons and Saxons? Do the settlement names predate or post-date the river name? Are they contemporary? Are we looking at the possibility of Frome, Somerset being in existence **before** the coming of Aldhelm?

1   Eilert Ekwall, *The Concise Oxford Dictionary of English Place-names* 4th edition, Oxford 1960.
2   P. Belham, *St Aldhelm and the Founding of Frome*, Frome Local Study Society, 1984.
3   H.M. Porter, *Saint Aldhelm, Abbot of Frome*, Frome Society for Local Study, revised 1984.

4   See T. Jebson, *The Anglo-Saxon Chronicle: An Electronic Edition.*

5   *Calendar of Deeds of Property in the Manor of Frome Selwood,* Frome Society Yearbook, vol 1 1987.

6   Gildas, *The Ruin of Britain, History from the Sources,* Editor: John Morris, Phillimore, 1978.

7   Watts, Victor (ed.), 2004, *The Cambridge Dictionary of English Place-names,* Cambridge University Press. And see R. Whitlock, *Somerset,* London, Batsford, 1975. Whitlock invites interpretation as "settlers by the sea-lakes" (Seo-mere-saetan). If we understand that the Welsh for *sea* is *mor* then we do not have to stretch to an anglicised spelling, *mere,* making it more likely that he is right.

Selwood Forest

'Selwood Forest....spanned the watershed between the streams draining westwards to the Bristol Channel and southwards to the English Channel; the Wiltshire portion rose on the greensand escarpment to nearly 250m, though on the Somerset side it extended onto the lower land of the Oxford Clay'.

James Bond in 'Forests, Chases, Warrens and Parks in Medieval Wessex' p 116 in *The Medieval Landscape of Wessex*, ed M Aston and C Lewis. Oxbow Monograph 46 1994.

1627-9:

Disafforestation:
James Bond, ibid p 132.

16th Century:

'The Forest of Selwood as it is now is 30 myles in compass and streachith one way almost unto Warminster and another way unto the quarters of Shaftesburi, by estimation a ten myles'.
Leland's Itinerary (Victoria County History, Somerset, ii. 555) dated 1540.

'The boundaries of this area merged imperceptibly with the Forest of Gillingham to the south and the Forests of Braydon and Clarendon to the east...'
Michael McGarvie, *The Bounds of Selwood*, Frome Society for Local Study 1978 p 1.

13th Century:

Perambulations, or 'walks' of Selwood Forest are published, describing the bounds of the Royal forest, reserved for the king.

M McGarvie, ibid p1.

10th Century:

Selwood is mentioned in the *Life of St Dunstan*, written about 1000, recording the escape from death of King Edmund while riding in a hunt at Cheddar Gorge.

8th and 9th Centuries:

Asser, biographer of Alfred, records in his *Life of Alfred* that Selwood was known as Coit Mawr, Great Wood, by the Welsh (Asser was Welsh).

Selwood is mentioned as a boundary by the *Anglo-Saxon Chronicle* in 709, 878 and 893.

Earlier:

There is no mention in the surviving written record of Selwood or Coit Mawr until the Saxon conquest, under Cenwalh, of the late 7th century (from 658 onwards, with the battle at the supposed site of Penselwood) and the establishment by Ine and Aldhelm, both Saxons, of the diocese of Sherborne *'to the west of Selwood'*. (A/S Chronicle 709).

Human Skeleton Found At North Hill, Frome, 1931

The Reverend H. Arnold Cook, of 33, Fromefield, Frome, reported to H. St George Gray on 6th June 1931 that a human skeleton had been found recently during road widening, at the point of a triangular piece of orchard at North Hill, where the Bath and Westbury roads divide, at the top of the rise from the town.

The workmen told him that the skeleton was buried face downwards. Some of the bones had already been carted away. Investigation found that the remains represented a strongly built man, of about 5 feet 9 inches. The size of the bones favoured a diagnosis of a Saxon burial, but the skull form suggested a Briton of the Roman period. The modelling of the lower jaw was that of a person fed on well cooked food.

From: H. St. George Gray, *Proceedings of the Archaeological and Natural History Society of Somerset* Volume 77 1931 p 139.

The bones are not at Taunton Museum (information given by Stephen Minnitt, curator, 2017) and are not at Frome Museum.

Benedictine Offices

Matins/Vigils/Nocturns	12 midnight.
Lauds	Dawn or 3am
Prime	6am
Terce	9am
Sext	12 noon
None	3pm
Vespers	6pm
Compline	9pm

The Wessex Dynasty of Ecgberht

Ecgberht (King:802-839) father of

Aethelwulf (King:839-858) father of

Aethelbald (King:858-860) brother of

Aethelberht (King:860-865) brother of

Aethelred (King:865-871) brother of

Alfred (King:871-99) father of

Edward the Elder (King:899-924) father of

Aelfweard (King:924 for 16 days) half-brother of

Athelstan (King:924-939) half-brother of

Edmund (King:939-946) brother of

Eadred (King:946-955) uncle of

Eadwig (King:955-959) brother of

Edgar (King:959-975) father of

Edward (King:975-978) half-brother of

Aethelred (King:978-1016)

The Three Wives and Children of Edward the Elder

1. Ecgwynn	2. Aelfflaed	3. Eadgifu
b. ?	b. ?	b.896
married c.890	married c.900	married c.920
d.?900	died or became nun	died 968, aged 72,
	at Wilton c.920	Canterbury.
Aethelstan and Eadgyth	Aelfweard and Edwin	Edmund and Eadred
	plus daughters	plus daughters

Battles and events in western Wessex from English and Welsh Sources

(All references are from the Anglo-Saxon Chronicle for the year given, unless stated)

577: Cuthwine and Ceawlin, pagan Saxons, *'fought against the Britons and slew three kings, Coinmail, Condidan, and Farinmail, at the place which is called Dyrham; and they captured three cities, Gloucester, Cirencester, and Bath'.*

6th century (or earlier): the founding of major monasteries, run by Irish monks, at Malmesbury and Glastonbury. Other Welsh monastic communities are in existence throughout Somerset, evangelised from south Wales monasteries e.g. Llantwit Major (St Illtyd Fawr), from the 5th/6th centuries.

658: Cenwalh fought at (probably) Penselwood *'against the Welsh'*, and drove them as far as the Parrett.

665: The second battle of Badon.

688: Ine, Christian descendant of Ceawlin, succeeds to the kingdom of Wessex. He *'built the monastery at Glastonbury'*.

709: Aldhelm, founder of the monasteries of Bradford-on-Avon and Frome and first Bishop of Sherborne, dies.

878: Alfred's battle with the Viking leader Guthrum at Edington, Wiltshire. The year of the cake burning and the scattering of Saxon forces into the Moors (mors) of Somerset. (*Asser's Life of Alfred*).

899: Death of Alfred of Wessex. Edward the Elder, Alfred's son, begins his reign.

922: The kings of Wales, including Hywel Dda, give Edward their allegiance as sub-kings.

924: Death of Edward. Accession of Athelstan, his son.

926: Athelstan annexes Northumbria. Hywel, (not Hywel Dda) King of the West Welsh (Devon and Cornwall) and other British kings submit to his rule.

934: The King's court meets for a witan on 16th December at the palace of Frome after returning from the attack on Scotland and a visit to the tomb of Cuthbert at Chester-le-Street near Durham. (n.b. not A/S Ch, but mentioned in a Winchester Old Minster archive and can be assumed to be correct. See Sarah Foote, 'Aethelstan', Appendix II p 263), and see Foot, ibid., p. 88.

937: Athelstan and his half-brother Edmund (aged about 15) fight a conglomeration of enemies of mixed kingdoms from the north, including the Scottish King Constantine, at the battle of *Brunanburh* (probably on the Wirral in Cheshire) and win. A poem is written to commemorate it.

939: Death of Athelstan. His half-brother Edmund becomes King of Wessex and of most of what has become recognisable as modern England.

946: Edmund is killed by Leofa 'the thief' (A/S Ch). His younger brother Eadred becomes king.

955: Eadred dies at Frome. Edmund's son Eadwig succeeds.

The Pelagian Heresy

Pelagius was a British priest active during the formative years of the Roman Church. Born in 354, dying in 420 or 440, he was a thorn in the side of dominant theologians who insisted that Original Sin was an essential part of man's (and woman's) nature. He argued that an individual was capable of choosing good or evil without any Divine aid or interference. For Pelagius and his many followers through the centuries, particularly in Britain, the human will and conscience was sufficient to guide an individual to live a sinless life.

The argument continues to this day.

The Frome Charter of 934

Internet ref: Sawyer 427 in Electronic Sawyer. Old English spelling is used.

The Charter is dated Frome, Somerset, 16 December 934. King Athelstan to the familia (servants) of Holy Trinity, Winchester; grant of 30 hides (cassatae) at Enford, Wiltshire; 10 (mansae) at Chilbolton and 10 (cassati) at Ashmanworth, Hampshire.

Held at the British Library, London.

The witnesses are: (2 kings, 2 archbishops, 15 bishops, 1 ealdorman and 25 ministers):

Aethelstan "rex et rector totius huius britannie insule" and "Ongolsaxna cyning and brytenwalda ealles yses iglandes" (King and Emperor of the whole of Britain).

Hywel Undercyning (Hywel Dda, Welsh sub king).

Wulfhelm Arcebisceop (Canterbury).

Wulfstan Arcebisceop (York).

Eodred bisceop (? Durham?)

Wulfhun bisceop (Selsey)

Aelfheah bisceop (Winchester)

Oda bisceop (Ramsbury)

Aelfred bisceop (? Sherborne?)

Aedelgar bisceop (Crediton)

Burhric bisceop (Rochester)

Cenwald bisceop (Worcester)

Aella bisceop (also called Aelfwine, Lichfield. May be "Athelstan A", the scribe, active 925-935)*

Wunsige bisceop (Dorchester)

Tidhelm bisceop (Hereford)

Cynaesige bisceop (Berkshire)

Wulfhelm bisceop (Hereford)

Aelfraed bisceop (? Sherborne?)

Alfwald ealdorman

Plus 25 ministers.

*The scribe known to academics as "Athelstan A" uses a particularly recognisable, florid style of writing and is considered to have been a close associate of Athelstan. The writing style is reminiscent of St Aldhelm, popular therefore with the King.

Athelstan Witans 930-939
from surviving Charters issued

(ref. D. Hill)

930
Lyminster (Selsey area) 5 April 930
Chippenham 29 April 930
Abingdon c.930
London 7 June 930
Whittlebury (north of Buckingham) c.930

931
Colchester 23 March 931
Wellow 931
Wilton ?931
Lifton, Devon 12 November 931

932
Amesbury 24 August 932
Milton (Kent) 30 August 932

933
Chippenham 26 January 933
Kingston 16 December 933

934
Winchester 28 May 934
Nottingham 7 June 934
Buckingham 12 September 934 (Constantine as witness)
Frome 16 December 934

935
Exeter 16 April c.935

Cirencester 935 (Constantine as witness)

936
No charters survive.

937
Dorchester, Dorset 21 December 937

938
No charters survive.

939
Dorchester? 15 April 939
Gloucester 27 October 939, Athelstan dies.

The Head of Oswald

It is possible that the lure of being able to unite the head of the seventh century king of Northumbria, Oswald, with most of the rest of his bodily parts would have been too great for Athelstan to ignore. His visit to Chester-le-Street on the way north in 934 and possibly also on the way south after the campaign would have given him a once in a lifetime opportunity to unite the nation symbolically as well as physically. He would never travel outside of Wessex and Mercia again, except to the unknown site of the Battle of Brunanburh in 937, which may have taken place near the coast in Cheshire.

Athelstan was pious and as Christian a king as could be expected in his time, but shenanigans involving relics were not unknown. At a later date, some monks of Peterborough stole an arm of Oswald from Bamburgh Castle and created a carefully guarded niche for it, acknowledging that others might do the same. At the Reformation, the monks of Durham may have substituted the body of Cuthbert for another recently dead brother to save it and buried it secretly, supposedly at Crayke abbey, near York. The Reformation probably caused a great deal of substitution and secret rescuing of well-loved saints' parts and this might have happened to Athelstan's corpse. William of Malmesbury, writing of Athelstan's exploits, regards him as a great and worthy king. Later worshippers at Malmesbury may have rescued him.

At least four heads of Oswald are known to have turned up on the continent. It may be the case that the Lindisfarne monks, in order to make considerable cash towards the restoration of their monastery, allowed eminent thieves to steal the head in Cuthbert's coffin and to replace it with others. Forensic enquiry would not be needed when both thief and victim knew what had been allowed to happen, but it may have come as a complete surprise to a royal thief or his agents to find that he may not have been first to the pot and particularly galling to find that he was being blackmailed by the Abbot for more cash.

A royal thief could lose his reputation as an anointed king if it were publicly known that he was guilty of theft from such a well-known and honoured source. Excommunication and Hell would be his destiny.

No remains of Oswald are mentioned in Exeter Cathedral's relic book which accounts for the extensive gifts from Athelstan's private collection, but any supposed parts of Oswald would have been placed at the Priory in Gloucester, in any case, there to remain, until the destruction at the Reformation.

If Athelstan did succeed in taking the head from the coffin in Chester-le-Street, the questions remain:

- was the head actually Oswald's or a head substituted earlier by another thief and
- did he substitute another relic head in its place, one which he already had in his collection?
- And does it matter?

Meet me at Ecgberht's Stone; a Tale of the Battle of Edington

ECGBERHT'S STONE.

No, not a tale, but true; I with my eye saw the whole of it, the onslaught by the foe, the devil Danes, creeping along the chalk hill bottoms, snake like, sure footed and dastardly. Riding on our hills as though they owned them, creatures of rolling moss and stone, coveting other men's land and goods, never wearying of hubris and dream, fed by their warlords and their idols. Impervious to conscience, careless of the wisdom of ages past and the cry of the Christian fathers, heeding only the lure of loot and the smell of fear and blood.

I was there. I watched, wheeling above, as the human creatures passed below me to their fates, waiting my turn to feast on the carrion of fallen warriors, pecking between the crushed metalwork at eyes and mouths no longer shouting.

It was the springtime of the year of Our Lord and the Blessed Virgin Mary, 878. Alfred and his troops, a king and his bishops. men of steel, men of the Book, chanting songs as they marched, the bishops reading aloud their magical words from their wagons, some astride. There were few horses; only the noble rode. The ground of Wessex beneath their feet, they moved slowly but certainly eastwards, northwards.

Men had walked and ridden from all quarters along the Roman roads, straight as they could, from Bath in the north, from the harried lands of Wiltshire to the east, from the Hampshire and Dorset forests and hills to the south, from the inland marshy seas of Somerset. The King came, gathering armed men, dogs, horses, as he travelled.

The bishops waved their wands as they rode. Their aestels, with the pommels of gold and crystal, makers of magic evoked the Saints and the Trinity, exhorting their assistance. Gods of war, gods to defend. Gods of promise exhorted, making the army a dense network of faith and belief protected by tutelary supporters, the relics which travel in the wagons alongside the men. Cuthbert was present, not in the flesh, but living in the King's mind and heart, all the company knew.

The bishops, mighty masters of the mind and deliverers of Paradise, read aloud, chanted the psalms of war, gelling together the men of Hampshire, Somerset, Wiltshire come to fight, to achieve the defence of Wessex or die trying. If ever support from on high were needed, it was now. An England bereft of the bloodline of Ceawlin and Woden would allow the Viking marauders, bloodthirsty, unthinking foreigners, into our rejuvenated centre of learning and literature, of Christian understanding, our history wiped out in a few nights of orgy, the sacred books torn, spat on, used to light camp fires. I watched the bishops as they waved their holy wands, bright jewels shining in the sun, drawing my winged compatriots as the anticipation of flesh and blood drew me. I cannot help the attraction of blood; I am the corpse cleaner, the raven. I am a friend of no man.

We came to Ecgberht's Stone at the crest of the hill of Coel, where the great Roman highways cross, men below, corvids above, large and small, black, black and white. We used to scavenge here, happily, on feast days in the past. The Saxons love the wooded valleys more than the high tops. There are spirits of the vanquished here, at Brixton. We watched as men arrived in large groups followed by our forces of the sky, alerted to their alarms of drum, song and shield. We shadowed the soldiers, sure of a feast wherever they stop, wherever the blood flows.

After the King's imprisonment in marshes during the winter despair turned to battle joy as Saxons anticipated a fight. They were a pitchforked army, but also metalled, shield clad. There were practised flesh-biters in their hands. They sang and gabbled, little knowing that we could understand their speech. Buoyed by their growing numbers and exuberance, they marched, sharing stories of sacrifice and suffering. Some had seen the terror of the banner of the Raven hordes, some had experienced it, the wanton waste of land and possessions, of thoughtless enjoyment of death, their death cult in action, the cult of young men.

At the King's fire, he told his best men of his tactics, as we sat on branches nearby. He was emboldened. He said that he had dreamed of St Cuthbert, who came to him, telling him of the coming victory over the Raven warriors. His fate was secure; he and his kin would rule over the English in security and wisdom. The best of saints, protector of the land, Cuthbert of Lindisfarne, removed from his beloved monastery because of the Raven ones, now would take his revenge.

We nodded and cawed. There would be blood, flesh and eyes to peck. Take Guthrum alive, he told his men. Spare the leaders of this Viking hoard. I will pacify them. Our victory will be followed by conversion. They will be taught fear of the Lord and Hell to come. Their minds will be infected by the glory of our conquest. The bishops applauded, the men at arms groaned. Death, we want, they said, not liberty for the devils. Flesh, blood, eyes, we cawed. But the Gospel and the Word, heard and then written, oaths taken on the Book, baptism at the font would prevail; it was the King's will. Food and feasting would cement mutual peace. Gifts would be offered to dazzle and bind. What man could resist both freedom, flattery and treasure? There would be gratitude and amazement at lives spared, the beginning of an end to the addiction to blood lust. The bishops cheered again, the ealdormen but did not refuse or complain. The King's vision of Cuthbert was too strong.

That night Alfred and his trusted scout Herelac, speaker of the Viking language, rode to the Danish camp at Edington, dressed and regaled as scops. They sang their way into the tents of Guthrum, told their tales and listened to the conversations of the resting Danes, noted their confident, overweening pride, their certainty of further success, their drunken ways. The duo returned with the comforting news of unpreparedness. The Danes were unready for the might of God and the Saints as well as the determined Saxon army.

In the first light of the day of battle, more news came from the scouts and from our brothers in the sky that the host of Guthrum was complacently awaiting events to unfold, certain of a superiority of will to hold and keep the land. Chippenham lay behind them, Alfred's former fortress. To Chippenham they could retire to sing their feast songs with his head nailed to the wall of the great hall, dripping gore. Let the King come to them, they would be glad of the chance to bring down this last kingdom of the south. Wessex would be no more. Guthrum would be unassailable, he thought, the banner of the Raven would fly over every royal fortress.

In the early dawn, the plans for the day confirmed, we left Brixton. Little did the Viking army understand of the strength of the Wessex King, the determination of the men of the south to defend the last kingdom. We birds, eager for the killing, followed above, our own scouts now ready in the trees at Edington, certain of the blood to come, sensing the stupor of the Viking camp. These would be the men who would be our food in days to come.

The wagons rolled, the bishops and priests in the harnesses of their books intoned, the men sang. There was no need for silence. The army marched steadily onwards, conserving its energy. From hilltop to hilltop the men marched and rode, growing quieter as the day wore on, travelling due northwards along the Roman road to our next camp at The Place. A place of fateful memory for both armies, in the sagas to be made.

CLEY HILL

Alfred travelled astride, a weary soul, having had little rest. His stomach troubled him, but Cuthbert was with him. On the summit of Cley Hill he would be safe, the steep slopes of the hill and fort atop deterring attack, a protective island of mountain in the soft south. Tonight the prayers of the priests and bishops would be the main event of the camp. The focus of the army would be to restfully prepare their bodies and souls for the final defence of Wessex. The Danish camp lay some miles further north-east, skirting the great chalk hills. The Saxon army could retreat to The Place from battle if necessary; the Vikings could flee if they must to the fortress of Chippenham.

The Saxons passed through the eastern part of the Great Wood, through the greensand glades, winding through the track of centuries to the lower slopes of Cley Hill. The bishops went ahead, relieving the sacred site of its former spirit inhabitants, speaking their magic words to remove ghosts and malevolent intent. Men feared to climb this hill, so full it is of the triumphs and tragedies of the ancient past, so full of the spirits of the dead. No pagan would dare to come near, no Christian, either, but with the magic of Cuthbert, this must be, if conquered in the name of God, the safest place close to the Danish camp as could be found.

The King's wife, Ealswith and the children Edward and Aetheflaed remained with guards at Ecgberht's Stone. Scouts would inform them of the outcome of the battle. If all was lost, a flight to Brittany from the shore to the south would have to be made. Alternatively, there would be exile in the marshes and mors of Somerset until Edward became a man. But there would be little of Wessex left. The dynasty of Ecgberht would be broken. Great dreams would have come to nought.

The Vikings had no plans. Their strategy was to act, enjoy what they had, to move as they could, to destroy what they could not take. They are by nature shipmen, they maraud, have no attachment to any land, but they will hold what they can, if they can, and plunder meanwhile. There is no dynasty to protect. Anyone may be a king; any pirate who bullies and shouts, he may be leader for a day.

Climbing the devil's place, The Place of ancient spirits, for the first time, the Bishops chanted psalms, puffing up steep slopes. We wheeled over the top, joined by kites and buzzards rising in the deep blue wells of the sky. Many men crossed themselves, deeply aware of the devilish spirits lurking in the psyche of the landscape, but the bishops and Alfred insisted that the living vision of Cuthbert would protect.

In the fresh green grass just below the summit the army unloaded and set up the last camp. The cooks were active now, preparing a wheaten feast with meat and cheese to build and cheer the heart and stomach. The priests and bishops, on high psychic flights of their own, forbearing to eat, dizzy with the climb, manufactured the magic necessary to protect the army and the King from the evil of The Place, to bring the joy of restful sleep for those who might die in the morning, to offer their souls a safe journey to heaven. They fasted and prayed. We pitched in the trees at the base of the hill, waiting our turn to prey.

The holy relics, carried round by the many black clothed priests, kissed by the men, fortified their spirits. The music of harps and drums, flutes and trumpets, softly played, soothed the fearful ones beneath the stars over the hill. Sleep followed. The King slept soundly, protected by Cuthbert, protected by his priests.

In the morning there was holy communion. All who wished it had the rites, connecting them with the holy ones and God, assured of Heaven, assured of life. Standards were raised, sharp sword scabbards were buckled. The blue and red Madonna was held high. Green and gold, the woven figures of saints preceded the coiled snake of men as they marched down the hill, the night of fear behind them. In the immediate future, a fight to the death. Drums rolled, men sang songs of holy might and now, too, battle songs, songs of companionship, of lust for the spearing and hewing of flesh, songs that bind, songs of belonging to Wessex. Horns were blown at random. We felt the rise in excitement, our time would be soon. On this day flesh would fall to earth.

The army marched in its correct order, the King first, accompanied by the ealdormen. The bishops and priests were near the front with the relic wagon; the fighters followed, led by the well trained thegns. The army moved north east, over the escarpment of chalk hills along the Ridgeway, stopping above the steep defile of Bratton to view the Danish camp below. Then, at the order, it descended rapidly to take the camp by storm. Time stood still as screaming men rushed by. Some fell, their feet slower than their wits. They ran and tumbled down, as if chasing the cheese.

There was much clamour in the early morning at the Danish camp; always spoiling for a fight, yet they thought that the Wessex forces would take longer to arrive. Guthrum ran like a rat, summoning his men; instantly they came to arms, donned their helmets, grabbed their shields. Alfred's men had drunk only the words of the Gospel and water in their fastness of The Place; Guthrum and his men had casks of ale with them from the King's cellars at Chippenham and they were now empty.

THE BATTLE
Saxons are running, steadied now from the fall from the great height, wits collected, swords at the ready. Spears are in position, shields held firm. At Edington, small cluster of mud buildings that it is, stands a shieldwall of drunken foe, west facing, forming around the buildings, unkempt but fierce, roused from sleep, furious at being caught unprepared. The old snarl at the young to keep in line, to wake up. Woden is loudly invoked, quickly summoned. It is a shabby shieldwall, but rocklike. Women crouch behind the buildings, screaming. Saxons are shouting and screaming with bloodlust. Swords are clashing on shields, an orchestra of bloody intent.

Guthrum, in front of the shieldwall, is on his horse, checking the line, barking consistency. Death will come to the breaker of the line. There are threats for his fellow players in this bloody game, the game of conquering a kingdom. There will be rewards, rings of silver. There will be a kingdom's worth of gold for those who fight and win.

Silent now are the two opposing shieldwalls, charged with the psychic might of their supporting gods and beliefs, their visions of heaven and hell before them. There will be no prisoners. Hell, Heaven or Valhalla will open their gates this day to greet the souls fresh to them. Guthrum, woolly haired, scowling, wheels his horse round and round, skulls hanging from his pommel flying out on their tethers. Alfred, astride a white horse, a banner of the Virgin in his left hand, rides his shieldwall line, ready for the death or restoration of a kingdom, certain of the assistance of Cuthbert, who rides in spirit on his shoulder, urging him on, his belly pains forgotten.

Guthrum, waving his sword high, signals to approach Alfred. Two of his men on horseback wait beside him, interpreters, protectors. He wants a parley. Alfred meets him in the space between the silent lines with two men of his own, a priest and an interpreter. The priest carries potent relics, symbols of power for all to see. Guthrum sees the priest and his burdens, spits, rattles the skulls hanging at his knees, laughs. Chalk and cheese, the pagan and Christian leaders meet, wheel around each other, stare into each other's eyes. Do not look away. Challenge with the eyes. Both know the power of the Look. Both are masters of Death, but one seeks it in battle, the other in his bed. Guthrum is festooned with metal rings incised with biting creatures on his arms, trophies of war manufactured from stolen gold and silver, booty from the monasteries of the Angles. Bones of stolen saints and murdered monks fly in his wild hair. Alfred, diademed, bedecked as a peace loving, erudite and wisdom seeking king should be, colourful, is clearly master in his place.

Cuthbert, he thinks, be with me now.

Would Guthrum retreat? If so for what price? He would not. This day he will erase Wessex as he had erased other English states. Today he will kill a king, send him to his God. The Danish kingdom of Britain will be completed, from sea to sea throughout the land. The Scandinavian devil will rule the saints. Woden will be supreme. No, he would not retreat, at any price. Would Alfred? No, he would not. The six men separate. A fight to the death, then. The leaders return to their lines.

Last orders and invocations are yelled by the group leaders of both sides, the shieldwalls tightened.

Suddenly, a shout rises from the Danish side. We birds scream and fly upwards into the clouds. A roar corresponds from Saxons, then there is a rushing sound as both walls run towards each other. Eyes opened wide glitter, flashing flesh cutting metal sings. Honour and glory are the only states that matter.

The walls collide, meet, thrust, yell, stab. The tussle of retreat and advance ensues, the shieldwalls waving like washing in a stiff breeze. From above the mess of men appears as a sea of hatred. Bodies fall, blood spurts, cries of pain fill the air. Numb warriors despair in the moments after the severing of an arm, the separation from all that a mother gave to her offspring, life and limbs. The earth is turning red. There is at first discipline in both walls, giving, taking, a timeless period of equality. Then there are suddenly more fallers at a point on the Danish side, no reinforcements to take their places.

The Danish wall, after a long period of exhausting stabbing, groaning, bleeding of both sides, weakens. Just one small part of the line of shields breaks and then is quickly closed by the men on either side. The gap mends, but is not fully repaired. The Saxons see the weak point, push against it, redouble their effort in the central portion where it appears.

The Saxons push, the Danish line breaks again, fails to fill its gap, stumbles over its own bloody, dismembered bodies on the ground. There is plenty there, we birds can see, for the feast after the battle. Guthrum screams to hold, but the line is beyond mending. The mushroom dreams and ale of the night before have had their effect. The will of the Viking is broken. There is too much blood, too many companions of the oars struck down, body parts distributed on fields of corn, too many already gone to Valhalla. The sight of it causes the thrill of blood lust to give way to fear. The pitiful cries for help of those halfway to Hell unnerves those still standing.

Guthrum shouts a retreat. Order is difficult to maintain when fear of defeat and pain return to men's minds. It gives way to panic as those on horseback turn their backs on the enemy to gallop back to the fortress of Chippenham. Northwards they flee, Guthrum now riding with them, the main body of the Danes on foot, running, discarding heavy metalwork as they go over the young corn, darting behind coppices, deep breathing, routed, ignominious, chased by the cavalry and infantry of the jeering Saxons. Once a rout, always a rout. Revel for one side, rout for the other. Shout the devil out. Out they will go, like rats, leaving the field of battle.

The Devil reaches Chippenham. In the fortress women wail at the change in fortunes of their bold brave men. He is followed by the army on foot for whom the gates are opened, swallowing the fleetest runners, leaving the wounded stragglers who cry outside in the fields, until they are silenced by the swords of the chasing Saxons. We begin to feast. The dead and living flesh, both are succulent.

Already the poet soldiers of the Saxon camp are composing sagas in their minds. Already Alfred is composing prayers of thanks to Cuthbert, his mind writing in the script of his court scop the tale of the valour of Wessex, the saving of the nation, the defeat of the upstart Guthrum.

But not yet; there is a siege to overcome. Chippenham was Alfred's stronghold until the Danes took it, forced him out in the preceding winter. Tit for tat, he has surprised Guthrum as Guthrum had surprised him. The difficulty now comes: how to cement this victory into a long-term acceptance of territory gained or lost? How realistic is it to expect the Danish kingdom of the east, so mercilessly won from the Anglo-Saxons but now full of interlopers to accept their lost mission?

While we consume the corpses, naked and stripped of their weapons and clothing, as the blood dries to brown on the corn and runs down to the streams, the men of the Danes and the men of the Saxons pause, planning their next moves. Not flesh now to dispute over, not numbers killed or maimed or prisoners taken nor ransoms given: but how to manage the future. In the event of success, how does a victorious army play out its legacy? And for how long? A generation of expectation of peace? Two generations? Can a grandfather plan for his grandchild's world? Their children's?

Alfred, almost mad with success, calls on the great saint on his shoulder to calm him. He paces the land in front of the gates. I see him, taking a rest from filling my gut on the plains to the west. At the beginning, as he reaches the gates of his own fortress, now slammed shut against him by the terrified Danes, perceiving their extinction, he shouts, swears, screams imprecations of revenge at his enemy. Revenge is sweet, after all that he has endured. Wounded and bruised, having lost some of their noblemen fighters in the shieldwall, the Saxons now wish to execute, to exterminate. Those who were overtaken by the chase to Chippenham are quickly despatched to Hell, young or old. A similar fate awaits those inside the gates of the fortress.

Before the gates and the watching Danes, Alfred carries out the rites of triumph, of thanks to the tutelary guardianship of the holy ones, to the banner of the Virgin, powerful lady of the skies. Guthrum, bereft of the help of Woden, is impressed by the ceremony of kissing the relics, by the gold and silver reliquaries which have played a part, it seems, in his defeat. A mightier force is on show today than he has met before in other lands. The battle has been won not on the might of men wielding swords or displays of virtue or tactics, but on the religious forces Alfred has been able to muster. If he is to survive this siege, he must think of this in future.

THE SURRENDER

The Saxons set up camp just beyond the range of spear and arrow, in sight of the fortress gates. For a fortnight they rested and held at bay the increasingly frustrated and despairing Danes within. We stayed to watch. Parleys from the towers to the interpreters below were held, beginning with defiance from the Danes. This, as they became hungrier and as ale stocks ran low, gave way to acceptance of their fate, not death in glory, but death by execution. Possibly extended death, as they would have treated Alfred. They have pretty ways of death, imaginative ways.

At the end of the fortnight, defeated in will as well as in body, Guthrum surrendered. He emerged through the gates, opening them wide, the pale, hungry remnants of his army, having eaten most of their horses, looking shabbier than ever, their demeanour dour, silent. They had come so far, ravaged the whole of Britain, only to be defeated by one man, whose vision and religious backing had proved greater than their own.

Alfred approached the Viking leader. To the latter's great surprise, he was not struck down in ignominy in front of his disappointed men. The King offered his hand in greeting, as though to an honoured nobleman of his own. They looked each other in the eye. Guthrum started. He now recognised the scop who had played the flute and sung in his tent before the battle. He ruefully smiled, accepted Alfred's extended hand and arm. Determination, resourcefulness and a more than adequate system of espionage could be added to this man's formidable fighting talents. A brain to admire, he grudgingly held, and said so to Alfred. The best man had won. Now he would submit to the will of Alfred, to his fate, to death.

Alfred would continue to surprise Guthrum. He and Cuthbert would use this fearsome leader, sober after two weeks of siege, to hammer home to all, his own followers included, that peace could be made even with the Devil. No show of force, or hate, was necessary. A cool exterior, diadem in place, stance erect, well fed, noble, magnanimous, could charm an enemy. Not death, then, but something else peculiar in the aftermath of war: friendship. No use of ligaments, no chains, but an arm around the shoulder, an offering of wine, of a cushioned couch.

Brought to Alfred's tent, luxury surrounding him, water to cleanse him and to drink, Guthrum and his chief men rested, while the remaining inhabitants of the fortress were relieved with food and water.

Danes lay in scattered groups, grateful to be spared death, offered life, clean pallets, recovering, exhausted by failure, speechless at the mercy which they were unexpectedly being shown. They were too weak to resent it, to wish for death, too hungry not to take the bread and cheese and even meat offered to them. In constant attendance, the priests and bishops performed their rituals, their presence a reminder of the psychic power, the Christian magic, behind the throne. Sickening, well organised, magnanimous orderliness was on show, a difficult pill for the Viking throat to swallow.

Fathers, brothers and sons, grizzled and fair, wept at their loss. They grabbed at offered food, suspicious of each armed movement of their guards, jumping at loud sounds, wincing at movement. Looking inward, distraught, seeing failure. Seeing nothing else, believing nothing. What is important in life to a starving man? Food, shelter, the needs of the body for fresh water. Women and children sighed and moaned with relief as they were attended by careful nuns. Saxons buried the remains of Viking brothers, fathers, sons, as though they were their own. There was less available for us birds, but we had already glutted.

THE PROMISE

Alfred, rested in body and mind during the siege of the fortress, was happy to wait for the inevitable, the crushing public capitulation, his new status in Europe as the only Anglo-Saxon King to defeat the mighty Vikings ensured. This would be a confirmation of the Pope's blessing given when he was a child. He sketched out his plans for the future on vellum prepared for this event. A list of boundaries. The place where the border between nations would be, the burghs and earthworks where the line would hold, to the security and comfort of both Anglo-Saxon and Dane. And in time the two peoples would merge. With different haircuts, different clothes, different languages, different upbringing, were we not otherwise the same people? Take two boys, one of mine, one of yours he said. Edward, small, fair, innocent. Your son, the same. They are like twins. They can be brothers. Brothers in Christ, the chief thing dividing us being our beliefs. Bring them together. We will live in peace. Let this be the last time we slay each other. See the priests, their books, their golden aestels. These can be yours, too, in a generation. Reading and writing will bind our nations, oaths will be promised, understood and acted upon. The laws of all our lands will be written, will be unassailable, the written word valid in the courts of our kingships. The law within signed charters will be maintained; no man can gainsay the written word. These are the coming times, when the sons of men will be educated. There will be scriptoriums full of the words we have spoken and agreed upon held for ever. Our regal requirements will be met by those who can read and feared by those who cannot, for the written word will be the first in requirement of proof of ownership or will. Saxon and Viking lords alike heard Alfred speak. The King's will was at its mightiest. God ruled with him.

Alfred was impressing Guthrum. He was wise in his own way, listened without comment. He would have to come to terms with this kind of conquest, the conquest of lifestyle. What would his son, his brothers, do to adapt to these new wiles? He was a prisoner. Woden had failed him. Perhaps the Irish and Welsh had it right; the way forward, to preserve the Danish hegemony, might be to accept the new religion, to follow the written way. Much could be preserved of the old ways; the oral saga tradition would never die. Viking deeds, the conquests and seafaring to the ends of the earth, their triumphs and empire, would never be lost as long as they had their language, as long as their words were spoken by the firelight. Viking villages and towns, trade creators for wealth for all, would have their names recorded for posterity on these charters that Alfred displayed. The land of the Angles would be ours to keep. What are a few promises? Better to agree and retreat, having secured more than we could ever have dreamed of in only a few short years.

There is much to take from this, less defeat than might have been, he thinks. I can persuade our young men towards this sharing approach. I will be King of this new way. I will take on the mask of this new religion. There is much to be learned from the priests, much of beauty and understated order which attracts. A life of wood and stone rather than ships and tents, always on the move, always sharpening swords, attacking as a form of defence. There will be wooden halls and seats, fields growing corn, not flames.

The wine, food and comfort brought Guthrum to the realisation that he was weary, sick to the bone of travelling, fighting, screaming imprecations. His throat was sore from it. When he was rested, his task would be to persuade his men that life without killing was worth having too.

Alfred's men watched closely as their lord offered the unexpected hand of generosity and brotherliness to his foe. He said he would act as Guthrum's parent in Christ at baptism, which would usher in the responsibilities of kingship in peace, of belief in the One, rejection of the Many. They argued that this approach would not work, that the Vikings were too far gone in bloodlust to be changed into angels of mercy, but as they watched the two kings they saw that one spoke, the other remained silent. They watched as a grudging mutual admiration grew. They saw the wilful, farsighted power of the Christian king dominating the disorder of the pagan. They began to believe that he could be right, after all. The defeat of the Viking leader was complete: he saw the error of his ways.

The interior of Alfred's tent was a palace in miniature, as richly embellished as the halls of his palaces before the Danes deprived him of them. Chippenham palace was now a mess, carcasses and urine and faeces stank, carvings, treasures and books lay scattered and sodden in rain water pools. The tent had the restrained atmosphere of an educated king's hall of central Europe. Rich materials hung from cross beams, slaves and servants bent to offer trays of delicacies to eat and drink before the honoured guests. This was the travelling home of a magnanimous leader of an empire who could afford to be serene, a leader who intended to be in charge for a long time to come. A mist of incense marked the place of an altar. Harp music accompanied the discussions of the future. Literature, colour and carving were everywhere to be seen. Alfred displayed his vision, the theatre of the mighty Christian world.

Messengers went ahead to prepare for the baptism of Guthrum and his chief men at Aller. He would be brought to the Somerset moors from where Alfred had recovered his zest, from where he had summoned his army, back to the little settlement of Athelney nearby and Langport, an area he and his kin would forever hold precious.

From Pagan to Christian

Still on the field of battle, Alfred made a gift to Guthrum. He bestowed him with a psalter and aestel, instructed him on Christian kingly rule, gave him a priest and teacher to begin an understanding of the written word and classical erudition. What Theoderic of the Goths and other pagans had achieved, Guthrum could, too. Guthrum's son would be educated. He would stay with the King, instructed by him personally.

The nations would be as one, able to live together under Christ and the Church with the protection of the Pope in Rome. As Alfred bent to pass the tokens of kingship to the Viking leader, his head shone with the diadem of power, a circlet, not of thorns or leaves, but of golden metal fashioned like the emperors of old, studded with gems, red and blue garnets and sapphires. His kingly robes, dark blue and green, embroidered with trees, flowers, the work of many exemplary maidens, enhanced the glittering emblems of power. His hair was combed and plaited, his beard neatly ordered, delicately shaped. Everything spoke of farsightedness and beauty combined.

Guthrum, swallowing his ale, bread and pride, stood upright. He staggered, making the prisoner's guard move forward in alarm, but daggerless and swordless, his personal threat was diminished, his physical strength gone. The height and stature of the man, only two weeks before imposing, had been reduced to a tottering middle-aged raggedness. He spoke with a croak.

'I bow to you, lord Alfred. On behalf of my men I give you honour, willing to admit your superiority in arms, willing to admit the superiority of your God. I agree to meet you for baptism. I agree that I will bring my men and our families with us to meet your maker and to make him ours, too. We will share this land between us and though I have little understanding of charters or books, yet I find that I can trust you and your oath. You will not harm the hostages while we are gone to our homes in the east. I will return to your place of choosing to begin this life of wisdom. I accept the presence of your scribes, priests and interpreter. They will accompany us to our homes. We will do them no harm, on the understanding that no harm will come to my son and the other chosen hostages. We will have a new arrangement of the kingdom. This I accept.' Then he swore an oath on the holy book which Alfred had presented to him.

Then Alfred let him go. Clean, fed, wined, stunned. Guthrum and his men promised, on the gospels of Alfred, watched by his priests, begged by the Viking women and their children, to return to the west in three weeks, to return to the heart of the lands they had intended to take and hold but could not. They would come west to Aller for baptism and to be seen to submit, to return to the hostages, to the young children, their future, which were taken into the care of the priests to begin the process of integration. Those under eight years old had the best chance of becoming peace-loving, of understanding the English tongue. Those older would have to learn to live without a weapon in their hands at all times, to learn to love writing and reading, to imbibe the holy words as quickly as possible.

At Aller, after three weeks, the Vikings returned as promised. The ceremony of Baptism took place. Guthrum was renamed Aethelstan. Aethelstan was now the adopted son of Alfred, the man he would have killed, raised to a place of high esteem, an equal in kingship. All would wear white for the duration of their alteration from pagan to Christian, the robes and filets would be worn continuously while the fast, repentance and awareness of the love of Christ was hammered home for eight days. For younger men, this was an interesting time; for the older, a struggle. For some it was a life-changing dream of the power of the inward life to effect change. For the most adaptable and able, it was a view of a career in future as scribes, priests and interpreters, attending the ordered presence of a king's court, forever at peace, comfortable. Making books, not burning them. Creating, not destroying.

Making books, not burning them. The Vikings were forced to see their own atrocities from another's point of view. The Saxon culture had been a fragile, tentative thing, robbed by vandalism of its best scholars, libraries and treasures. The greed and reckless violence of their pirate forebears had nearly destroyed all that they now saw was good. A converted soul can be an enthusiastic extremist when turned. The white robes and filet of transformation had this effect for some of Guthrum's younger warriors, who took up the pen with great enthusiasm. At the official unbinding of the robes after eight days of fasting and intensive exposure to the priests, the new relationship with Wessex was cemented with feasting at the royal palace of Wedmore. For a further twelve days, Alfred, Guthrum and the men of Wessex, together with the reunited hostages, children, wives and mothers, laughed together, hunted together, learnt something of each other's languages, attended mass, shared beauty in the written word and illustration, left their spears and swords outside the halls and listened together as scops, bards and musicians soothed their way to a better understanding.

The feathered corvid army, my brothers of the sky, move on, waiting and watching for the next feast of human flesh. We watch and wait for discord, for the shining swords and shields of imminent battle. They will return.

Bird-lore

' **E**thologically speaking...it is very probable that ravens and wolves learned to associate groups of armed men with food, and that they appeared before the fighting broke out.'

Birds and Bird-lore in the literature of Anglo-Saxon England (unpublished Phd thesis by Mohamed Eric Rahman Lacey, p.118.)

Quoted by Tom Holland in *Athelstan, the Making of England*, Allen Lane, 2016, p. 97.

The Ritual Shriek

Welsh lore and law talks of a way of including a kinsman in the sharing of a kindred's land. He must give "a shriek over the Otherworld"; "and then the law hears that shriek and grants him inclusion...that is to say, as much as each of their number who are settled there before him".

Llyfr Iorweth, ed. Wiliam, p.85-86, quoted in T.M. Charles-Edwards, Wales and the Britons 350-1064, Oxford University Press, 2013

"I will give three shouts at the entrance to this gate such as will be no less audible on Penryn Penwaedd in Cornwall..."

Culhwch, in *How Culhwch Won Olwen*, in *The Mabinogion*, trans. Jeffrey Gantz, Penguin 1976, p. 138

Later Welsh law may here have, in fossilised form, an ancient form of protest by the disowned or excluded Celt or Celts.

Perhaps the horse and rider brooch with its open-mouthed horse and rider, dated to the first and second centuries AD and found in sites throughout southern England including Cold Kitchen and Lamyatt, represents a cry of objection to Roman rule. If you wore this brooch, were you a supporter of a guerrilla or religious movement to claim the land back from the Empire, to show you were included in a British cultural idealogy, belonging to a kin and a landscape?

Later Britons may have employed the Shriek in the culturally overlapping real and Otherworld to focus on removal of the Saxons from their lost land, Lloegr. It may have operated as resistance, something akin to the late 19th century ghost-dance rituals of the North American Indian. The Welsh Armes Prydein (The Call to Arms) poem also talks of shouting.

The Armes Prydein, a prophetic poem from the Book of Taliesin, was written in the early tenth century. It recorded how the Welsh felt about their English overlords. It describes a future where all of the Brythonic (Welsh speaking) peoples are allied with the Scots, Irish and Vikings of Dublin under Welsh leadership to attempt to drive the Anglo-Saxons from Britain forever.

Hywel Dda was particularly targeted for his collaborative stance with the English kings of Wessex. He named one of his sons Edwin, like Edward the Elder's second son with his second wife.

The modern Welsh name for Britain is Ynys Prydain.

Shouting or shrieking is part of the ritual of Clipping the Church, as rememberered in:

'Rode Revel, Beckington Rout,
The Devil's in Frome
And cannot get out'
Folk song, anonymous

The church clipping ritual was carried out within living memory at Rode, Somerset.

A note for the reader: there are no notes in the fictional story, for the sake of readability.

Comments on the origin of information and references for further reading are supplied in the Bones section. Where possible, original sources have been consulted and incorporated. Sites have been visited, items in museums viewed, archaeological papers have been read. A lifetime of thinking about, living in and painting the landscape of Selwood and several courses and talks researched and given by me on its content have informed, inspired, and rooted me.

The activities of the characters of **Flesh** are fictional, but I have tried to use original historical sources as well as secondary sources and surprisingly there is a considerable amount for a more than bones only account of Wessex during the Saxon period. The amount of flesh, however, that I have applied to those bones is variable and as many academic authors must do for these times, I am forced to say that supposition and uncertainty are the order of the day. Imaginative constructions have played a large part in the story of Flesh. I have tried to indicate the amount of it, with obvious fictional characters mixed in with real ones and plotting regarding the Oaken Chest and the fictional events of the (fictional) Reliquary of St Radegund. Without imaginative reconstruction there would be little to thread together to make a readable story and it has been my aim to try to bring to life, for the general reader, something of the flavour of the post-Roman and early Middle Ages in this south-west part of England and to suggest where others might begin to investigate in their territory. The story of the drowning of Edwin remains subject to rumour and innuendo of the time; no-one knows for certain whether Athelstan intended or ordered his death. I have taken the liberty, for the sake of the storyline, of having his body washed up on the shore at Studland in Dorset rather than the official version of northern France.

Much of what I relate is based on the bones of fact; the flesh of the storyline is only intended to make the reading experience more accessible, a case of reading between the lines. The appendices and discussion in Bone are all fact and research based. The illustrations are my own, based on contemporary items or constructions based on contemporary style.

Place-name evidence has been the key to unlocking my own research information of the history and prehistory of the local landscape and others might find that pronunciation, rather than the reading of names only, may give clues to the palimpsest of landscape history wherever they are, revealing layers of settlement by different peoples with various approaches to life, culture, language and belief.

I hope that you will enjoy and perhaps be inspired to view the legends in your own place through a synthesis of the clues provided by place-names as well as local history, geography, archaeology and folklore. You need to be aware of the impact of writing on a formerly oral culture.

A strong feeling of belonging to a place also helps.

Annette Burkitt, Frome, September 2017

Selected Bibliography

General:
Michael McGarvie, *Book of Frome*, Barracuda Books ltd. 1980.
Michael Wood, *In Search of England, Journeys into the English Past*, Viking and Penguin Books 1999 and 2000 and *In Search of the Dark Ages*, BBC Books 1981.
Nicholas Higham and Martin J. Ryan, *The Anglo-Saxon World*, Yale University Press 2013.

Primary Sources:
Asser, *Life of King Alfred*.
The Anglo Saxon Chronicle.
The Early Lives of Dunstan, edited and translated by Michael Winterbottom and Michael Lapidge, Oxford University Press 2012.
William of Malmesbury, *Chronicle of the Kings of England and Deeds of the Bishops of England*.
Nennius, *British History and the Welsh Annals*, ed. and trans. by John Morris, Phillimore 1980.

Secondary Sources:
Peter Berresford Ellis, *Celt and Saxon, the Struggle for Britain AD 410-937*, Constable and Company 1993.
John Chandler, *A Higher Reality, the History of Shaftesbury's Royal Nunnery*, Hobnob Press 2003.
T.M. Charles-Edwards, *Wales and the Britons, 350-1064*, Oxford University Press, 2013
Eilert Ekwall, *The Concise Oxford Dictionary of English Place-names*, Oxford 1936.
Peter Ellis. Ed, *Roman Wiltshire and After*, Wiltshire Archaeological and Natural History Society 2001.
Eric L Fitch, *In Search of Herne the Hunter*, Capall Ban Publishing, 1994.

Sarah Foot, *Aethelstan, the First King of England*, Yale University Press 2011.

David Hill, *An Atlas of Anglo-Saxon England*, Blackwell 1981.

N J Higham, ed, *Britons in Anglo-Saxon England*, Boydell Press 2007.

Tom Holland, *Athelstan, The Making of England*, Allen Lane Penguin 2016.

Ronald Hutton, *Pagan Britain*, Yale 2013.

Susan M. Pearce, *The Kingdom of Dumnonia. Studies in History and Tradition in South Western Britain AD 350-1150*, Lodeneck Press 1978.

H M Porter, *The Saxon Conquest of Somerset and Devon*, James Brodie 1967.

Ann Ross, *Pagan Celtic Britain*, London: Constable, 1967.

Ben Snook, *The Anglo-Saxon Chancery*, Boydell and Brewer, 2015.

Pauline Stafford, *Unification and Conquest, a Political and social History of England in the Tenth and Eleventh Centuries*, Edward Arnold 1989, 'The King's Wife in Wessex 800-1066', published in *Past and Present* Volume 1 1981 pp 3-27.

Barbara Yorke, *Wessex in the Early Middle Ages*, Leicester University Press 1995.

The interested reader could go to Devizes Museum to see items recovered from Cold Kitchen Hill and Taunton Museum for those from Lamyatt Beacon. The Warminster Jewel (aestel) is on display at Salisbury museum. The major sites associated with Athelstan, Gloucester Cathedral, St Oswald's Priory, Winchester Cathedral, Milton Abbas church and Muchelney Abbey (another Athelstan foundation) can all be visited. The remains of Cheddar palace can be viewed at Kings of Wessex School. At Frome there are two pieces of a Saxon cross shaft in the church of St John, both of which appear throughout this book.

Acknowledgements

Thank you to my friends for listening and for your patience while the book grew and for sharing in the enjoyment of our unique landscape over many years, particularly Jane Harwood, Jean Lowe and Christine Deed. I hope my obsessions didn't weigh too heavily.

Thank you to the local keepers of specialist knowledge and awareness, Revd Colin Alsbury of St John's church of the parish of Frome Selwood, Revd John Hodder and to Professor Michael Wood, who know Frome well and have provided some comments and advice.

Thank you to the inspiration of the late Anglo-Saxon archaeologist David Hill who was a friend in my early days, to the late local historian and Frome native H M Porter and to the late Revd Patrick Cowley of St John's in the '50s where it all began for me.

Thanks also to Silver Crow readers of Frome and Gill Harry particularly who got me started with the writing up of lectures given twenty years ago in Frome.

Victor Strode Manley who collected Wiltshire folklore in the early twentieth century and whose notes are kept at Warminster Library gifted me much information, including games played on Cley Hill in former times.

My thanks to Longleat House Archives, Somerset Map 70, for permission to reproduce the 1813 Cruse map of Frome. Copyright Marquess of Bath.

Many thanks to Dr John Chandler of the Hobob Press, for his patience and hard work in preparing the manuscript for publication.

Thanks to Frome itself and its special sacred landscape, which has always been my home.

And lastly grateful thanks to my friend and husband, Tim, for his willing ear, shared interest in things of the deep past and without whom this book would not have come about.

The Illustrations are the author's freehand drawings.

The Author's watercolour of Cold Kitchen Hill looking east from Packsaddle, Frome.

Celtic style raven.

Based upon a horse and rider brooch found at Lamyatt during excavation. The Excavation of a Romano-Celtic Temple and a Later Cemetery on Lamyatt Beacon, Somerset by Roger Leech, Britannia 1986 v.17, pp 259-328

Based upon Saxon cross shaft carving in St John's church, Frome.

Based upon Saxon cross shaft carving in St John's church, Frome.

Based upon bust of Athelstan on a coin in the British Museum, ref. M.M. Archibald and C. Blunt, Sylloge of the British Isles 34: British Museum AngloSaxon Coins V, Aethelstan to the reign of Edgar, 924-c.973 (London 1986).

Based upon bust of Athelstan on a coin in the British Museum, ref. M.M. Archibald and C. Blunt, Sylloge of the British Isles34: British Museum AngloSaxon Coins V, Aethelstan to the reign of Edgar, 924-c.973 (London 1986).

Based upon a relief of mother goddesses in the Corinium Museum, Cirencester.

Celtic style boar.

Based upon a coin of Edward the Elder, said to be a tower or reliquary type, ref. Blunt, C.E., (1989), Coinage in Tenth-Century England from Edward the Elder to Edgar's Reform, Oxford: The British Academy.

St John's Church, Frome, in 2017: view from King Street.

Lightning Source UK Ltd.
Milton Keynes UK
UKHW01f1024040718
325211UK00001B/102/P